"Go back to your reading, but read out loud," Alex said.

He closed his eyes as he settled deeper into the mattress with another sigh. "I like your voice."

Sarah would have enjoyed the compliment if she hadn't been so horrified by the thought of reading the scene he had just interrupted. She couldn't possibly continue from where she'd left off. Rachel and Kee had been *doing it*.

"I—ah—I'll just read you the first chapter, since I only started this book this evening," she said, marking her page and quickly leafing back to chapter one.

"What kind of book is it?"

"A . . . it's sort of a mystery," she whispered. "Written by a woman who lives right here in Maine. It's set on the coast. There's a bit of romance in it, too."

His mouth slashed into a grin, and his eyes opened when he lifted an eyebrow. "Any good stuff? Any heavy breathing and groping?"

The Seduction of His Wife is also available as an eBook

JANET CHAPMAN

The
Seduction of
His Wife

POCKET STAR BOOKS
New York   London   Toronto   Sydney

An *Original* Publication of POCKET BOOKS

 A Pocket Star Book published by
POCKET BOOKS, a division of Simon & Schuster, Inc.
1230 Avenue of the Americas, New York, NY 10020

This book is a work of fiction. Names, characters, places and incidents are products of the author's imagination or are used fictitiously. Any resemblance to actual events or locales or persons, living or dead, is entirely coincidental.

ISBN-13: 978-1-4165-0527-3
ISBN-10:   1-4165-0527-X

This Pocket Star Books paperback edition July 2006

10 9 8 7 6 5 4 3

POCKET STAR BOOKS and colophons are registered trademarks of Simon & Schuster, Inc.

Cover design by Min Choi

Manufactured in the United States of America

For information regarding special discounts for bulk purchases, please contact Simon & Schuster Special Sales at 1-800-456-6798 or business@simonandschuster.com.

To Esther Rauch,
for your generous spirit
and much cherished friendship.

The
Seduction of
His Wife

Chapter One

❉

Alex Knight fought the fatigue weighing on his eyelids and brushed an unsteady hand through his hair in an attempt to wipe the fog from his brain. He needed to stay focused on the road ahead, to avoid the final irony of cheating death in the jungles of Brazil only to die in a car wreck less than ten miles from home. He rolled down the window of the rented sedan and sucked in the crisp November air, hoping the scent of fir and spruce and pine would perk him up. Not three days ago, he'd thought the rotting jungle would be the last thing he smelled and screaming monkeys the last thing he heard.

But he was home now, thanks to a healthy amount of luck and the determination not to die in that stinking jungle at the hands of some crazy rebel bastards. Well, luck and the thought of his father and brothers who needed him, and his two would-be orphaned children who needed him even more.

Alex came fully awake the moment he turned onto the Knights' private logging road, anticipation quickening his pulse and making his foot heavy on the gas as he passed the sign that said he was entering NorthWoods Timber land. Only eight miles of blessedly familiar gravel road, and he would be back in the bosom of his family.

Alex dodged frozen puddles as he picked up speed, guiding the car around a sweeping curve and thumping over the solid wooden bridge that crossed Oak Creek. He'd rebuilt that bridge two summers ago with Ethan and Paul, and he remembered the arguments he'd had with his brothers over the bridge's design. Ethan had wanted to use steel beams, Paul had wanted to make it single-laned, and Grady, their father and patriarch of their little clan, hadn't cared *how* it was built as long as it got done before a loaded logging truck ended up in the creek.

Alex frowned as he pushed the car recklessly faster. Where in hell was everyone, anyway? He had called home countless times from the U.S. embassy in Brazil three days ago; he'd tried again from Mexico yesterday, and yet again this morning when he'd landed in Maine. No one had answered, and this morning all he'd gotten was a mechanical voice saying the message machine was full.

Some homecoming this was going to be. He was back from the dead, dammit, and nobody knew it! The company he'd been working for in Brazil had told Alex they'd sent two men to Oak Grove eleven days ago, to tell his family he had been killed and that his body had likely been swept downriver when a murdering band of rebels had attacked the dam site where he'd been working as a road engineer. Which meant everyone should be home mourning their loss instead of running around the countryside, but it appeared that the five people he loved were about to miss his miraculous resurrection.

Alex slammed on the brakes when the dense forest suddenly opened to reveal a spectacular view of the lake, then waited for the frozen dust to settle as he stared out the open window. He sighed long and painfully hard, emotion welling in his chest at the sight of Frost Lake's northernmost cove stretching deep into the densely forested mountains. The view never failed to move him, and this morning it was especially sweet.

Completely unbidden, Alex remembered another homecoming ten years ago, when he'd brought home his bride. He'd stopped in this same spot, and they'd talked about their future—Charlotte about her plans to update the lodge's kitchen and Alex about his hope to expand their landholdings by another hundred thousand acres within two years.

He shook his head at how naive he'd been at twenty-two. Or, rather, how blinded he'd been by Charlotte's beauty that he hadn't seen the dollar signs in her eyes. She'd left him and their two children five years later, once she had finally understood that profits went into land and equipment purchases and that redecorating meant only a new stove. Four months later Charlotte had died in a car wreck, leaving Alex a widower and the sole parent of Delaney and Tucker. Delaney was ten now, and Tucker had turned seven only three months ago.

Yes, marriage was one mistake he was in no hurry to repeat. He had his kids, his father and brothers, and their logging business; he had everything a man could hope for in life. A life he was getting a second chance at and would never take for granted again, Alex vowed as he stared at the Knight homestead, snuggled in a stand of old-growth pines three miles up the rocky shoreline.

He could just make out the dock jutting off the south side of the peninsula, and he noticed that the floatplane was gone. But there was smoke rising from the chimney of the seventy-year-old lodge, which meant someone was home. So why weren't they answering the phone?

Alex heard the 22-wheeler coming toward him just moments before he saw it, and he stepped on the gas and spun the sedan to the side of the road. He rolled up the window to avoid the dust storm that arrived along with the deafening blast of an air horn as the tractor-trailer loaded with sawlogs went speeding by.

It was Wednesday, Alex realized, so the crew was hauling today. And tomorrow was Thanksgiving, which meant Delaney and Tucker had this week off from school and that his father had likely taken them to Portland in the floatplane as he did every year. Grady must be trying to give his grieving grandchildren some sense of normality, hoping to get their minds off their loss for a little while. Ethan would have gone in Alex's place as their pilot, and Paul was likely taking advantage of having the house to himself, dealing with his own grief by sitting in front of a crackling fire with a lady friend.

Alex headed home with a grin, thinking about the little tryst he was going to walk in on. He soon turned off the main hauling artery and onto a narrow lane for the last mile of his fantastical journey, which had begun with the sound of gunshots thirteen days ago in the mountainous jungles of Brazil. He'd spent the next eleven days in that hellhole of a rain forest, trying to make his way down to civilization while hiding from the murdering rebels hunting for foreign hostages to fund their personal war. Then there'd been two days of embassy red tape and unanswered calls home, and all day yesterday and last night spent in a succession of airports as he made his way back to Maine.

Alex finally pulled into the yard at the back of the lodge, shut off the engine, and unfolded his aching six-foot-two body out of the rented sedan. He absently brushed down the front of the jacket he'd bought at the Cincinnati airport and scanned the dooryard with a frown. All four pickups were parked beside the machine shed, which meant the loggers working farther up the road were on their own. That wasn't unusual, as the experienced crew was more than capable of cutting and loading the pulp and timber onto the trucks without supervision.

So he must have guessed right: Grady and Ethan and the kids were gone in the floatplane, and Paul had shut off the phones to hide out with his girlfriend. Alex leapt over the single step onto the back porch but stopped with his hand on the screen door handle. Should he just barge in on them? He'd likely give his baby brother a heart attack.

Hell, Paul deserved a good scare for drowning his sorrow in the arms of a woman while he thought his brother was floating facedown in some jungle backwater. Alex opened the screen door with a grin of expectancy and twisted the doorknob to burst inside with all the drama of a returning ghost.

But his shout of hello ended with a grunt when he came to a halt against the solid wood door. Alex stepped back and rubbed his forehead as he twisted the knob again, only to realize that the damn thing was locked.

They never locked their doors! It was an unwritten code of the woods never to lock a house with a telephone inside in case of an emergency. Alex pounded on the door so hard he rattled its frame. "Paul!" he shouted. "Get the hell out of bed, Casanova! It's past noon! Paul!"

His only answer was silence.

"Paul, open up!"

Still silence.

"Dammit, don't make be break down this door!"

"Paul's not here," came a soft, barely audible reply.

It took Alex a good five seconds to realize the voice he'd heard was female, and several more seconds to notice the face peeking from a crack in the curtain of a nearby window.

He stepped over and grinned down at the unfamiliar brown eyes staring up at him. "Where's Paul?" he asked in a more civil tone.

"He's in Augusta, lobbying against a tree-harvesting bill."

"And who are you?"

"Mrs. Knight."

"Mrs.?" Alex repeated, straightening in surprise. "You're married to Paul?"

She gave a small shake of her head.

"Ethan?" he whispered. "Ethan got *married?*"

She shook her head again.

He took another step back. *"You married Grady!"*

Her eyes widened at his shout, and she violently shook her head with a yelped "No!"

Alex stepped up to the window and bent at the

waist to put his eyes level with hers, finding a perverse pleasure in seeing her lean away and the curtain close. "Then who in hell did you marry, lady? There are no more Knights."

"I married Grady's oldest son, Alex. I—I'm his widow."

Alex reared back with a frown, momentarily wondering if he was still in the jungle and this was some sort of delirious nightmare. Either that, or he had hadn't heard right.

Alex scrubbed his face and sucked in a calming breath. "Lady," he said evenly, "Alex Knight left here five months ago to work in Brazil, and he was not married when he got on the plane."

A tiny crack appeared in the curtain again, just enough for him to see one large brown eye. "We were married a week ago this past Monday by proxy, by Judge Elroy Rogers," she said, her stilted voice sounding as if she were repeating a well-rehearsed line. "But then last Thursday, his father was told that Alex had been killed. Paul will be back tomorrow. If you want to talk to him, you'll have to come back then."

The curtain closed, and Alex saw the shadow of a small body move away from the window. He could only stand there in utter disbelief. He'd been married by proxy nine days ago? Then declared dead three days later?

But the men from the company he worked for had come here *eleven* days ago, they'd told Alex at the embassy, and his father had known *Saturday* that he was dead. So how in hell had Alexander Knight gotten married the following Monday? And by proxy. That wasn't even legal, was it?

The hell he was married! The little impostor was lying. Alex stepped back to the door and pounded on it again. "Open up!" he shouted, this time making even the windows rattle. "I swear I'll call the sheriff if you don't open this door."

"I already called him," she said from the window. "So you better leave right now."

Alex immediately moved back to the window, but instead of a pair of frightened eyes looking out, he found the business end of a shotgun pointing through the curtain. He choked on a laugh. He *must* be lying facedown in the rotting jungle, raging with fever. He was not standing on the back porch of his own damn house, having his own damn shotgun pointed at him by a woman he had married by proxy two days after he was supposed to have died.

The gun barrel clinked against the glass. "You better leave if you don't want Sheriff Tate to haul you off in handcuffs," she warned, her suggestion sounding more desperate than threatening.

"It'll take John an hour to get here," Alex snapped, placing his hands on his hips as he faced the window. He recognized his old shotgun by the missing sight on the tip of the barrel and knew the damn thing didn't have a firing pin. "And when John does show up, you'll be the one leaving in handcuffs." A thought suddenly struck him. "Hey, what's your first name?"

"It—it's Sarah."

"Sarah," he repeated. "Sarah Banks, the housekeeper Grady hired this summer? You came back from the coast with him at the end of their vacation." Alex dropped his hands to his sides, his indignation evaporating on a relieved sigh. "Sarah, it's okay. I'm Alex Knight, Delaney and Tucker's dad. They told me all about you in their letters and phone calls. How you ran the bed-and-breakfast they stayed at on Crag Island last August, and how my father talked you into coming back with them to keep house for us. It's okay, Sarah. I know all about you, because it's me, Alex."

The shotgun barrel lowered only inches. "You're not Alex Knight!" she denied. "Alex died in Brazil six days ago."

"Go get my picture off the mantel," he said, stepping back and unzipping his jacket. "Go on, get it so you can see for yourself."

The curtain closed, and Alex saw her shadow disappear into the kitchen. He took off his jacket and smoothed down the front of his rumpled shirt, combed his fingers through his overlong brown hair, then straightened his shoulders and waited. The curtain finally opened again, this time with a small picture frame appearing against the glass, and Alex realized that Sarah was comparing him to his photo.

"I've lost a good twenty pounds, and I haven't shaved in three days," he pointed out. "But look past the cuts and bruises on my face. My eyes, Sarah. They're the same. And my nose and jaw," he said, lifting his hand to rub his stubbled cheek. "It's me, Alexander James Knight. And I'm not dead."

The curtain closed, the shadow disappeared again, and Alex was left standing for what seemed like several minutes before he finally heard the dead bolt softly click. He stepped back to the door, opened the screen, and turned the knob to step inside.

Sarah stood across the kitchen near the swinging door leading into the great room, her large doe eyes framed by a porcelain face as white as new-fallen snow. She was still holding the shotgun, though it was pointed at the floor now instead of him, and Alex knew he really *was* in the jungle, delirious with fever and having a dream beyond his wildest fantasy. If this was what the angel of death looked like, he would follow her into hell itself.

She was beautiful. Utterly, stunningly perfect. From her long, lustrous hair the color of sunshine framing her china-doll face, down every inch of her petite but definitely well-endowed body, the woman was a vision of feminine perfection.

He should probably say something instead of just staring like an awestruck teenager, but for the life of him, Alex couldn't find his voice. For one insane but vividly imaginative moment, he wished he really *were* married to her. What in hell had his father been thinking, bringing this package of female perfection home to three bachelors?

"You can set down the shotgun," he said softly. "It doesn't have a firing pin." He frowned. "Don't you know that pointing a useless gun at someone is the best way to get yourself shot? If I *had* been an intruder, I could have been armed."

He hadn't thought it was possible, but Sarah paled even more. Alex set his jacket on the bench by the door, ran his hands through his hair with a calming sigh, and stepped all the way into the kitchen.

"Sarah," he said when she stepped back against the swinging door to the great room, making it open. "I really am Alex Knight, so there's nothing to be afraid of. I just want to take a long hot shower, eat most of whatever that is I smell cooking, and sleep until my kids get home."

"They don't know you're alive," she whispered. She leaned the shotgun against the wall without taking her gaze off his, her face flushing with color as she raised her hands to her cheeks. "Delaney and Tucker don't know you're alive! And Grady! Oh, my God, you've got to call them!" She rushed to the kitchen table and picked up a piece of paper that she held toward him. "This is the hotel they're staying at in Portland. You need to let them know you're not dead!"

He was finally getting somewhere. Her concern for Delaney and Tucker had overridden her shock, and she slid the portable phone across the table to him, tossing the paper down beside it when the stove timer started buzzing.

"Call them," she said, rushing to the stove and picking up a pair of oven mitts. She was bent over to lift something from the oven—and Alex was admiring the view—when the wail of a siren suddenly pierced the air. "Oh, no," she squeaked, turning with a pie in her hands, her stricken gaze darting to Alex. "That's Sheriff Tate."

Alex also turned as the sheriff's cruiser came to a stop mere inches from the porch in a cloud of spitting gravel. John Tate was out of the car before it finished rocking, one hand on his holster and his eyes pinned on the screen door.

"Step out of the house, mister," John ordered, drawing his weapon. "Now!"

Alex used his toe to push open the screen door, stepped onto the porch with his hands raised, and smiled at his friend.

"Sarah!" John hollered. "Sarah, where are you?"

"She's taking pies out of the oven, John," Alex told him. "And this, my friend, is not the welcome home I was expecting."

John straightened from his threatening stance and squinted through the sun reflecting off the settling dust. "A-Alex?" he whispered.

Alex nodded but kept his hands raised. "How many of our trucks did you run off the road?" he asked. "You must have set a speed record getting out here—unless you were hunting deer at one of our old cuttings again."

"Alex?" John repeated, a bit stronger this time, lowering his gun. "But Grady said you were dead!"

Alex dropped his hands and shook his head. "Almost. But it'll take more than a few crazy bastards to finish me off." He touched a cut on his forehead. "Though the jungle nearly did me in."

John holstered his gun, leapt onto the porch, and gave Alex a hug that would have strangled a bear. "My God, man, it's good to see you," he said, his voice raw with emotion as he slapped Alex's back. John suddenly stepped away and looked toward the kitchen. "Sarah?" he asked, moving his gaze back to Alex.

"She's fine, though I think I scared two years off her life." Alex broke into a grin. "You been trying to work up the nerve to ask out our housekeeper, Tate?" Alex threw his arm over John's shoulder to guide him inside. "Don't wait too long, my friend, or I just might beat you to it," he added softly as they walked into the kitchen. "Sarah, was that an apple pie you pulled out of the oven?"

But before Sarah could answer, John moved to stand between them, facing Alex with a look of confusion.

"You okay, Sarah?" he asked without looking at her. "The dispatcher said you sounded frightened and that someone was trying to break in."

"I'm okay, Officer Tate," she said, going to the cupboard and taking down two plates. "I just didn't recognize Mr.—ah—Alex at first." She pulled two forks from a drawer, set them on the counter, then started cutting the pie. "It's going to be messy because it's still hot," she warned with her back to them, her long blond hair hiding her face.

What in hell was going on here? *Officer* Tate? Was Sarah trying to pretend there was nothing going on between her and John? "Have a seat, John," Alex said, pulling a chair from the table and sitting down, then using his foot to shove another chair out for his friend. "And tell me how many people showed up for my funeral." He gave John a guileless smile. "I did have a service, didn't I?"

His old high-school buddy paled and slowly shook his head. "Grady scheduled it for next Wednesday."

Alex kicked out the chair a little farther and motioned for John to sit down. "Good," he said. "I didn't miss it, then. You suppose Clay Porter will show up?"

John finally sat at the table with a relieved grin. "Porter will likely be the first one there, and not leave until after he spits on your grave."

Sarah brought over two heaping plates of pie, set them in front of the men, then rushed back to the stove when a different timer started buzzing on the counter. She shut it off, opened the oven door with her mitts, and pulled out a large covered pan from the bottom rack—this time while both men enjoyed the view, Alex noticed.

But the smell tickling his nose finally got the best of him, and Alex picked up his fork and looked at his plate. Honest to God, he hadn't known so many apples could fit in one piece of pie. Dispensing with manners, Alex drove his fork into the center, leaned down to meet his hand halfway, and shoveled the dripping, crust-covered apple into his mouth. He didn't even wait until he was done chewing to repeat the process, and only after his third mouthful did he notice John staring at him.

"It's been five months since I've had apple pie," Alex defended while chewing. He patted his belly with his free hand. "And I've got twenty pounds to gain back."

"Where have you been for the last six days?" John asked. "Grady said your work site was attacked by rebels last Thursday and that you were killed."

"Thirteen days," Alex corrected after swallowing another mouthful. "They attacked thirteen days ago, and I spent the next eleven days trying to get back to civilization without getting captured or eaten by jungle beasts."

"Thirteen?" John repeated, glancing over his shoulder at Sarah, whose back stiffened.

What in hell was going on here? John was acting more confounded than a teenager in a whorehouse.

A sense of dread suddenly shot through Alex, making the pie he'd eaten settle like lead. "Sarah?" he said, then waited until she looked at him. "How come you called yourself Mrs. Knight when I showed up? Did Grady tell you to say that to strangers to give you some security when you're alone here?"

Her large brown eyes just stared at him.

"She *is* Mrs. Knight," John interjected, drawing Alex's attention. "You were married a week ago this past Monday."

"I was running for my life a week ago Monday."

"By proxy," John clarified. "Grady told everyone in town that Judge Rogers married you and Sarah in his chambers the same day Sarah adopted Delaney and Tucker."

"She *what?*" Alex bolted up from his chair, sending it skidding across the floor as he turned to Sarah.

John also stood and moved to stand between them again, his expression even more confounded. His eyes suddenly narrowed. "You didn't know," he whispered, glancing over his shoulder at Sarah, who was now pressed against the counter, her hands gripping her apron and her eyes as big as silver dollars. John looked back at Alex. "That wily old bastard," he said, shaking his head. "Grady told everyone that you met Sarah last spring when you went to check out Crag Island for their summer vacation. And that you decided not to wait until you got home from Brazil and married her by proxy last Monday."

"I spent two weeks in *Brazil* last spring, looking over the dam site," Alex said evenly, glaring at Sarah before turning his glare on John. "I had never even heard of Crag Island until Dad told me where he was taking the family this past summer."

John rubbed the back of his neck and frowned. "Then he must have been trying to protect Delaney and Tucker," he thought out loud. "You said he'd been told you were dead on Saturday?" John asked, and Alex nodded. "So he didn't say anything until after he got Sarah married to you, so she could adopt the kids. Then he waited three days to announce your death."

"Protect them from what? I made a will before I left, giving custody of Delaney and Tucker to Ethan if anything happened to me."

John cocked his head, his expression speculative. "To protect them from your in-laws, maybe?" he offered. "We all know Charlotte's parents would have contested your will and come after those kids. Hell, they tried to get custody of them when Charlotte died. Grady must have talked Rogers into fudging the paperwork, to marry you to Sarah before word of your death got out. That would have given your in-laws less of a chance in a custody battle."

Both men looked at Sarah, who was clutching her stomach, her face blanched with worry.

"Y-you can't tell anyone, Mr. Tate," she said, her gaze darting to Alex, then back to John. "If the truth gets out, Grady will get in trouble for forging all those papers. And it could end Judge Rogers's career." She stepped closer, looking directly at Alex. "We thought you were dead, and Sheriff Tate is right. Grady was afraid your late wife's parents would come after your children, and he didn't want Delaney and Tucker to be put through any more upset."

"So he married me to you and then had you adopt them?" Alex whispered, unable to believe what he was hearing. The terror of the jungle was nothing compared to the mess he'd just walked into.

His father, along with their good friend Judge Elroy Rogers, not to mention their equally guilty housekeeper, would be brought up on charges if he didn't go along with this insane—though amazingly inventive—conspiracy. And his kids would be dragged through even more trauma.

"Grady was desperate," Sarah said, taking another step closer. "He was only thinking of the children."

"And you?" Alex asked ever so softly, as anger born of desperation tightened his chest. "Were you thinking about my children, Sarah? Or were you picturing a real nice future here as my widow?"

"That's uncalled for," John said, stepping between them again. "She's not Charlotte, Alex."

Alex turned on John. "No? Then exactly who is she?"

"Your wife," John snapped, tucking his thumbs into his belt and glaring right back at him. "At least until Grady gets home and you can decide what to do about this . . . this . . ." John's defenses suddenly crumbled, and he shot Alex one last confounded look before he turned to Sarah. "I won't say a word to anyone, I promise," he told her. "The way I see it, this is a personal matter, and no one's business but your own."

"Thank you," she said with a nod, turning back to the counter. "I'm going for a walk," she suddenly said, taking off her apron as she changed direction. And with her head down so that her hair hid her face, she scurried past John and Alex and onto the porch and ran into the yard.

Both men were left standing in silence, staring out the screen door as it banged shut.

John softly whistled through his teeth, looked over at Alex, and shrugged. "Well, my friend," he said with a sheepish grin. "I'm damn glad you're home safe and sound, though I don't know whether to feel sorry for you or envious."

Alex stepped up to the screen door to watch Sarah run down a narrow path into the woods. "Neither do I, Tate. Dammit to hell, what has Dad gotten me into?" he asked, staring at the spot where his *wife* had disappeared.

Chapter Two

❊

Talk about good deeds coming back to bite her! Holy smokes, she had a *husband!* A very-much-alive husband, who apparently wasn't any happier to find himself married than she was.

Sarah ran down the forest path as if the demons of hell were nipping at her heels, then picked her way along the lakeshore until she came to her thinking rock. Trembling uncontrollably, she climbed up the huge boulder and sat down in the deep bowl sculpted into its side facing the lake. Only then, once she was settled in her private little hidey-hole, with her knees pulled up to her chest and her face buried in her hands, did she finally break into gut-wrenching sobs.

A husband. What in the world was she supposed to do with a towering, broad-shouldered, blue-eyed husband? Alex Knight was even taller than his equally imposing

brother Ethan and as forebodingly scary as Paul was boyishly charming.

This was Grady's fault, dammit, for talking her into
marrying his dead son. What had looked like a perfect
way to get the children she'd always wanted without the
usually requisite husband had turned into her worst
nightmare when Alex Knight had come back from the
dead. Actually, he looked as if he'd crawled his way back;
his face and hands were covered with cuts and bruises, he
was as gaunt as a ghost, and his eyes—though they definitely matched the eyes in his photo—looked downright
hunted.

Sarah was honestly happy that Delaney and Tucker
had their dad back, and sincerely glad for Grady and
Ethan and Paul. The Knights had been devastated by the
loss of what Sarah had come to realize was the foundation of their family. Alex Knight seemed to have been
the anchor that held them all together, and his death
had cast them adrift with nothing to cling to but their
mutual grief. But that would change tomorrow, when
they arrived home to a Thanksgiving feast that truly
would be a celebration.

Yet she was now in an extremely awkward position.
She knew exactly what Alex was feeling—arriving home
to a wife he'd never met much less wanted—because she
was feeling just as angry, frustrated, and confused. But
most especially angry.

She had subtly probed her new employers—mostly
Paul—in the two and a half months she'd been here and
had learned that Alex's marriage to Charlotte hadn't exactly been wedded bliss and that he'd been quite content
being a single father for the last five years. Just as Sarah

had been happily widowed for four years, since her marriage to Roland Banks had been no picnic.

Sarah wiped away her tears, then hugged her knees to her chest to hold in what warmth she could to her shivering body. She couldn't believe how quickly John Tate had figured out Grady's plan to protect Delaney and Tucker. Grady had warned her that people in town might question her marriage, but if they all stuck to their story, there wasn't much anyone could do about it. John had visited enough for her to realize he was a close family friend, and she believed he would keep his promise not to tell anyone. And knowing what a close-knit family the Knights were, Sarah didn't think Alex was about to run around town denouncing his marriage, either. Which meant that for the time being, she was stuck with another husband she didn't want.

Roland Banks had been quite full of himself, and quite convinced that a naive seventeen-year-old bride had been the perfect solution to his problem, as well as a good way to keep his dragon of a mother off his back. Sarah had spent the next twelve years with Martha Banks hanging on *her* back instead, while being ignored by her husband for the eight years before he'd drowned at sea. Well, ignored except when Roland needed a pretty wife to show off.

Youthful ignorance, misplaced gratitude, and a warped sense of duty had locked Sarah into a terrible mess at seventeen, and it had taken her twelve years to get free. And what had she done with her newfound freedom? She'd placed herself right back in another heart-wrenching trap. How could she just walk away from Delaney and Tucker? She couldn't love those kids more if she had given birth to them herself. But she couldn't stay married to a stranger, either.

Maybe she could quietly divorce Alex and go back to being their housekeeper until she got her sporting camps up and running in the spring. Yes—she could keep to her original plan to reopen the lodge and eight cabins, three miles down the shoreline, which Grady had offered to lease to her when he'd stayed at her bed-and-breakfast on Crag Island in August.

But she couldn't live in the same house with her ex-husband until spring; that would be much too awkward. Dammit! Grady had better come up with a solution when he got home tomorrow. He'd made this mess, and he needed to fix it!

"Sarah! Sarah, where are you?"

Uh-oh. Her ghost-husband had come looking for her. Sarah scrunched into a ball to make herself as tiny as possible. She didn't want to talk to him. Not yet—preferably not ever.

"Sarah, you didn't take a jacket, and it's getting cold out here. Sarah! Show yourself!"

The man sure did love to shout. First he'd yelled at Paul to open the door, then he'd yelled at her when he'd found out Paul wasn't home, and he was *still* shouting. Sarah slid deeper into her seat. She'd rather freeze to death than face him right now, and she'd go home when she was good and ready, dammit.

"Look, I'm sorry I shouted at you back there," he hollered. "And I'm sorry if I scared you. I promise to be a gentleman if you come back to the house, where it's warm."

Sarah could tell he was only several yards away by the

sound of his voice. She pursed her lips together and refused to answer.

She heard him growl under his breath and let out a frustrated sigh. "Okay," he said loudly. "I'll just leave your jacket on this bush, and you can come home when you're ready. I promise, I'm not angry anymore."

That was a flat-out lie. Mr. Alexander Knight was very angry: because he had a wife he didn't want, because he'd been anxious to see his kids and family and they weren't here, and because she wasn't listening to him. Well, she didn't care; she wasn't going home until she had worked up the nerve to spend an entire evening and night alone in the house with a virtual stranger.

Sarah's watch started beeping, and she slapped her hand over her wrist to muffle the sound, frantically poking the buttons to make it stop. A rock farther down the shoreline rolled against another rock, and Sarah prayed the lapping waves had drowned out the alarm.

"Sarah?" she heard him say from about thirty yards away. She held her breath for what seemed like forever before a snapping branch told her he'd finally gone into the woods.

Still, she didn't move, just in case it was a trick to make her think he'd left. She scowled at her watch; it was five minutes to four, and the alarm had been to remind her that Oprah's show was coming on. Sarah leaned her head against the boulder with a frustrated sigh. So much for her plans to watch Oprah and then a quilting show on satellite TV. After that she had intended to sit in front of a crackling fire and work on her plans for the abandoned sporting camps she intended to turn into a first-rate tourist destination. And then she'd planned to go to bed and finish the novel she'd started last night.

Sarah stared up at the clouds rolling in from the northwest and thought about the heroine in the book she was a third of the way through. What would Rachel Foster do if she found herself in this position? Sarah gave a soft snort. Rachel sure as heck wouldn't be hiding in a hole in a rock, freezing her tail off. She'd be standing on tiptoe right in her unwanted husband's face, telling him to quit shouting.

Oh, to be like one of those women who seemed to pop right off the pages of the books she couldn't get enough of. Ever since she'd discovered romance novels in the mail-order library catalog nine years ago, Sarah had been trying to live up to their wonderful examples. Even though she knew they were fictional, those women always seemed to be smart, feisty, and ever so sure of themselves. They had the bravado to love manly men, were confidently sexual creatures in their own right, and went after their dreams with the tenacity of salmon swimming upstream.

She'd *almost* been living her own dream. She had found her slice of heaven here in these beautiful mountains, with two children who needed her and two brothers and a father figure she could love. And come spring, she would be a competely independent businesswoman and run her sporting camps the way *she* wanted to run them. Yes, she had found happily ever after, just like one of the women in her books.

Well, except for the handsome hero part. But she wasn't even thirty yet; there was still time for a flaming affair. In the historical romances especially, being a merry widow meant a woman was free to indulge in affairs of the heart. And that's what Sarah had been planning on doing once she worked up the nerve.

"Okay, enough dreaming," she scolded herself in a whisper. "What would Rachel Foster do if she found herself married to a complete stranger?"

Rachel was a fictional architect who lived on the coast of Maine, who had sworn off men—or at least passionate men. So Rachel probably wouldn't care *what* her back-from-the-dead husband thought of being married to her. She would just go about her business as if he didn't exist, wouldn't she? Yeah, Rachel Foster would simply ignore the shouting man, and maybe even pretend he was still dead until everyone got home tomorrow.

That certainly sounded doable to Sarah. She could just go back to the house and finish her preparations for tomorrow's feast, watch her shows on the kitchen television, and then head to her room and lose herself in Rachel's story. Alex Knight wouldn't exist for her; he could have the great room to himself and the entire upstairs of the house.

Sarah sat up with a resigned sigh. She should probably feed him, though. He had said he just wanted to shower, eat, and sleep until his kids got home. She could fix him a tray of food and serve him in the great room, so he could eat in front of the fire and not in her kitchen. Maybe . . . maybe she'd pour him a drink—or even two—of Grady's whiskey. That should knock him out for the night.

Come to think of it, maybe she'd pour herself a tall glass of whiskey mixed with a bit of lemonade and sip her way through the awkward evening ahead. Rachel Foster would have a drink, wouldn't she?

Sarah turned to peek over the top of the boulder and spotted her jacket hanging on a branch. She climbed down onto the shoreline, stepping from rock to rock to avoid getting her feet wet, grabbed the jacket, and slipped it on. Then, with the fictional Rachel Foster giving her courage, Sarah marched back to the lodge with all the dignity of a smart, feisty, confident heroine.

Alex leaned back on the couch with a sigh of utter and complete satisfaction, lacing his fingers over his full belly as he stared at the empty plates on the coffee table. He'd literally licked them clean, not willing to miss even one drop of the most delicious pork gravy ever to grace a potato. And the stuffing! In a million years, he wouldn't have thought he'd like toasted almonds and dried cranberries in his pork stuffing, but the taste lingering on his tongue had been divinely inspired.

Alex spotted a carrot curl that had fallen off his plate and sat up to pop the thin, perfectly steamed ribbon into his mouth. Then he picked up the second glass of whiskey Sarah had poured him when she'd brought in fresh ice cubes a few minutes ago, and swirled the contents.

The large wooden tray teemed with empty dishes, a tall glass of what had been lemonade, and a tiny vase arranged with some berry-laden twigs, all sitting on a crisp white linen place mat. The napkin accompanying the meal had been folded to look like a bird.

Alex had stayed at a few five-star hotels in his time, and he couldn't remember ever being served a tastier dinner in finer style. No wonder his dad had hired Sarah to keep house for them, if this was how they had been treated last summer.

When Sarah had returned to the house, she'd gone straight to the fridge while reminding him to call his father, and she'd started making dinner without even giving him a glance. She'd been a completely different woman from the one who had run from the house in a panic. This Sarah was calm, politely aloof, and all business. She was still working in the kitchen; he could hear pans rattling and cupboard doors opening and closing occasionally, all over the sound of the television blaring out some sort of how-to program. After listening closely for several minutes, Alex realized that Sarah was watching a cooking show. Which made sense, as the smells that spilled through the swinging door whenever she came floating in with more food or drink made Alex wonder if he wasn't having a culinary dream. At this rate, he'd gain back his twenty pounds—along with several extra—in less than a month.

He took a sip of whiskey and leaned back on the couch to gaze around the great room, cataloging the many changes, some of them subtle and some obvious. The curtains were new, Grady's favorite old chair had been reupholstered, and the windows gleamed spotlessly as they reflected the interior lighting. There wasn't one dust bunny or cobweb to be found. The furniture was the same and his mother's knicknacks were all still here, but everything had been tastefully rearranged and polished to an almost blinding shine. Hell, the place looked like a staged photo from *Better Homes and Gardens*.

Actually, it looked like a very upscale bed-and-breakfast.

"Have you been able to reach Grady yet?" Sarah asked as she came floating through the swinging door, this time carrying an armful of wood that she dropped into the box by the hearth.

"You don't need to lug in wood, Sarah," Alex said, setting down his glass to stand up.

She shook her head and waved at him to stay sitting. "Don't move," she ordered, picking up the tray of empty dishes. "I don't mind carrying in wood. I always wanted a fireplace back on Crag Island, but all we had was an ancient potbellied stove in the parlor." She set the tray against one hip to free one of her hands and leaned down to top off his glass of whiskey from the bottle she'd left on the table. "You just sit back and enjoy being home. Did you find the towels for your shower okay? I moved them into the hall closet, where there was more room."

He'd noticed that the closet in the bathroom had been set up for everyone in the house to have his own shelf, labeled with their names. There was one empty shelf, and Alex assumed it was to have been his when he returned on schedule in a couple of months.

"Excuse me?" he asked, frowning up at her when she asked him another question.

"Were you able to reach Grady?"

He shook his head. "No. They must still be out. I left a message with the desk clerk for Dad or Ethan to call home when they got in."

Sarah shot him a broad grin that made Alex catch his breath. Damn, she was beautiful when she smiled. "They're going to jump right on that plane and fly home tonight, once they hear your voice," she said.

Alex shook his head again. "They could take off from the airport in Portland, because the plane is amphibious, but Ethan won't land on the lake in the dark. Not with the kids on board, anyway."

"Oh. So they will have to wait until morning."

Alex nodded, his attention drawn back to the tray when she pulled it off her hip to hold with both hands. "Do you spoil everyone this way, Sarah, and wait on them as if they're at your inn? Good Lord," he said, rolling his eyes. "You're going to turn my kids into spoiled brats."

She looked confused, if not a bit insulted. "I don't spoil anyone. I just do my job well."

"You've turned this old house into a showcase, and you haven't stopped working since you came back from your walk. Or are you trying to impress me, afraid I might tell my father that I think you should leave?"

For a moment, Alex was sorry he'd said that. But dammit, she'd spent the last four hours acting as if she were serving the lord of the manor, and he didn't like it one bit.

"I'm not trying to impress you or anyone," she said tightly, her back rigid with anger—which only served to accent her lush figure, Alex couldn't help but notice. "Just because I like to keep a nice house and cook nice meals doesn't mean I have a hidden agenda."

"Look, I'm sorry," he said, lowering his eyes so he'd quit trying to picture what was under that pretty pink sweater. "The house is beautiful, and the meal was wonderful. And the whiskey," he added, picking up his refilled drink, "was a very thoughtful and much appreciated addition."

"You're welcome," she softly snapped, turning and marching through the swinging kitchen door.

Uh-oh. She had definitely noticed him noticing her chest. Well, dammit, a blind man would appreciate the way she filled out a sweater! He winced at the sound of several pans loudly clanging together, then again when a cupboard door slammed shut and the television volume was turned up higher. So his curvy housekeeper-wife had a bit of a temper, did she, as well as an aversion to being ogled? How . . . interesting. Alex tucked both those little facts away with a smile and saluted the kitchen door with his drink before he took another long sip.

Chapter Three

❖

The jerk! Sarah took a long swig of her whiskey-laced lemonade and glared at the closed door. The arrogant jerk—implying she'd spent the last four hours buttering him up because she was afraid of being fired! Alex might be the heir apparent, but Grady had given Sarah his word that she would have a home here on Knight land for as long as she wanted.

Sarah took an angry swipe at the moisture suddenly welling in her eyes. Grady had even called her *daughter* last week and given her a fatherly hug when they'd come out of Judge Rogers's chambers. Ethan and Paul had hugged her, too, and they had called her *sister*. Just because Alex Knight had the nerve to be alive didn't mean she would be sent packing. She was not some disposable pawn, just because she was no longer needed to protect the children. And she sure as heck would never lower herself to groveling to keep her position.

Sarah took another swig of her drink. She'd spent twelve miserable years indebted to Martha Banks and eight years trying to be invisible to that dragon's bully of a son. The day she buried Martha last June, Sarah had walked away from the cemetery vowing never, ever, to let anyone make her feel inadequate again. Burying Martha had ended Sarah's last obligation to her deceased father and had finally freed her to become the heroine of her own story.

And when Grady Knight had landed on Crag Island in August, along with his grandchildren and two younger sons for a month's vacation at her inn, he had presented Sarah with the opportunity to take the first important step toward her new life. Come keep house for them over the winter, Grady had offered, while she worked on reopening the abandoned sporting camps he'd acquired when he had bought the land they sat on several years ago. Grady's only stipulation at the time had been for the sporting camps to be their little secret until he could convince his sons that they *should* be reopened.

If there was one thing Sarah had never doubted, it was that she was an excellent innkeeper. And she was not going to let Mr. Jerk in there, she thought with another poisonous glare at the closed door, belittle her talents.

She wasn't turning his kids into brats, she was civilizing them. Delaney was learning to sew and finally taking an interest in what she wore and how she did her hair. And Tucker was finally able to cut his own meat without endangering himself or anyone close by. Even Ethan's and Paul's manners had improved. Grady had confessed to Sarah that his wife, Rose, had drilled manners into her sons from birth but that they may have grown a bit lax since her death seven years ago.

Not that they were barbarians, they just needed some feminine input, Grady had explained. Rose had died just months after Tucker was born, and since Charlotte had run off two years later, the whole family had grown sort of ragged around the edges.

Mr. Alex Knight could use a refresher course in manners as well, Sarah decided as she tilted her glass to catch the last drops of lemonade before turning to the counter to cut up more lemons. She quickly made another pitcher and refilled the bottom third of her glass with whiskey from the extra bottle in the pantry, then topped it off with lemonade, hoping Alex was gulping down his own whiskey. If he felt half as exhausted as he looked, the whiskey should knock him clean off his feet until tomorrow morning.

Sarah smiled as she sipped her new drink, quite proud of her plan to ply Alex with liquor until he passed out. It was amazing what one could learn from novels, and she couldn't wait to climb into bed so she could find out how Rachel Foster was going to get out of the mess she was in. When Sarah had stopped reading last night, Rachel had been sneaking through the secret tunnels of the beautiful mansion she'd helped her father design, trying to replace a stolen emerald earring. Tonight Sarah hoped to reach the part of the story where the sexual tension that had been building between Rachel Foster and Keenan Oakes finally exploded.

Sarah swirled the ice in her half-empty glass and eyed the great-room door. Too bad Alex was such a jerk. He was a little on the thin side and a bit banged up, but he had the overall look of a romance hero. Especially those crystal blue eyes that could get a woman all hot and bothered if he ever turned on the charm. Assuming he *wanted* a woman's attention, because he sure as heck hadn't been trying to charm her!

Sarah had caught him staring at her chest, but then, most men did. It was the main reason Roland Banks had married her; showing up with a curvy blond wife on his arm had been a great disguise. But Alex Knight was just a typical lech.

When the phone rang in the other room, Sarah immediately rushed to the door, pressing her ear against it to listen.

"Hello," she heard Alex say. "Ethan! Ethan, it's me, Alex!"

There was a moment's silence, and then Sarah heard, "Ethan, listen, it really is me. I'm not dead, brother," Alex said softly. "I didn't get shot, because I escaped into the jungle. It took me eleven days to make my way out. . . . No, no, I'm fine, I promise. I tried calling home from the U.S. embassy in Brazil, but no one answered. Is Grady there? And Delaney and Tucker?"

There was an even longer silence, then Sarah heard Alex pull in a shuddering breath and softly say, "No, don't wake the kids. You'll never get them back to sleep. I want to talk to Dad. Put him on. Wait! Tell him first, so he doesn't have a heart attack when he hears my voice."

Sarah straightened and took a large gulp of lemonade as she fought back tears. She could just imagine Grady and Ethan in their hotel room in Portland, Ethan telling Grady that his son was alive.

"D-Dad," Alex said, his voice thick with emotion.

"Jesus, Dad, don't cry. I'm okay. I'm home, and I promise you that I'm perfectly fine."

Sarah pressed her ear up to the door again, wiping a tear running down her cheek. She was so happy for Grady and Ethan, though sad that their reunion had to be taking place over the phone. But tomorrow would be a great celebration. And she would make sure it was extra special for them, when the *whole* family sat down at the table again.

"Yes, Dad, I met Sarah." Sarah pressed her ear closer. "Yes, she's very sweet, though I was surprised to find my-self married to her. . . . No, I didn't make a scene."

Another flat-out lie! Alex Knight was a compulsive liar.

"Yes, of course I will be a gentleman. . . . No, Dad, I won't say anything to her until you get here. . . . I *promise* you that I'm fine. I'll tell you all about it when you get home. . . . Yes, we'll discuss the situation then. Give Delaney and Tucker a kiss for me, will you? Lord, I can't wait to see them. . . . Okay, then, good night. I'll be wait-ing on the dock for you at daybreak. I love you, too," he finished thickly.

Sarah had to use her apron to dry her tears this time, and she gulped down the last of her lemonade as she made her way back to the counter. Good grief, she was going to be a bawling geyser tomorrow when Delaney and Tucker saw their daddy.

"Sarah! Do you have any Band-Aids?"

There he was shouting again, not two minutes after promising Grady he'd be a perfect gentleman.

"Yes!" Sarah shouted back, only to slap her hand over her mouth. She never, ever shouted. She set her glass on the counter and reached into a top cupboard for the first-aid supplies, grabbed the box of Band-Aids and a tube of salve, and spun around to march into the great room before the jerk shouted again.

But Sarah had to grab the counter instead when the kitchen suddenly started spinning. Uh-oh, she probably shouldn't have had that third glass of lemonade. She took a deep breath, blinked several times to get back her focus, then slowly and deliberately walked to the door and opened it.

"The whiskey went straight to my legs," Alex said, giving her a lopsided smile. "Or I would have come into the kitchen and asked nicely."

Sarah could only stare, amazed at how a simple smile could change a man so drastically. Now Alex looked more like his girl-crazy brother Paul than his serious brother Ethan. "That's okay," she said, carefully walking up and dropping the salve and Band-Aids onto the couch beside him.

She turned to leave, but Alex caught her by the hand and pulled her back to face him. Only she didn't exactly face him but lost her balance and fell onto his lap.

"Whoa!" he said with a grunt of surprise, catching her in his arms with a laugh. "Don't run off. I want to tell you that I spoke with Grady."

"I-I heard," she whispered, utterly mortified as she tried to scramble off him.

His arms tightened around her, and his smile widened until there were two dimples showing on his cleanly shaven cheeks. "They're going to leave Portland early, so they can be home by daybreak."

"I see," Sarah barely got out, feeling heat climbing up

her throat. Holy smokes, she was sitting on his lap! And he didn't appear ready to let her go anytime soon.

Her blush kicked up several notches as their eyes met, and just as she'd suspected, when Alex Knight decided to turn on the charm, the woman on the receiving end definitely got hot and bothered. Sarah was near burning up. And there wasn't one weak muscle in his body, she quickly discovered; his arms around her were rock solid, his chest felt as hard as stone, and . . . uh-oh, his eyes had just lowered to her mouth.

"I wanted to ask if you'll wake me up in the morning," he said softly, still staring at her mouth. "But I've decided to . . . I've decided . . ." His eyes finally lifted to hers. "To kiss you," he whispered, pulling her against his stone-hard chest as he settled his mouth over hers.

Some long-buried feminine instinct compelled Sarah to hold perfectly still. *Now* she understood why the women in historical romance novels swooned; she couldn't seem to catch her breath! Tiny pinpricks of awareness shot through her, tightening her skin and making her heart race as Alex's lips moved over hers. He tasted like pork gravy and whiskey and smelled of flannel and aftershave.

Was he ever going to stop?

Did she really want him to?

Sarah suddenly surprised herself by softening against him and unpursing her lips.

The moment she did, he broke free and leaned away—though he didn't loosen his hold on her, and he was back to staring at her mouth. Sarah wanted in the worst way to squirm, but that same instinct kept her still again.

His gaze finally rose to hers, his eyes a deep, dark blue under heavy eyelids. "I'm drunk, Sarah. Drunk on happiness from finally talking to my brother and dad, and drunk on the whiskey you've been pouring down me all evening. Don't read anything into this."

The heroines in her books would have slapped his face. Sarah braced her hands on his shoulders and shoved off the arrogant jerk, smiling in satisfaction when she heard him grunt. She glared at him, her hands on her hips and her chest heaving over her racing heart.

What in heck could she possibly say? *No problem, I like a pulse-pounding kiss as much as any bimbo?* Or *Think nothing of it, Mr. Knight, I enjoy being mauled by a drunk?*

Sarah gave him one last narrow-eyed glare that should have sent him back to his grave, spun on her heel, and marched to the kitchen door as steadily as she could. Alex Knight's quiet chuckles were the last thing she heard as she slapped open the door, only to have it swing closed behind her with a soft, anticlimactic *swoosh*.

He was a bit more drunk than he realized. But damn it to hell, the woman was beautiful. Alex scrubbed his face with both hands, trying to rub away the feel of her lips. He'd only wanted a little taste to satisfy his curiosity, but he'd gotten a nuclear reaction that had nearly backfired on him. Sarah had felt like molten heat in his arms when she had softened against him. She had also tasted of lemonade that definitely had been laced with whiskey, which meant the woman had been pouring liquor down her own throat all evening, as well. Alex gazed at the still swaying kitchen door. Would she tell Grady tomorrow that he'd made a drunken pass at her?

Alex had heard the protectiveness in Grady's voice on the phone tonight. And as emotional as his dad had been to learn Alex was alive, dear old softhearted Grady hadn't been so overwhelmed that he couldn't warn Alex to be nice to Sarah.

Alex frowned at the dying fire in the hearth. His father had been complaining for years that they needed a woman around, that Delaney needed a role model and Tucker needed mothering. So when it appeared his sons weren't going to accommodate him anytime soon, Grady had gone out and found his own woman—whom he hadn't hesitated to make a daughter-in-law not two days after getting the news of his son's death.

Alex scrubbed his face again, trying to think straight. Okay, he had to give his dad credit for picking a great housekeeper. But what had Grady been thinking to bring such a tempting woman home to his three bachelor sons?

Unless . . . unless that was precisely why Grady had brought Sarah here. The wily old coyote. He'd been *hoping* to rile his sons, and likely hadn't cared which one, as long as he got a daughter-in-law in the end.

Alex threw his head back against the couch and stared up at the moose head hanging over the mantel. The whiskey was making him see the obvious benefits of staying married to Sarah. She hadn't exactly fought his embrace, so he'd kissed her. And she'd been just about to kiss him back when he'd come to his senses. Maybe Sarah wasn't as averse to this marriage as he thought. Maybe she had fallen in love with Delaney and Tucker and simply couldn't give them up. After all, she'd quickly gone along with Grady's plan to protect them. Maybe that was why she hadn't run away for good, as any sane woman would have, instead of coming back from her walk and feeding him.

The house had grown quiet, and the kitchen lights had been turned off. Sarah must be in her room off the kitchen, which had been turned from a sewing room into the housekeeper's bedroom after his mother died.

Alex closed his eyes and thought about heading to bed himself. He finally got up from the couch with an exhausted sigh, checked to make sure the dying embers in the hearth were banked, and headed upstairs. For eleven horror-filled days, he'd dreamed of falling asleep in his own bed to the sound of the breeze stirring the tall pines outside his window, and tonight he was finally getting his wish.

Chapter Four

"**Do** you remember what I told you in our workout room, right after you kissed me?" Keenan asked, reaching behind her and gently lifting her braid, pulling it over her shoulder.

"I—" Rachel swallowed and tried again. "I don't remem—what did you say?" she asked hoarsely, trying to see his face through the shadows. She couldn't see a damn thing, so she looked down—and could only watch, mesmerized, as he deftly opened the clasp, pocketed her barrette, and then slowly twined the freed ends of her hair around his fingers.

"I told you the next time we reached this point, that I intended to finish it."

"And we . . . we're at that point now?"

Slowly, and with such gentle precision that Rachel tingled all the way down to her toes, Kee began undoing her braid.

"We're past that point, Rachel."

Her skin tightened in awareness.

The braid slowly unfurled, and his hand moved higher.
Breathing became difficult.

And when his fingers finally reached the nape of her neck,
he cupped her head, leaned down, and brought his lips to
hers—not kissing her, not quite touching her—just close
enough to bring every nerve in her body alive in anticipation.

"Either smack me with your flashlight, Rachel, or kiss
me."

The flashlight clattered to the floor.

Sarah stopped breathing, her eyes glued to the page as
the hairs on her body stirred. "Don't do it, Rachel," she
whispered. "You go to bed with him, and there's no turning back. He's going to demand more than you're wanting to give. Don't do it."

But Rachel *did* do it, right there in the next sentence,
when she threw herself at Keenan Oakes and kissed him
with the urgency of a passion she could no longer deny.
"Now you've done it," Sarah muttered as she pulled her
own hair over her shoulder, twisting it into a tail as she
read on, her eyes widening in shock. Holy smokes, Kee
was going to take her right there, right against the wall!
And not only was Rachel letting him, she was demanding he hurry up!

He shoved her jeans down to her ankles at just the same time
she pushed his down. He lifted her up, moving her back
against the wall like before. Rachel wrapped her legs around
him, this time gasping at the shock of having nothing between
them.

Nothing but glorious, quivering heat.

He positioned her higher, then stopped suddenly, the tight muscles of his arms twitching, his eyes closed, sucking breaths rasping from his lungs.

Rachel realized he was fighting for control.

She didn't want that. She dug her nails into his skin to make him look at her, and stared up past the angular planes of his face in the moonlight, into dark blue eyes blazing with primordial need.

"It's not trespassing if you've been invited," she told him, shooting him a crooked smile. "Or do I need to clarify that point as well?"

A shudder ran through him, shaking them both.

Rachel tilted her pelvis, relaxing her thighs to lower herself until she could feel the tip of his shaft probing the wet folds of her opening.

And still, he held back.

"I've always had a thing for cavemen," she whispered.

His eyes burned at her reference to their first meeting, his nostrils flaring and his hands biting into her thighs. He swore, hotly and crudely, grabbing a fistful of her hair as he braced one forearm on the wall behind her and captured her mouth in a hard and consuming kiss. He moved that kiss to her cheek, then her throat, then buried his face in the crook of her neck and thrust forward, and upward, not stopping until she—

"Sarah. Sarah!"

"What!" Sarah snapped, looking up with a glare. Then she gasped, slapping the open book to her chest. "What are you doing here? This is my bedroom. And where's your shirt?" she squeaked when Alex walked up to the foot of her bed.

"What in hell are you reading?" he asked, one eyebrow raised as he looked at the book covering her chest. "I've been calling to you, and I knocked on your bedroom door loud enough to raise the dead."

Sarah couldn't stop staring at his chest, even as she felt a blush climb into her cheeks. He was . . . he . . . holy smokes, his shoulders were broad. And his muscular chest was dusted with soft-looking hair. And his belly was flat enough to—

"Earth to Sarah," he said, moving to stand right beside her. He waved a hand in front of her face, then bent at the waist and squinted into her eyes. "Exactly how much whiskey did you have?"

"Wh-why are you looking for me?" she whispered, forcing her eyes up from his rippling stomach to his frowning face.

He straightened. "None of the beds upstairs is made, and the mattresses have some mealy purple stuff all over them."

Sarah tried to focus on what he was saying and not on the fact that he was towering over her in nearly naked glory, until his words finally sank in. "Oh, I forgot. I stripped the beds when everyone left so the mattresses could breathe. That's lavender buds all over them, to make them smell nice."

The face she was forcing herself to look at—so she wouldn't look at his chest—slackened in disbelief. "You're letting them *breathe* and making them smell like lavender?" he asked. He scowled. "What in hell for?"

"It's common practice to air mattresses several times a year," she said, scowling right back at him. Where, oh, where was her blanket? Too mortified to actually find out, Sarah could only hope it was tucked up under her book and not crumpled down at her waist. Her nightgown was paper-thin, and she just knew she was blushing furiously enough to make it transparent. "I was taking advantage of everyone being gone."

"So where am I supposed to sleep?"

"Ah . . . I-I'll go make your bed."

He didn't move, so she didn't even try to get up. Instead, they stared at each other, until Sarah's gaze slipped down to his chest again. She immediately snapped her eyes back up and found that his gaze had also lowered—and she doubted he was looking at her book.

"You have a double bed," he said ever so softly, slowly lifting his gleaming—or more likely whiskey-glazed—eyes to hers. "Maybe you could read to me until I fall asleep. I don't think I have the strength to climb those stairs again."

Sarah pressed her book even harder against her breasts. What would Rachel Foster do? Throw her book at him? *Carry* him up the stairs if she had to?

No, Sarah thought with a mental shake of her head. A smart, feisty, confident heroine would probably scoot over if a handsome man with gleaming blue eyes made such a provocative offer. Besides, what could the man possibly be capable of in his condition? He'd finished off half a bottle of whiskey, he was worn out from two weeks of running for his life, and he had said he only wanted to sleep.

She was not such a shrinking violet that she couldn't let him lie on top of the covers beside her, was she? *Begin as you intend to go on*, she was constantly reminding herself. Well, she certainly didn't intend for Alex Knight to think she was some frightened little mouse, much less a twenty-nine-year-old prude. Maybe it was only the whiskey giving her courage, or maybe it was Rachel Foster whispering in her ear, but Sarah suddenly scooted over, smoothed out the blankets, and patted the bed beside her.

Alex Knight didn't move.

Sarah took one of the pillows propping her up and set it in place for him—keeping her book pressed to her chest—then patted the bed again without looking up.

"Do you know what you're doing, lady?"

Now what would Rachel say? "Sure," Sarah said with a negligent shrug of one shoulder. "If you're too tired even to climb the stairs, I think that says it all. You're at least a foot taller than the couch is long, so that's out. You stay on top of the blankets, and I'll stay on my side of the bed," she told him, giving the bed one more pat.

When he still didn't move, Sarah suddenly felt empowered. Was she really capable of making this man back down simply by calling his bluff? Whew, this heroine business was heady stuff!

She shot Alex a grin that would have made Rachel proud. "I promise not to take advantage of you, Mr. Knight, if that's what's worrying you."

The scowl Alex gave her should have sent Sarah running for the woods, but she merely widened her smile. With the shadows from the bedside lamp making his scowl look more cartoonish than menacing, Alex finally crawled on top of the covers and settled beside her, lacing his fingers over his flat belly with a tired sigh.

Sarah went utterly still as she felt the hot weight of his body pressed against hers with only a thin blanket between them. *I can do this, I can do this,* she repeated to herself over and over, until her racing heart finally slowed down enough that she could gently wiggle away.

"Go back to your reading, but read out loud," Alex said, closing his eyes as he settled deeper into the mattress with another sigh. "I like your voice."

She couldn't possibly read the scene he had just interrupted; Rachel and Kee had been *doing it!*

"I—ah—I'll just read you the first chapter, since I only started this book this evening," she said, marking her page and quickly leafing back to chapter one.

"What kind of book is it?"

"A . . . it's sort of a mystery. Written by a woman who lives right here in Maine. It's set on the coast."

She looked over to see that Alex had his eyes cracked open, looking at her. "You like gory mysteries?"

She shook her head. "This is more of a woman's mystery. There's a bit of romance in it, too."

His mouth slashed into a grin, and one eye fully opened when he lifted his eyebrow. "Any good stuff? Any heavy breathing and groping?"

Sarah tamped down the blush creeping up her throat. "It's a mystery," she repeated. She looked back at the book and started reading before he could say anything else. "*Using her cane for support, Rachel Foster limped down the steps of the library and headed for her truck, eager to get home and take a long soak in a tub of steaming water. The torn cartilage in her knee was nearly healed . . .*" Sarah read softly, her voice picking up the rhythm of the prose.

She made it to page twelve before Alex's breathing evened out and Sarah realized he'd fallen asleep. She stopped reading and smiled. Holy smokes, she'd done it;

she had a real live man in her bed instead of a fictional hero! He was passed out, so she felt safe enough, and having a few drinks of her own appeared to have given her the courage to call his bluff. She only had to make sure she was out of bed and dressed by daybreak, so she could wake him up to greet his family.

Sarah was just leafing back to her old place in the book when she let out a jaw-wrenching yawn. She shut the book with a sigh, secured the cloth sleeve she always slipped over the racy romance covers so nobody would realize what she was reading, set the book on her nightstand, and shut off the light.

Sarah carefully scooted under the covers near the edge of the bed, yawned again, and quickly fell into sleep with a smug smile.

Her muscles were leaden, her mind foggy with colorless images. Sarah only vaguely sensed she was floating in that ethereal gap between conscious awareness and deep sleep, where surreal dimensions materialized in a way that caused dreams to seem real.

She was reliving Rachel and Kee's passionate lovemaking, her vivid imagination filling in the blanks from where she'd stopped reading. Only it wasn't Keenan Oakes her dream had conjured but the equally imposing Alex Knight. And it wasn't Rachel Foster boldly stroking his body, it was Sarah's fingers running through the downy-soft hair on his chest.

This was the fun and the safety of dreams, Sarah decided as she leaned over her dream hero and touched her lips to his chest. A wave of warmth shot through her when he shuddered, encouraging Sarah to let her fingers wander up his shoulder to his neck as she kissed him full on the mouth.

His arms came around her in a heated embrace, and his tongue enticed her lips apart. Her own passion exploded with pulsing energy, so that when her hero rolled Sarah onto her back and covered her with his body, the ache in the pit of her stomach made her wrap her legs intimately around him. His thick, throbbing manhood pressed through his pants against her panties, and Sarah caught her breath at the appearance of the barriers.

Rachel was already naked, wasn't she, and had helped Kee out of his own pants? Right after she'd dropped the flashlight?

Strong, probing fingers ran under Sarah's nightgown to the elastic at her waist and slowly pulled her panties down over her hips. Ah, yes, now she remembered. Kee had helped Rachel undress.

Sarah pushed her panties low enough that she could slide them off with her toes. Her dream hero fumbled with his own pants, then immediately moved back between her thighs. Sarah wrapped her legs around him again, throwing her head back with a moan of delight when he suckled one of her nipples right through her nightgown. He captured her wandering hands and held them to the pillow as he settled more deeply against her—*this time making her gasp at the shock of having nothing between them.*

Nothing but glorious, quivering heat.

He stilled suddenly, the taut muscles of his arms twitching.

"It's not trespassing if you've been invited," Sarah whispered.

A shudder ran through him, shaking them both, and Sarah tilted her pelvis, lifting herself until she could feel the hot tip of his shaft probing the wet folds of her opening.

He captured her mouth in a hot, consuming kiss, his lips then trailing down to her throat. He thrust forward, and upward—

Sarah's gasp of surprise brought her fully awake, and she could only stare wide-eyed as Alex Knight reared up in equally wide-eyed shock. Holy smokes, she wasn't dreaming! She was making love to Alex for real!

Well, *almost.* Was he really awake? Could a . . . could a man actually *do it* in his sleep?

"No, don't stop," she rasped, digging her fingers into his shoulders to back up her demand. "Finish it," she desperately cried as she lifted her hips toward him, her entire body aching to feel him fully inside her.

A growl erupted from deep in his chest as he pushed through her barrier. Sarah felt a moment's discomfort, and then he was fully, deeply inside her. She held herself still, not even daring to breathe, until he started to move in a rhythm that began rocking Sarah in waves of blossoming passion.

Oh, merciful heavens, yes! It felt so good, so beautifully wonderful to be so *full.* Sarah thought she might die of wonder as she answered his thrusts with tiny moans of encouragement, every nerve in her body focused solely on what she was feeling, each tremor of pleasure surprising her with its intensity.

Her insides clenched, tightening inward and upward as she began to sense something—something amazing— just beyond her grasp. But then Alex suddenly stilled above her, and Sarah opened her eyes to find his head thrown back, his muscles corded with tension as he pulsed his release.

He quietly collapsed against her with a growled sigh, and Sarah could only blink at the ceiling in disbelief. That was it? They were done?

Well, *he* was done, apparently.

But she'd just been getting started. She had been about to finally experience *it*. *Fulfillment*. The big O. Dammit, he couldn't be done!

Sarah pushed at his shoulders. "I can't breathe."

Alex rolled to the mattress with a groan but pulled her with him until she was tucked up against his side. He brushed her hair back from her face, and lightly—if not somewhat negligently—kissed her forehead before he let his head fall back with a deep, contented sigh.

Sarah stared past his rapidly rising and falling chest. They were going to *cuddle* now? With her nightgown up around her armpits, his heat scorching her breasts and thighs, and her body still tingling with . . . with . . .? Oh my god, what had she done?

She'd slept with her husband!

And just consummated a marriage neither of them wanted!

"Sorry about that," he suddenly murmured. "You kind of caught me by surprise." He patted her naked backside. "Just give me a minute, and I'll see if I can't take care of you."

Take care of . . . good God, he didn't even realize what they'd done! He was still half asleep, still drunk, or quite possibly both.

"I—ah—I need to go to the bathroom," she muttered, wiggling out of his grasp and sliding off the bed.

He made a halfhearted attempt to stop her. "Hurry back," he mumbled when he failed to catch her.

"Sure," she agreed, fumbling through the dark to the bathroom, scurrying inside, and quietly closing the door behind her. She didn't even dare turn on the light, for fear of what she'd see in the mirror.

What madness had compelled her to invite Alex into her bed to begin with, and then what devil had made her start stroking him? She had actually *begged* him to finish it.

Sarah slapped her hands to her fevered cheeks. How was she ever going to face him in the morning? What could she possibly say in her defense? *Sorry, Alex, I really didn't mean to seduce you? I was just a sexually frustrated, twenty-nine-year-old virgin in need of a lay?*

And Grady. How would she ever explain this to Grady?

Sarah stiffened her spine and balled her hands into fists at her sides. She wasn't explaining anything to Grady, because she wasn't telling a soul what she'd done. And Alex just *had* to promise not to tell anyone, either.

But he wouldn't be any more eager to let people know what had happened between them, would he? After all, she hadn't exactly *dragged* him into her bed, and she hadn't *poured* all that whiskey down his throat. He was just as guilty of poor judgment as she was, wasn't he?

Sarah heard movement in the other room, and a bright light suddenly shone under the crack of the bathroom door. Alex was awake? He seemed to be walking around the bedroom.

Sarah snapped on the bathroom light, then quickly checked to make sure her nightgown completely covered her.

She heard what sounded like her closet door banging open. What *was* he doing? She heard hangers sliding, and then something bumped against the bathroom wall. She twisted the doorknob and opened the door to see Alex, wearing only his pants, toss her suitcase onto her rumpled bed.

"Get dressed," he said without looking at her, apparently too busy pulling her clothes off their hangers. "You're out of here."

"*What?*" Sarah asked as he dropped her clothes on top of the closed suitcase.

She came to an abrupt halt when he spun to face her. And for the first time since meeting Alex Knight, Sarah was actually afraid of him. He looked fully awake and completely sober and angry enough to . . . to kill someone. How had the man gone from a sleepy, sated cuddler to a fire-breathing monster in less than two minutes?

Sarah eyed the doorway leading into the kitchen, but Alex walked over and slammed it shut, planting himself in front of it.

She immediately backed up to the wall of her bedroom and held out her hands. "It—it's not what you think. I was dreaming, Alex. I-I thought you were someone else." She gave him a tentative smile to let him know that *she* wasn't mad. "Let's consider it no point, no foul, and I'll go spend the rest of the night on the couch."

"Dreaming?" he repeated ever so softly, his anger laced with disbelief. "You thought I was someone *else?*" He took a step forward. "No point, no foul?" he said in a near shout. "*You were a fucking virgin!*"

Sarah lifted her chin and said, "I think that's an oxymoron. Look," she quickly added when he took another step closer. "Nobody has to know I was a virgin. Nobody even has to know we slept together, for that matter."

He folded his arms over his chest, his expression saying she might as well have told him she was the president of the United States. "But wouldn't that ruin your plan, if we don't tell everyone we've consummated our marriage?" He nodded toward the rumpled bed. "Isn't that the reason you staged this little seduction?"

Sarah gasped. "There you go again, accusing me of having an agenda." She pointed an unsteady finger at him. "I do not want to be married to you! I only went along with Grady's plan because I thought you were dead."

"And now that I'm not? What's your plan now, Sarah?"

"I don't have a plan," she snapped, walking over to her bureau and opening a drawer to pull out a sweater and a pair of pants. It was damn hard to defend herself wearing only a nightgown. And since having her back to him seemed to have a calming effect on her, Sarah went back to pretending he didn't exist.

But she spun around when he started pulling more clothes from her closet and throwing them on the bed. "Pack up your stuff. You're out of here."

"You can't really mean to kick me out."

He nodded. "I can, and I am. You can go to the hotel in Greenville. Grady will come down and see you . . ." He looked up at the ceiling, then back at her. "Saturday. He'll see you Saturday or Sunday, after we've had a nice, *private* family reunion."

"But it's the middle of the night!"

"The pickups have lights. Take whichever one you want."

Stunned, she sputtered, "But—but the turkey. I have to put it in the oven at six. And all the other food—it's only half prepared."

He opened the suitcase and started stuffing her clothes into it. "You're out of here, lady. I don't trust you any farther than I can spit. I intend to have a nice, long talk with my father, and I intend to be *alone* with him when I do."

"But Delaney and Tucker. They won't understand."

He pointed a piece of her clothes at her. "You leave my kids out of this, or I'll make you sorry you were even born."

Sarah spun back to the bureau. Holy smokes, he was mad. She knew from personal experience how angry men could get when they thought they were being manipulated—especially by a woman—and she'd rather spend the rest of the night braving the cold, dark woods than this man's anger.

So Sarah pulled out most of her undies and socks, walked over to the bed without looking at him, and dropped them into the suitcase. She made several more trips back and forth, stuffing everything she possibly could into the suitcase and the backpack she'd grabbed from beside the bureau.

She felt Alex's dark, accusing eyes on her the whole time, and it wasn't until she snapped the suitcase closed and zipped up the backpack that he grabbed the two bags and walked out the bedroom door. "You have two minutes," he said as he strode into the kitchen. "Then I'm kicking you out with whatever you're wearing."

Sarah picked up the clothes she'd set aside, ran to the bedroom door, and shut it. But dressing proved difficult, what with her shaking so violently. As she was bent over trying to slip into her panties, she noticed the blood on her thigh. That's when she finally lost what little composure she'd been clinging to and silently started to weep.

How had everything gone so terribly, horribly wrong? Not twelve hours ago, she'd been bustling around her kitchen, anticipating Thanksgiving dinner with every intention of making it special for her family.

Only they weren't really her family, were they?

Sarah slipped into her jeans and zipped them up, then walked over to the bed and sat down to put on her socks. Her book was sitting on the nightstand, and she picked it up and flung it as hard as she could at the wall. "This is all your fault, Rachel Foster," she hissed. "Filling my head with your foolishness. There are no heroes in this world, and being smart and feisty only gets a woman in trouble."

"Time's up," Alex said through the door.

"I'm coming!" Sarah yelled back, swiping her face with the back of her hand. "I'm putting on my socks!"

She stood up, took a deep breath, and, with her head held high, opened the door and strode through the kitchen. She stopped at the already open back door, slipped into her jacket and boots, picked up her backpack and suitcase, and pushed through the screen door without looking at Alex. The screen door banged behind her just as the inside door slammed shut, and Sarah shuddered when the dead bolt snapped closed.

She stood blinking into the black night until her eyes slowly adjusted and she could finally make out the boundaries of the dooryard. She looked at the four pickups parked beside the machine shed, then stepped off the porch and started walking down the driveway. She stopped at the edge of the forest, zipped her jacket up to her chin, hefted the pack over her shoulders and picked up her suitcase, and started walking the eight miles to Oak Grove.

Chapter Five

❊

It was the water that woke him. Cold November water straight from the lake, Alex knew as he sat up with a roar; Grady's weapon of choice whenever he was mad at one of his sons. This morning his father was in a full rage, judging by the looks of him. Well, what Alex could see. His eyes felt as if they were filled with sand, and the bright morning sunlight made it difficult to focus. The sledgehammer pounding in his head wasn't helping much, either.

"Nice to see you, too, Dad," Alex croaked, his throat begging for some of the water dripping in his eyes.

"What in *hell* have you done?" Grady shouted. "I talked to you not ten hours ago, and you promised me everything was fine and that you'd be on your best behavior with Sarah." He pointed his finger at Alex. "Where is she? And what in hell are you doing in her bed?"

Alex raised one eyebrow. "I'm alive and well."

"I can see that," Grady snapped. "Where's Sarah?"

Alex raised his other brow. "My wife, you mean?"

"Yes, your wife, you jackass! She's gone, along with a good deal of her clothes," he said, pointing toward the closet. He leaned in real close. "Where is she?"

Alex closed his eyes. "I kicked her out," he whispered. "I told her to go stay at the hotel in Greenville until she heard from you."

His father said nothing, though Alex could see a vein throbbing in his temple when Grady spun around and strode out of the room. Alex sat on the soaked bed, his whole body as limp as the sheets. This still wasn't the homecoming he'd been expecting. "Where are Delaney and Tucker?" he asked, after finally getting up with a groan and walking into the kitchen.

"In Oak Grove with Ethan," Grady said from where he was standing at the sink, staring out the window.

"But why? You knew I couldn't wait to see them."

Grady looked over his shoulder and scowled. "Because I may be old, but my brain still works." He turned to face Alex, his eyes narrowed. "After we talked last night, I got to thinking about you and Sarah being alone here all night, and I started worrying that you'd say or do something to upset her." He nodded at Alex's affronted scowl. "So I had Ethan land in Oak Grove, and I borrowed Mary's truck to come here." He took a step closer. "You just couldn't wait for us to get home and we could talk this out, could you? Where'd you take her?"

"I didn't take her anywhere. I made her pack her bags and go to Greenville."

Grady's face paled. "When?" he whispered. "What time did she leave?"

"Around three this morning," Alex said with a confused frown. "I told her to take one of the trucks and that you'd go see her at the hotel in Greenville on Saturday."

Grady's ashen face turned toward the window, then he looked back at Alex. "She didn't take one of the trucks, son," he said softly. "Sarah doesn't drive."

"*What?*" Alex looked out to see all four pickups parked beside the machine shed. He looked back at his father. "What do you mean, she doesn't drive?"

"She lived her entire life on Crag Island," Grady said. "It's two miles long and one mile wide, so she never needed to learn to drive." He stepped up and poked Alex in the chest. "You threw a defenseless woman into the night three hours ago, eight miles from nowhere. You go find her, you hear?"

Alex backed up and rubbed his chest. "That woman is not defenseless. She has more balls than a brass monkey. She got me drunk last night and seduced me, so she wouldn't lose her lucrative little setup here."

Grady shot his gaze toward the bedroom before he looked back, his face turning a dull red. "Sarah can't even handle Paul's flirting with her; she sure as hell wouldn't have the courage to stage a seduction. She was married to a bullying brute for eight years, so I doubt she even cares for men very much."

"Married?" Alex repeated. "Is that what she told you? That she was a widow?" He narrowed his eyes. "She was a damn *virgin*! And if that doesn't prove just how far she's willing to go to stay married to me, then you *are* old."

Grady paled again. "*Was* a virgin? Oh, God," he whispered. "What have you done?" He shook his head. "Sarah doesn't have a calculating bone in her body. She fell in love with Delaney and Tucker so much that she was willing to marry a dead man to keep them safe."

Alex used his fingers to knead his pounding temple. Dammit to hell. What *had* he done? And why in hell hadn't the woman told him she didn't drive?

Because she'd been scared to death, that's why. She had just been accused of seducing him, then forcibly packed up and kicked out. Could it have happened exactly the way she had said it did? Had he been so stupid as to crawl into her bed, and they had started making love in their sleep?

Alex lowered his hands when he felt his father's arms settle around him. "I can't tell you what it means to have you home," Grady whispered as Alex wrapped his own arms around his dad. "I thought I'd lost you. We all did, and a good part of us died with you." Grady leaned back and looked at Alex with misting eyes. "You're never leaving again."

"I won't. I promise."

Grady patted Alex's back. "And now you'll go find Sarah and fix this? You'll bring her home where she belongs?"

Alex let out a resigned sigh. "I'll fix it."

Grady's face finally relaxed into a smile. "I realize it must have been quite a shock, but marrying you to Sarah was the only thing I could think of to make sure we didn't have to fight for Delaney and Tucker."

Alex returned his smile. "Actually, it was a rather ingenious plan. I doubt you had much trouble talking Rogers into helping you?"

Grady walked over to the porch door. "Rory had one or two run-ins with Charlotte's parents before they moved away. He was more than happy to help."

Alex walked to the door Grady had opened and faced his father. "Sarah said she doesn't want to be married any more than I do," Alex told him. "So even though I'll bring her back here, you can't keep her as a daughter-in-law."

Grady slapped Alex's shoulder, leaving his hand there. "Now that you're home, that's between you and Sarah."

Alex gave him a worried look. "Maybe you should be the one to go get her."

Grady held up his hands, palms forward. "You kicked her out, you need to be the one to apologize and bring her home."

"I was pretty hard on her, Dad. I said a few things I shouldn't have." He suddenly frowned. "How did you get in? I distinctly remember . . . ah, locking the door," he finished lamely.

Grady pointed at the key in the lock. "We all carry keys now, after I suggested Sarah keep the doors locked when we're not here. John Tate said there's been some strangers hanging around Oak Grove and that the border patrol asked him to keep an eye on them."

"The border patrol?"

Grady shrugged. "Beats me what it's about. John said the men have been showing up and leaving several times over the last few months. They're pretending to be hunters, but no one's ever seen them come back to town with game they've shot."

Alex spun on his heel and headed toward the great room.

"Where are you going? You have to go after Sarah."

"She's been gone three hours; another two minutes won't hurt. I need to change into dry clothes," Alex called over his shoulder as he pushed open the swinging door and jogged toward the stairs. Dammit, Sarah had been out there alone in the dark for more than three hours, and there were strange men hanging around who were of interest to the border patrol. But what worried Alex the most was that the Knight land sat directly between Oak Grove and the Canadian border.

He ran up the stairs and into the bathroom, chased four aspirins down his throat with a long drink of water, then strode to his bedroom, stripped out of his wet clothes, and threw them onto the bed—only to have a cloud of lavender buds shoot into the air and onto the floor. "Dammit," he growled, trying to supplant his guilt with anger as he pulled on dry pants. "Nobody lets their mattresses *breathe*. This is not the Ritz!"

Alex laced his boots and threw on his shirt, buttoning it up as he ran back down the stairs and into the kitchen. "How far do you suppose a woman can get on foot in three hours?" he asked as he slipped on his jacket.

"In the dark, alone, and constantly looking over her shoulder because every little noise she hears scares her to death?" Grady returned. "Four, maybe five miles."

"Then you should have passed her on your way in."

"Not if she heard me coming and hid in the woods." Grady sighed, his face softening. "Sarah's a bit of a mouse, Alex. She's been working here for nearly three months, and she isn't anything like the other house-keepers we've had. It's as if Sarah's trying to be invisible while making everything perfect for us." He looked back at Alex. "She's always watching those crazy how-to shows on satellite television and practicing everything they preach to the point that it's beginning to drive Ethan and Paul crazy. She's got all our clothes, even our socks and underwear, sorted by color and season, she's sewn new curtains for all the windows, and every night we sit down to a four-course meal."

"So you're saying her being a perfect housekeeper is driving everyone nuts?"

Grady nodded. "Well, yeah. Everyone is afraid to mention any little thing to her, for fear they'll come home to find it fixed or improved. Hell, she even built a cupboard out by the hot tub for towels. We wrap the towels around ourselves to walk back to the house, and the next day they're washed and folded and back in the cupboard when we go to use the tub again."

"And this is bad . . . how?"

"Because she's trying too damn hard," Grady said with a scowl. "It's as if Sarah's only goal in life is to please everyone. She actually told me that making us happy makes her happy." He stepped out onto the porch. "We've all tried to get her to stop fussing over the details and have a bit of fun, but she just laughs and says she *is* having fun."

Alex stepped off the porch and turned to look at his father. "So do you want her to stay on as our housekeeper or not?"

"Sarah is the best thing that's happened to this family since your mama died," Grady said. "She just needs loosening up." He suddenly smiled. "And if you're even half the man I know you are, you're exactly the person to do the loosening."

Alex lifted a brow. "And if I don't want to be that person?"

"You spend one month around Sarah and *then* ask me that." He waved Alex away. "Just go find her and bring her back. I'll call Ethan at Mary's, and Delaney and Tucker will be here when you get back with Sarah. And Alex?"

"Yes?"

"You compose a damn good apology while you're looking for her, and deliver it on your knees if you have to. Drunk or not, you don't sleep with a woman, accuse her of treating *you* badly, and then kick her out into the night. You'd better hope she *can* forgive you."

Alex hung his head. "I know. I'll bring her back. You just have my babies here when I do."

He ran to the first pickup in line, jumped in, started it up, and headed toward town. He would definitely get down on his knees, if that's what it took to make Sarah believe he truly was sorry—about everything.

Finding Sarah was proving about as easy as finding a needle in a haystack, Alex discovered after thirty minutes and only four miles of driving. The ground was frozen solid, and he had a hard time seeing the infrequent clues that told him she had gotten even that far. Three times he had found a turned rock, crushed grass, or a broken bush where Sarah had gone into the woods, only to reemerge maybe thirty feet down the road. He'd discovered the first such sign about a mile from the house, not far from where their lane merged onto the main hauling artery. Alex had stopped and searched the woods for five minutes before he'd found where she had stepped back onto the road.

She'd done the same thing two more times. Grady's passing had probably been one of those times, but who had been the second and third? Hunters heading out to get to their favorite spot before daybreak? Or the strangers in town?

At mile five, Alex saw where Sarah had gone into the woods yet again, only this time he didn't see any sign that she had come back out. He continued driving around a curve before pulling the truck to the side of the road. He shut off the engine, got out, and quietly closed the door, then headed into the woods while keeping his eyes on the road.

In less then two minutes, Alex saw Sarah step out from behind a large tree, look up and down the road, and start walking toward Oak Grove again. He stood in the early-morning shadows, frozen in place, utterly ashamed of himself.

She was shivering, her large brown eyes sunken in her pale white face, her collar pulled up against her tangled hair, as she slowly made her way toward Oak Grove. She was wearing her backpack, but she wasn't carrying her suitcase. Remembering how heavy it had felt when he'd carried it out of her bedroom, he guessed she'd stashed it in the woods during one of her detours.

Alex closed his eyes and hung his head. Damn, he was a bastard. The woman had walked five miles down a wilderness road in the freezing cold, most of it in the dead of night, just because he had been afraid of . . . of what? Her? Sarah didn't even come up to his chin, and he outweighed her by at least sixty pounds.

Hell, Grady and John were right: he had judged Sarah simply based on his experiences with Charlotte. Without even knowing her, he had decided Sarah had seen their thousands of acres of timberland and thought her beauty and charm would be enough to get her a share of the Knight empire.

She didn't look like much of a gold digger as she walked past him. She looked miserably cold and scared to death, if not completely defeated. Yeah, he was a bastard, all right. Alex waited until Sarah had disappeared around the corner before he stepped onto the road and silently followed her. When he rounded the corner, he found her stopped, staring at his truck. She turned and saw him, and her face paled even more the moment she realized who he was.

"I'm sorry, Sarah," he said from about fifty feet away. He lifted his hands from his sides in a helpless gesture. "I am truly sorry."

If she hadn't looked so unconvincingly brave and so damn cold that she couldn't stop shivering, Alex would have smiled when she lifted her chin, squared her shoulders, and gave him a glare that could have toasted them both. Then she simply turned away and continued walking down the road.

"You could have told me you don't drive," Alex said as he started after her, his longer strides slowly closing the distance between them. "I wouldn't have thrown you out if I'd known you couldn't drive yourself to Greenville."

She kept silent and kept walking.

"Grady's home, and he wants you to come back."

Still no reaction.

"I want you to come back. And so do Delaney and Tucker."

"Delaney and Tucker will be fine without me, now

that you're home," she said without bothering to look over her shoulder.

Alex was within twenty feet of her now, and he noticed she'd picked up her pace a bit. "Grady's waiting for you, and he's probably going to put the turkey in the oven, and we're all going to die of food poisoning tonight."

She still kept walking and said nothing.

A floatplane suddenly buzzed overhead at treetop level, catching them both by surprise. Sarah stopped, tilted her head to watch it fly over, then turned to glare at Alex. "You just keep telling one lie after another, don't you? They haven't even made it home yet."

"That's Ethan, with Delaney and Tucker," Alex explained. "Grady had them land in Oak Grove, and he borrowed the store owner's truck and came home alone. Didn't you see him drive by one of the times you hid in the woods?"

"Why would Grady have done that?"

"Because he knows me so well."

"Because he knows you're a shouting, lying jerk, you mean?"

Alex clasped his hands behind his back. "Yes, because he knows I get a bit loud when I'm angry." He shook his head. "It's all bluster, Sarah. I would never hurt a woman. Not intentionally," he quickly clarified, dropping his hands to his sides. "I really *am* sorry for what happened. I never should have come to your bedroom, much less crawled into your bed. And being drunk is no excuse; I take full responsibility for what happened. I'm also sorry for how I reacted after. I shouldn't have kicked you out in the middle of the night like that."

She seemed to consider his apology, then obviously decided she didn't believe him, because she turned away and started walking again. Alex took several long strides and caught up with her, grabbed the top of her backpack, and pulled her to a halt. She stood quietly, staring at the road in front of her.

"I'm sorry," he whispered to the back of her head. "I promise you, Sarah, I am not that person from last night or this morning. I'm really much better than that. Please come home."

"Fine," she said, still looking ahead. "I accept your apology, but I'm not going back. I'm going to Mary's, and then I'm going home."

"Home?"

"To Crag Island."

Alex continued to talk to the back of her head, finding it easier for him and knowing it had to be easier for her. "Back to your isolated life on your isolated island?"

She pulled in a deep breath and let it out on a shuddering sigh. "I'm going home to regroup, and then I'm going to move . . . someplace," she finished in a barely audible whisper. She stiffened. "Let me go."

"Please," he softly entreated. "Wait until spring. Give me until March—give us all until then. Regroup here, and if you still want to leave come March, then we'll get a divorce, and I'll take you back to Crag Island myself."

She let out another shuddering sigh. "It will only make it harder on Delaney and Tucker if I stay all winter. It's best if I leave while they have the excitement of your being back."

He was getting absolutely nowhere, his patience was waning, and this was obviously a job for Grady. Alex lifted her backpack off, set it on the ground, then took off his jacket and settled it over her shoulders.

She immediately pulled the jacket around herself with a whispered "Thank you."

"I think it's only fair that you turn in your resignation to the man who hired you," Alex said, turning her toward his truck. "If you want to quit, you tell Grady and Delaney and Tucker that you're leaving. Then you can run back to your island."

He guided Sarah around to the passenger side of his truck, opened the door, and lifted her in before she could do more than squeak in surprise. "I am dying to see my kids," he said, handing her the buckle of her seat belt. He looked directly into her eyes. "Let me get home and see them, and this evening we'll all sit down and have a talk. And if it's decided that you're leaving, one of us will take you back to Crag Island. Deal?"

Alex knew it was his mention of seeing Delaney and Tucker that got to her. She took the buckle from him and snapped it shut, and Alex quickly closed the door, ran back to get her pack, and jumped into the truck before she could change her mind. He made a three-point turn in the road and quickly brought the truck up to speed. "Where's your suitcase?" he asked.

"In the woods, not far from ho—from your house. I left it at the base of a large tree near the turnoff."

Alex slowed the truck a bit. "Are you okay?" he asked softly, watching the road. "I mean physically, did I . . . are you hurt?"

"I'm fine."

She looked down at her lap, and Alex reached over

and turned the heater fan on high. "Grady said you were married for, ah, eight years, I think. If that's true, how come you were still a virgin?"

"Because I was married to a man who didn't particularly like women," she told her lap, her face going bright pink. She looked at Alex. "And if your next question is why did I marry Roland Banks, the answer is it's none of your business." She lifted her chin. "Anything else you want to know?"

Alex opened his mouth but just as quickly snapped it shut. He'd gotten her into the truck without any kicking and screaming, and he didn't need to give her a reason to start walking to Oak Grove again the moment they got home. So he simply stepped down a little harder on the gas.

Grady had Sarah all wrong. She wasn't a meek little mouse; she was quite possibly the most well-disguised tigress Alex had ever met. Under her eager-to-please exterior, he had seen several hints of a steel backbone.

Dammit, his father must have seen it, too. In the month he'd stayed at her inn, Grady had seen the real woman inside that beautiful body, and that's why he'd brought Sarah home.

His father was always scheming. Always—which was why Alex broke into a cold sweat as he sped home. For all of Grady's crazy ideas, the old man was almost never wrong when the final results came in. Hadn't the Knight landholdings grown from two hundred thousand acres to five hundred thousand on Grady's watch? Even when they hadn't had two nickels to rub together, Grady had managed to keep buying land. Marrying their housekeeper to his dead son to protect Delaney and Tucker had been another one of his father's brilliant schemes.

And Grady's bringing Sarah here initially?

That's what really worried Alex.

Chapter Six

✴

All Sarah wanted to do was stand under a hot shower for three hours, crawl into her bed, and stay there for the next three months. But she had six very ecstatic people to feed, six mattresses covered with lavender buds to vacuum and make up, and probably a hundred dirty dishes to wash and put away after dinner.

She stood in the middle of her bedroom in a dazed stupor, staring at her wet bed as she listened to the shouts and squeals coming from down at the dock. The wet bed she understood; she'd had to dry out Paul's mattress last month when Grady had abruptly awakened his youngest son the morning after Paul had fired one of their crew without discussing it with anyone.

Sarah suddenly smiled at the realization that Alex had gotten the same treatment this morning. Good. She hoped he had come awake with a pounding headache that throbbed as much as hers still did.

Sarah finally forced herself to move. She pulled off the wet sheets, dug around in her closet for the fan she had thought she wouldn't need until next spring, and set it on the nightstand to blow on the wet mattress. Then she walked into her bathroom, stripped off her clothes, turned on the shower, and stepped under the heavy spray. She had time for a quick warm-up, and then she had to get that turkey stuffed and into the oven. As it was, they weren't going to eat until five, where before she'd planned on having dinner at three.

Sarah stood under the steaming water, groaning at the feel of her bones thawing. It had taken every bit of willpower she possessed not to start crying when Grady had opened her truck door. He had helped her out and taken her into his large, gentle embrace, all while whispering that he was sorry for not being there for her earlier. Sarah had given him her best smile and assured him she was perfectly fine and that he had nothing to apologize for. Then she had walked into the house and stood staring out her window when Alex silently dropped off her bags before softly closing her door.

She'd had plenty of time to think during her long walk this morning—when she hadn't been jumping at every little sound, that is—and had come to the conclusion that she simply couldn't stay here. Heck, she wasn't even sure she could stand living in the old sporting lodge three miles away. Not now. Not after what had happened between her and Alex.

If they hadn't slept together, if they hadn't *done it*, she very easily could have gotten an annulment and gone back to being just the housekeeper for the rest of the winter. But she couldn't possibly live under the same roof with Alex while trying to pretend she didn't know what it felt like to be held in his arms, to have his mouth on her breasts, to feel him so very intimately *inside* her.

For as shocking as it had been to wake up and find her dream was real, Sarah couldn't help but remember how nice it had been. Well, *almost* nice. For all the trouble she'd gotten herself into, she could have at least experienced the big O. Sarah threw back her head and let the water carry her hair down her back. She was glad she was no longer a virgin. She finally knew what it felt like to have a man make love to her . . . albeit briefly and without the man really knowing he was doing it.

Sarah heard Paul's shout right through the outside wall and smiled at the realization that the youngest Knight brother had just arrived home to the biggest surprise of his life. She quickly rinsed her hair. She had a great celebration to orchestrate! On a scale of one to ten, her future was a four compared to what the Knights were experiencing. Alex was alive, Delaney and Tucker had their dad back, Grady had his son, and Ethan and Paul had their brother again.

Sarah dried off, grabbed some clothes out of her suitcase, and rushed out to the empty kitchen. She pulled the turkey from the fridge and set it in the sink, then got out her ingredients for the stuffing.

"Mom! Mom!" Tucker shouted, banging through the swinging door, making it bounce back so that it nearly smacked Delaney, who was running in behind him. "Did you see him? Daddy's home! He's alive!"

"I've seen him," Sarah said quietly, wiping her hands on her apron before she pulled Tucker into her arms. "And I knew he was your daddy the moment I saw him.

He looks just like his picture." She reached out and hugged Delaney with her free arm. "I am so happy for you two," she said, giving them both a quick squeeze before letting them go.

"So now we got both a mom *and* a dad," Tucker said, his large blue eyes shining up at Sarah.

"Not really, Tuck," Delaney said before Sarah could respond. "They're just meeting for the first time. They don't even know each other."

"But they're *married*," Tucker shot back. "Gramps married them to each other last week. That makes us a family, 'cause Judge Rory said Sarah signed the papers that made her our mom. He said we're supposed to tell everyone she's our mom now."

Tucker looked at his father, who was standing in the doorway, utterly still and pale. "We got dressed in our best clothes," Tucker continued, his chin rising defensively. "I wore my suit and was your best man. Gramps said I was. And Delaney stood next to Sarah. We all got married." He took a step toward Alex, who paled even more. "Tell her, Dad. Tell Laney that Sarah's our mom."

"What's all the hen squawking in here?" Ethan asked, walking past Alex and up to Tucker. He swept the seven-year-old off his feet with a laugh and folded him over his shoulder. "You put a young man in a suit, and he suddenly thinks he's got the whole world figured out," Ethan said as he carried Tucker back into the great room, past his silent brother. "If I were you, Tuck, I'd be more worried about explaining that *Unsatisfactory* you got in math to your daddy instead of . . ."

Ethan's voice trailed off, leaving Alex staring at Sarah, who was acutely aware of Delaney standing between them.

"He'll figure out it wasn't a real wedding," Delaney said. She looked at Sarah. "That it was just to keep Grammy and Grampy Mayhew from trying to make us go live with them."

"Y-you knew?" Sarah asked.

Delaney broke into a wide grin as she tossed her long brown hair over her shoulder. "I'll be eleven in five months," she reminded Sarah. "Of course I knew." She shrugged one delicate shoulder. "The heat register in my bedroom runs up from the kitchen. I heard everyone talking about what Gramps wanted to do."

"You knew your father was dead six days before we told you?" Sarah asked in horror. "Delaney, how come you didn't say anything? How could you act as if you didn't know?"

Alex suddenly strode up and sweeped Delaney off her feet to hug her tightly against his chest. "Ah, baby," he whispered.

"I didn't believe it, Daddy," Delaney said into his neck, fiercely hugging him. "I knew you weren't dead. I knew it!" She leaned back in his arms and took his face in her hands, staring directly into his eyes. "I knew you'd come home."

"Ah, baby," he repeated, burying his face in Delaney's hair and rocking her back and forth. "That's exactly why I came back—because you and Tucker were waiting for me." He brushed her hair off her face. "And I promise you, no more hiring out to engineering jobs. I'm not leaving these woods again unless you and Tuck are right beside me," he finished thickly, stroking her hair as he held her against his chest. "You were my guardian angel for eleven days, baby. I heard your prayers."

"I prayed every night, Daddy," she whispered. "Sometimes all night."

Sarah had to turn away to dab her eyes with her apron. Lord, oh, lordy, she had known she was going to turn into a bawling geyser today.

"Come on, baby," she heard Alex say. "Let's you and me and Tuck take a walk to our secret place."

"Okay, but we can't stay long," Delaney warned. "I have to help Sarah set the table. I sewed all the place mats myself, and I sewed one for you, too, because I knew you'd come home."

"You sewed the place mats?" Alex asked, incredulous. "When did you learn to sew?"

"This fall. Sarah's been teaching me."

Sarah started running water in the sink to wash the stuffing bowl, knowing Alex was looking at her.

"Come on, Daddy. Let's go now," Delaney said. "Sarah and I have a ton of stuff to do today."

Sarah broke into a smile after the door swooshed open and shut. Delaney had sewn the place mats, as well as the table runner for their Thanksgiving dinner, and Sarah had never seen prettier or more crooked mats in her life.

Their Thanksgiving feast went by in a blur. After dinner, on her way through the great room to make the beds upstairs, Sarah stopped to stare, openmouthed, at Alex sitting on the couch. Tucker was on his lap facing him, Delaney was cuddled beside him but twisted around to see better, and Grady and Paul and Ethan were all standing in front of the couch, leaning over so they could also see.

Alex had his shirt unbuttoned and was rubbing his fingers over his chest. Sarah couldn't figure out why everyone was so interested in it, until he said, "It must have been over twenty feet long and as thick as my waist." He looked directly into Tucker's wide-eyed stare. "Anacondas aren't venomous, so they kill their prey by squeezing the breath right out of them," he said in a dramatic whisper, squeezing Tucker in a giant hug until the boy squealed.

Alex sat back and pointed at several small cuts on his chest again. "But they do bite. So I pulled my knife out of my belt and started hacking at its head," he continued, raising one hand to make slashing motions in the air. "I ate him for supper that night, but I had to eat him raw because I couldn't build a fire."

"Eewww," Delaney said, leaning away. "Daddy, you didn't eat a raw snake!"

Alex grinned and patted her leg. "It tasted almost as good as the turkey we just had, baby. Only chewier."

Sarah couldn't decide which horrified her more—that Alex had fought off a giant anaconda or that he was giving his children a blow-by-blow account of the battle.

Realizing that Alex was watching her staring at his chest, she spun away and ran up the stairs. She grabbed the vacuum cleaner from the hall closet, thinking about the shows she'd seen about anacondas on the Discovery Channel.

Alex had actually tangled with one of the massive beasts? And not only had survived but had eaten it— raw! And it had tasted *almost* as good as her turkey. Sarah couldn't decide if that had been a compliment or an insult. She plugged in the vacuum and started sucking up the lavender buds off Grady's bed.

The vacuum suddenly went off, and Sarah spun

around to find Alex dangling the plug in his hand. "We'll vacuum up this stuff," he said. "You've put in a long day, Sarah." He held up his hand when she opened her mouth to protest. "I think we can figure out how to make our own beds, including Delaney and Tuck. And we'll take care of the dishes."

"That's very nice of you to offer, but I'll do the dishes." She didn't want anyone messing with her kitchen; she'd have to spend the whole next morning putting everything back in its place. "And I'm supposed to have my talk with Grady tonight."

Alex leaned against the door frame and continued to dangle the vacuum plug from his hand. "About that. I'm asking again if you would please postpone telling Grady you're leaving. His mind is still reeling from the shock of having me home, and so is everyone else's. Could you give us at least until after the first of the year before you head off to begin your new life?"

"But—"

"Meanwhile, you could make good use of your time here by exploring where you might like to go."

Sarah eyed him suspiciously. "Why are you being so adamant that I stay?"

He dropped the plug to shove his hands into his pockets, then dropped his gaze to the floor. He finally looked at her after a long silence, his eyes beseeching, if not a bit sad. "I don't want what happened between us to stand on its own," he softly told her. He leaned back to look down the hall, then stepped fully into the room and closed the door. "Sarah, if you leave here remembering me for only what I did to you, you'll be condemning me to a lifetime of guilt. I need you to know that I'm not that person who came to your room last night and took advantage of you."

"You didn't take advantage me," she said, darting a glance at the closed door before stepping closer to him. "I started it. I was the one who was dreaming and started touching you." She reached out but stopped just short of touching his arm, appalled to think he was taking the blame for *her* foolishness. "Alex, I don't blame you for anything. And I don't blame myself, either. It just . . ." She shrugged. "It just happened."

"I never should have gone to your bedroom in the condition I was in, and I certainly had no business getting into your bed. I knew better."

"So did I."

He turned away and walked over to stare out the darkened window. "Please stay until after the first of the year," he repeated. "If not for me, then for the others."

Well, spit. One month? Five or six weeks, tops? She'd spent twelve years saddled with a duty she hadn't asked for and hadn't wanted; surely she could handle six weeks.

"Do you like working here?" Alex asked into the silence, still staring out the window. "Or *did* you like it before I showed up?" He turned to face her. "You must have, if you agreed to Grady's plan to marry me and adopt the children. So other than my being alive, has anything changed?"

"Well . . . no," Sarah said with a frown. "I like living out here, and I love the children. But everything's changed now."

"Just me. I'm the only thing that's changed. And if I hadn't almost died, I'd have come home in the spring, and you wouldn't have thought anything of it. I would have been just one more Knight to keep house for." He took a step closer. "Give me a chance to prove I'm not the man you met last night." He grinned crookedly. "I'm not asking you to give this marriage a try, I'm only asking that we pretend it's real so that Grady can save face. After a reasonable amount of time has passed, we'll get a divorce, and you can go start your new life."

"So we'll pretend you knew about the marriage all along?" she asked. "When we go to town, we'll have to act married?"

He nodded. "Yeah, otherwise everyone will know that Grady was just working another one of his schemes and that Rogers was in on it with him. Just until January. Just until we can make it look like our marriage simply didn't work out. We can tell people you got homesick and missed the ocean or something."

Sarah stared at him, not ready to agree but even more reluctant to say no. Grady was just like a father to her, and she certainly didn't want to get him in trouble. And her sporting camps—she really, really wanted to open those camps.

"Why don't you sleep on it and give me your answer in the morning?" Alex opened the door, stepped to the side, and waved her out past him. "Go on, go to bed. I'll muster the troops, and we'll have this stuff vacuumed up and the beds made in no time." His smile widened. "And Ethan and Paul can do the dishes."

"But I—"

"Oh, but I insist," he said. "And you can sleep late tomorrow morning." He pulled her to a stop at the head of the stairs by taking hold of her shoulders. "I wasn't acting

when I told Delaney I was impressed with the place mats.
Thank you for teaching her to sew. I've taught her to
drive a skidder and a snowmobile, but it never crossed
my mind that a young girl should also learn to sew."

"She loves it," Sarah said, trying very hard not to
notice how warm his hands felt on her shoulders or how
they caused her stomach to clench. "With practice, she'll
be able to make some of her own clothes."

"Thank you, Sarah," he said softly, his breath stirring
the hairs on top of her head. "Now go to bed, and don't
so much as pick up a pot or a pan on your way through
the kitchen."

Sarah wondered if he was trying to send her to bed because he wanted to be alone with his family. She *should*
turn in for the evening, so he could spend private time
with his kids and tuck them into bed himself.

"Good night." She set her foot on the top step, effectively stepping out of his hands. "I'll see you in the morning."

Several hours later, Alex lay in his bed, which happened
to be directly over Sarah's, and thought about the unexpected twists and turns his life had made in the last
couple of weeks. He'd cheated death, only to come home
to find himself married to an unusual woman his father
seemed convinced was exactly what they all needed.
Alex couldn't decide what he thought about Sarah,
though he was sure of one undisputable fact: the woman
was every man's fantasy. One look at her enticing body
brought a man's mind to long nights and rumpled
sheets. He could still remember the look and feel and
taste of her, and he felt himself grow heavy with desire

for her even now. No man in his right mind, drunk or sober, would have walked away from her last night.

But Sarah also had not deserved being initiated into lovemaking by a drunken stranger. Despite her claim to the contrary, Alex knew he was just as much at fault for what had happened, and he needed to make things right with her.

It would take patience to get back into her good graces, and Alex only hoped he could ignore her beauty long enough to gain her trust. Yet just thinking of her full breasts, as he'd felt them last night, brought a sheen of sweat to his forehead and a doubt to his resolve. Even though their marriage would end in divorce, Alex didn't want Sarah to leave with the memory of last night's ill-fated lovemaking standing between them.

He wondered about her first husband. She had told him Roland Banks hadn't particularly cared for women, and her virginity certainly had been proof of that. Why had she married the man to begin with, and why so young? Sarah had to have been in her teens when she married Banks. What father in his right mind would let his daughter marry so young? Come to think of it, what about her father and mother? How come there had been no mention of them? Could she have been a teenage orphan Roland Banks had preyed upon?

So many questions. So many pieces to a puzzling woman whose cooking was divinely inspired, as Alex had discovered yet again at dinner. A perfect little housewife packaged in a fantasy body.

But what about the real woman inside that body? What made Sarah tick? Surely she had dreams, wants, needs of her own? She was somewhere around thirty years old; surely she wanted more out of life than caring for someone else's family.

He'd have to sit her down and talk with her—if he could corner her long enough. She had done a good job of avoiding him all day, hiding in her kitchen and behind her housework. Except when he'd caught her staring at his chest, when he'd been telling Tucker about his battle with the anaconda.

Alex smiled into the darkness. He had started to make up for last night's debacle by offering to do Sarah's chores and telling her to sleep in. He would have to be sneaky in gaining her trust, so she wouldn't realize what he was doing. Alex knew he could be charming when he wanted to be, and he would use every last trick in his book so he'd have a clear conscience when she left.

And maybe . . . maybe he could even get back into her bed before she left, just to show her how good lovemaking could be. Grady had said Sarah needed loosening up, and what better way to do that than to show her how fun lovemaking can be between two consenting—and awake—adults?

Alex sighed, closed his eyes, and snuggled into the bed he'd been dreaming about for two hellish weeks. He would have to let Sarah go eventually, but why not send her away with some pleasant memories to replace the unpleasant ones?

He wouldn't mind having a few pleasurable new memories himself.

Chapter Seven

❈

S*arah woke up at nine* and quickly dressed to make everyone breakfast, but she found only an empty house. A note on the table said that Grady and Alex and Delaney and Tucker had gone to Greenville, which was thirty miles past Oak Grove, and Ethan and Paul were out at the cutting, checking on their crew. The note also said not to expect any of them home until late afternoon.

So Sarah ate cold cereal and spent the rest of the morning convincing herself that she'd made the right decision to stay. Just the thought of leaving made her heart ache, she loved Delaney and Tucker so much. And she still wasn't ready to give up her dream of opening the sporting camps, despite knowing that whether it was three miles separating them or three hundred miles, she would never be able to get Alex Knight out of her head.

When she had thrown her sheets into the washer, she

had blushed the whole time, unable to forget the feel of
his mouth on her breasts. How was she going to survive
living under the same roof with Alex for the next six
weeks? The way her heart was pounding just thinking of
him, she'd be throwing herself into his arms within a week.

With her sheets drying on the line, Sarah went about
putting everything in her kitchen back where it
belonged, while she absently listened to Martha Stewart
on television explaining how to clarify butter. Sarah
spent ten minutes searching for her roasting pan before
she finally spotted it on the top shelf of the pantry; she
frowned, wondering how Ethan and Paul could possibly
have dented the heavy pan. She must have fallen into a
catatonic sleep the moment her head hit the pillow last
night, not to have heard the roaster getting dented.

With the kitchen finally put back the way she liked
it, Sarah shut off the TV and headed into the great
room, turning on the TV in there to watch a quilting
show while she picked up the school projects Delaney
and Tucker had dug out to show their father. The phone
rang, and Sarah was undecided about whether or not she
should answer it. Nine calls out of ten related to the
Knights' logging business, which she knew absolutely
nothing about. But after having Alex show up without
warning because she'd let the machine take the calls,
Sarah decided she should start answering the phone.

"NorthWoods Timber," she said.

Silence answered her.

"Hello?"

Still nothing. But Sarah knew the line was open,
because she could hear fast-moving traffic in the back-
ground. "Hello?" she repeated. "Who's there?"

There was a sudden click, and the drone of the dial tone was all that answered her.

Sarah set down the phone with a frown. This was the first time this had happened to her, though it had happened to Paul once and to Grady twice in the last two weeks. Who kept calling, and why didn't they say something?

The clock in the corner chimed noon, and Sarah shook off her concern, deciding the Knights must have a number similar to someone else's. She turned the TV to a music video channel, and Toby Keith's voice filled the great room. Sarah picked up her dust rag and went back to work.

Ten minutes later, as she was standing on a stool in front of the hearth to give the moose's antlers a good dusting, a pair of large hands suddenly wrapped around her waist like an iron band. Sarah gasped in surprise and nearly fell; she'd been singing along with the TV and hadn't heard anyone come in. She twisted around and looked down to find herself chest-to-nose with Alex. She tried to step away, the stool wobbled, and his hands on her waist tightened.

"You shouldn't be climbing on stools when no one is home," he said, plucking her off and setting her on the floor.

"I think I'd survive a three-foot fall," she shot back as she scurried away. The phone rang again. "Aren't you going to answer that?" she asked when he didn't move.

"You're the housekeeper, you should answer it."

"It's probably for you," she said when it rang for the third time. Her heart still racing from the feel of his hands around her waist—not to mention that her

breasts were still tingling from bumping into his head—
Sarah gave Alex a brilliant smile. "It's probably one of
your old girlfriends, calling to welcome you back from
the dead."

He said nothing to that.

The phone rang for the fifth time, and Sarah plucked
it off the coffee table and hit the talk button. "North-
Woods Timber," she said. "Yes, this is Mrs. Alex
Knight. . . . Well, thank you, Mr. Porter, for your condolences. No, Grady's not—"

Alex snatched the phone from her. "What in hell do
you want, Porter?" he growled into the receiver. He suddenly smiled, not a very nice smile. "Yeah, it's me," Alex
continued, his voice as dangerous as the look on his face.
"I'm not dead, so don't bother coming out to give your
condolences to my widow. And the answer's still no. We
catch anything other than your logging trucks on our
roads, and we'll sue you for trespassing."

Without so much as a goodbye, Alex punched the off
button and tossed the phone onto the couch before turning his dangerous look on Sarah. "If Clay Porter calls
again, you hang up the moment you realize it's him. And
if he dares to show up here in person, you point your
shotgun at him."

It seemed Clay Porter wasn't one of Alex's favorite
people. "Would that be the shotgun I'm not supposed to
point at anyone because it doesn't have a firing pin?"

His scowl deepened. "Just don't let him in," he said,
turning on his heel and heading into the kitchen. "Is
there any pie left?"

Sarah followed him through the swinging door.
"Who is Clay Porter?" she asked, gaping when he strode

to the counter and picked up a piece of pie with his bare hands.

"He's our land neighbor to the north," Alex told her after taking a bite, practically inhaling the pie. "His logging trucks use our main hauling artery to get his pulp and timber to market."

"And you want to sue him for trespassing?"

"Only if he uses our roads for anything other than hauling trees."

"What else would he use them for?"

"Moving heavy equipment," Alex said around another mouthful of pie. He leaned against the counter, his expression still menacing as he chewed and finally swallowed. "About ten miles farther up, the artery has deteriorated, and Clay wants to rebuild it."

"And you don't want him to improve your road? But why?"

"We don't need it rebuilt yet. We won't be cutting that far out for another three years."

Sarah was thoroughly confused. "But why not let Mr. Porter fix your road for you now, if it will benefit you eventually?"

"We have to let him use our main hauling artery because of an agreement Grady signed with his father twenty years ago, but that agreement doesn't say anything about making it easy for him."

"And letting him rebuild your road would be helping the competition? Is the logging market that tight?"

Chewing the last of his piece of pie, Alex shook his head.

"Then why not let him fix the road?" she asked again, her patience waning.

Alex swallowed and then smiled, again not very nicely. "Because we don't want to." He pushed away from the counter and stepped closer to glare down at her. "You stay away from Clay Porter, understand?"

No, she didn't understand a darn thing, but looking up into Alex's dark eyes, Sarah simply nodded and changed the subject. "Where are Delaney and Tucker? Your note said they were with you."

"Grady took the kids out to the cutting. He dropped me off to get one of our pulp loaders out of the shop to transport it to the cutting." His smile softened. "Ethan's going to let Tucker drive one of the skidders since no one's working today."

"*Drive* it?" Sarah squeaked. "But he's only seven."

"I was driving skidders at five. And Delaney's been driving them since she was six."

Sarah thought that Alex and Ethan were idiots for letting children drive such a monstrous machine. She walked over to the wall of pegs and took down her jacket. "I'm going for a walk," she said as Alex scooped up the last piece of pie.

Sarah woke three days later to a cold, driving rain laced with sleet. But the sun was shining inside her with the memory of a wonderful weekend, so she didn't care how bad it was storming outside. Delaney and Tucker had been glued to their father since he came home, and Alex couldn't seem to be happier about it.

Sarah had quietly stayed out of everyone's way, content to watch the whole family enjoy their reunion. Even Paul seemed reluctant to leave home and had forgone his usual Friday and Saturday night dates. The men played with the kids all day, and after Delaney and Tucker went to bed, they would head into the office off the great room, share a couple of drinks, then all head outside to soak in the hot tub before going to bed themselves.

Neither Grady nor Alex had asked Sarah if she was staying or not, so Sarah hadn't bothered to tell them she was. She didn't know if Alex was assuming she was staying or if he was afraid to ask for her answer. Then again, maybe he was as embarrassed over what had happened between them as she was and had adopted her strategy of pretending they weren't married.

So far, it seemed to be working well for both of them.

Sarah finally got out of bed and quickly dressed to make breakfast and put up six lunches. The kids had to return to school today, and the men had to go back to work in the woods—even in the rain. Fried eggs and bacon and crisp toast greeted the Knights as they trailed into the kitchen, a sleepy Tucker bringing up the rear.

"I don't want to go to school today," Tucker said. "I want to go to work with you, Dad, and drive the skidder again."

Alex smiled at his grumpy son. "I'm not going to the woods today, Tuck. I have to run into town for parts, and then I'm working in the machine shop to fix one of our trucks. You'd be bored."

Tucker scowled at his eggs, then suddenly brightened. "The tube for my bike tire might be in. Will you pick it up for me? And put it on my bike?"

Alex promised he would, and peace reigned for the rest of the meal, forks and glasses clinking amid quiet conversation, until everyone left. Alex took the children to the end of the lane to catch the school bus, Paul headed out to the shop to start tearing apart the truck engine, and Grady and Ethan headed out to the cutting to check on the crew.

As soon as the house was empty, Sarah started picking up the breakfast dishes, smiling as she thought of how particularly handsome Alex had looked this morning. His eyes were finally losing that haunted look, and he seemed to be gaining weight. She liked to think it was her cooking that was helping Alex recover from his grueling ordeal. The best medicine was a loving family and good food, Sarah's mom had always said.

But Sarah's careful attention to meals hadn't been enough to stop her mom from dying when Sarah was only fourteen. Nor had her wonderful soups enabled her daddy to recover from his fall from the roof when she was sixteen. He had lingered for nearly nine months and had died just before her seventeenth birthday. Five weeks later, Martha Banks had managed to talk Sarah into marrying her son.

As Sarah started stacking the dishes in the dishwasher, her thoughts turned once again to Alex. He could have been exactly the kind of man she had once dreamed about being married to. It wasn't until her wedding night with Roland that Sarah had realized her dream of a loving home filled with children was never going to happen.

But she had two lovable children now. And she had a *temporary* husband. And come spring, she would be running her very own business and living in her own lodge three miles up the lake—close enough to stay in contact with Delaney and Tucker but far enough away to avoid their father. So, for a little while at least, Sarah could live out her dream.

She snorted to herself. Alex would undoubtedly bring up their divorce as soon as some woman in town caught his eye and he realized he couldn't very well ask her out while he still had a wife at home. He'd likely file for divorce on January 2—he couldn't live like a monk forever.

Sarah quickly finished the morning dishes and went upstairs to make the beds and clean the two bathrooms. When she came barreling into the kitchen two hours later, her arms full of dirty towels, she saw a vase of pink roses sitting on the kitchen table. She stopped in her tracks, dropped the towels right in the middle of the floor, and stared at the beautiful flowers.

A card was nestled in their center. She leaned over the table and tried to read it, but the card was in an envelope. She went to the sink window, saw Alex carrying a box of parts into the shop, and then walked back to the table. Careful not to disturb so much as a petal, she inched the envelope out and opened it. The card read: *To the sweetest woman this side of the Canadian border.*

She smiled. Paul must have an important date tonight and had asked Alex to pick up some flowers for him. Lucky girl. Sarah slipped the note back into the envelope and returned it to its nest. At least she could enjoy the roses for the day, she decided as she picked up the towels and headed to the laundry room.

Grady and Ethan came back from the woods around noon, and all four men came in for lunch. Sarah usually packed them a giant basket of food to take to the woods, but they had told her they needed to work on the equipment this afternoon, so they'd be home for lunch.

"My, my. What pretty flowers," Grady said as they all sat down.

Sarah beamed at him. "Aren't they the most beautiful roses you've ever seen?" She turned her smile on Paul, only to have him wink at her. Not surprised by Paul's flirting—he just couldn't seem to help himself—she darted a glance at Alex and found him looking back at her expectantly.

She smiled.

He lifted one brow, as if he were waiting for her to say or do something. She refilled his glass with milk, but instead of thanking her, Alex frowned.

Sarah sighed, not knowing what was bothering him. Maybe it was the fact that Paul was going out tonight and Alex couldn't openly date until they got their divorce. Maybe he envied Paul and Ethan their freedom.

Conversation was light, and the meal was short, the men having plenty of work to get back to. They soon started for the door, Grady whistling, Ethan trying to hide his smile, and Paul openly grinning.

"Well, guys," Paul said. "I hate to leave you in the lurch, but I promised Jane Trott I'd drive her to Bangor this afternoon. Don't set a place for me for dinner, Sarah." He winked at her again. "Or at the breakfast table. We'll probably stay the night in Bangor."

Sarah turned from setting some plates in the sink. "Wait, Paul, you forgot your roses."

"My roses?" he said, looking confused.

"Aren't you taking them to Jane?" she asked, a bit confused herself.

Ethan snorted. "Paul hasn't bought a woman flowers since his senior prom."

Alex closed his eyes and leaned his forehead against the door casing. Grady started laughing, pushing first

Ethan and then Paul through the door before slapping his oldest son on the shoulder on his way by.

"Alex bought the roses," Grady said.

Alex bought them?

Alex closed the door and turned to her. "Yes, Sarah. I bought the roses for you."

"Me?" she squeaked, bringing her soapy hands up to her face, which made her sputter to spit out the bubbles. "Why would you buy me roses?"

Alex's eyes glittered with amusement. "I wasn't aware I needed a reason to buy my wife roses."

"Oh," Sarah said, suddenly understanding his gesture and feeling a bit deflated. "You bought them to make people believe we really are married." She forced her smile. "That was smart. Did anyone see you carrying them to your truck?"

"That's not why I bought them, Sarah."

"No?" She darted a glance at the beautiful roses, her mind turning a mile a minute, then bunched her apron in her hands and looked back at Alex. "You didn't have to buy me flowers to get me to stay," she softly told him. "I've already decided to stay until spring."

Alex just stared at her. Was he surprised that she had seen through his gesture so easily? No, he looked . . . disappointed. Maybe even hurt. He just kept looking at her with those lake-blue eyes of his, and for the life of her, Sarah couldn't tell what he was thinking.

He suddenly turned and opened the door, then looked over his shoulder. "The only reason I bought you roses, Sarah, was because I wanted to," he said softly, quietly closing the door behind him.

Sarah clutched her apron to her chest and stared at

the door. She *had* hurt his feelings. Instead of trying to dissect his gesture, she should have just said thank you.

But nobody had ever given her flowers before. She hadn't even gotten a corsage for her senior prom, because she hadn't gone to it—because she'd been getting married to Roland that weekend. Come to think of it, she hadn't even had a wedding bouquet. So how was she supposed to know how to react to Alex bringing her a dozen roses?

"You thank the man, dummy," she said with a groan, closing her eyes. "And you let him know how much you appreciate his gesture by . . . by . . ."

Dammit, how *was* she supposed to show her appreciation?

On TV and in her romance novels, women usually gave the guy a kiss. "Uh-uh," Sarah muttered, shaking her head. She wasn't going there. If she started kissing Alex, she might not stop for ten or twenty minutes. Maybe thirty.

Sarah snapped open her eyes. Was that what Alex had been looking for? A kiss? Had he brought her flowers to see if maybe she had recovered from their bedroom debacle, hoping she'd give him some sign that she forgave him?

Sarah walked to the table and picked up the vase, holding the roses to her nose. Did it really matter why he'd given them to her? They were beautiful and smelled divine, and she cherished them, no matter the reason.

Sarah spent the next hour foolishly smiling at the roses, all because of what Alex had written: *To the sweetest woman this side of the Canadian border.* She carried the roses into the great room and set them on the table by her chair, turned on the television, and watched Martha Stewart pot outdoor plants to bring inside for the winter. She looked around the great room for someplace to set out a few plants. Everything had turned brown outside with the fall frosts, so maybe she should buy some flowering plants the next time she went to Greenville.

Sarah picked up the roses and set them in her lap to enjoy their smell as she learned how to care for a Christmas cactus. And when the show was over at two o'clock, she took her vase of beautiful roses and climbed the stairs to the attic.

Wind-driven rain battered the roof, but she was so intent on her project that she didn't even notice. She set the vase on a nearby table, pulled a chair up to another table, then opened her pad of paper and proceeded to sketch out a pattern that would transform her beautiful flowers into a tiny quilt. But she wasn't sending this quilt to Clara in New York. No, this one was going to hang in Sarah's private suite at her sporting lodge.

Chapter Eight

❋

O_n *Tuesday morning,* the first day of December, Sarah found herself standing in front of a monster. The darn thing actually had a ladder built into it for climbing up into the cab, and it was such an ugly green that it looked like a seasick monster. Heck, even the tires were taller than she was.

But what truly alarmed Sarah was that Alex was smiling at her with the same expectant smile she often saw on Tucker whenever there was trouble brewing. What was Mr. Alex Knight up to now? He had pulled her aside after breakfast this morning and asked if she would like to come to the cutting with them today, adding that maybe he would even let her drive his skidder.

Surprised by his offer, though admittedly more curious than anything else, Sarah had said yes without even stopping to wonder *why* he was offering. Besides, if Delaney and Tucker could drive a skidder, she wanted to learn how.

Which was why she was standing in a logging yard full of downed timber, suddenly uncertain as she eyed the ugly green monster. Then she looked at Alex and found him inspecting her. Sarah tucked a loose strand of hair behind her ear, remembering that he had told her to braid and pin it out of the way. It was dangerous work they did in the woods, and loose clothing and long hair were a no-no.

Apparently satisfied that she passed inspection, Alex plopped a hard hat on her head that covered her eyes. He laughed and removed it, adjusted the inner band, and plopped it down again. "Climb aboard," he said, bowing formally and gesturing with his hand. "Your chariot awaits."

"This," Sarah said as she climbed the ladder, "is the ugliest chariot I've ever seen."

Alex helped her along by placing his hands on her hips to give her a lift. "This is my Mean Green Machine, lady, and don't you insult it."

Sarah stopped climbing when she reached the entrance to the cab, trying very hard to ignore the heat of his hands on her hips as she looked inside. "Ah, are you sure we'll both fit in here?"

"Sure we will, providing you keep your elbows to yourself," he said as he climbed up behind her.

Oh, Lord. Now his chest was cradling her bottom, and Sarah closed her eyes and gritted her teeth. She'd been doing so well this last week about keeping her attraction to Alex in check, and here she was with his arms holding the ladder on either side of her, wrapping her in an embrace of heat and denim. Sarah scrambled into the cab, sat down in front of the steering wheel, and stared at the array of switches, dials, and levers.

She looked at Alex, who was still standing on the ladder. "About the only thing I recognize is the steering wheel. I'll never be able to drive this," she muttered, her voice betraying her disappointment.

Alex dismissed her worry with a smile of assurance. "Sure you will. I'll teach you in no time," he promised as he climbed into the cab. He picked her up, ignoring her squeak, and sat her back down on his lap.

Alex groaned. And then, like any sane man, he carefully set Sarah beside him, pinning her between his thigh and the cab wall, and calmly let out his breath—until she suddenly squirmed. Alex buried his second groan in the grinding of the large diesel motor as he brought the huge skidder roaring to life.

This may not have been one of his more brilliant ideas. Spending the morning plastered against Sarah might be more than his overactive imagination could handle. But how in hell else could he seduce a woman who had mastered the fine art of being invisible? Getting Sarah alone had been an exercise in frustration for the last six days. If she wasn't busy running the Knight Bed-and-Breakfast Inn, she was giving Delaney sewing lessons or helping Tucker fix up his room to look like the inside of the space shuttle. And when she wasn't being indispensable to everyone, the woman kept vanishing into thin air.

Sometimes she went for walks in the woods, Alex knew, because he would find carefully arranged bowls of twigs, moss, birch bark, and pine cones placed throughout the house. And other times, when he'd pop home unexpectedly in the middle of the day—with an unexplainable need to make sure she hadn't run off to Crag Island—Alex would call her for two or three minutes before Sarah came down from upstairs dressed in a heavy sweater, her cheeks red with cold and her eyes looking as guilty as a mouse in the pantry.

So this morning he'd come up with what he thought was a brilliant way to get Sarah all to himself. Now, though, he wondered if he was brilliant or masochistic. Alex ended up groaning a hundred times that morning. It may have been only thirty-five degrees outside, but it might as well have been a hundred degrees inside the cab. The skidder had a heater, but he'd shut it off after the first half-hour. Between his raging hormones and Sarah's squirming backside, there was no need for artificial heat. She had shed her own jacket two hours ago, and Alex could only hope she was suffering as much as he was.

The woman was all over the place. If she wasn't turning this way or that to see everything at once, she was sticking her head out the window to watch the trees dragging behind them, thus sticking her cute little backside in his face. Alex gritted his teeth and hauled her back into the cab for the hundredth time in as many minutes.

She was smiling more than he'd seen her smile since he met her. And she kept asking him dozens of questions about everything, acting worse than his kids. Alex knew he was finally seeing the real Sarah—the real woman behind her eager-to-please facade. That fool Roland had to be responsible for her having learned to hide her emotions so well. It was obviously a defense she had polished so well that Alex suspected Sarah didn't even realize she did it.

But she was coming alive today, driving him nuts in the process. Sarah was a stunningly beautiful woman at her worst times, but today her glowing face left him speechless. She had also left his crew speechless when she had asked them one question after another during their morning break. Caught up in her own curiosity, she hadn't noticed the way the men could only stare, not knowing exactly what to make of her. They had all solemnly tried to answer her questions but had smiled foolishly whenever she turned her back. They'd also given Alex a few envious looks.

Not that he could blame them. Sarah's jeans fit her like a second skin. And Alex knew exactly how thin they were, because those jeans had been burning a hole in his thigh all morning. His only saving grace with the men was that Sarah had put on her jacket when she'd gotten out of the skidder.

Alex pulled her inside the cab yet again, this time with a stern look to stay put. Honest to God, he hadn't had this much trouble on Tucker's first ride when the boy was two.

Lunch was a repeat of the morning break, the men all sitting on downed logs in the loading yard to eat their meals. Ethan suddenly cursed. Alex followed his stare, then cursed as well. Sarah had taken off her jacket as the weak noon sun had brought the temperature up to a blistering thirty-six degrees. She was bent over the food basket, her perfectly molded fanny facing them. Alex heard a few choked coughs as coffee went down the windpipes of several men, and he grabbed Sarah's coat and stood up to throw it over her fanny. Or her shoulders. Or her head. He wasn't sure what he should cover, since every inch of her was enticing. He spun her around, stuffed her into the jacket, and zipped it up to her chin. "I—ah—I don't want you to catch a cold," he said at her questioning look.

But when Alex thought he heard someone softly mutter the words "chest cold," he decided lunch was over for Sarah and himself. He grabbed her hand and hauled her toward the skidder.

Sarah smiled over her shoulder at the crew as they watched Alex drag her off. "Alex is in such a hurry because he's going to let me drive his Mean Green Machine," she called back.

"Hell!" Ethan yelped.

"No!" Paul shouted.

Grady stepped in front of his sons. "Not one word, you understand? Don't either of you say anything to Alex," he commanded. And then he smiled. "He'll find out soon enough about Sarah's driving abilities."

"But dammit, Dad, that's a skidder, not a truck. She's going to take ten years off his life, not to mention shave all the bark off every tree we own," Ethan argued.

Grady beamed brighter. "Lord, I hope so. Giving Alex a go at teaching her to drive will do him, and me, a world of good."

The two brothers nodded, their worry turning to grins as they sat down to watch the show. They were not disappointed. They heard the engine start and the gears grind as the powerful green beast suddenly lurched forward, digging up the ground as it roared into the forest. All the men wore stunned expressions that turned to pained winces when they heard small trees snapping and saw large trees shuddering. If they listened very carefully, they could hear colorful curses scorching the air, but nobody was sure if it was Alex yelling . . . or the forest.

Well, so much for *that* bright idea. Alex downed his fourth beer amid the swirling waters of the hot tub and pictured his excited wife in the house, likely crying her eyes out.

God, he'd yelled at her. He'd even cursed her. Alex closed his eyes, trying to block out the images of their hair-raising ride this afternoon. The crazy woman only knew one speed, apparently, and that was full speed ahead. No matter if there were a few trees in the way— she simply drove right over them. Alex figured North-Woods Timber had at least three new logging trails, one of them coming damn close to the lake. That was when he had finally lost it and grabbed the wheel.

It had been the longest fifteen-mile ride home he had ever taken. Sarah had sat silently beside him in the pickup, and Alex had felt like a bigger monster than his skidder for turning her bubbling excitement into head-hanging shame. When they'd gotten home, she hadn't even been able to look him in the eye but had walked quietly into the house.

Damn it to hell. He'd been making such progress.

Maybe more roses?

Dinner was a quiet affair that night, Sarah's glaring absence reminding everyone that all roads occasionally had bumps. Alex felt as if he'd driven into a major washout. Sarah was sitting in the great room, watching another one of those incessant how-to shows while mending shirts, saying she wasn't hungry. Delaney and Tucker were merely pushing their food around on their plates, when they weren't scowling at Alex.

Grady, Ethan, and Paul were somber but understanding. Each of them had tried to teach Sarah to drive, Grady had finally admitted. No one had fared any better than Alex, but they had never reached the yelling stage. However, they had never put Sarah behind the wheel of a ten-ton skidder dragging two tons of logs through the forest.

"We told you Sarah can't drive," Ethan said into the silence. "Is there any particular reason you decided to start her lessons in a skidder?"

Alex looked down the table at his father, then at Paul, Delaney, and Tucker, before looking back at Ethan and shrugging. "I thought she just couldn't drive on state roads because she didn't have a license. How in heck can anyone not have the sense to steer around immovable objects instead of through them?"

"It's not the steering Sarah can't get a handle on," Paul said. "It's the speed. She can't seem to coordinate the two."

"She won't push softly on the gas," Ethan clarified. "She's either got the throttle shoved all the way to the floor, or she's slamming on the brakes and driving our faces into the dash."

"She's the same with the sewing machine," Delaney softly interjected, her cheeks tinged pink for tattling. "She keeps breaking needles because she's always got the machine going at full speed. That's why she does most of her sewing by hand."

"She drives a bike real good," Tucker piped up. "She

rides down our lane to the artery with me all the time. But she does like to go fast," he admitted with a proud grin. "I have to pedal really hard to keep up."

"You need to apologize for yelling at her," Delaney added, "because it's not Sarah's fault she doesn't know how to drive. You just need to teach her." She scowled at Ethan and Paul. "They gave up after only a few tries."

"Yeah," Ethan said evenly. "She's your wife, you teach her. But in a pickup, not a skidder."

Alex had had enough. He really hadn't done anything wrong this afternoon, other than react like any normal, terrified man. He pushed away from the table with an overloud sigh and headed into the great room to straighten out the mess he'd made, with encouraging smiles from his offspring and snickers from his brothers following him through the swinging door. He quietly walked up to the television, shut it off, then walked over to Sarah and held out his hand.

It took her a minute to look up from her mending, and then she simply stared at his outstretched hand.

"Come for a walk with me, Sarah."

"I have to finish mending this shirt for Grady," she said, looking back at her work.

Alex gently pulled the shirt out of her grasp, set it on the table beside her, and held out his hand again, wiggling his fingers. "Your mending will be right here when you get back. I promise, Grady won't do it himself."

She finally looked at him, and Alex felt a spurt of hope that the large brown eyes meeting his were not filled with shame or embarrassment but with impatience. "You're not actually afraid of me, are you?" he asked before she could say anything, keeping his smile to himself when her chin came up. "I mean, my yelling today didn't leave any bruises, did it?"

She tapped the side of her head and cupped one ear toward him, her eyes guilelessly wide. "Excuse me?" she said a bit loudly. "Could you please repeat that? I seem to be deaf in my left ear."

Alex reached down with a bark of laughter, captured her hands, and pulled her to her feet. "Come on, brat. Let's get out of here before Ethan and Paul realize they're stuck with the dishes again."

"I don't want them doing my dishes," she said as Alex all but dragged her into the kitchen.

"I'll help," Delaney offered, scrambling away from the swinging door and picking up her plate from the table. "I know where everything goes." She beamed a smile at Sarah. "You and Daddy go for a nice, long walk."

Alex frowned as he led Sarah over to the wall of jackets. Delaney was acting a little too eager for his liking. He glanced at his family sitting at the table. Hell, they all looked too eager. Alex handed Sarah her jacket, then slipped into his own, fully aware of the five sets of expectant eyes watching them.

Dammit, he had warned his dad and his brothers that the marriage was only temporary and had told them not to read anything into his actions concerning Sarah. Delaney and Tucker, however, were proving to be a more delicate matter. Alex had tried, but he couldn't seem to get through to them that Sarah would be leaving in January and that they shouldn't get their hopes up. Tucker kept insisting Sarah was their mom now and that she would never, ever leave them. Delaney only smiled her young lady smile and silently patted Alex's arm.

Just when had his little girl grown up?

"I'll wash the pots," Sarah said over her shoulder as Alex herded her out the door. She stopped on the porch to glare up at him. "They dented my roaster the other day."

He took hold of her hand. "It will still roast with a dent in it," he said, letting her go when she wiggled her fingers to get free. "Let's walk this way," he suggested, taking the path around the house that led to the lake.

"Where are we going?" she asked, falling into step beside him.

"Just for a walk. It's a beautiful night, and I want to see the moonlight on the lake."

"You didn't have to bring me on a walk to apologize. A simple 'I'm sorry for yelling and cursing you out' would have been sufficient."

Alex stopped and faced her. "I have no intention of apologizing for anything. There's not a man alive who wouldn't have reacted exactly the same way. You tore up nearly two miles of woods and murdered thousands of trees, Sarah." He turned away and started down the lawn. "It's a miracle we're both still in one piece."

"Then why didn't you stop me?" she asked, running to catch up. She pulled him to a halt by grabbing his sleeve. "What took you so long to grab the wheel?"

"I was frozen in horror. Hell, Sarah, all you had to do was slow down and turn the wheel whenever you came to a tree. How could you not grasp that simple concept?"

She glared up at him, the moonlight bright enough for Alex to see her cheeks were pink with anger. She pushed on his arm as she let go of his sleeve and shoved her hands, which were fisted, into her jacket pockets. "Then if you have no intention of apologizing, why are we going for a walk?"

"So you can apologize to me."

Her jaw dropped on a gasped "What?"

Alex turned so she wouldn't see his smile and started walking toward the lake again. Again, she ran to catch up and grabbed his sleeve. But instead of stopping, Alex simply captured her hand and continued walking, ignoring her attempts to get free.

"What am I supposed to apologize for?" she asked, her voice as stiff as her fingers digging into his.

"For scaring ten years off my life today." He stopped at the narrow ramp to the dock and guided her ahead of him, then took her hand to lead her past the wing strut of the floatplane. "I need to know you weren't intentionally trying to scare me to death."

She tried to pull them to a halt, but Alex continued to the end of the dock, then stopped and turned to face her. "Okay. This is a good place for you to apologize. We're all alone, and the moonlight is bright enough that I can see your sincerity."

"I am not apologizing. I wasn't the one cursing and shouting."

Alex fought his urge to laugh. "Two simple words, Sarah. 'I'm sorry.' And then you can kiss me."

Her jaw dropped again, and her shoulders stiffened. "I am not kissing you."

"Why not?"

"Why *not?*" she repeated, her expression incredulous.

Alex nodded. "Yeah, what's wrong with two consenting adults—who happen to be married to each other, by the way—sharing a kiss in the moonlight?"

"We are not married. Not legally," she said, dropping her gaze to his chest.

"It's legal as long as I don't dispute it," he reminded her, lifting her chin to look at him. "Do I frighten you, Sarah?"

"Yes. No," she said more firmly, pulling her chin free. "I'm not afraid of you because of what . . . of that first night."

"I don't believe you," he softly told her. "You've been avoiding me all week."

"I went with you today."

"Only because your curiosity got the best of you. One kiss, Sarah, just so I know I didn't turn you off men."

She actually snorted. "If Roland Banks wasn't able to turn me off men, you certainly can't."

Alex's grip on her shoulders tightened. "Was he abusive?"

Her eyes widened, and she shook her head. "He never laid a hand on me."

"Abuse isn't always physical. What did he do to you?"

"Roland was a bully and a jerk, but his bark was worse than his bite. Just as I have with you, I soon learned to ignore his outbursts."

Alex ignored her little dig and stayed on the subject. "Why did he marry you, if he didn't care for women?"

"Because he didn't want anyone on the island to find out he preferred men." She angled her head to stare up at him. "What better way to disguise the fact that you're gay than to marry a pretty seventeen-year-old who is too naive and filled with grief to know any better?"

"This is the twenty-first century, Sarah. Gay men don't hide behind marriage anymore."

"They do if they live in a small, isolated fishing village that hasn't evolved in a hundred years. Roland would have been ostracized if anyone found out, and his mother would have been humiliated."

"Why didn't you divorce him once you realized your mistake?"

"Because by then it was too late." She dropped her gaze to his chest. "And I had a debt to pay off."

"What debt?"

She looked up. "To Roland and his mother. They sold their house and moved in with me when my father fell off our roof. They helped me run the inn and take care of Dad for the nine months before he died. It was Martha Banks's idea that Roland and I get married, and I couldn't very well say no and kick them out after all they'd done for me. They had no place to go."

She stepped out of his grip and turned her back to him, facing the lake. "It took me nearly a year to come out of my fog of grief and finally figure out that Martha hadn't cared about me or my father but had only coveted our inn." Sarah looked over her shoulder at him. "But by then, she had convinced me to put her and Roland's names on the deed."

Alex pulled in a deep breath and let it out slowly. "So you stayed married to a bully for eight years out of gratitude?"

"And I lived with his dragon of a mother for four years after that. Martha died this past June, and that's why I was free to accept Grady's offer and finally get off Crag Island."

"Only to get yourself trapped in another marriage," Alex said, shaking his head when she turned to face him.

"And you don't know what to do with this new husband, either, do you? Especially considering that I happen to *like* women."

Her response to that was a smile. "I'm not seventeen years old this time. And I am not afraid of you, Alex Knight. I apologize for scaring ten years off your life today, but I'm not going to make this more of a mess by kissing you."

"Then I guess I'll do the kissing," he said, reaching out and gently cupping her face, lowering his mouth to hers.

Alex wasn't sure if Sarah would recoil in disgust or give him a sharp kick in the shin, but she merely went perfectly still, her hands gripping his jacket sleeves and her lips unmoving. Deciding that no response was actually a good sign, he moved one arm around her shoulders to pull her into his embrace and ran his fingers into her hair to deepen his kiss—all the time being ever so gentle, careful not to scare her off.

Alex couldn't believe it had been ages and ages since he'd wanted so badly for a kiss to be perfect. But it was surprisingly important to him that Sarah respond, that she *like* the feel of his arms around her and his mouth on hers.

He almost shouted when she softened against him, parted her lips on a tiny sigh, and slid her hands around his waist. His victory was short-lived, however, when Alex realized that instead of worrying about Sarah's reaction, he'd better start paying attention to his own. Without even trying, the woman was igniting a fire inside him.

He knew better than to continue to kiss her but was unable to stop. Sarah tasted so sweet, felt so good in his arms, and fit so perfectly against him that he was one second away from going too far. He straightened, holding her head against his pounding chest.

"Okay," he said into her hair. "Maybe that wasn't such a bright idea, either. You might be right about this getting messy." He kissed her hair, then set her free. "You must know that I want you, Sarah."

"I know," she whispered, her face flushed, her lips swollen, and her expression direct. "Most men do."

"What?" He took a step back.

Sarah studied him calmly. "Which surprises you more? That I know you want me or that I'm not shocked by it?" She smiled. "I've been running a bed-and-breakfast since I was fourteen. Do you have any idea how many men have said those same words to me?" She shook her head. "I've spent nearly half my life being propositioned by men from twenty to ninety years old. I know exactly how enticing long blond hair, large brown eyes, and a stacked chest are. Heck, I was married because of my looks."

Alex frowned so hard his face hurt.

"I'm sorry if my bluntness upsets you," she continued before he could say anything. "Or appalls you. But you're not exactly in a minority." She smiled again. "Although you certainly got a lot farther than any of the others."

Alex felt heat rising up the back of his neck. Was he angry that Sarah was lumping him in with all those men or angry at himself for being no better than they? How in hell could she stand there smiling at him, mocking the fact that he had been the only one of dozens actually to have scored? And the fact that he obviously wanted to score again? Hell, why wasn't she shoving him into the lake?

"Don't worry," she continued, again before he could say anything, not that he could have strung two words together if he'd wanted to. "As soft as my skin is, it's grown quite thick over the years. None of those men wanted more than just a romp in bed, either. I wasn't long figuring out that bodies like mine are for fulfilling fantasies, not marrying."

Alex was seconds away from throwing *himself* into the lake.

She smiled again, her face stunningly beautiful in the moonlight as she gazed up at him. "If it's so important that I forgive you for what happened that first night, then I forgive you, Alex. And I'll stay here long enough for our marriage to appear real for Grady's sake. But that's as far as it goes between you and me. I don't have the courage to have an affair, and I won't stay in another loveless marriage."

She looked at him expectantly, but dammit to hell, what could he say? That he was a bigger jackass than Roland?

Her chest rose and fell at his silence. She shrugged one delicate shoulder in resignation, then turned and silently walked down the dock. Alex could only watch as Sarah made her way up the lawn, her body washed in moonlight, until she disappeared into the shadows at the side of the house.

They didn't want more than just a romp in bed, either, she'd said so matter-of-factly. *A body for fulfilling fantasies?* Hell, he hadn't stopped fantasizing about Sarah since he'd stepped into the kitchen that first day.

Alex turned to face the lake and let out a frustrated sigh. Talk about feeling like a jackass; she'd nailed his intentions exactly. But the woman didn't have a clue about men if she dared to admit she didn't have the courage for an affair.

She hadn't said she didn't want to, only that she was *afraid* to. Most men would consider that a direct challenge. And if that was how he took it, what did that make him?

Alex snorted. It made him no better than any one of those damn bastards who had propositioned Sarah over the years.

Chapter Nine

❈

Sarah forced herself to walk calmly across the massive front lawn until she reached the safety of the shadows. Then she started running, not slowing down until she reached the edge of the dooryard, where she finally stopped with her hand over her racing heart.

Alex Knight wanted her!

Well, he wasn't getting her, dammit. She'd been rail-roaded into one marriage without realizing the implications; she was not letting herself get seduced into thinking this one would turn out any better.

Sarah stood outside the reach of the porch light and stared through the kitchen windows at Delaney and Paul as they did the dishes. Alex hadn't said anything about keeping their marriage permanent; he'd only admitted to wanting her.

Sarah shoved her fists into her pockets and silently shook her head. She was throwing every damn romance novel she owned into the trash tomorrow, and she was never buying another one of those foolish dream weavers. They were turning her mind to mush, spinning fairy tales in her head, and making her wish for something beyond her grasp. Those fictional heroines weren't smart and feisty, they were foolish to throw themselves into the arms of the first handsome man to catch their eye. Happily ever after only happened in books.

Sarah scowled at Grady, sitting at the table sipping his tea. She was cornering that scheming man tomorrow and demanding he tell his sons she was reopening the sporting camps. She needed to move out of this house as soon as possible, to get away from Alex Knight before she did something stupid like actually fall in love with him.

The camps were supposedly winterized; the people who ran them before Grady bought them had rented the cabins to ice fishermen and snowmobilers in the winter. Since she intended to run a year-round business, why couldn't she go live in one of the cabins now?

Sarah stepped behind a large tree when she saw Alex walk around the side of the house and onto the back porch. He stopped with his hand on the screen door and looked around the moonlit yard, then finally went inside. Sarah scurried along the perimeter of the yard, keeping the row of pickups between her and the house, and then carefully made her way down the shadowed path that led to the hot tub.

If she moved into one of the cabins, she'd put three miles between her and Alex and still be close enough to see Delaney and Tucker several times a week. Well, the camps were actually four miles by way of the main artery, which meant that either she or the kids would have to walk that far to see each other. But that had been the plan all along, hadn't it?

Sarah stepped onto the deck that held the hot tub and lifted the cover off the steaming water. Her small savings from her salary here, along with what she'd managed to tuck away from her bed-and-breakfast and the few checks Clara had sent her from New York, would quickly get used up if she moved now instead of in the spring. The camps wouldn't generate any income for several months, and she had planned on using her savings as start-up money.

Maybe she could continue to clean and cook for the Knights several days a week—while they were at work, so she wouldn't have to see Alex any more than necessary.

It was a sad fact that Sarah was close to broke, all because Martha Banks had left her share of the Crag Island inn to her second son, Brian, despite being estranged from him for more than fifteen years. (Sarah considered Brian the smart one for having run off to Boston at age seventeen.) So she couldn't even sell her inn to raise money to start her new business, since she couldn't find her silent and as yet unsuspecting partner. Martha's lawyers had been looking for Brian Banks ever since the dragon had died, and Sarah could only hope that the man was found soon, so he could buy her half of the inn. That's why leasing the sporting camps from Grady was so important to her. For twelve years, she'd had to share her inn with Martha Banks, but the camps would be completely hers, run the way *she* wanted to run them.

Sarah shed her jacket, kicked off her shoes, and went perfectly still as she looked around and listened, making sure she was alone. Then she stripped off her clothes, climbed into the tub, and sank into the water up to her chin.

This was her bravest concession to decadence: getting into the hot tub without a swimsuit. It had taken her a whole month to work up the nerve to strip off and finally slide in, even though Grady had repeatedly encouraged her to use the tub. But oh, how nice it felt to let the steaming water swirl over her naked skin. How daring and naughty she was.

Sarah smiled as she reached an arm over her floating breasts and pushed them below the surface. She'd laughed hysterically the first time she'd snuck out of the house, after everyone had gone to bed, and gotten into the tub. She'd never imagined boobs floated, but the darn things were worse than fishing bobbers. When she had turned on the jets the first time, she'd nearly been slapped silly by her own anatomy.

Sarah leaned her head back on the rim of the tub with a sigh and stared up through the swirling steam at the moonlight filtering through the pines. Tomorrow morning, after everyone left, she was going up to the attic to go over every page of the business plan she'd made so far. It was nothing more than a loose-leaf binder filled with various lists at this point: Maine guides she could hire for fishing and hunting and wildlife safaris, supplies she'd need for each of the eight camps and the main lodge, and New England newspapers and magazines she could advertise in. The last list, the budget for start-up, was the only thing still giving her trouble. She needed a lot more than the measly eight thousand dollars she had saved up, one thousand of which she'd already spent on material for the quilts, tablecloths, and curtains she'd been sewing for each of the cabins.

She had taken the Knights' small boat up the lake several times in early fall, while the men were at work and the kids were in school, to measure the windows and to catalog what furniture and equipment had been left and was still usable. The cabins were well furnished, mostly with antiques, which had given Sarah the idea to showcase them as quaint, deep-woods camps from a bygone era. She had three quilts made so far, plus several tablecloths and enough curtains for two of the camps.

But it was hard to plan a business in secret. She needed to order towels and linens and new mattresses, and she wished she could spend more time up the lake cleaning and painting. Yes, tomorrow she was cornering Grady long enough to make him—

"Sa-rah! Sarah, where are you?"

Sarah bolted upright at Alex's shout, sucking in a mouthful of water as she slid under the surface with a sputtered gasp. Drat the man, he was always looking for her!

She sure as heck couldn't let him find her in the hot tub. Not naked. Not with her boobs floating around her ears!

"I'll be in in a minute!" she shouted, spinning around to climb out of the tub into the darkness.

"Maybe I'll come in instead," he said softly, his amused voice not ten feet away.

Sarah quickly dropped back into the water, folding her arms over her breasts as she sank into a fetal position, even though it was pitch black out and she hadn't turned the underwater lights on. "Go away," she said through gritted teeth, just barely able to see the silhouette of Alex leaning against a nearby tree.

"That was a quick trip inside to get your swimsuit."

"Go away," she repeated, sinking deeper when he stepped onto the deck. "I don't have anything on."

"Really?" he whispered.

Sarah could see his hand reaching for the controls, and she cupped her hands and sent a wave of water splashing against his chest and face—just as the jets kicked on and she suddenly shot across the tub. She reached out and slapped at the controls until the turbulence finally stopped in a flurry of rising bubbles.

"What did you do that for!" she sputtered, clinging to the edge of the tub.

"Because you made me mad down on the dock," he growled, pulling his shirttail out of his pants and bending over to wipe his face.

"Now there's a news flash," Sarah said, eyeing her clothes on the bench and gauging her chances of reaching for them without exposing herself. "You've been mad at me since we met."

He straightened and glared at her, the chiseled planes of his face looking menacing in the scattered moonlight. "I am not a lecher, and I don't like being lumped in with the rest of your fan club."

"Oh, then please excuse me," she said sweetly, inching toward the bench, "for misunderstanding when you asked what was wrong with two consenting adults kissing in the moonlight and then telling me that you want me."

Sarah couldn't be sure, but she thought she saw two flags of color darken his cheeks. "I thought I was giving you a compliment," he muttered, running a hand through his wet hair.

Sarah reached out and grabbed a fistful of her clothes. Alex lunged to stop her, but she scooted across the tub, dragging her clothes through the water with her, and turned her back to him. "Then please accept my apology for misjudging you," she said as she found her soaked sweater. "I'll have to work on keeping my mind out of the gutter."

She wrestled the wet sweater over her head, pulled it down to her hips, then turned to face him. "Anything else you need to clarify for me that can't wait until I've dried off?"

"Yes, as a matter of fact, there is," he said softly, placing his hands on the edge of the tub. "Why haven't you put a label on my shelf in the upstairs bathroom?"

Sarah stilled with her pants at her knees. "Excuse me?"

"I want my name on my shelf, just like everyone else. I've been home a week and a half, so why don't I have a label?"

Oh, she had a label for him, all right, but it wasn't something she wanted Delaney and Tucker to see. Sarah got her pants pulled up just as he leaned closer, his head and chest hanging over the water directly in front of her. "And everyone has one of those silly little bowls of twigs and cones that smell so nice in their bedrooms," he whispered. "Except me. How come I don't have one?"

Sarah braced one foot on the wall of the tub, grabbed his shoulders, and gave a powerful yank. She scrambled out of the way and over the side just as Alex's yelp of surprise ended in a gurgling splash. She slapped her hand down on the jets and then ran flat-out for the house, breaking into a smile as his angry roar followed her down the path.

"Take that, Mr. I-was-giving-you-a-compliment," she muttered as she ran onto the porch and slammed through the kitchen door. She immediately slowed to a walk, keeping her eyes on her bedroom door as she squished barefooted past Grady and the gaping Delaney and Paul.

Grady downed the last of his tea, then dabbed his mouth with his white linen napkin to hide his smile. Damn if things weren't going well.

"What do you suppose happened to Sarah?" Delaney whispered.

"She must have fallen in the lake," Paul returned softly.

The back door slammed open again, and Alex strode inside like a marauding Viking. Grady noticed that his son was equally wet, and he also noticed the tiny bit of lace Alex had crumpled in his right fist. But where Sarah had appeared quite pleased with herself, despite her condition, Alex appeared ready to commit murder.

"It's a bit cold for swimming, isn't it?" Paul asked, handing his brother the towel he'd been using to dry the dishes. "Still trying to get rid of that jungle heat?"

"Where is she?"

"Probably in the shower by now," Grady said, taking his cup to the sink before walking over to Alex. "I heard her door lock behind her, and I prefer not to have to fix the casing, so don't even think of breaking it down."

"That—that woman—" Alex stammered, pointing at Sarah's door while glaring at Grady. "What in hell possessed you to bring her home like some stray . . . some stray . . ."

"Mouse?" Grady finished with a chuckle, patting his son's wet shoulder and then giving him a nudge toward the great room. "Looks to me like she's got a bit of a roar," he said, shoving Alex through the swinging door. He pulled his hand back and rubbed his fingers together. "Feels warm for lake water. I told you it's not wise to use the hot tub twice in one day."

All Grady got for answer was a glare before Alex finally plodded, wet boots and all, up the stairs without answering Ethan when he looked up from his book and asked what had happened.

Grady smiled at Ethan. "Seems Alex and Sarah are getting to know each other," he said, wrapping his arm around Delaney when she came up and leaned against him. He turned his smile on her. "You keep saying your prayers, little girl. They seem to be working."

"It's a good thing, then, that they had a fight?" she asked, wrapping her arm around his waist.

He tapped the end of her nose. "It's not really a fight if everyone wins."

"Then what is it?"

"It's courtship," he told her, ruffling her hair. "You'll find that out yourself, one day. Not for many, many years, I hope." He gave her a nudge toward the stairs. "Go up and make sure Tucker brushes his teeth, will you? Then your daddy will read you both a story—assuming he can string two words together by then."

Seemingly pleased that Alex and Sarah were courting, Delaney skipped across the room and disappeared up the stairs at a run.

"The only reason I'm keeping my mouth shut," Ethan said as Paul walked through the swinging door, "is because as long as you're focused on Alex, I'm safe."

Grady shot Ethan a feral grin. "For now," he agreed.

"Was that a bra Alex had in his fist?" Paul asked them both, his own grin lecherous. "Sarah's bra?"

Ethan snorted and stood up. "It sure as hell wasn't his." He shook his head. "Why is he pestering her? She's going to quit, and we'll be back to eating canned beans and boiled ham while we look for yet another house-keeper."

Grady eyed Ethan speculatively. "You worried about your belly or about Sarah?"

Ethan closed his book with a snap and tossed it onto the couch. "Neither," he hissed, heading for the kitchen. "I'm going to town."

"Whew," Paul whistled when the porch door slammed closed. "I think someone has a crush on Sarah."

Grady nodded. "If Ethan wouldn't take so damn long to warm up to a woman, he might have better luck."

"Like me, you mean?" Paul asked. "I don't have any problems in that department." He suddenly sobered. "Sarah's the first woman to catch Ethan's eye in years."

Grady shook his head again. "She's already spoken for. Ethan will have to find his own."

"Before you find one for him?" Paul asked, backing toward the stairs with his hands raised in surrender. "Just as long as you don't worry about me, Pops. I'm doing fine on my own."

Grady headed for the office off the great room, smiling as smugly as Sarah had. Yup, things seemed to be going well. He just wished Sarah and Alex would hurry up and decide they actually *liked* each other, before he had to break the news that Sarah was opening the sporting camps come April.

Chapter Ten

✵

Cornering Grady was like trying to catch fish without bait. He'd slipped out of the house the last three mornings before Sarah had even gotten out of bed, and in the evenings he locked himself away in the office right after dinner, then headed straight to bed from there.

Avoiding Alex, however, was even harder than cornering Grady. The man wouldn't leave her alone. Having told her he wanted her and being told he'd have to get in line seemed to have turned the Knight family darling into the family pest. Sarah had thought she was merely being honest but now realized she'd become a challenge. It seemed the more she was around Alex, the dumber she got.

Like this morning, when he'd suggested she spend a few minutes sitting in one of the pickups to get familiar with it, so that when he popped home for lunch, she'd be ready for a driving lesson. Sarah had planned to head up the lake and start cleaning one of the cabins to live in and had told Alex she didn't have time today, but maybe tomorrow.

He'd told her to be sitting in the pickup at noon.

Sarah glanced at her watch, saw it was one o'clock, and smiled as she looked around the cozy cabin she'd been cleaning all morning. By now, Alex had found her note taped to the windshield of the red pickup, saying that tomorrow was really a better day for her driving lesson. Drat the man, she was not going to let him get into the habit of bossing her around, much less interfere with her business plans.

And if she didn't corner Grady in the next few days, he would learn right along with the others that she had moved to the NorthWoods Sporting Camps. She had more than a thousand dollars and countless hours already invested, and moving now instead of next spring made sense. It would take her the rest of the winter to whip all the cabins into shape, and then she still had to get at least the front room and the kitchen of the main lodge ready for guests.

Sarah checked the ancient potbellied stove in the corner to make sure the fire was dead, then slipped on her jacket and headed outside. She stopped on the narrow porch of Cabin One and took a moment to soak in the view of the deep, pristine lake rimmed with lush, evergreen-covered mountains marching all the way past the Canadian border. "Perfect," she whispered on a deep breath of pine-scented air. "Just perfect. I can lure tourists here from as far away as Europe and Asia."

Sarah walked to the bicycle leaning against the cabin and checked that the old red wagon was tied securely to the seat post. She'd used it to haul cleaning supplies, a quilt and bedding, and the curtains she'd hung up this morning. "I'll need to set up a Web site to draw international guests," she thought out loud as she pulled the bike upright and swung her leg over the seat. She pushed off, the empty wagon rattling behind her. "One more expense to add to my budget. But maybe the Web site can wait until I see how my first season goes."

Satisfied that her business plans were progressing nicely, Sarah pedaled out the half-mile lane that led to the main hauling artery. Alex had likely returned to the cutting site by now, hopping mad from her note, she hoped, and she had plenty of time to get home and start dinner. They were having lamb tonight, since Sarah knew Alex hated lamb.

She didn't really understand why she liked pushing Alex's buttons, but she did know it was fun. She couldn't remember ever feeling so provoked by the opposite sex— in an exciting, butterflies-in-her-belly sort of way, that is.

Sarah raced down a short hill and madly pedaled to make it up the next knoll, the wagon bouncing on the frozen road behind her. Maybe she should write a book. Not one of those trouble-causing romances, but a book on running an inn, with recipes and little anecdotes about memorable guests. Lord knew, there could never be enough how-to books.

Sarah pulled onto the main hauling artery, making a wide swing because she was going so fast, and the wildly bouncing wagon nearly pulled her off balance. She just pedaled harder, picking up speed with a laugh of delight. Life was good. She had Delaney and Tucker to love and the excitement of a new business venture looming ahead, and for the first time in her life, she finally felt in charge of her destiny. Almost like a heroine in one of her books.

Almost. It was just the hero part that kept plaguing her. But she was a modern woman, not a damsel in distress who needed rescuing. She was damn well capable of rescuing herself.

Sarah saw the empty logging truck headed toward her long before she heard it, because the wagon behind her was making so much noise. She steered to the side of the road, and the truck sped past, the driver giving her a big smile as he reached up and blasted his air horn. Sarah pedaled faster. Drat. The driver would surely tell Alex he'd seen her, and then Alex was going to ask her what she was doing so far from home in the opposite direction of town, and why in hell she had been dragging a wagon behind her.

Well, so be it. He would know about her opening the camps in a couple of days, anyway, when she moved into Cabin One. She'd be safely settled in her new home when the explosion came, when Grady told his sons about his plan to let her reopen the camps. None of them wanted the camps reopened, because they didn't want tourists clogging their roads and traipsing through their forest taking pictures of moose. Maybe she should invite Delaney and Tucker over that first night, so they wouldn't have to listen to the heated discussion.

Sarah approached the sharp curve that was half a mile before the lane leading home. That reminded her that she'd have to put up a sign with an arrow at the fork in the road, so her guests didn't end up at the Knight homestead. She was just thinking she could take a shortcut through the woods, since her wagon was empty, and cut a good mile off her trip, when she rounded the corner and spotted a car parked on the side of the road. It was right beside the shortcut, and Sarah quickly decided to take the long way home.

She steered to the opposite side of the road as she neared the car, noticing it had Massachusetts plates. Probably out-of-staters hunting grouse, the only game open to hunting right now. Deer season had ended two weeks ago, and thanks to Ethan, Sarah had a freezer full of venison.

Just as she was approaching the car, two men emerged from the woods. Sarah's first impression was that they looked out of place. They weren't dressed for the woods but wore black leather jackets and sneakers. One was trying to fold a map; the other one was carrying a hunting rifle.

Not a shotgun, which was used for grouse, but a rifle.

Sarah picked up her pace. The men seemed startled to see her and stopped on the edge of the ditch. They stood there as she pedaled past, staring at her with narrowed eyes. She gave them a short smile and a quick wave and kept on pedaling.

Sarah didn't look back when she heard their car doors open and close; she merely pedaled harder, wanting to get to the turnoff as fast as she could. Had Grady hired surveyors to cruise this section of woods for harvesting? Sarah had met one or two of the foresters they usually used, and they were local men, dressed for the woods.

She was just a quarter-mile from the lane when she looked back and saw the car speeding toward her, leaving a plume of frozen dust in its wake. She didn't know why the men disconcerted her; she only sensed that they hadn't liked her catching them walking out of the woods. She looked back again to find that the car had slowed down behind her. This was not good. In fact, it was starting to get downright scary. Why didn't they just pass her?

She heard the engine rev just before the car sped by and came to a sliding halt not fifty feet in front of her. Sarah steered her bicycle straight into the ditch, jumped off, and ran into the forest at an angle that would take her to the path that led home. The fallen leaves, frozen and dried crisp, made a lot of noise under her feet, but that also allowed her to hear them following. She heard when they suddenly stopped to listen, and she immediately stopped, too.

She didn't dare move. She looked around the forest, hoping for a place to hide, and spotted a large pine tree with several low-hanging limbs. Watching where she placed her feet, Sarah moved toward the tree, all the while listening for signs of pursuit.

One of the men said something she couldn't make out, and they both started running in her direction.

Sarah sprinted the last twenty feet to the tree and grabbed the bottom branch to swing herself up, then climbed high into the concealing branches until she could barely see the ground. The men stopped not ten feet away from the base of the tree, and Sarah went perfectly still. They slowly scanned the area as they listened for sounds of her running. Both had guns; one of them had the rifle he'd been carrying earlier, the other a handgun.

"Come on out, honey!" one of them yelled.

Sarah saw him put the handgun into his pocket as he motioned for the other man to set down his rifle. The other guy set the rifle on the ground, then the first man kicked some leaves over it. "We don't want to hurt you," he said in a heavy accent as he looked around. "Are you lost? We can give you a ride to town. Come out, lady."

Just then, Sarah heard a truck coming down the road—a pickup, by the sound of it. It was going quite fast, and she would bet her shoes it was Alex racing home, hoping to catch her pedaling down the road.

The pickup came to a sliding stop, the tires chittering as they dragged on the frozen gravel. The two men below her instantly reacted. One pulled his handgun from his pocket; the other retrieved his rifle from the leaves. Both men spun to face the road.

"Sarah? Sarah! Where are you?" Alex shouted.

Oh, God. Alex was coming into the woods to look for her. And he was heading straight toward the two men!

"Sarah!" Alex shouted again.

She had to do something. The men had their guns pointed in his direction, and if he got any closer they might shoot him.

Sarah started climbing down the tree and stopped just above the men when she heard one of them say something in a language she didn't recognize. One man started to sidle to the left, as if he planned to ambush Alex.

Dammit, she had to do something. "Alex, they have guns!" Sarah yelled, just as she leapt onto them. Both men went rolling to the ground with grunts of surprise, and Sarah yelped at the pain of her knee connecting with a hard shoulder. The man beneath her lashed out with his gun, striking her in the ribs.

The other man rolled to his feet and grabbed her hair,

pulling her up in front of him. She kicked back and connected with his shin, elbowing him in his belly at the same time. She then kicked the first man, who was now pointing his gun toward the road, and Alex shouted again.

"Alex! They've got guns!" she yelled, as loud as she could.

The man behind her grabbed Sarah by the shoulder and yanked her to the ground. A shot cracked through the woods, and Sarah screamed before realizing the sound had not come from either of the men beside her. They were crouched, motionless, looking toward the road, the one man pinning her down with his knee.

"Leave her," the man with the handgun said, grabbing his partner off Sarah and shoving him deeper into the forest.

Stunned by her unexpected freedom, Sarah buried her face in her hands, her whole body shaking uncontrollably.

"Sarah? Sarah, where are you?"

She lifted her head and took a shuddering breath, trying to stop trembling. "Alex? I'm here. Th-they ran away, but I don't know where they are!" she yelled.

Alex broke through the dense underbrush and dropped to his haunches beside her, scanning the woods around them with his gun poised to fire. Sarah scrambled to her knees and buried her face in his jacket.

Alex rocked Sarah back and forth in one arm, crooning nonsense to her as he scanned the woods. *They*, she had kept shouting, which meant there had been at least two men. Alex watched the woods for several minutes, his scowl darkening when he glanced down and saw the pieces of bark and leaves in her tangled hair. "What happened, Sarah?" He squeezed her softly when she didn't answer and scanned the forest again. "What are you doing out here all by yourself?"

The sound of a car starting drew his attention, followed by the violent revving of an engine and the sound of tires spinning on gravel.

Alex eased Sarah away so he could see her face. "How long had they been chasing you? Did they hurt you?" he asked softly.

When he realized she wasn't going to say anything, only shake her head, Alex tucked his gun into his belt, stood up, picked Sarah up, and carried her back to his truck. He set her in the passenger's seat and closed the door, unloaded the handgun, shoved it under the driver's seat, and climbed in. But instead of starting the truck, he stared out the windshield at the bicycle and Tucker's old red wagon lying in the ditch.

"You shouldn't ride a bike on this road, looking for your twigs and stuff," he said, using every ounce of patience he had to soften his voice. He saw that Sarah was trembling uncontrollably, and his anger immediately vanished. He started the truck and put it in gear, then pulled Sarah against his side and headed for home with his arm wrapped tightly around her.

He had come back to the house two hours ago, hoping to spend time alone with Sarah by giving her a driving lesson—and getting her to see that he wasn't just another member of her fan club. But all he'd found was her note on the windshield. Angry, though not really surprised, he had conceded this round in their battle of wills and gone back to work.

But then one of the drivers had climbed out of his rig at the logging yard just half an hour ago, unable to quit grinning as he told Alex that he'd seen his wife pedaling down the road like a cat with its tail dipped in turpentine, dragging an old wagon behind her.

Alex had sped back toward the house, hoping to catch her. When he'd found the unfamiliar car sitting by the side of the road, he'd started to worry. Seeing the bicycle and the wagon lying in the ditch and finding two sets of large footprints going into the woods, Alex had pulled out the handgun they always kept under the seat.

"Where were you, Sarah, when you yelled that the men had guns?" he asked, now that her trembling seemed to be easing, though she had her face buried in his side.

"In—in a tree."

"You climbed a tree?"

She nodded against his jacket.

"And then what?"

"I jumped on them," she whispered.

Alex was speechless. She'd jumped on the men with guns in their hands? "Why?" he croaked.

"They were going to ambush you."

Alex felt the tremor begin deep in his chest before it worked out to his fingers and toes. She'd left her hiding place to save him? Holy hell, was she an idiot!

She suddenly pulled away, and Alex realized he'd spoken out loud. He tightened his arm around her and glared out the windshield as he turned onto their lane. "You do not jump on men with guns."

She hit him with her own angry glare. "So I was supposed to sit there and watch them ambush you?"

Alex couldn't for the life of him pick which emotion

was in charge at the moment. He was violently shaking over what she'd done, but it might be anger tying his gut in a knot. She tried to sit up again, and he let her.

"Fine," she said. "Next time, I'll just let them shoot you."

"Why were they chasing you?"

"I don't know. I was pedaling down the road just as they came out of the woods."

"You've never seen them before? In town? At Mary's store, maybe?"

"No."

"They were coming out of the woods, they saw you pedaling by, and they just started chasing you?"

She nodded.

"Did you talk to them?"

"No, I just waved at them and kept going," she said, looking down at her hands as she gripped the knees of her dirty jeans.

Alex pulled into the yard, shut off the truck, and turned in his seat to face her. "You waved at them," he repeated evenly.

His voice must have betrayed his anger, because she flinched. Alex closed his eyes and took a slow breath. "Sarah, you can't go waving at strangers you see in the middle of nowhere."

"No! It wasn't like that. They didn't follow me because I waved. I think they didn't like the fact that I caught them coming out of the woods."

"They were probably just hunting. Why in hell would they chase you for catching them hunting?"

"They were on the shortcut that leads to home. And they weren't hunting. One guy was folding a map, and the other guy had a rifle, not a shotgun. And they were dressed in leather jackets and sneakers." She shifted to face him, anger rising in her face. "I didn't say anything to them. I just acknowledged their presence and kept pedaling. I couldn't just ignore them."

"Yes, you could."

She started to open her door, but Alex reached out and took hold of her arm. "Sarah, you have no idea of the effect you have on men. When you smile, the pope himself would forget his vows."

"So this is my fault?" she asked, her voice rising in disbelief. She jerked from his grip and folded her arms under her breasts. "Because I was foolish enough to smile and wave at those men, I *invited* them to chase me through the woods? With guns?"

"No. That's not what I'm saying."

"Then what exactly are you saying?"

Alex blew out a frustrated breath and rubbed his face with both hands. Dammit. He needed Sarah to promise never, ever to put herself between him and danger again.

Hell, what he really needed was to kiss every scratch and bruise on her body and assure himself she really was all right.

Her door opened, and Alex silently watched her stalk into the house.

He finally followed her, went over to her closed bedroom door, and stood listening to her quiet sobs for a full five minutes—every tick of the old kitchen clock echoing his escalating urge to lash out. Then he walked away before he broke down the door.

Sarah didn't see Alex again that day, and it was nearly midnight and he still wasn't home. He hadn't returned to the work site, the others had said when they came home for dinner. After Sarah had told them what had happened, Ethan started cursing, then grabbed his jacket and stormed out, with Paul right behind him.

Grady had paced for twenty minutes as he made Sarah repeat exactly what had happened, before locking himself in his office. Sarah had kept Delaney and Tucker busy making Christmas decorations at the kitchen table after dinner.

But now it was nearing midnight, the kids were in bed, Grady was nursing a bottle of whiskey in his office, and Sarah was the one pacing the kitchen floor, fretting and worrying and blaming herself.

A truck finally pulled into the dooryard at a quarter to one. Sarah ran to the back door and saw three men get out and make their way to the porch. Their footfalls were heavy and unsteady, and one man was being supported by the other two. Sarah threw open the door just as Grady rushed into the kitchen.

Alex was between his brothers, his head bent as he cradled his ribs. When he looked up, Sarah couldn't stifle her groan.

He was a mess. His face looked as if a skidder had hauled a load of logs across it; one eye was swollen almost completely shut, his other eye squinting below a bandage that covered his forehead. His left hand, holding his ribs, was also bandaged. His shirt was torn, there was blood on his collar and sleeve, and his lower lip was split. The smell of antiseptic wafted into the kitchen ahead of him.

Ethan and Paul all but carried Alex to the table, then carefully settled him onto a chair. Grady, who had been speechless up to now, started cursing.

"What happened?" Sarah asked past the lump in her throat.

"You're what happened," Ethan snapped, turning on her.

"Ethan!" Alex said, only to suck in his breath.

Ethan ignored him, bringing his anger back to Sarah. "He went looking for those men who chased you today and spotted their car at the Greenville hotel." He pointed at Alex. "The man's not even near his full strength, yet he went looking to avenge you. When those bastards fled, my jackass brother tore after them. We found him and his truck wrapped around a tree!"

"That's enough!" Alex shouted, slamming the table with his fist. He moaned in pain but never took his eyes off Ethan. "This is not Sarah's fault," he bit out with deadly softness.

"That's enough from both of you," Grady ordered. "It's no one's fault, except maybe Alex's for going off half cocked."

Ethan glanced at his battered brother, then stormed back out the door, his angry footfalls fading to a deafening silence. Alex's groan broke the tension.

Sarah stepped to him and cupped his cheek, turning his face toward her as she examined him through blurry eyes. "Oh, God, I'm sorry, Alex."

Alex groaned when Paul and Grady moved to help him stand up. "If this had been last year, those men wouldn't have stood a chance when I'd caught them," he boasted, which he ruined with another groan.

"No," Paul assured him. "But then, you wouldn't have had to go after them last year, would you?"

"Get a glass of water, and bring those pills, Sarah," Grady said over his shoulder, nodding toward the tiny brown bottle Paul had set on the table as they helped Alex through the swinging door. "We'll get him into bed."

It seemed forever before Sarah was sitting by Alex's side and the two of them were finally alone. The doctor had declared his ribs were bruised but not broken, Paul had explained. Alex also had six stitches over one eye, three cracked knuckles, and a banged knee. Sarah sat on the bed, a glass of water and two pain tablets in her hand.

Alex gave her a lopsided smile. "Ethan is really a sight to behold when he's angry, isn't he?" he said, obviously trying to make light of his brother's scene downstairs.

Sarah shivered.

Alex reached for her hand. "Don't take his words to heart, Sarah. He's not mad at you. He's mad at me for wrapping my truck around a tree, and madder still at the thought that I might have caught up with them."

"Oh, Alex. You shouldn't have gone after those men."

Alex said nothing, and she closed her eyes. "One of them spoke with an accent. And they had a map and a rifle when they first came out of the woods."

"It doesn't matter, Sarah. All that matters is that they're gone and I'm basically okay. I'm busted up a little bit, but I'll be fine.

She reached out and took his bandaged hand in hers. "I won't bicycle on the road again."

"This isn't your fault, Sarah."

She just sniffled, and he lifted their joined hands, then said mischievously, "If you kiss my boo-boos, I bet I'll feel better."

That jolted Sarah out of her tears. Did the man think she was dumber than dirt, not to realize he was taking advantage of his situation? Then she saw the twinkle in his eyes. Though she hadn't done anything wrong, he *had* gone after those men because they'd gone after her.

She lifted his hand to her lips and gently kissed the back of his bandage.

"Ohhh," he moaned. "I couldn't feel a thing. The bandage is in the way." He pointed to his swollen eye. "Kiss me here?"

Sarah grinned and softly kissed his temple.

"And here?" He touched his lips. "If you kiss me here, I know I'll feel good enough to go to sleep," he cajoled.

Sarah looked at his poor, swollen mouth, then lifted her gaze to his. "How long ago did the doctor give you a pain killer?"

Alex looked fuzzy. "I don't know. A while ago."

Sarah hesitated the briefest of seconds, then leaned down and gently touched her lips to his.

Alex leaned forward to deepen the contact, then dropped back onto the pillow. "Now I feel better," he whispered, his eyes closed and his battered face wearing a pained smile.

Chapter Eleven

Sarah put her plans to move up the lake on hold, to take care of Alex for the next several days. She sat in the great room with him for hours each day. Sometimes they'd watch her how-to shows together, sometimes she would read to him, but sometimes they'd simply sit and talk—mostly about her, since that seemed to appease his growing restlessness. She didn't know how it happened, but Sarah found herself telling Alex all about her life growing up on Crag Island, about her parents, and about the twelve years the Bankses had plagued her. She, however, was only able to get bits and pieces of Alex's life, since every time she asked about his childhood, he always managed to turn the conversation back to her. The man should have been a CIA agent instead of an engineer.

Alex was initially an amiable patient, although he grumbled whenever he limped to the bathroom. He entertained his kids after school by checking their homework and planning their approaching Christmas vacation, just one week away, and told them hair-raising tales about his eleven-day hike through the jungle—though Sarah suspected he softened the desperate parts and embellished the heroic ones. All in all, she found dealing with Alex on a daily basis to be surprisingly easy and sometimes downright rewarding.

Like when she trounced him at chess eight games out of ten. She had teased Alex that just as in chess, being a successful innkeeper required not only discipline and strategy but the ability to recognize impending disasters and the smarts to head them off. And like when Alex sent her to the attic to find his scruffy old pack basket of ice-fishing equipment, and she had sat mesmerized as he replaced all the line on his fishing traps while explaining how they worked.

Sarah found herself looking forward to New Year's Day, when ice-fishing season started. The next time she went to Mary's store in Oak Grove, she was buying herself a set of ice traps so she could try her hand at freshwater fishing. It couldn't be any more difficult than saltwater fishing, Sarah had blithely declared. This resulted in Alex issuing her a fishing challenge for New Year's Day.

The stakes? A kiss lasting at least two minutes if Alex won, an evening of dinner and dancing in Greenville if Sarah caught more fish. Sarah started rethinking her prize within minutes of shaking hands on their wager. Dinner and dancing was basically a date, wasn't it? So who was actually winning what?

After six days of inactivity and being fed gallons of nutritious soup, Alex's mood began to change from compliant to cranky. Sarah would just start on a chore when she would be called—not by the bell she'd given him but by a shout—into the great room. "Read to me," he would demand. "Or give me a sponge bath," he'd petition, his no-longer-swollen eyes now looking anything but pained.

But the crankier Alex got, the more diabolical Sarah became. She would patiently read him articles from forestry magazines and engineering journals, instead of one of her romance novels as he kept asking for, and on more than one occasion, Sarah simply gave him his dose of pain pills and patiently waited until they put him to sleep. Then she would escape to the attic to work on another quilt hanging to send to Clara in New York City.

There had been a close call two days ago, when Alex had answered the phone and Clara Barton had asked to speak to Sarah. Sarah had immediately grabbed the phone and gone into her bedroom for privacy; Alex was the last person she wanted speaking to Clara. And though she knew Alex had been curious about who was calling her, he'd been polite enough not to ask, and Sarah hadn't offered any explanation. She had learned long ago that the less said, the better.

Too bad she hadn't remembered that little truth when Alex had been probing about her life with Roland and Martha Banks.

Alex had spent the last six days lying on the couch, surrounded by enough Christmas decorations to fill the White House and staring at a Christmas tree large enough to be in Rockefeller Center, with plenty of time to think about the two men who had chased Sarah. Just thinking of her jumping on those men would make Alex's blood boil, sending cold chills down his spine.

John Tate had been called the next morning, and he had come out and taken Sarah's statement, reassuring her that the men were likely long gone after Alex's foolish attempt to catch them. But as soon as Sarah had gone upstairs to make the beds, John had told Alex and Grady and Paul that he would contact the border patrol as well as Daniel Reed, the local game warden, to pass on the information, and that he would start making their logging roads part of his daily rounds.

Ethan hadn't been there to hear John's concerns, because he hadn't returned after storming out that first night. John said he'd seen Ethan in Greenville and that if he ran into him again, he'd bring him up to speed on what was happening. Two days later, Ethan had stopped into the house just long enough to pack some clothes and camping equipment. He'd had nothing to say to Sarah— who had gone to her room when he'd come through the back door—and very little to say to Alex, except to inquire how he was feeling.

Alex hadn't pushed the issue, knowing Ethan would apologize to Sarah as soon as he figured out why he'd gotten so mad at her to begin with.

But it was Sarah's daily escapes that really puzzled Alex. She seemed to take a lot of walks, though she assured him she was staying in the woods and not walking their road. But sometimes when she disappeared, Alex would hear soft footfalls coming from the attic. She would always check to see if he was sleeping—which he always made sure he appeared to be—and then she would quietly head up to the attic. He figured Christmas presents were her secret there.

Alex marked his page, stuffed the romance novel between the couch cushions, got up with a muttered curse at his still sore knee and ribs, and limped to the office. It was time he went back to work, even if that meant sitting at a desk instead of in his skidder. He sat down at his drafting table with a sigh and smiled in anticipation of his own present for Sarah, which was being delivered Christmas morning.

Alex absently shuffled through the road maps he'd been working on before his accident, contemplating what he'd learned about his wife these past six days. He couldn't decide if he was more amazed by her unbroken spirit, despite the nosedive her life had taken since her mother's illness, or by her choice of reading material.

The romance novels had been a real eye-opener; the fact that he'd found them in the trash was even more enlightening. He'd read four in the last six days, sneaking them from under the sofa cushions when Sarah escaped outdoors or upstairs.

Alex felt he finally had an idea how Sarah's mind worked. Hell, he certainly understood how their bedroom disaster had happened that first night. Some parts of those books were downright erotic. But they also presented an insight into Sarah's indomitable spirit, if she considered the women in those novels to be role models. The heroines were intelligent, which Sarah certainly proved she was at chess; they were brave to the point of being reckless, which she had proved by jumping on those men; and they were hell-bent to go after what they wanted in life, which . . . Well, Alex wasn't sure Sarah had mastered that trait yet. He wasn't even sure Sarah *knew* what she wanted.

She obviously wanted a family, judging by how she'd jumped at Grady's offer to marry a dead man and adopt Delaney and Tucker. But what about the men in the books she read? Didn't Sarah want a hero of her own? Didn't she want to love a real live man, instead of just reading about it?

He'd been trying to get a few simple kisses since he'd met her, and she shied away from even that small intimacy. What in hell was she afraid of? Not him personally; she was way too prickly and provoking to be afraid of him.

Alex frowned as he reshuffled the maps, unable to find the one that showed the tote roads their construction crew had rebuilt this fall so they could move their operation there in February. He got up and searched Grady's desk, the file cabinet, and the back wall of shelves, littered with everything from Delaney's and Tucker's school projects to broken skidder parts.

"Sarah. Sarah!" he shouted as he limped out of the office and over to the bottom of the stairs. "Sarah!"

It was a good two minutes before she appeared at the top step, her face flushed with the cold of the attic, and softly asked, "What?"

"Have you been cleaning the office? I'm missing one of my maps."

She shook her head. "Grady's first rule when I came here was that I don't touch his office," she said as she came down the stairs.

Alex stepped out of her way, turning to walk back to the office. "Help me look, then," he said. "I can't find the map for the section we're cutting in February."

Alex turned to see Sarah stopped in the office doorway, her hands on her hips and her expression horrified. "It's a wonder anyone can find anything in here, much less one single map."

"I was working on it last week. It should be right here," he said, frowning down at his drafting table.

"Maybe Grady has it in his truck," she offered, stepping up to the large desk in the center of the room and scanning the mess of papers. "Or Ethan might have taken it when he came home. Maybe he's camping out in that section for . . . for a while," she finished softly, turning away to open a file drawer.

But she didn't turn fast enough for Alex to miss her look of sadness. "I don't think Ethan has it," he said. "I was sitting on the couch the whole time he was home, and he never entered the office."

"And Grady?" she asked with her back to him.

"He might have taken it," Alex conceded, sitting behind the desk. "But he would have mentioned it to me. He knew I was working on plans for a bridge we need to build before the spring thaw."

Sarah closed the file drawer, saw it bounce open, and used her shoulder to slide it shut as she looked at him. "Do you need a map to design a bridge? Don't you just draw it out or something?"

"The map has the grades I use to determine the height and span of the bridge."

"Grades?"

"Elevations," he explained, "that show the slope of the land leading down to the brook." He glanced at his watch and suddenly brightened. "We could go out to that section, and I could reshoot the grades. It's only nine.

We'd be back long before Delaney and Tucker get off the school bus."

"Why *we?*" she asked, looking alarmed. "Surely you're able to drive now."

"I need you to hold the elevation stick," Alex told her, warming up to his idea. "And I'll give you a driving lesson on the way out."

Sarah's expression went from alarm to horror, and she started backing out of the office. "You're not giving me a driving lesson. Not in your condition."

"What does my condition have to do with anything?" he asked, stalking her out the door.

"You're going to get your good knee banged up right along with your bad one," she said, backing toward the kitchen. "That's assuming I don't smash your face into the dash." She stopped with her back against the swinging door. "I nearly wrecked Paul's fancy Mustang, and Grady was shaking so badly after my lesson with him that he could barely speak. Ethan didn't even last to the main hauling artery; he made me walk home. I just can't get the hang of driving."

Alex folded his arms over his chest, being careful of his ribs. "It's not rocket science, Sarah," he said with a reassuring smile. "There's a gas pedal, a brake, and a steering wheel. If you can coordinate three pots cooking on a stove while something is roasting in the oven, right along with everything else it takes to put on a meal, you can drive."

"It's the engine," she muttered, lifting her chin. "I can't seem to run anything with an engine. I broke four power-saw blades and burned up the sander when I made the hot-tub cabinet."

"You run an electric mixer, don't you? I don't see food flying all over the kitchen when you make cookies."

She had started to back through the swinging door but stopped. "That's because the mixer has speed settings, not a gas pedal. I can set it on whatever number I need, and it doesn't get away from me."

"Then we'll set the shifting lever to low gear, just like on your mixer," he said, stepping forward. He didn't relish the idea of driving to the new cutting in first gear, but if that's what it took, he'd simply grit his teeth. "Put on some long johns and a pair of tall boots. You're going to have to wade across the brook if it's not frozen solid yet, so I can shoot grades on the other side."

She looked as if she wanted to shoot him.

"I need to get that bridge designed so our road crew can build it by February, Sarah."

"Can't you call Grady on the radio to see if he's got your map?" she asked desperately.

"I already called him," Alex lied, determined to give her a driving lesson. "He's not in his truck."

Sarah gave him a look of such defeat that it was all Alex could do to contain his grin. She shot him one last scowl, then marched into her bedroom. Alex limped over to the back door, grabbed his jacket off a peg, and headed out to the machine shed to get his surveying gear— merrily whistling the whole way.

Sarah sat behind the wheel of the red pickup with her sweaty hands balled into fists on her knees, fighting the urge to smack Alex upside the head with her dented roaster. She had spent six days practically glued to his side, and now he wanted her to spend all day with him in the front seat of a truck and then in the woods.

It was bad enough that she couldn't even escape him in her sleep; the man kept invading her dreams, which had been growing progressively naughty. She hadn't read a romance novel in weeks, and she still kept waking up hot and bothered, hugging her pillow to her breasts, her heart racing. She'd gotten so stressed lately that she had actually run into the bathroom and thrown up three nights in a row. She'd had to resort to taking naps in the middle of the day, because she spent the night staring up at the dark ceiling, literally *aching* to feel his skin rubbing against hers, his weight pressing her into the mattress, his warmth making her blood boil.

"Ready to fire her up?" Alex asked as he slid in beside her.

She was so fired up she was going to combust! Sarah dropped her head so her hair hid her face, reached out and twisted the key, and heard a loud screech.

Alex immediately reached over and pulled her hand off the key. "You only hold the key halfway on while the glow plugs heat up the fuel, because this is a diesel engine," he told her. "That was the starter you heard grinding. So now, put your foot on the brake," he instructed. "And once the glow plug light goes out, start the engine."

Sarah did what she'd been told.

"Good. Now, while your foot is on the brake, pull the shifting lever all the way down until the arrow is on the one."

Sarah brought the shifting lever to one.

"And slowly release the brake."

She did that, too, and nothing happened. The truck merely idled in place.

"Good. Now put your foot on the gas, and press it down only a little bit," he instructed. "Just so that we start creeping forward."

Sarah stepped down on the gas, the engine revved violently, the truck lurched forward, and she immediately slammed her foot on the brake pedal. Alex's shout of "Easy!" ended with a grunt when he slammed into his seat belt. "Put it back in park."

Sarah wrestled the gear shift back up to the P, staring at the dash.

"O-kay," Alex said. "Let's try the gas pedal while we're still in park. See that large dial to the left of the speedometer? That's the tachometer. It tells you how fast the engine is turning. Softly step on the gas again, and see if you can make that needle stop on 2000."

She finally looked over at him. "Why?"

He smiled. "Because it'll give you something to aim for. Never mind about anything else. If you can keep that tach under 2000 when you're in first gear, the truck won't go faster than fifteen or twenty miles per hour."

Sarah eyed the tachometer. "Why didn't Grady or Ethan or Paul tell me about that dial?" she muttered, stepping down on the gas, only to see the needle shoot up to the number five.

"Ease back on the pedal," Alex shouted over the roar of the engine.

Sarah relaxed her foot, and the tachometer needle dropped to 1000. She pushed on the gas again, and the needle shot up to the number four this time. She smiled, eased up on her foot, and the needle wobbled down below the two before settling just a hair's width above it.

"That's it," Alex said. "Feel it in your foot, Sarah. You control the engine; it doesn't control you. Practice bringing the tach up to 3000, then down to 1000."

Sarah slowly curled and uncurled her toes inside her boot and watched in amazement as she was able to make the needle go to any number she chose. "That's it?" she said with a delighted laugh. "It's as simple as picking a number on the tachometer and using my foot to set the needle on it?"

He nodded, his own smile reflecting her excitement. "Just like your food mixer," he said. "Forget about all the other dials, Sarah. You keep that tach under 2000 rpm, and you'll be able to control the truck."

"But I can't watch the dash *and* the road," she pointed out. "I have to see where I'm going."

"That's right, but with only a little practice, you'll know from the sound of the motor what the tach is doing. The numbers are only a benchmark. See that red line under the four and the five? If you keep the needle in that red area very long, you could blow the engine."

Sarah eyed the tachometer.

"Okay, foot on the brake again, pull the shifter down into first gear, then slowly step on the gas until the needle reaches 1500 rpm. That's a good speed to start out."

Sarah pushed down on the brake, pulled the gearshift down to the one, then stepped on the gas and shot them forward with a jerk. But instead of slamming on the brakes, she relaxed her foot while glancing at the tachometer, then out the windshield at the driveway, then back at the tachometer. The needle finally started hovering between 1000 and 2000.

"I'm driving!" she yelped, breaking into a smile as she steered toward the lane. "And we're not crashing. If I wasn't so busy *driving*, I'd hug you!"

"I take rain checks," he said with a chuckle, pulling back the hand braced on the dash and relaxing into his seat. "That's it. Keep glancing at the needle, and keep it around 1500."

Sarah snuck a peek at the speedometer and saw she was going only fifteen miles an hour. Well, hey, it sure beat the heck out of bouncing in and out of the ditch at fifty. Holy smokes, she was driving!

"What's your tach reading?" Alex asked loudly two minutes later. "It's up to nearly 4000, Sarah. Ease off the gas."

Sarah pulled her foot off the pedal, and Alex had to brace his hand on the dash again when they nearly lurched to a stop. "That's good; you didn't slam on the brakes this time," he said, only to suck in his breath when she overcorrected and they jerked forward, the needle shooting all the way to five.

But Alex didn't say anything, likely because he was busy cursing under his breath as they continued down the lane—sometimes with the engine revving loudly in the redline, sometimes with the truck barely creeping along.

"Stop and put it in park," he said when they came to the main artery. "I'll take over from here."

Sarah stepped on the brake a little too hard, pitched them both into their seat belts, and shifted into park as the truck rocked to a halt. "But I'm just getting the hang of it," she said, looking over at him with a frown, just now noticing the fine beads of sweat on his forehead.

"Yes, you are," he said as he unfastened his seat belt and opened his door. Then he gave her a boyishly crooked smile. "And eventually, *I'll* get the hang of your driving."

Chapter Twelve

❈

He was going to have to make some modifications to Sarah's Christmas present, Alex realized as he turned onto the newly built logging road. Continuing the driving lesson, he explained to Sarah that he was shifting the truck into four-wheel drive because of the five inches of unplowed snow. Though she'd done fairly well today, she was a long way from mastering the gas pedal. She would start out well enough, determined to get the tachometer exactly on 1500 rpm, but the moment she looked out through the windshield, she would start pressing harder and harder on the gas, as if she were trying to catch up with something.

Life, maybe? Did Sarah feel she had to rush headlong at life before it left her behind? From what she'd told him of her childhood growing up on Crag Island, Alex could well understand Sarah's addiction to satellite TV. Almost everything she knew about the real world she had apparently learned from watching television and reading. It rather alarmed Alex to think that Sarah's perception of life was based on sell-me-a-dream TV and larger-than-life fictional characters. But the truly scary part was that the woman actually thought she was worldly wise because of it.

Hell, Delaney was less naive than Sarah was, especially when it came to men. His daughter had grown up in an all-male household and had seen the good, the bad, and the ugly sides of real men. Sarah's experience had been a parade of lechers, a bully of a husband, and a father who had lost his will to live when his wife died. From that decidedly narrow paradigm, Sarah had apparently concluded that real heroes only existed in books and on television and that looking for one for herself was a waste of time.

Alex stopped the truck and shut off the engine when the road came to a babbling brook. "Did any of your fan club ever mention love, Sarah?" he asked as she started to open her door.

Her hand stilled on the handle. "What?" She looked at him, her brow wrinkled in confusion. "Love? What do you mean?"

"Just that. Did any of them ever say they loved you?"

"Well, sure," she said dismissively. "Quite a few. What better way to get a girl into bed than to say I love you?"

"So several men over the years told you they loved you, but you simply didn't believe them?"

She opened her door and slid out. "What they *loved* was my body. What brought this up?"

Alex shrugged and opened his own door. "Nothing,

really," he said as he got out. "I was just thinking about something Delaney told me this week."

"What did she tell you?"

"There's this boy at school who said he loves her."

"Just before he tried to kiss her, I bet," Sarah muttered. "I'd better have a talk with her."

"I already took care of it," Alex said, holding his hand up to halt her growing concern. "She'd be embarrassed if she knew I told you about the boy."

"But why? This is girl stuff."

"No, it's father-daughter stuff," Alex returned with a laugh, reaching into the bed of the truck and lifting out his surveying equipment. "She asked *me* because I'm a boy—in case you haven't noticed. Delaney wanted to know if she punched the kid, if that would end his pursuit or only encourage him."

"And you said?"

Alex gave her a wink. "I told her the truth, that men just *love* a challenge."

Sarah stared at him nonplussed, then suddenly reached into the bed of the truck and grabbed the surveying stick that was at least two feet taller than she was. Alex had a moment's worry that she was thinking about smacking him with it, but she spun on her heel and started marching toward the stream.

He set up his tripod with a chuckle and attached the transit. "Be careful going through that brook," he called to her. "The rocks are icy."

"I've been climbing over slippery rocks since I was three," she snapped over her shoulder, wading into the stream while using the stick for support. Alex watched her carefully make her way to the other side, where she stopped and turned to face him. "Now what?"

"Look for an orange tag tied to a tree several yards up the road." He lifted his tripod and carried it down to a flat rock next to the stream for a reference point. "Once you locate the tag, start scuffing the snow just below it. You should find a metal stake driven into the ground."

She scanned both sides of the ditch as she slowly walked up the gently sloping road. She was about forty yards away when she stopped, plodded to the right side of the road, and started kicking the snow with her boots.

"I found it. Now what?"

Alex looked through the transit lens. "Place the bottom of your stick on the ground beside the stake," he called out. He straightened with a smile and waved his hand in a twirling motion. "The other bottom end of the stick, Sunshine. The numbers are upside down."

She snapped her gaze to him in obvious surprise at the nickname, then spun the stick and held it beside the stake. "Okay. It's set."

Alex jotted down the number in his transit's crosshairs, then straightened. "Keep going up the road another twenty yards, look for another orange tag, find the stake below it, and do the same thing."

"That's it? Just hold the stick? Tucker could have done this for you after school," she said as she started up the road through the fluffy snow. "What's it mean when there's a green tag on a tree?" she shouted as she turned and walked backward.

"Green?"

She stopped and pointed. "There's a small piece of green ribbon tied to the limb of that tree. Is there a stake under it?"

"We don't use green tags for anything. This is a spruce forest; we'd never be able to see them."

She shrugged and started up the road but stopped again, walked over to a tree opposite where she'd seen the green tag, and touched one of the branches. Alex looked through the transit lens, turning the focus until he could clearly see what she was touching. He straightened with a frown. Nobody used green ribbon in an evergreen forest.

"Scuff the snow under the tag," he shouted. He looked through the transit again, angling the lens to see her feet.

"There's nothing here," she called back. "There seems to be some sort of path leading into the woods, though." She looked across at the other tag, then back into the woods where she was standing. "It crosses the road right—"

Sarah dropped the stick with a startled yelp and started down the road toward Alex at a flat-out run. "Something's in there!" she screamed as she splashed through the brook without even slowing down, her eyes wide with terror.

Alex braced himself for the impact and caught Sarah as she sloshed out of the stream. He immediately tucked her against his side and moved off the road before setting her down at the base of a large tree. Before he could even crouch beside her, she scurried further behind the tree and yanked him down. He landed with a startled *whoosh* just as Sarah wrapped her arms around him tightly enough to make his ribs hurt.

Alex grinned through his wince, not willing to squander this opportunity to hold his wife. His smile widened as he watched a large bull moose step into the road right where Sarah had been standing.

"Easy now, you're safe," he whispered into her hair when he recognized this particular moose. "I won't let anything hurt you."

She squirmed, trying to see up the road, but he tightened his arms as he watched the majestic bull look across the brook at their truck. Alex let out a barely audible, guttural grunt.

The moose, sporting a rack of antlers that spanned five feet, perked his ears and focused his large brown eyes on the tree they were hiding behind. "Shhh," Alex whispered against Sarah's hair. "Don't make a sound."

The bull gave a soft grunt of its own, then started walking toward the stream, its cavernous nostrils flaring as it tried to catch their scent. Alex waited until it stepped into the stream, then slowly turned Sarah around—still holding her protectively in his arms—and whispered, "The rut's over, but this guy is obviously still hopeful. Have you ever seen anything like him, Sarah?"

She sucked in her breath and tried to shrink even smaller against him. "Why is he coming toward us?" she whispered.

"Because he thinks he just heard a lady moose."

"Y-you called him?" she squeaked. "When you grunted? But why?" she cried in a whisper, trying to look up at Alex while still keeping an eye on the moose.

The bull stopped at the front of their pickup and started licking the road salt off the bumper. Alex gave another soft grunt that made the moose lift its head, zero in on their location, and take several steps toward them.

Sarah squeaked again. Alex stood up with her still wrapped in his embrace and moved to put the tree between them and the moose standing less than ten yards away, eyeing them curiously. The large beast was so close that they could hear him breathing. Alex could also hear Sarah's heart pounding.

"Sarah, meet Thumper," he whispered in her ear. "Tucker named him. About three years ago, Thumper came to visit us at the lodge when he was a two-year-old adolescent. He hung around for nearly a week and kept butting his head into one of the skidders parked in the yard, so Tucker started calling him Thumper."

"H-how come your talking isn't making him run away?"

"Because even though he's five now, he still hasn't gotten any smarter. If anything, he's grown bolder."

"Will he charge us?"

"Maybe," Alex teased, tightening his arms. "If he's disappointed to learn we're not the girl moose he heard."

Sarah sucked in her breath again.

"Then again," Alex continued, working to keep the amusement out of his voice, "he might decide a pretty little blonde with big brown eyes is even more appealing."

Sarah leaned to her right to put more of the tree between them and the moose. He felt her heave a calming sigh. "He's not my type," she whispered, never taking her eyes off Thumper.

"No? He's a handsome fellow in his prime, considered quite a catch among the lady moose in this area. Look at him," Alex said, leaning them back to the left. "If he grunts again, he's saying he loves you." Alex bent over Sarah's shoulder just enough for her to see his smile. "Will you believe him?"

"Just as much as I believed all those other males," she

whispered tightly, darting her gaze to him briefly before looking back at Thumper. "He's no different. He's just interested in a good time before he starts looking for his next victim."

The venom in Sarah's voice punched Alex square in the gut.

"Go find your own girl, Thump," he said loudly, waving an arm in the air. "Go on, get!"

Thumper jerked his head with a startled snort, took several steps back, then spun on his rear legs and headed for the stream in a trot that sent clods of snow shooting into the air behind him.

Alex turned Sarah to face him. "Which one of your infamous fan club broke your heart?" he asked. He gave her a gentle squeeze when she only looked up at him mutely. "What did he do—tell you he loved you, take you to bed, then go his merry way? No," Alex said before she could answer. "He definitely didn't get you into bed. So how did it play out? What stopped you at the last minute?"

Sarah gave a heavy sigh. "I actually had my bags packed," she said quietly, her face pale with the obviously painful memory as she looked up at him. "I'd been married to Roland for only two years, and James had been staying at the inn for a week when he swept me off my feet with his offer to take me back to Boston with him."

"But?"

"But I heard him on the phone in the parlor the day we were supposed to leave. The ferry stopped running at six, so I'd made arrangements with a friends's husband to take us to the mainland at midnight."

"But?" Alex repeated, forcing himself to relax his grip.

"But James was talking to a friend in Boston, boasting about how he was bringing his buddy back a hot little surprise from Maine." Sarah glared up at Alex. "James told him to change the sheets on his bed and clear his calendar, because he wouldn't want any distractions for at least two weeks. And that he couldn't ever complain again that James never brought him any souvenirs."

Alex reared back in surprise but didn't let go of Sarah. "The bastard was bringing you back to his friend? While making you think you were running away with him?"

Her eyes answered for her. Alex pulled her forward and wrapped his arms around her, holding her head to his chest. Holy hell, no wonder she didn't trust men. She had to have been, what, nineteen? "And so you've painted every man since James with the same brush."

"Just like you think every woman is like Charlotte," she said into his chest, her body as rigid as stone. She gripped the back of his jacket and tugged until Alex released her enough that she could glare up at him. "Or are you going to stand here and tell me you didn't immediately decide I was just like her?"

"No more than you're going to tell me I'm like James."

Sarah went soft in his arms and smiled. "Does this mean you're not going to tell me you love me?" she asked, batting her lashes.

Alex let go, stepping back as if he'd just been punched again, and gaped at her. "Not on your life, lady," he finally said. "Three feet of snow will be covering hell before you ever hear those words from me."

Her smile turned smug. "Then you just keep on grunting at moose," she said, stepping around him and walking over to the truck. "Because, like Thumper, you'll eventually come across a female you can charm," she finished as she got in and closed the door.

Alex stood staring at her for a full two minutes before he finally walked down to the brook, ignoring the icy water that soaked his feet as he waded across and angrily plodded up the road.

Dammit to hell, she'd done it to him again. The maddening little witch had given him just a peek inside that beautiful head of hers, only to suddenly turn her provoking smile to full wattage and completely disarm him.

It was a defense, he suddenly realized. Blunt, catch-you-off-guard humor backed up by a disarming smile was Sarah's weapon of choice whenever she found herself in a tight situation. Hadn't she tried to defuse the tension that first morning in her bedroom by claiming no point, no foul? And down on the dock, when he'd kissed her, hadn't she suddenly smiled and calmly stated that most men wanted her? And at the hot tub, she'd caught him off-guard by suddenly changing from a cornered victim to a smiling fury.

Whenever things started to get a bit heated, Sarah simply went all soft and feminine on him. Oh, yeah, she knew exactly what an unexpected smile from a drop-dead beautiful woman did to a man. And besides having no compunction about using her considerable charm to disarm a guy, she was damned good at it. If she had smiled at Thumper, they'd probably be sitting in a tree right now, trying to get rid of a lovesick moose.

He was going to have to be more careful in the future. But being forewarned, he would be forearmed the next time Little Miss Dazzling Smile tried to turn the tables on him.

Alex reached down and picked up the surveying stick she had dropped, his mind shifting to how it must have felt when Sarah had realized she was nothing more than a vacation souvenir being brought back to a friend. Damned hurtful all the way to the soul; not that dissimilar to how Alex had felt when Charlotte had told him that getting pregnant with Delaney and Tucker had been nothing more than calculated gambles that hadn't paid off.

Yeah. Long-term hurtful.

Alex's absent gaze strayed down the path where Thumper had come out, and he frowned. Instead of broken branches, as there should have been on a well-traveled game trail, he could see where a hatchet had taken off the limbs of several trees. He walked down the trail, rounded the corner, and saw that it continued up the mountain ridge, hatchet marks clearing the way as far as he could see.

He'd dismissed the green tags the moment Thumper had stepped onto the road, deciding a hunter had tied the camouflaged ribbons to mark an active game trail. It wasn't uncommon for Maine guides to scout an area for deer or moose, and as long as his crew wasn't cutting an area, the Knight land was open to hunting.

But no hunter ever messed with game trails by cutting them wider. In fact, they were careful not to disturb anything. So who had marked and widened this path? Not snowmobilers. Grady wouldn't have given the local snowmobile club permission to make a trail through a section they'd be logging later this winter.

A breeze stirred the trees overhead, sending a flurry of snow down Alex's collar just as the sun disappeared behind a cloud. A deep chill of foreboding raced up his spine as he stood in the center of the man-made trail, and Alex zipped his jacket up and headed back to the road. He waded through the stream, then picked up his tripod and carried it on his shoulder back to the truck. There he removed the transit, put it into its protective case, and set everything in the bed of the truck.

He stood staring up at Whistler's Mountain, rising above the trees, then finally climbed behind the wheel. He didn't know which worried him more, the fact that Sarah might never see him as anything more than a horny bull moose or the unsettling feeling that something dangerous had invaded his woods.

Chapter Thirteen

❈

If the ride home was filled with tension so strong it hummed, the rest of the day proved even more intense. Grady had been home when Sarah and Alex returned at noon, and he had told them someone had broken the windows out of their equipment at the cutting and slashed all the hydraulic hoses. He'd been on the phone since ten, calling for parts to repair them, and Paul had gone looking for Ethan.

Everyone, including Ethan, sat down to dinner that evening and attempted to keep the conversation light for Delaney and Tucker's sake. Even though the kids knew what had happened, the men suspected it was likely a bunch of bored teenagers causing trouble again, which had been the case three years ago, Sarah learned.

"Delaney has decided to join our fishing challenge," Sarah told Alex, attempting to keep the mood light. "She said she would love an evening of dining and dancing with her father when we catch more fish than you."

Alex smiled at his daughter, then turned his piercing blue eyes on Sarah, obviously not pleased she'd gotten around their date by including Delaney. "You don't consider it cheating, two against one?"

Sarah filled her fork full of mashed potato. "You can choose a partner if you want. Or Delaney and I will limit ourselves to only five traps to match your five."

"I'll be your partner, Dad," Tucker piped up. "We can beat the girls."

"What challenge?" Paul asked, looking from Sarah to Alex. "I want to be included if we're having a fishing contest."

"What's the prize?" Tucker suddenly asked in alarm. "I don't want to go dancing."

"If we win, we can pick our prize," Alex assured him after giving Sarah one last promising look. "Maybe the women will have to wait on us hand and foot for a week."

Paul snorted. "They pretty much do that now."

"They can do my school project that I'm supposed to finish over vacation," Tucker said. "I don't want to make a stupid book about what everyone does around here. I'd rather spend my vacation riding the snowmobile Santa's gonna bring me."

"Why don't you take pictures of all the logging equipment?" Sarah suggested. "That way, you wouldn't have to draw everything. You can make a photo album of everyone's job, and even include a picture of yourself driving the skidder on the cover."

Tucker instantly brightened and looked at his father. "Can I use your digital camera?" he asked.

"Sure, Tuck."

"Sarah, can you remind me to order a new bulb for the ozonizer on the hot tub?" Grady said. "The bulb burned out, and the water's all fogged up and starting to smell." He looked around the table. "The tub's out of commission until we get the bulb replaced, so don't anyone use it."

"How long will that take?" Delaney asked, obviously not liking that the hot tub couldn't be used during vacation. "That's how I warm up after ice fishing all day."

"I'll have it overnighted," Grady promised.

"Sarah met Thumper today," Alex said, changing the subject. "He seems to have survived another hunting season okay."

Paul chuckled. "It's a wonder, considering he's got the brains of a bullfrog. I found him standing in the middle of the road the other day, and he didn't even have the sense to move when I drove right up to him. He just started licking the bumper of my truck. If some hunter didn't get him, one of our logging trucks sure as hel—heck will," he finished, amending his language in deference to the children.

Sarah was appalled at how they could talk so callously about an animal they had named. "He's beautiful," she said. She held her arms out as wide as she could. "He had antlers this big, and he sounded like a freight train coming through the woods. I ran screaming down the road when I heard him."

"Thumper wouldn't hurt you," Tucker assured her. "He's too dumb to hurt anyone." He looked at Alex. "Tomorrow's Christmas Eve, and it's snowing again, so I'll be able to ride the snowmobile Santa's bringing me. You said there's got to be at least a foot of snow to run it."

"If we get another six inches," Alex agreed. "And *if* Santa brings you a snowmobile. But you can't ride it on the lake. The cove might be frozen over, but as long as there's open water still showing in the center, you're not even allowed to *walk* on the ice. That's the rule."

"I know," Tucker said with a frown of impatience. "I'm not as dumb as Thumper."

"Ethan, could you help Sarah carry her Christmas presents down from the attic after dinner?" Alex asked his brother, breaking into a forced smile when Sarah kicked him under the table. "She asked me to help her, but I need to help Tucker finish a project he's working on."

Ethan forced his own smile. "Sure," he said, filling his mouth with ice cream.

Sarah tamped down the heat inching toward her cheeks. Great. Just what she wanted to do, spend time in the cramped attic with Ethan. What was Alex up to? She hadn't asked for help with her presents. For that matter, how had he even known she had presents stashed in the attic?

The moment everyone finished eating, Sarah jumped up and started clearing the table, only to have Alex volunteer to help her with the dishes.

"What in God's name made you ask Ethan to help me carry down my presents?" Sarah asked in an angry hiss as she shoved silverware into the dishwasher.

Alex passed her a plate. "It was the only thing I could think of."

"Only thing for what? Payback for this morning?"

"This morning?" he asked, looking confused.

"When I compared you to Thumper," she impatiently explained.

He grinned. "Hell, no. I'm much more inventive about getting even for insults. I'll also get even for your scheme to avoid dinner and dancing in Greenville," he added, and leaned closer. "Not that it matters, because I'm still holding you to that kiss when I win."

"You still haven't explained Ethan," she said, refusing to respond to his threat. Or was it a promise?

Alex sobered. "I want my brother back," he said softly. "I know what I'm asking might be hard for you, but just this once, just for the span of this evening, could you please not question my motives?"

Sarah started packing the dishwasher. He was asking her to trust him? For Ethan, who hadn't said two words to her since he'd been home? The tension in the house since he'd returned had been so thick Sarah wasn't even sure a chainsaw could cut it.

"Okay," she softly conceded. "I'll let him help me."

Alex pulled her forward and kissed her quickly on the forehead. "Thank you," he said, spinning around and walking into the great room, conveniently ignoring the rest of the dishes.

Sarah finally made her way up to the attic, a silent Ethan treading behind her. She immediately went to her stash of Christmas gifts, picked up several brightly wrapped boxes, and turned to hand them to Ethan.

"Sarah," he said softly. "Sarah, I'm sorry."

He set the boxes on a table, then took hold of her shoulders. "I am so damned sorry for what I said the other night. I was an ass for getting angry and storming out, and it had absolutely nothing to do with you. Of course it wasn't your fault Alex drove off half cocked and got into a wreck. That was his choice."

"I didn't ask for those men to chase me," she said tightly.

"I know," he said, hugging her gently. "My big brother has kindly reminded me that I'm dumber than Thumper. I never should have implied any of it was your fault." He lifted her chin. "Will you forgive me?"

Sarah buried her face in his chest and nodded.

Ethan squeezed her in one more enormous hug, then kissed the top of her head and released her. He grabbed the boxes off the table and walked over to the attic stairs, nodded at his brother standing halfway down them, and quietly walked past him when Alex nodded in return.

Alex quietly walked into the attic and up to Sarah. He gently set his hands on her shoulders. "Thank you," he whispered. "For everything."

"What's Ethan got against women?" she asked, turning to stare out the dark attic window.

"Men's hearts get broken, too, Sarah," Alex told her softly. "A girl shattered Ethan's heart several years ago, to the point that it may never mend."

She turned to face him. "Is that why Grady brought me here? To . . . to . . . was he hoping I'd catch Ethan's eye?"

Alex chuckled. "He brought you here because he thought we boys all needed our eyes opened." He rubbed his hands together. "So, which one of these pretty packages is your gift to me?"

Sarah gave him a sweet smile. "I didn't bother to wrap your gift," she said, heading toward the stairs. "Why waste good paper on a lump of coal?"

* * *

Christmas morning arrived with record-breaking cold. The cove had been frozen for weeks, but this morning the whole northwestern bay of Frost Lake was solid ice. Tucker was ecstatic, all but jumping out of his socks to hurry outside to drive the downsized snowmobile Santa had brought him. Alex seemed equally ecstatic over the ice-fishing basket Paul had gotten him, along with a promise to help him with the contest on New Year's Day.

Sarah eyed the beautiful fishing traps Alex gave Ethan and fretted about her much smaller, cheaper ones. But it didn't take fancy equipment to catch fish; it only took skill. And she hadn't lived on an island all her life without learning how to fish. Saltwater or fresh, Sarah figured most fish thought alike, and she intended for her and Delaney to trounce the men, whose team had grown to include Alex, Tucker, Paul, and Ethan, making the odds two to four against the women. Grady was staying neutral.

Sarah had sewn dark green chamois shirts for all the men and had embroidered the NorthWoods Timber logo on the pockets. She had also put a lump of coal in Alex's stocking hung on the mantel, along with a note from Santa that said if Alex tried harder this coming year, maybe he'd get something better next Christmas.

Everyone had agreed that Santa was a very smart man.

Sarah had made a rag doll with a dried apple head for Delaney as a decoration for her bed. Sarah remembered being almost eleven and wanting to explore her burgeoning decorating skills, so she included material for curtains and pillows so Delaney could have the pleasure of sewing them herself.

Tucker, the little imp, had also wanted an Atomic Man backpack. On a trip into Greenville months ago, Sarah had found silver material, and she had made Tucker the fanciest Atomic Man backpack ever seen. Even he said so.

She was taken aback by the lavish gifts the Knights gave her. Sarah opened packages of beautiful clothes, a brand-new roasting pan, and enough novels to keep her reading for months—including a romance novel from Alex, the sister book to Rachel and Keenan's story.

When Alex handed Sarah one last gift, the entire room suddenly went silent. She unwrapped the tiny box with trembling fingers and opened the lid to discover a simple gold wedding band sitting in a bed of satin. She could only look at Alex, unable to find words to express her . . . her . . . Oh, God, he'd bought her a wedding band!

Alex smiled, darted a quick glance at his father, and told her a wife should be wearing a ring if she didn't want every male this side of Canada hitting on her when she went to town.

Sarah finally found her voice and thanked him for his very thoughtful gift, tucking the box beside her other gifts with a promise to wear it whenever she went to town.

Later she set a large ham and homemade bread on the table, since Grady had told her it was tradition to have build-your-own sandwiches for Christmas lunch. They were just beginning to fill their plates when a noise outside interrupted their meal.

"Wow!" Delaney said, beating her brother to the window. "What a beautiful truck—and it has a bright red bow on it!" She looked at her father, her smile widening. "I wonder who it's for."

"Maybe there's a card," Alex offered, walking to the window with everyone else. "Sarah, why don't you go out and see?"

With a sense of dread and a sharp look at Alex, Sarah threw on her jacket, slipped into her boots, and went outside.

"God save us all," she heard Paul whisper as she left.

Ethan muttered a curse.

Delaney and Tucker were in their coats and out the door right behind her, the four men following them.

Sarah, her hands shaking as she held the card and the title document to the powder-blue SUV, croaked, "It— it's mine?"

Alex nodded. "It's yours."

"But it must have cost a fortune!" She shoved the card and the title at him. "I can't accept something this expensive."

"The truck is yours, Sarah," he told her, tucking his hands behind his back. "You can leave it to rot where it sits, or you can drive it."

Sarah looked at the sea of faces watching her. Ethan and Paul looked horrified, Grady looked happier than a cat with a belly full of cream, and Delaney and Tucker looked as if they couldn't imagine why anyone would want to refuse such a beautiful gift.

Alex looked . . . dammit, he looked even more expectant than he had when he'd given her the roses. Sarah stepped up to the diabolical jerk and kissed him on the cheek. "Thank you for the lovely gift, Alex. I just love it."

Chapter Fourteen

❖

They'd gotten another eight inches of snow, and the New Year arrived with enough sunshine to bring the temperature up to thirty degrees. Perfect for fishing and riding a baby snowmobile on Frost Lake, Grady had declared at breakfast. Sarah's determined smile caught Alex's eye, because he had no idea what the crazy woman had to smile about.

She had come out of the lodge with five of the most pathetic-looking fishing traps he had ever seen, and Paul had taken to a fit of laughing when he recognized them as white elephants that Mary had been trying to sell for years. But Alex had quickly ended Paul's amusement with one well-placed snowball, which started a storm of frozen missiles flying at everyone.

Except for Sarah. She was already on the lake, carrying her woebegone traps under her arm, a bait pail and ice scoop in one hand and a chisel in the other. Alex groaned. She was going to be one of those serious fishermen, he could tell from her no-nonsense walk. He headed out onto the lake after her, his finely crafted traps in his new pack basket slung over his shoulders. "Wait up, Sarah. Do you even know where you're going?"

"Yes, and I'm going to catch tonight's dinner."

Oh, God. She was going to be so disappointed. Frost Lake was slow fishing on its best days, and Sarah was expecting to catch a whole platter of fish with her pathetic traps? Alex groaned again as she walked away. Peeking out of her pocket was an old book on ice fishing she must have found in the attic.

Well, he'd simply have to keep her mind off fishing and on fun instead. Being an experienced ice fisherman, Alex had a kite in his basket along with his traps. Whole hours could pass without so much as a wind flag; the fish were either biting or they weren't. And any good ice fisherman worth his salt always carried plenty of toys.

Sarah stopped a good forty yards from him, nearly two hundred yards from shore, and slowly looked around. She studied the new blanket of snow, she studied the cloudless sky, and then she slowly scanned the shoreline.

"What," Ethan asked Alex, "is she looking for?"

Alex shrugged. "She's got an old book on ice fishing," he said, as if that explained everything.

Ethan broke into a smile for the first time in days. "A serious fisherman." He slapped Alex on the back. "We'd better set up if we don't want to lose. Hey, where's Delaney going?"

Paul and Tucker stopped beside Ethan and Alex, and they all watched Delaney carrying her fishing traps over to Sarah.

"She really *is* going to desert us," Paul said. He looked down at Tucker. "You know what this means, Tuck?"

The boy just shook his head.

"This means war!" Paul said with a laugh, grabbing Tucker and swinging him up in a high-flying circle. "And we're going to blow them out of the water."

Grady arrived then, shaking his head. "I don't want anyone's feelings hurt," he warned. "Besides, what kind of men would you be if you took advantage of them? Between the two of them, there's only ten years of ice-fishing experience, and all of it belongs to Delaney. So play nice."

Paul stopped swinging Tucker to gape at his father. "Are you nuts? They'll have us doing dishes until spring."

Everyone turned at the sound of ice being chopped.

"Alex," Ethan said. "Delaney knows we have a gas auger. Why are they chopping the ice with that chisel?"

"It's a real *old* book," Alex reminded him.

The men went to work drilling holes, which they did at the rate of twenty-five holes to one of Sarah's. They set out their traps and baited them and then went about making a camp out of the coolers, food basket, and folding seats they had brought. And then the younger Knights got out their kites, along with some of the largest, knottiest balls of string ever seen. Fishing was fun, but kiting was serious business.

Tucker was starting on the next generation of kite flying, and he had Grady to thank for the new spool and crank that made hauling in the long lengths of twine easier. Ethan's kite was by far the largest, but he said that was so it could carry all the string he intended to put on this year.

Alex took a quick look at Sarah before he opened his own colorful kite. She was sitting on a folding chair, studying her trap. She also had that silly book opened on her lap. Alex hurried to get his kite in the air, tied it off on a stick he sank in an ice hole, and then walked over to show Sarah how to set her trap.

He didn't make it two steps before he was stopped by his father's hand on his arm. Alex followed Grady's gaze and saw a game warden coming toward them on a snowmobile, headed straight for Sarah and Delaney. Alex started toward them again, when he suddenly remembered he'd forgotten to get Sarah a fishing license, but Grady tightened his hold.

"Let her fight her own battles," he said at Alex's questioning look. "Besides, if that's Daniel, this could be fun."

Alex decided his dad was right. Daniel Reed was a bachelor, and no more immune to a pretty face than any of them. Alex couldn't wait to see if Daniel didn't melt into a puddle of testosterone at Sarah's feet.

Paul and Ethan came to stand beside Grady and Alex, Paul still holding his kite in his hand. They broke into collective grins when Sarah stood up as the uniformed officer got off his snowmobile and approached her. Alex's grin went especially wide when Delaney inched closer to Sarah and took her hand.

"Ma'am," Daniel said, tucking his gloves into his pocket as he looked at the pathetic ice trap sitting in the uneven, undersized hole. "I'm Daniel Reed, the game warden around here." He touched his hat brim as he finally looked up—and choked in surprise.

She was beautiful. Stunning. Gorgeous!

"Officer Reed," she acknowledged warmly.

And her voice was like honey! Daniel looked at the Knight men, who were obviously enjoying his discomfort. He cleared his throat and finally found the nerve to look back at the beautiful woman. "Could I see your license, please?"

"License?" she repeated. "I need a license?"

Daniel nodded, only to realize he was being impolite— or, more likely, dumbstruck. "Yes, ma'am," he finally got out. "But not if this is Delaney's trap," he hurried to assure her.

Daniel sighed when she shook her head. He had known Delaney wouldn't be caught fishing with that contraption.

"It's mine," the gorgeous angel with the honey voice said. "My book didn't say anything about a license," she continued with a frown. "I never needed one on the coast."

The woman held a book out to him. Daniel took it, scanned the cover, then turned to the first page and grinned. "They didn't need licenses when this book was printed," he explained as he thumbed through the ancient study. "Today," he informed her, realizing that as long as he wasn't looking at her, he could at least string a sentence together, "you need one in freshwater. But," he continued in a rush when he foolishly glanced at her worried face, "I'll let you go this time, seeing how you've only got one . . . ah . . . that one trap set." Not that it would ever catch a fish. "Just make sure you get a license before you come out again, okay?" he offered, feeling brave enough to look at her again.

She gave him a smile that made him go weak in the knees.

"Does Delaney need a license?" she asked.

"No," he said, shaking his head. "Not until she's sixteen. Are you visiting from the coast?" Daniel asked, his curiosity making him bold when he noticed she wasn't wearing a wedding ring.

"No, I live here. I'm Sarah—ah—Knight," she told him. "I'm married to Alex. We live over there," she said, pointing at the lodge in the distance.

Everything suddenly clicked into place for Daniel. So this was the woman Alex had married. But why hadn't the lucky bastard put a ring on her finger? Daniel decided he sure as hell would have, if she belonged to him. "I know your husband," he said. "I'll leave you to your fishing, then, and go visit the others. Have a fun day, Delaney. Mrs. Knight," Daniel said with a nod as he climbed back onto his snowmobile.

He was shaking his head when he stopped in front of the four grinning Knight men. "You guys ought to be ashamed of yourselves," he scolded. He leveled his gaze on Alex. "She says she's your wife."

"She is," Alex said, his hand outstretched.

"Business slow?" Daniel asked, returning Alex's handshake.

"No."

Daniel scanned the twenty-five large, expensive ice traps sitting in perfectly drilled holes. "You got a thing against women ice fishing?"

"No."

Daniel looked at Alex's beautiful wife, who was cutting another hole for Delaney with a rusty old ice chisel. He looked back at Alex, one eyebrow lifted.

Alex sighed. "She's got this book," he started to explain.

Daniel held up his hand. "Say no more. She's one of those serious fishermen, I take it," he said, grinning at the kite Paul was holding.

"She's going to catch our supper," Alex said.

"Hope you brought hot dogs," Daniel returned with a chuckle as he headed back to his sled. "And, Alex? You might want to buy her a license tomorrow. That gorgeous smile of hers won't help her with the female wardens."

The three men went back to work on their kites the moment Daniel drove away, and Grady helped Tucker get his kite airborne. Delaney suddenly let out a loud, excited whoop, and Alex turned to see his daughter jumping up and down in front of Sarah, who was madly pulling line up from a hole. A fish suddenly shot through the ice, fighting mad at being yanked from its watery home. It was a damn big fish, too. Alex turned to look at his brothers.

They were all standing over their own traps with dumbstruck expressions on their faces. Alex laughed and walked over to congratulate Sarah . . . and maybe eat a little crow.

The five men reached Sarah and Delaney at the same time, and they all stood silently as Sarah expertly took the beautiful landlocked salmon off the hook and bopped it on the head. She turned a proud, stunning smile on them without saying a word, then bent down to rebait her hook.

Alex watched in amazement as she dipped into the bucket of minnows, netted one out, then held it between her fingers while she carefully attached the tiny fish and placed the baited hook, line, and sinker back down the hole. She watched the fish to make sure it was lively enough, then fed out the thick line until she came to a button threaded through it. She wound the remaining line around the rickety reel, reset the flag, and carefully set the trap down over the hole on its rickety legs.

Alex glanced over at his five traps. Then he looked at Paul, Ethan, Tucker, and Grady's traps. All of them had been in for more than an hour, and not one flag had gone up.

Just then, Delaney's flag shot up about ten yards away. Four grown men groaned, and Tucker tried out his first curse.

"Excuse us," a very smug Sarah said as the two women rushed to the waving flag, where Delaney landed a lively—and large—lake trout. This time, both girls beamed at them, and Tucker's second curse was downright appropriate. All five men scrambled to their traps, their kite flying suddenly forgotten.

The Knights sat down that evening, red-faced from both sunburn and total humiliation, to a platter of perfectly cooked fish. The women tried to be humble and gracious in victory but were unable to keep their pleased smiles from escaping. If it hadn't been for them, they'd all be eating hot dogs, since there wasn't even one active flag for the men all day. Twenty-five traps had sat for nearly five hours, their stubborn flags refusing to budge. It was a silent meal that night, the beautiful fish indeed tasting like crow.

And Alex realized he'd have to watch Delaney more closely now, because she was getting a smile on her adorable face that would have him beating the boys off with a stick.

"Sarah, we're going to have our yearly NorthWoods Timber meeting this evening after the kids go to bed,"

Alex said as he pushed his empty plate away. "We can have our dessert then."

"I'll have the coffee ready," she assured him, getting up and walking into the great room with Delaney. "Just make sure not to dent any pots when you clean up," she added sweetly, pushing a giggling Delaney ahead of her.

Chapter Fifteen

✤

The meeting began at eight-thirty. Tucker and Delaney were already sound asleep after a full day of fresh air and sun, fish battling, snowmobiling, and kite chasing. Sarah had the table set, and the aroma of fresh coffee and apple crisp filled the kitchen. She poured the coffee, dished out the crisp, and headed for the great room to watch TV.

"Sit down, Sarah," Alex said, pushing out the chair beside him. "You're involved in what's been going on around here as much as we are, so you might as well give us your input."

"About what?" Sarah returned and sat down beside Alex. "I really don't have anything to say."

"Oh, I think you have something to say to Grady."

"I do?" she asked, glancing at Grady, who was giving his oldest son a questioning look.

Alex pulled a large red binder from his lap and set it

in front of his father. "I imagine you want to remind Grady that he has yet to tell us about your plans to reopen the sporting camps."

The silence lasted exactly two seconds before Paul shot to his feet. "What?" His glare moved from Sarah to Grady. "We agreed those camps would stay closed. We don't want tourists running around our woods."

Grady reached out and slowly opened the binder in front of him, silently studied each of the pages, then looked across the table at Sarah and grinned. "This is quite a business plan you've put together. I knew I made the right decision last August."

Fully aware of the three sets of eyes locked on her, Sarah swallowed the lump in her throat and said, "Thank you."

"Wait a minute," Ethan said, his voice deadly soft. "Are you saying you made this deal with Sarah last summer? That she didn't come here to keep house for us but to reopen the sporting camps?"

Grady nodded.

"But we agreed the camps would stay closed," Paul repeated, softer this time but no less angry as he pulled his chair back to the table and sat down.

Sarah was painfully aware of Alex's silence, more damning than Ethan's and Paul's strongly voiced objections.

"Where did you find this?" Sarah asked, pulling the binder toward her and softly closing it.

"In the attic, in a box near the window."

"A box that had my name written on it?"

He nodded. "I was looking for a case of fishing lures and wasn't paying attention to what was written on anything. It wasn't until after I found the binder that I looked more closely at the box it was in."

"We've only had two minor accidents in all the years we shared our roads with the sporting camps' previous owners," Grady said, drawing everyone's attention back to the subject. "And it pains me to see that business just sitting there, rotting into the ground, when it could be bringing us revenue."

"How?" Paul asked. "If Sarah's running the camps, she's the one who will be making the money."

"She'll pay us rent based on a percentage of her profits."

Ethan shook his head. "That won't amount to squat. Those cabins are too old and need too much work. Sarah will lose money the first five years she's open."

"Actually," Alex interjected, "I think she could make them pay." He glanced briefly at Grady, then looked at his brothers. "I studied her plan, and if Sarah stays on budget, does most of the work herself, and pulls in the client base she intends to target, she'll show a profit within two years."

Sarah nearly fell out of her chair. "You're in favor of my opening the camps?"

Alex shook his head. "No, I agree with Ethan and Paul. I don't want a bunch of tourists on our roads. I'm just saying that you've planned everything out quite well, and with your innkeeping experience, you can make a go of it."

"I've thought about the problem of the camps being in a working forest," she told him. "I plan to educate my guests about what you do, and I'll make sure they don't interfere."

"Opening those camps will also bring money to Oak Grove," Grady added. "The whole town will benefit."

"Especially our insurance company," Ethan said. "Our rates are going to skyrocket the first time one of our trucks flattens a car of tourists."

"Your trucks travel the state roads without any problem," Sarah pointed out. "Why wouldn't your drivers be as careful on your logging roads as they are on the state's?"

"The state roads are designed for heavy traffic," Ethan countered. "They're wider than ours, and they're paved. Do you have any idea how long it takes a loaded 22-wheeler to come to a stop on gravel?"

"It's already a done deal," Grady said, leaning forward to set his clasped hands on the table. "Sarah and I shook on it last August." He let his gaze roam to each of his sons, ending with Alex. "Sarah doesn't own the inn on Crag Island. Her brother-in-law inherited Martha Banks's half of it, so Sarah needs a new place to call home and a new business to run. Are you saying that we should kick her out and send her back to a home she doesn't even own, just because we can't share our roads with a few automobiles?"

Silence descended, and Sarah held her breath until she realized it was making her head throb. She stared at the closed binder in front of her while she waited for the three men who held her dream in their hands to decide.

"Where's your brother-in-law?" Ethan asked.

"Nobody knows. Martha's lawyers are trying to find him. When they do, I hope to sell him my half of the inn. That's what I planned to use for capital to update the cabins and to buy new boats and motors."

"You're willing to sink all your money into those camps?"

Sarah nodded. "Because I know I can make them work."

A sigh heavy enough that she actually felt the air move came from Alex. "I say we table this decision until we've had time to think about it and Ethan and Paul have had a chance to read Sarah's business plan."

Well, spit. That wasn't what she wanted to hear. "How long will it take for you to make a decision?" she asked, looking toward Ethan and Paul. "Because I need to move to the camps now, to start getting them ready if I want to be open by April first."

Alex shook his head. "You're not moving to those camps right now."

"I'll come back here three days a week to clean and cook for you until April. But it'll be easier for me to work on the cabins and the main lodge if I'm living there."

"You can't move now," Ethan said, silently communicating with Alex before looking at her. "Until we know what's really going on around here with those strangers and this vandalism, you shouldn't be living there all alone."

"You have your own truck now," Alex pointed out. "You can drive to the camps and work there several hours a day, as long as you're back here by dark."

Well, at least they were talking as if they intended to let her open the camps. And having her own transportation *did* make staying here workable—except for putting some distance between her and Alex.

"It's settled, then," Grady said, giving her a confident wink. "Now, on to new business. I want NorthWoods Timber to own a lumber mill."

All three sons blinked in disbelief.

"A lumber mill!" Ethan said. "Are you crazy? Do you know the start-up costs for opening a lumber mill?"

Grady smiled. "It's already built. Loon Cove Lumber is for sale." He sat forward in his chair. "And Clay Porter is trying to buy it."

That little bit of information got a heated reaction from Alex. "What in hell does Porter want with Loon Cove Lumber? He's in the logging business, like us."

"Exactly," Grady said. "And like us, he's dependent on Loon Cove to buy his timber. Without that mill, we have no place to send our sawlogs." He pointed a finger at Alex. "And if Porter buys Loon Cove, you can be damn sure he won't be milling *our* trees." He looked at Ethan and Paul. "So if we don't snatch it out from under him, our only market will be the paper mills. And pulpwood doesn't earn us nearly what timber does."

"Are there other sawmills around here, other than Loon Cove Lumber?" Sarah asked. "If Mr. Porter buys it, can't you just sell your trees to someone else?"

All four men shook their heads. "The next closest mill is ninety miles away," Alex said. "Cheaper Canadian lumber has caused most of the small mills around here to close. Loon Cove is one of the last holdouts."

"Then won't Loon Cove eventually close, too, if Canada's lumber is cheaper?" she asked.

"We can compete with Canada," Grady told her, "if we own both the timber and the mill. That's why Porter is going after Loon Cove."

"He'll have to mortgage himself up to his eyeballs," Alex said.

"So will we," Grady warned. "But I say it's worth the

gamble." He leaned back in his chair and folded his arms. "Or do you want to be dependent on Clay to put food on our table?"

"Loon Cove is bigger than we need," Paul said.

"We'll buy the trees we need from Porter," Grady explained, mischief dancing in his eyes.

"How much time do we have?" Alex asked.

"None. Old man Bishop wants to sell quickly, which is in our favor. There aren't too many people out shopping for mills right now, and the price is good. I say we vote."

"Vote?" Ethan said. "You just spring this on us and ask us to vote?"

"Vote," Grady said again.

"I vote yes," Paul said, grinning at his scowling brother. "You're just afraid you'll have to turn in your chain saw for a band saw."

"I vote yes," Grady said.

"Yes," Alex echoed.

"Oh, all right," Ethan conceded. "But I'm not becoming a millwright, and that's final."

"I'm glad it's unanimous," Grady said with a smug smile. "Because I've already signed the purchase agreement and put down a hefty deposit."

As Ethan and Paul swore, Sarah gaped at Grady. What was it with this man, always scheming behind his sons' backs?

"Loon Cove is thirty miles by road, but it's only fifteen miles if we follow the shoreline and head up the river," Grady reminded his sons. "And it comes with a few thousand acres of timberland that borders our land, so we can build a road that will let us haul larger loads than the state roads allow us to. This is a wise move," he assured them.

"And just who's going to run the mill?" Ethan asked, still sounding angry. "You said Bishop was anxious to sell. Why?"

"His health is failing." Grady grinned at Ethan, rubbing his chin. "And I've been wondering, myself, who might run the place for us."

"Dammit to hell," Ethan growled.

"You'll go?" Paul asked with surprise. "But you hate mills."

"I'll go," Ethan said, looking at Alex.

Alex nodded agreement.

"When?" Ethan asked.

"We own it as of March first."

"Looks like we're in for one hell of an interesting spring," Alex said, sliding his chair back and standing up.

Sarah also stood up, and, ignoring the table full of dirty dishes, she headed straight for the back door.

Alex beat her there. "And just where are you going?" he asked, grabbing her jacket before she could. "It's ten degrees outside, and it's dark."

"Just out for a walk," she said, lifting her chin.

Alex moved so that his back was to the others heading into the great room. "Ethan's not running away," he quietly assured her. "Have you considered that maybe he's running *toward* something?"

"I still don't like it."

He held up her jacket, nodding for her to turn around and slip it on. Sarah slid her arms into the sleeves, and Alex reached for his own jacket. "I think I'll join you," he said, opening the door and waving her ahead of him.

"Ah, on second thought," Sarah said, making a production of peering outside and then unzipping her jacket.

"It's colder than I thought. I think I'll go read in my room instead."

Alex quickly ushered her out onto the porch, closing the door behind them and looping his arm through hers. "Nonsense," he said with a chuckle. "It's a wonderful night for a walk." He led Sarah across the yard and over to her SUV, then leaned against its fender. "I noticed this truck hasn't moved from where Paul parked it when he plowed the driveway. How come? Don't you like it?"

"I like it." She grinned. "I'm just waiting for the kids to go back to school."

"Why?" he asked, his gaze lowering to her mouth.

"So there won't be any witnesses."

He laughed and brought his gaze back to hers. "Along with your binder of business plans, I also found a small quilt that looked a lot like the bouquet of roses I bought you. Did you sew it?"

She lowered her gaze. "Yes."

"It's quite intricate and must have taken you hours. How come you put it in that box, after all that work? Why aren't you displaying it?"

"I planned to hang it at the sporting lodge," she told him, her gaze locked on his jacket zipper.

He lifted her chin for her to look at him. "You're quite an artist."

"Thank you."

"How come you aren't wearing your wedding band?" he asked, tucking his hands behind his back.

"Because I haven't gone into town."

"I saw Daniel Reed checking out your hand. He noticed you weren't wearing a ring."

"Daniel Reed?"

"The game warden who couldn't bring himself to ticket you for not having a fishing license." He shook his head. "Do you do it on purpose or just by instinct?"

"Do what?"

"Bring men to their knees with that thousand-watt smile of yours. Don't raise your hackles at me," he said with a laugh. "I'm merely pointing out an obvious fact. I want you to wear my ring, Sarah. It'll look better for all of us whenever one of our crew or someone from town comes to the house."

The thought of slipping that ring on her finger was more than Sarah could bear. She had pulled off Roland's ring the day he'd been declared drowned at sea and had finally taken her first real breath in eight years. Sarah decided it was time to change the subject—well, sort of. "It's the first of the year. When are you going to file for divorce? Or should I be the one to file?"

Alex straightened from the fender. "If anyone files, it'll be me," he said. "But not yet."

"You have to do it soon, if only for the kids. Tucker keeps calling me Mom, because Grady told him to call me that when we got married so people would believe the wedding was real. And Tucker still thinks it's real and keeps asking me when I'm going to move into your bedroom like a real mom. You need to talk to him and Delaney."

"No."

"Parents divorce all the time," she continued, ignoring Alex's black look, illuminated by the porch light. "I'll be living just up the lake, so they can visit regularly. And I'll make sure they know I still love them. It's not fair to give them false hope by keeping up this pretense."

"I'll deal with my kids."

"And so will I," she shot back. "I love them, and I don't want them hurt."

"Then don't get a divorce."

"Are you nuts? You don't want to be married any more than I do."

Alex leaned against the fender again, crossing his feet at the ankles and folding his arms over his chest. "Maybe I've changed my mind."

"You can't do that! We have a deal." Didn't they? Dammit, hadn't they agreed they'd get a divorce after the first of the year? "You asked me to pretend the marriage was real until enough time had passed so Judge Rogers and Grady wouldn't get in trouble."

He shrugged. "I don't recall what I said exactly," he said. "If I did make that deal, then I've changed my mind."

"You can't!"

"Why not?"

"Why—" Sarah snapped her mouth shut, yearning to wipe that maddening grin off his face with the palm of her hand.

"You can always file the divorce papers," he told her, his calm voice only making her angrier. "If I do it, every man north of Boston will think I've lost my mind."

"That's it?" she barely got out in a choked whisper. "You want to stay married to save *face?*"

"There's also the traffic on our roads to consider," he continued. "If you were to suddenly become available, there'd be more local pickups heading to your camps than tourists."

Sarah rolled her eyes. "Of all the absurd—"

"And then there's the matter of the divorce settlement," he continued, rubbing his chin. "What do you suppose you'd be entitled to? Maybe the deed to the sporting camps?"

"I don't want anything in the divorce," she said, her anger turning to desperation. "I just want my life back."

He locked his gaze on hers. "Which life would that be, Sarah?" he softly asked. "The one where you live all alone in that big old sporting lodge, taking care of everyone but yourself?" He took hold of her shoulders. "Or a husband and family of your own? It's a lot safer to read about happily-ever-after than it is to go after it, isn't it, Sarah?"

"I found the books you stuffed in the couch," she told him. "You think just because you've read a few romance novels, you've got me all figured out?"

He smiled.

"They're fiction, Alex. Make-believe people in a fictional world. And they don't have anything to do with our predicament. Neither one of us wants to be married to the other."

"Speak for yourself, Sunshine." He leaned down and settled his mouth over hers.

Holy smokes, he was doing it to her *again!* Knocking her off-balance by turning her mind to mush. Every salacious dream she'd had in the past month reared its tempting head, and Sarah found herself right back in the middle of them as his lips moved over hers, sweet apple crisp and the smell of pine pitch assaulting her senses. Her insides clenched, and her lips parted of their own volition, her hands gripping his jacket to pull him closer instead of pushing him away.

Run for your life! her mind screamed, but Sarah heard

it as only a whisper drowned out by the roar of blood coursing through her veins. Her heart violently pounded against her ribs, or was that Alex's heart beating so strongly against hers?

His tongue moved inside her mouth, his hand sliding down her back and pulling her tightly against him. She was so lost in a sea of sensations that she moved her hips against him—and felt herself caught in a tempest of chaos that brought her crashing to shore.

No. No, that was definitely something more solid than a hand on her backside, and some tiny, still working part of her brain told Sarah she was sitting on the fender of her SUV, her legs wrapped around Alex and her tongue shoved halfway down his throat.

She needed to think of something else—anything but the feel of Alex Knight's body clinging to hers. No, *she* was clinging to *him!*

The man weaving fantasies through her runaway imagination finally lifted his mouth, and Sarah dropped her head to his chest, sucking in gulps of frozen air. With each breath, Sarah finally regained her control, until she was able to rear back and shove him away.

She slid down the fender, surprised that her legs worked well enough to keep her from slithering to the ground, and started toward the house. But she hadn't taken three steps before he caught her and stopped her.

"I'll let you run this time, Sunshine," he whispered against her hair. "As long as you understand it's not me you're running from, but yourself."

Chapter Sixteen

❈

S*arah sat motionless behind* the wheel of her SUV, little clouds of condensation filling the cab as she stared out the windshield at the imprint of her backside on the right front fender. *Understand it's not me you're running from, but yourself,* Alex had told her last night, his words echoing long after she'd run to her bedroom.

She hadn't even bothered to clear the table from their meeting, she'd been so flustered. And after a restless night's sleep with Alex's warning repeatedly whispering through her dreams, she'd gotten up early and cleaned the kitchen before making breakfast.

Sarah had thought breakfast would never end. The kids didn't want to go back to school, the two younger Knight brothers were still trying to come to terms with being mill owners, and Alex had been so silently *there* that every nerve in Sarah's body had hummed in awareness. Even Grady had been subdued, his mind on the few parts they still hadn't been able to get for their vandalized machinery.

And then there was the trail Sarah had found the day they'd been out shooting grades. Grady had mentioned this morning, before the kids had gotten up, that he'd told both John Tate and Daniel Reed about the trail. John had promised to tell the border patrol, and Daniel had promised to see where it led. And then there was the map that was still missing.

By the time the house had emptied of Knights, Sarah's nerves were so frayed she'd run to her bathroom and actually thrown up. Deciding she needed to stay busy to calm down, she had gone out to the hot tub and changed the ozone bulb that had finally arrived in the mail two days ago. But the frustration of trying to get that stupid bulb properly seated in its stupid little box had only made her more angry.

Sarah rubbed her eyes with her fists and glared through the windshield at the fender again, the imprint of her backside blatant evidence of her foolish behavior last night. *It's not me you're running from, but yourself. Then don't get a divorce*, he had said with such deadly calm.

What in hell was Alex up to?

Why did he seem so determined to seduce her?

But maybe more important, why did the mere thought of making love to Alex cause Sarah to break into a cold sweat one minute and be hot and bothered the next? Could he be right? Was she really afraid? Of him? No, he didn't scare her. She felt drawn to him the way a moth was drawn to a flame. So did that mean she *was* running from herself?

It's easier to read about happily-ever-after than it is to go after it yourself, isn't it? For a man with an engineering degree, Alex sure had been busy analyzing her—or, rather, trying to explain why she wouldn't let him sweep her off her feet. It couldn't have anything to do with *him*, he had apparently decided, so *she* must be the one with the hangup.

"Let it go," Sarah told herself, her angry puff of heated air turning to frost on the windshield. She reached down and finally twisted the key in the ignition, starting the SUV. "I am being a perfectly sensible woman," she muttered, looking for the defrost button and jabbing it on. "I don't have a hangup about sex. I just want to make love to a man for all the right reasons. And just because Alex Knight is good-looking and has been nothing but sweet to me since he brought me back doesn't mean I'm falling in love with him."

Sarah snorted. Sweet? Heck, the guy had been acting as if he were God's answer to her prayers. And it was driving him crazy that she wasn't tripping all over herself to jump back into his bed so she could feel his strong arms around her, the weight of his heated body covering hers, the . . . the . . . dammit, he was the crazy one, not her! She was *not* falling in love with Alex Knight! He was only attracted to her beauty, not her heart and soul and mind. He was just like all the other men.

Wasn't he?

Did it matter that the card accompanying the roses he'd given her had said they were for the *sweetest* girl this side of Canada, not the prettiest? And he had given her this truck so she could be independent; he had to have been thinking about her feelings then. And it sure did seem as if he wanted them to stay married. Why else would he have given her a wedding band just a few weeks before they were supposed to get their divorce?

"Let it go," she told herself again. "The man is just determined to drive me crazy!"

Sarah pressed down heavily on the gas pedal at that thought, but the tachometer needle only rose to 3000 rpm. She scowled at the dial and pressed harder, but the needle wouldn't go one rpm higher.

She had realized the truck wasn't new and could see it already had sixty thousand miles on it. But the tachometer went up to 6000 though, so why wouldn't the needle go above 3000?

Alex had bought a lemon. Sarah wiped the frost off the inside of the windshield with a laugh. "You got rooked, Mr. Smarty-Pants. Somebody sold you a sick truck."

Not that she cared at the moment. The truck still worked, and 3000 rpm was enough to make it go. Sarah stepped on the brake, pulled the gear lever down to one, let off the brake, and slowly stepped on the gas, then turned the wheel and guided the truck onto the lane leading to the main artery.

She was driving! All by herself!

Sarah decided that *she* was clearly not the problem; the Knights were. They made her nervous. She was doing a much better job driving on her own than when someone was sitting beside her, telling her what to do and when to do it.

She was free! She could go to her camps and even into town once she got the hang of it. Heck, she could drive all the way to Greenville if she chose. Sarah gave another laugh and decided that even though Alex made her crazy one minute and mushy the next, she had to give him points for giving her independence.

Sarah drove down the lane, her speed increasing with her confidence. All she had to do was keep the truck between the snowbanks, and she'd be at her camps in no time. She came to a skidding halt at the main artery, looked both ways for traffic, then turned to the left and stepped on the gas. Since she might meet loaded logging trucks on their way to the mill, she kept her truck to the side of the road, at the same time trying to keep the right tires out of the snowbank.

And she was doing a pretty good job of it, until she rounded a corner and saw a green pickup speeding toward her. Sarah slammed on the brakes, turning the wheel to the right to get out of the way. Only her truck didn't stop; it spun around—and around and around and around.

Everything came to a sudden halt when her truck slammed into the oncoming pickup. Sarah was thrown against her seat belt, her right hand struck the dashboard, and her right knee also connected with something solid.

Then there was silence, except for the sound of her loudly rapping engine. Sarah blinked, looked out through the windshield, and saw Game Warden Daniel Reed looking back at her from behind his own windshield. Their two trucks were smashed together nose-to-nose, as if they were kissing. Though it wasn't at all funny, Sarah started laughing hysterically, burying her face in her hands with a wail.

*   *   *

Daniel jumped out of his truck and scrambled over to the SUV. The woman inside had her face buried in her hands, and he hoped she wasn't seriously injured; they were at least ten miles from Oak Grove and forty miles from the nearest hospital. He pulled open her door.

"Are you okay?" he asked, reaching in and shutting off the truck, then bending down to check on her. He sucked in his breath when wide, shocked eyes met his and he found himself face-to-face with Mrs. Alex Knight. "Are you okay?" he repeated.

She nodded and tried to get out, but her seat belt stopped her. Daniel closed his eyes in thanks that she was wearing it. They had hit each other with a jolt, but he didn't think she was seriously hurt. He reached around her and undid her belt, then carefully helped her out.

She nearly fell once her feet touched the ground, and Daniel caught her as he realized she couldn't put any weight on her right leg. He set her back in her truck, facing him, and hunched down. "Mrs. Knight . . . Sarah, isn't it?"

She nodded.

"Where are you hurt?"

"My knee got banged, and my right hand hit the dash, and it hurts something fierce," she whispered.

Daniel took her hand in his and found it was already starting to swell, two of the fingers looking particularly bad. He smiled at her. "I hope these weren't your whistling fingers," he said with false cheer. "Stay here, and I'll call for help. I have a radio in my truck, and I'll have the sheriff out here in no time. We'll take you to Greenville, to the hospital."

"The hospital?" she repeated, and she shook her head. "I just want to go home."

"Sarah," Daniel said, frowning at her. "Those fingers look broken, and your knee is hurt. You need to have a doctor check you over."

She continued to shake her head, looked at their smashed trucks, and gave a shuddering sniffle.

Daniel cringed. She'd better not start crying; he was worthless when it came to crying women.

"I just got this truck." She sniffled. "And now I've smashed it up. Alex gave it to me for Christmas."

"Now, Sarah, Alex will only care that you're all right." He gave her a smile in hopes of heading off her tears. "It's just a dented fender and a busted radiator. Nothing that can't be fixed."

She sniffled again.

Not knowing what else to do, Daniel walked to his truck and called John Tate, who arrived twenty minutes later, much to Daniel's relief. Sheriffs were trained to deal with distraught women; game wardens dealt better with pissed-off poachers.

"I need to warn you, John," Daniel said before they approached Sarah's truck. "Near tears or not, you are about to have your day made."

Eyeing Daniel suspiciously, John hunched down in front of Sarah, then looked back at Daniel and smiled. "We've met," he told Daniel before turning back to Sarah.

"Can you tell me where you're hurt?" John asked her softly.

"I banged my hand and knee. But I'm okay," she rushed to say. "I just want to go home."

John took her cradled hand and examined it. "You need to see a doctor."

"I wrecked my new truck."

John patted her uninjured knee. "Alex will only care that you're okay," he promised. "Is your driver's license in your purse? I'll need it for my report. Daniel and I will take you to Greenville, and we'll stay with you until Alex arrives. I'll do my paperwork on the accident there."

Sarah blinked at John. "My driver's license?"

"You do have a license, don't you?" John asked.

She shook her head.

Daniel laughed softly, then helped John get Sarah into the passenger's side of the cruiser before they moved the wrecked trucks off the road.

"She doesn't even have a license," John said, shaking his head.

Daniel looked across the top of the car. "She didn't have a fishing license, either."

Both men broke into grins, then climbed into the cruiser and headed for Greenville, their beautiful passenger softly sniffling behind them.

"Where is she?"

John and Daniel stood up from the waiting-room chairs and hurried over. "She's fine, Alex," John assured him, holding out his hand in greeting.

"Where is she?" Alex repeated.

"Alex," Dr. Caleb Betters said as he walked into the waiting room. "Thank God you're here."

"Where *is* she?" Alex growled.

"Sarah's okay," Caleb assured him. "She's in Room Two. But I want to talk with you before you see her."

"Why?"

"Don't worry, I just have a few things to discuss, that's all. How are the knuckles?" Caleb asked.

Alex shrugged and started for the room that held Sarah. He was stopped by a restraining hand on his arm. "My office first," Caleb said.

"After I've seen her."

"No," Caleb said, tightening his grip.

Alex looked again at the door where Sarah was, then followed Betters down the hall.

"I want to talk to you before you leave," John called after them. Alex raised his hand in acknowledgment, then slipped into the doctor's office.

"Take a seat," Caleb told him.

Alex remained standing. "How bad is she hurt?"

The aging doctor stared at Alex, staying silent until Alex sat down in the chair. Caleb sat on the edge of his desk. "She's got two broken fingers, and her right knee is swollen and sore but not seriously damaged." He held up his hand when Alex started to rise. "But that's not what I want to talk to you about. When you see her, you may be shocked that both of her eyes are bandaged."

Alex stood up.

"This, too, is not serious," Caleb assured him. "She's got welder's flash."

"Welder's flash!"

Caleb nodded. "It took some doing, but I finally figured it out. As you know, welder's flash means you've sunburned the eyeballs. But looking at a welding arc isn't the only way it happens. Any exposure to strong ultraviolet light can do it. Your wife," he informed Alex, "changed the ozone bulb on your hot tub this morning.

Since it takes a few hours to feel the effects, it wasn't until she was here that she complained she couldn't see well and that the lights were bothering her."

Alex started pacing. "Welder's flash hurts like hell," he said, knowing from personal experience. "Is she in a lot of pain?"

"She wouldn't be if she'd quit crying. She keeps soaking the bandages I put on and washing out the salve with her tears," the obviously frustrated doctor told him.

Alex headed for the door.

"Wait," Caleb said, grabbing his arm. "There's more."

"More?"

"You need to know that Sarah's five weeks pregnant."

Every drop of blood in Alex's body pooled in his feet, and he groped for the chair, slowly sat down, and silently dropped his head into his hands.

Caleb touched his shoulder. "Sarah didn't realize it, either. I don't want you going in there and riling her up," he warned. "Pregnant women are at the mercy of their hormones, and that's probably why she can't seem to stop crying, now that she's started. But I need to put more salve in her eyes, and I want the bandages to stay dry this time. So promise her the moon if you have to—just make her stop."

Alex could only sit there, stunned beyond words, having no idea what he should be thinking, much less what he should be feeling.

Or, heaven help him, what Sarah was thinking.

She was five weeks pregnant. Of all the things that could have happened to her! Alex couldn't imagine what she was feeling right now. Used? Or more likely trapped by a far bigger obligation than marriage? Alex closed his eyes, praying for understanding. *Her* understanding. He had crawled into Sarah's bed drunk on whiskey and lust and gotten her pregnant.

Alex finally got himself under control enough to make his way into the hall, then stood outside Sarah's door, wondering what he should say. Once he realized nothing he said was going to change anything, he quietly opened the door.

She was sitting on the exam table with her bandaged right hand held to her chest and her beautiful eyes covered with soggy bandages. Silent tears were leaking out from beneath the peeling medical tape. He quietly walked up beside her, and Sarah jumped when she felt his presence.

"Who—who's there?"

"It's me," he told her, setting his hand on her shoulder, which made her jump again. Alex carefully gathered her into his arms, careful of her hand, and cradled her against his chest. "I'm sorry, Sarah," he told her. "I'm so sorry."

"You're sorry? *I'm* the one who should be sorry."

He shook his head, realized she couldn't see him, and said softly, "You've got nothing to be sorry about, Sunshine."

"I wrecked my new truck."

"To hell with the truck, as long as you're okay."

"I wrecked Daniel Reed's truck, too."

"We're insured."

"And John Tate seemed upset that I don't have a license."

Alex stifled his groan.

Sarah sniffled.

"Crying only makes your eyes worse, Sarah. I know it hurts, Sunshine," he told her, "but you have to stop crying so Betters can put more salve in them."

"Did he tell you what happened to my eyes?" she asked, turning her head in his direction.

Alex found his first smile. "He said you sunburned them on the ozone bulb."

She nodded, then dropped her head on another sniffle.

"No more tears, Sarah."

"Did he . . . did he tell you anything else?"

"Yes."

"Oh."

Alex smiled again. That one little "Oh" had a whole world of worry behind it. He didn't need to see her eyes to know Sarah was unsure if it was a good yes or a bad yes he'd given her. He decided to help her decide.

"How do you feel about it?"

"How do *you* feel?" she softly asked back.

"How *should* I feel?" he countered, his smile widening.

She actually harrumphed. He could tell she was trying to frown, but the wet bandages made it impossible. Alex gently nudged her shoulder.

"I haven't decided yet," she snapped.

He brought his mouth close to her ear and whispered very softly, "Well, I've already decided."

Just then, a knock came at the door, and Caleb walked in. "Okay, people, if we've got the watering pot turned off, let's put some salve on those eyes and replace the bandages for the third time," he said tiredly. He shoved several prescription bottles at Alex, then stepped up to his patient. As he worked, Betters issued instructions for tending broken fingers, banged knees, and sunburned eyeballs. He also threw in a few tips on growing a baby, just for good measure.

When he was finished, Alex picked Sarah up and headed down the hall, but he had to stop when he ran into Reed and Tate in the waiting room. Alex glared at John, who just frowned back.

"She doesn't have a license," John told him.

"I own the road she was driving on, so she doesn't need one," Alex shot back.

"Alex," John said, only to hesitate at Alex's lethal look. "I'll talk to you later."

Alex continued out of the hospital, Sarah held securely in his arms—just as securely as she was entrenched in his heart.

Chapter Seventeen

❖

Still reeling from the news that she was five weeks pregnant, Sarah absently picked at the bandage on her right hand. Though she wasn't quite ready to admit it to Alex, she was ecstatic to be having a baby. She didn't care if it was a boy or a girl, as long as it was as happy and healthy as Delaney and Tucker.

Sarah's only regret was that her baby would be born right in the middle of a crazy, mixed-up mess of circumstances. But Alex was a good man as well as a great father, and she didn't doubt for a minute that he would do the right thing for their baby.

But what exactly *was* the right thing? Would he insist they stay married for real now? Or would he pay child support when they divorced and settle for visitation rights? Being a single mom wasn't quite how Sarah had envisioned her future, but then, not much in her life had gone as planned since she'd turned fourteen.

"Have your eyes stopped hurting?"

"Yes."

"And your hand?" Alex asked, his own covering hers to make her stop picking her bandage.

"It only throbs a little. Dr. Betters gave me something for the pain that he promised wouldn't hurt the . . . the . . ." Sarah wanted to kick herself for inadvertently broaching the very subject she wanted to avoid.

Alex's hand moved from her bandage to her leg, and she felt him pat her uninjured knee. "Our baby?" he finished for her. "Have you decided yet how you feel about being pregnant?"

"Not yet."

"Poor Sarah. It seems you keep shedding your obligations only to find yourself neck-deep in more. But you take each of them in stride, don't you? From your mother's cancer and your father's death, then your marriage to Roland Banks and his mother, all the way up to marrying a dead man who comes back from the grave and gets you pregnant."

"I am not a victim," she said, lifting her chin in his direction.

He gently patted her knee again. "No, you definitely have never been a victim."

"Can—can we not tell anyone about the baby for a while? It'll only confuse Delaney and Tucker."

"I was going to suggest we wait," he agreed, his hand lifting off her knee just before Sarah heard the blinker come on and felt the truck slow down. She realized they were turning onto the NorthWoods Timber road.

"I'm sorry about my truck."

"It's only a truck. They sell them every day."

"Actually, I think someone sold you a lemon," she told him. "I couldn't get the tachometer to go over 3000 rpm." She turned her head toward him. "In fact, that might be why I lost control when I saw Daniel Reed coming toward me. I think whatever's wrong with that truck is what caused the accident. My driving was perfectly fine until then."

"I'll have them check out the truck when they do the repairs," he promised. "So, it looks like our roles are reversed for a few days," he said much too cheerily.

"What do you mean?"

"You can't see or walk, so that means I get to take care of you, just like you took care of me."

Holy smokes, she didn't want Alex taking care of her! "Delaney can help me."

"After school. I can't leave you sitting at home alone all day if you can't even see."

"I'll sleep."

"And if you have to use the bathroom?"

"I can limp from my bed to the bathroom."

"What if someone comes to the house?"

"They'll just think no one's home."

"And if it's whoever broke in and stole my map?"

Sarah snapped her head toward him. "What makes you think someone broke into the house?"

"You said you caught those men coming out of the woods on the path that led to the house and that they were folding a map," he explained. "That was around the same time my map went missing."

"But it wasn't one of your white drafting maps they were folding. It was a regular map."

"I know you were still shaken up when we got home

that day, but did you notice anything unusual in the house that evening or the next day? Anything out of place?"

Sarah frowned, trying to remember. "I remember that I had to mop the floor because there were muddy footprints leading from the back door to the great room. I figured one of you guys didn't take off your boots when you ran into the office to get something. Grady sometimes forgets."

"They were all out at the cutting that day, and when I went through the house looking for you, I took off my boots."

"You think those men I saw coming out of the woods broke into the house?" she whispered. "But why only steal a map of your roads?"

"It was the section we're moving to next month. And that trail Thumper came walking out of is not a game trail but man-made. Then there's the vandalism to our equipment," he added. "Grady, Ethan, Paul, and I have been thinking about it, and we've been wondering if it wasn't teenagers, if there's something else going on. If you add together the missing map, the man-made trail, and the vandalism, it looks like someone's trying to slow us down from cutting in the new section."

"But why?"

"That's what we can't figure out. Daniel Reed followed the trail and said it didn't lead anywhere. It went up Whistler's Mountain and seemed to feather out to nothing."

"What about in the other direction?"

"It crossed the road where we took the grade elevations, then continued on until it met up with an interstate snowmobile trail."

Sarah fell silent as she thought about what Alex was saying. "Then I don't want to stay home alone if I can't see."

"I'll stay and entertain you," he promised, again much too cheerily. "Maybe I'll read to you from the new romance novel I got you for Christmas. You know, that sister book to the one you've already read?"

Oh, Lord. She couldn't let him read that novel out *loud.* "Actually, I've already read it," she lied. "Maybe I'll just listen to videos on the television while you . . . cook and vacuum and do the laundry," she finished, suddenly a bit cheery herself at the thought of Alex doing the housework.

Concerned faces greeted Sarah at the door. Alex shook his head to tell his father and brothers not to say anything, then carried Sarah to her bedroom and laid her down on the bed.

"You can take a nap while I start dinner," he suggested, motioning for everyone to leave the room quietly. "Just as soon as the kids get off the bus, Delaney can help me cook, and Tucker can set the table."

"Tucker needs reminding which side the fork goes on," she murmured, rolling onto her side. "And don't let him carry more than two plates at a time to the table. They're too heavy," she finished in a whisper, tucking her good hand under her cheek with a sigh.

Alex straightened with a smile. Always the housekeeper and mother, Sarah couldn't stop worrying about the kids, even though she was half asleep from the pain medication.

She appeared so small and helpless and utterly

defenseless. Seeing her bandages scared him so badly that Alex started to shake.

He loved her. There was no way around it, not anymore. This dynamic little whirlwind who had introduced herself as Mrs. Alex Knight only five weeks ago had captured his heart without even trying. And if he had any say in the matter, she would remain Mrs. Knight until the day they died.

Alex took the blanket off the nearby rocking chair and covered her up, carefully tucking her in as he bent over and softly kissed her hair. "Sweet dreams, wife," he whispered before reluctantly walking away.

"It's not as bad as it looks," he told his father and brothers as he came into the kitchen and found them sitting at the table with worried faces. "She's got a couple of broken fingers and a bruised knee is all. She was wearing her seat belt."

"And her eyes?" Grady asked.

"It's welder's flash."

"How in hell did she get welder's flash?" Ethan asked.

Every one of them, at some time or other, had had a touch of welder's flash. It hurt like the devil for a few days, the eyelids feeling as if they were lined with sandpaper.

"She changed the bulb in the hot tub. The bulb puts out ultraviolet light, and she must have gotten too close to the new one once she got it working."

"I told her I'd change that damn bulb," Grady said, sounding angry at himself. "Dammit, she's always rushing to do stuff if we even mention something needs to be done!"

Alex smiled. "Hey, we have to love her just the way she is, good intentions and bad driving included."

Stunned silence settled over the kitchen, and Alex grinned like the lovesick fool he was as he looked at his father. "You asked me to give her a month, but I don't think it took three weeks before the thought of getting a divorce started turning my stomach." He moved his gaze to include his shocked brothers. "I'm keeping her."

"Sarah doesn't exactly act as if she wants to be kept." Paul grinned. "In fact, she's been acting as if being married to you turns *her* stomach. I've actually seen her turn green once or twice."

"I can change her mind," Alex drawled, leaning back in his chair. "But I need to get her alone to do that, and I'm thinking now is the perfect time. Being completely dependent on someone has a tendency to make a person more . . . ah, cooperative."

"That's a bit devious, don't you think? Even for you," Ethan said with a lifted brow.

Alex shrugged. "All's fair in love and war."

"So what's your plan?" Grady asked, rubbing his hands together, obviously not the least bit worried about his son's deviousness.

"After everyone leaves for work and school tomorrow, I'll take Sarah up to her sporting camps. I'll tell her that I want to look around before making my decision on whether they should be opened." He grinned at his brothers. "If my truck battery happens to go dead and we get stuck there, well, I guess we'll just have to spend the night."

"She knows we have radios in all the trucks," Paul warned.

"Radios are useless if the battery's dead."

Grady was shaking his head. "It won't work. You'll be

spending all your time trying to stop her from worrying about us worrying about you."

Alex frowned. "Then I'll say I got through to you, but you couldn't come pick us up because—" He thought for a minute. "Because one of the skidders broke down, and you're going to spend all night fixing it. Paul, can you come home early tomorrow to be here when Delaney and Tucker get off the bus?"

"Sure, I'll watch them."

"Did you see Sarah's and Reed's trucks?" Alex asked.

"We saw them," Grady said. "Neither one can be driven."

Alex looked at Paul again. "Get Sarah's truck towed into town for me tomorrow? Cane Motors can fix it fairly quickly."

"When we tried to move Sarah's truck, I noticed a block of wood taped underneath the gas pedal," Ethan said, his brow rising again with his smile. "She must have been going, what, twenty miles an hour, tops?"

"I've learned from an old pro," Alex said, nodding toward Grady.

"What about what's been going on around here?" Ethan asked, turning serious again. "Maybe you shouldn't go to the camps."

"I'll bring my rifle," Alex promised. "But we should be as safe there as anyplace. The camps are at least two miles from the main snowmobile trail." He sat forward, leaning his arms on the table. "Any news from the border patrol? Do they have any idea what's going on?"

"John told me there might be a smuggling ring working in the area," Ethan said. "But the border patrol wants to keep their speculation quiet. They don't want everyone jumping at every stranger in town and tipping them off. John said they might be planning on using snow-mobiles to cross the border in remote areas. The Canadians are looking into the matter on their end."

"Smuggling what?"

Ethan turned his hands palms up. "They have no idea. Could be drugs, people, or weapons. Hell, they don't even know which direction the smuggling is going, in or out of the U.S."

"But if they're using snowmobiles to cross the border, what's the trail leading up Whistler's Mountain for, if it doesn't go anywhere?"

"Beats me," Ethan said with a shrug. "I'm only telling you what the border patrol told John. Maybe the smugglers haven't finished cutting the trail yet. I've been keeping an eye on that trail since you found it, and there've only been animal tracks in the snow. If the smugglers cut it, they aren't using it yet."

Alex sat back and rubbed his chin. "If it weren't for that trail, I might think it was Clay Porter who keeps messing with our equipment."

Ethan snorted. "Porter's not brave enough to start an all-out war. Besides, he doesn't know he's lost his bid for Loon Cove Lumber yet."

Alex looked at Grady. "Who have we got sleeping at the cutting now?"

"Richard, Harley, and Frank," Grady said with a nasty grin. "They're sorely hoping those bastards come back for another go at it, so they can smash a few faces. You know how possessive Harley is of that delimber. I thought he was going to cry when he saw its smashed windows and cut hoses."

Alex stood up when he noticed the yellow school bus pulling into the yard and turning around. "Then we're doing all we can to protect ourselves. Time for me to start supper."

All three men groaned.

Alex turned back to them. "Unless one of you has suddenly learned how to cook?"

"Let Delaney and Tucker fix supper," Paul suggested. "At least they won't poison us."

Alex walked to the door with a laugh and immediately hushed his kids when they came banging onto the porch. "You have to be quiet. Sarah's sleeping," he told them.

"In the middle of the day?" Delaney asked in surprise.

"She got in a small truck accident this morning, and she's a bit banged up," Alex explained, helping them out of their backpacks and jackets. "She's okay, just sore and sleepy because the doctor gave her a pill to make her more comfortable."

"Like you took?" Tucker asked in a loud whisper, his eyes rounded with worry.

"Just like I took. But if you're both real quiet, I'll let you peek in her room so you'll see for yourselves that she's okay. Can you be real quiet, Tuck?"

Tucker nodded.

Alex led his kids over to the door, slowly opened it, then quietly herded them inside. Delaney immediately walked up to the opposite side of the bed and frowned at Sarah before looking up to her father. Alex touched his finger to his lips, took Tucker's hand, and motioned for Delaney to follow them out.

"Why are her eyes covered up?" Tucker asked the

moment Alex closed the bedroom door behind them. "Is she blind?"

"Only for a few days," Alex assured his kids. "Do you remember what happens when you get a sunburn on your arms?"

Both children solemnly nodded.

"Sarah changed the bulb in the hot tub, and the light from the bulb gave her a sunburn on her eyes. They'll heal fine, and in a couple of days the bandages will come off."

"What about her hand?" Delaney asked.

"She broke two of her fingers," Alex explained. "Just like I cracked my knuckles a few weeks back. They'll heal, too," he assured them, holding up his still taped but usable right hand.

"She'll be okay?" Delaney's chin quivered.

Alex gathered both of his babies into his embrace. "She'll be just fine," he promised.

"I—I want to start calling her Mom," Delaney whispered.

Alex squeezed his eyes shut and squeezed his kids. "Then call her Mom," he agreed. "And both of you can help make her recovery easier these next few days."

"How?" Tucker asked, his head popping up.

"By fetching things for her, reading to her, helping her get around. And she won't be able to do any chores for a while, so you can help with those." He gave each child a knowing look. "I don't think she's going to like not being able to work, do you? Sarah's not used to sitting back and letting people wait on her, so we need to make sure she enjoys the experience."

Each of his very astute children gave Alex a conspirator's wink. Tucker's wink was with both eyes, but he got his point across.

"And you can start by helping me get dinner on the table. Then, after supper, Tuck, you can read Sarah a story, and Delaney, you can help her get ready for bed."

"But if she can't see," Delaney said, "what if she has to get up in the night to use the bathroom? I think I should sleep with her tonight."

Alex couldn't have been more proud of his daughter if she'd just discovered a cure for cancer. "That's a great idea, baby. I know I'll sleep easier knowing you'll be there for Sarah." He kissed the top of her head, then kissed Tucker. "Go wash up and get back here to help me with supper."

And on that note, the kitchen experienced a mass exodus, including three men who suddenly remembered they all had something important to do. Alex walked to the fridge, opened the door, and stared at the neatly stacked containers that could be full of anything from leftover lamb from two days ago to venison stew from the day before that.

Then he saw the hot dogs they hadn't needed last night and decided they'd make an excellent supper. He pulled out the hot dogs, hesitated, then pulled out the other leftovers. Lamb, venison, and diced hot-dog stew sounded even better—and would require washing only one pot.

Chapter Eighteen

❈

Sarah woke up to someone softly snoring in bed beside her and remembered after a moment Delaney was sleeping with her. But when she couldn't figure out why it was so solidly dark in her bedroom, it took a full minute before she remembered her eyes were bandaged. She carefully tested her right knee and found that it hurt to bend it, but most of her muscles were so stiff she didn't even want to think about moving.

Lord, she was pathetic. She couldn't even drive five miles down a private road without smashing into the one vehicle she met. Her only saving grace was that she'd hit a pickup and not a loaded logging truck; she doubted she'd be waking up at all if she had.

Sarah decided she needed a five-minute pity party before she began the seemingly insurmountable task of facing the day ahead. She must have slept on her injured hand, because her fingers were throbbing like the devil.

Her right knee felt as bloated as a watermelon, and her eyes were watering again, though she couldn't be sure if that was because they had a pound of sand in them or because the thought of being at Alex's mercy made her want to burst into tears.

Yup, she was pathetic all right, and she hadn't even gotten to the baby part of her problems.

Sarah had immediately taken to Delaney and Tucker when they had arrived on Crag Island and had soundly fallen in love with them over the following months. But she didn't have a clue how to deal with a newborn baby. She would have to start watching more of the health channel. She'd seen a few of their birthing shows but had always thought they were something she'd pay more attention to *someday*.

Well, someday was here.

Sarah lowered her good hand to her belly and ruined her pity party by breaking into a wide grin. A miracle was happening inside her. It was probably only the size of a raisin right now, but it was definitely her and Alex's baby.

So, how did she *really* feel about the Alex part?

Well . . . if she had to share her baby with anyone, Alex Knight was as good a father as Sarah could hope for. It would be part of a wonderful family and be brought up in an interesting, beautiful place. She could raise a baby and run her sporting camps, couldn't she?

So why did she have this terrible ache in her chest? She decided it wasn't dread tightening her chest but . . . awareness. Maybe even anticipation making her ache with wanting. She yearned to *really* make love to Alex, with both of them fully aware and enjoying it.

Sarah moved restlessly. It was going to happen; she had felt his intentions humming through the air when Alex had lifted her onto the fender of her truck and kissed her as if he really meant it, as if he wasn't kissing a pretty face attached to a fantasy body but kissing *her*.

"Do you have to pee?" Delaney asked over a yawn.

"I guess I do," Sarah said with a smile. "Is the sun up? What time is it?"

The mattress moved. "Six-thirty," Delaney said. Another layer of blankets landed on Sarah when her nursemaid got out of bed. "And it's snowing again. I hear Daddy in the kitchen already. I'll help you get dressed before I go upstairs and get ready for school."

"I love you, Delaney," Sarah whispered. "Thank you for sleeping with me."

Her declaration was met with silence. "Can I call you Mom, Sarah?" Delaney whispered, her voice uncertain.

Sarah felt her eyes fill with tears again. "You sure can, sweetie," she said thickly. "I'd like that."

"I know your marrying Daddy wasn't real," Delaney said. "But even if you do get divorced, you'll still be my mom. Right?"

"That's right," Sarah softly agreed. "Your dad can't dispute the adoption without getting your grandfather in trouble."

That was another mess they'd eventually have to straighten out, but Sarah had a feeling Delaney was mature enough to handle it. Tucker wouldn't be quite so understanding. What a mess they'd made for the kids.

"Then come on, Mom," Delaney said, as Sarah heard her padding around the bed. "Let's get you up and dressed, so I can get out there and make sure Daddy doesn't burn the toast. It's a wonder any of us survived between housekeepers over the years."

Sarah chuckled softly but quickly frowned when she realized it wasn't toast she smelled burning but—oh, Lord—she smelled onions scorching over high heat. What *was* Alex cooking?

It took some doing, and no small amount of effort not to curse, but Sarah made it into the bathroom by leaning on Delaney, washed herself up, then hobbled back to the bedroom, again using Delaney for a crutch. She was ready to scream by the time they finally got her dressed and she hobbled into the kitchen.

She was suddenly swept off her feet and carried over to a chair at the table. "Good morning, Sunshine," Alex said as he set her in the chair. "How are you feeling this morning?"

"Probably better than my frying pan," she shot back. "It will have to soak in baking soda for a week to get rid of that onion taste."

"Uh-oh, somebody needs a happy pill," he said with a laugh, and a tiny pill was suddenly pressed to her lips and a glass placed in her good hand. "Delaney, can you get Tuck up and dressed?"

"Maybe I should take the day off from school," Delaney said. "And stay and help you take care of Sa— Mom."

"Other than having socks duct-taped over your hands, you and Tucker survived my nursing when you got poison ivy," Alex said cheerily. "I think I can handle Sarah."

But could *she* handle *him?* Sarah wondered, quickly washing down her pill, setting her glass on the table so she could cross her good fingers on her lap. *Please, please let Delaney stay home*, she silently begged. But Sarah heard the great-room door swoosh and knew her fate was sealed. She was doomed to spend the day at the mercy of a much too eager nursemaid.

The door swooshed again, and the kitchen started filling up, Ethan and Paul and Grady alternating between showing their concern and making jokes about her looking like an alien from outer space. But she was a sweet alien, Grady assured her, just before he gave her hell for changing the bulb in the hot tub.

The joking didn't stop until Tucker came running into the kitchen with a bang, rushing up and hugging Sarah so hard she squeaked. "I wanted to sleep with you, too," he said, as Sarah felt his small hand touch her bandaged eyes. "Do they hurt?" he whispered, overloud. "What's it like not to see?"

"It's very frustrating," Sarah told him, groping to find his cheek to give him a pat. "Can you bring me one of the sticks we found that the beavers had stripped, Tucker, so I can use it to feel my way around?"

"Never mind, Tuck," Alex said from someplace near the stove. "She can't walk, so she doesn't need to feel anything."

"How are you going to write?" Tucker asked. Sarah felt him touch her bandaged right hand. "You can't hold a pencil."

"I'm left-handed, just like your daddy," she told him. "Not that it matters, if I can't see."

"Oh, I hadn't thought about that. Are they going to peel?"

"What?"

"Daddy said you sunburned your eyeballs. Are they going to peel like my arms did when I got sunburned?"

"They won't peel, Tuck," Alex said with a chuckle, this time from beside the table. "Sit down and eat, so you don't miss the bus."

And so it went for the next half-hour, teasing conversation intermingled with speculations about what they were eating. From the taste of it, Sarah guessed Alex had made cheese and mushroom omelets laced with burnt onions, to complement the burnt toast. When the kitchen emptied, the men going to work and the children rushing out to the bus honking its horn in the driveway, a sudden silence settled over the kitchen like a lead weight.

"Has your pain pill kicked in?" Alex asked, apparently near the sink.

"It must have, because my taste buds are numb."

"Uh-oh," he said from right beside her. "We're in for a long day if you're going to take pot shots at my cooking."

"That wasn't cooking," she pot-shot back. "That was murdered food forced on defenseless peop—" She yelped when she was suddenly picked up again. "Cut that out," she snapped at where she thought his face was. "You have to warn me first."

"But where's the fun in that?" he asked, kicking the swinging door open to carry her into the great room. "You sit and listen to videos while I clean up, then we'll head over to your sporting camps."

"What? Why?"

"So I can have a look around. I haven't been there in almost a year, and I've never really looked to see what condition the place is in."

"But there's at least two feet of snow on the road leading into those camps."

"I'll plow my way in. The road should be opened anyway, in case of fire." Sarah sensed him leaning down close to her. "Are you still determined to open the camps, even with a baby on the way?"

"Yes," she whispered. "I can still run them with a baby."

"Then we should find out what kind of money it's going to take to get them up and running, don't you think?" he asked, his mouth still close.

"G-Grady said they were in fair shape."

The air in front of her suddenly felt empty. "It doesn't matter what Grady thinks," Alex said from someplace above her. "Ethan and Paul have given me final say on whether you open the camps or not." He was just as suddenly right back in her face. "And if you even hint that I'm expecting something in exchange for letting you open those camps, I will make Roland and Martha Banks look like saints. Understand?" he finished in a growl, his breath all but setting her cheeks on fire.

Sarah mutely nodded.

"That's a smart girl," he whispered, his lips touching hers briefly—and then the air was suddenly empty again, the television coming on with the twang of country music.

Holy smokes, what had that been about?

Sarah sucked in her breath. He thought she would actually consider sleeping with him to open her camps?

How would he put it? Oh, yeah. *Hell would be covered in three feet of snow* before she ever went anywhere near his bed!

* * *

Alex smiled openly, since Sarah couldn't see him. He'd never met anyone so easy to rile, nor had he ever seen anyone looking so pathetically outraged. He broadened his grin when Sarah started picking at her bandaged hand as she scowled at nothing, before he quietly turned and walked back to the kitchen. As much as he hated to see Sarah hurt, he was not about to waste an opportunity to get past her defenses and back into her bed.

Alex knew how easy it was for a person, especially someone disillusioned by life, to become overbusy taking care of everyone else, because it was so much safer than having to deal with her own shattered dreams. Hadn't his kids become his whole world after Charlotte had left? But today Sarah's injuries would force her to sit blindly in the main lodge of her sporting camps, with nothing to do but focus on her past tribulations, her present situation, and her future.

If she wanted to eat, she would have to trust Alex to feed her, and if she wanted to get from point A to point B, she'd have to trust him to carry her. And if Sarah finally wanted to be the heroine of her own story, she would have to drop her defenses long enough for Alex to prove that she could trust him with her heart.

Hoping desperately that his plan would work, Alex threw on his jacket, went outside, and started loading the bed of the plow truck with enough firewood to warm up at least the main room of the sporting lodge. Whether it took half a cord of wood or half a dozen cords, he wasn't bringing Sarah back home until she was ready to put his wedding band on her finger for real.

As soon as he finished with the firewood, Alex went back to the house and quietly peeked into the great room to find Sarah still sitting, still scowling, and still mad as a wet hen. Mad was good; it was a hell of a lot better than wary.

Alex headed to the pantry, found a large bin, and started loading it with food. He spotted a bottle of wine on the top shelf and grabbed it, blew off the dust, and set it in the bin. But then he remembered Sarah was pregnant and shouldn't have wine, so he grabbed one of the bottles of sparkling grape juice instead before carrying his load out to the truck. He went back into the house and into the great room, asking how she was doing as he walked to the stairs. Without stopping long enough to hear her reply, he ran upstairs and stripped off his bedding, rolling it up and setting it in the hall. He went into the bathroom next and stuffed towels and toiletries into a pillow case.

He made another trip out to the truck with his cache, then came back inside and into Sarah's room to grab some of her clothes. He opened the top drawer of her bureau to find her undies and noticed the tiny box that held the wedding band he'd given her. He picked it up and was stuffing it into a pillow case when he suddenly heard a bell tinkling.

Why in hell was a bell ringing?

Then he remembered the bell Sarah had set on the coffee table for him to call her when he'd been laid up. Not that he'd used it, when shouting had gotten him a much more interesting response.

"You rang, madam?" he drawled, walking into the great room.

"What are you doing?" she asked. "It doesn't sound like you're cleaning the kitchen."

"You're one of those micro-managers, aren't you?" he said to avoid answering her. "You're going to need a staff to run your camps, but you won't keep anyone more than a month if you start micro-managing them. Especially the guides. They're independent people who don't like being bossed around. That's why they're guides."

"I can handle a staff. It's you I'm worried about. You forgot to put salve in my eyes and change the bandages." She held out her good hand. "Just give me the salve. I can do it myself."

"But you can't put on new bandages by yourself. Your right hand is one big ball of gauze."

She dropped her good hand and went back to scowling.

"I'll put your salve on before we leave," he said, going back to packing the truck, again smiling openly.

In twenty minutes, he was down to just Sarah's medicines left to load, as well as Sarah herself. Alex breezed into the great room, shut off the TV, and walked over and found her lying on the couch, softly snoring. He'd be inclined to sleep, too, if he couldn't even see his own nose.

He hated to wake her; she needed the sleep to heal. He'd put her salve on at the sporting camps. He made yet another trip out to the warmed-up truck with Sarah's coat and medicine, then came back in, took the blanket off the back of the couch to cover her, and carried her out to the truck. She didn't even wake up but immediately snuggled into her jacket lying on the seat and started snoring again.

Alex finally climbed into the truck himself, blew out a tired sigh, and headed out the driveway. Seducing one's wife took a lot of leg work and planning—but sometimes a man just had to do a bit of huffing and puffing to impress a woman.

Chapter Nineteen

❈

Sarah woke up to the soft, rhythmic voice of someone reading out loud. But even as she tried to surface through the ethereal fog of confusion, she became lost in the scene painted by words. She was sitting in a pub in Puffin Harbor, trying to explain to Rachel Foster that the sexual drought she was experiencing was making her desperate enough to start soliciting dates on the steps of the state capitol.

But she didn't have a sister named Rachel. And her name wasn't Willow Foster, and she couldn't remember ever waking up in Duncan Ross's bed.

Sarah snapped open her eyes to solid blackness, gasping at the pain ripping through her right hand when she tried to use it to sit up. The reading stopped.

"Easy, Sarah. You're okay," Alex said, his voice moving closer. "You're on the floor of your sporting lodge, on a mattress in front of the fireplace. Don't make any more sudden moves," he continued gently, his strong hands on her shoulders laying her back down. "You've been sleeping for hours, and you're disoriented."

"Hours?" she said, her good hand going to the buttons on her blouse.

"What's the matter?" he asked, his voice deadpan. "You worried I might have undressed you while you were passed out and had my wicked way with you?"

"I . . . I . . ."

Warm, soft lips touched hers. "I didn't even peek—though don't think I wasn't tempted." He feathered his mouth over hers. "You'll always tempt me, Sunshine," he whispered against her lips before pulling away and running his hands down her arms. "I'd better give you only half a pill from now on. You were passed out like a hibernating bear."

"I really slept through your bringing me here?" she asked, turning her head as if to look around, hating the fact that she couldn't see. She was never, ever taking her eyesight for granted again.

"You even slept through my plowing the road, and for at least two hours right here in front of the fire."

"But why did you bring me to the main lodge?" she asked. "I have Cabin One all cleaned up and ready to stay in."

She felt more than heard his sigh. "How in hell would I know that? I've spent the last two hours trying to get this tomb of a room warmed up."

Sarah relaxed into the mattress with a smile. "But it's such a beautiful room, don't you think? I can already picture my guests gathering here in the evening, talking about their day's adventures."

She felt the mattress dip beside her, and when Alex spoke, she could tell he was facing the fire instead of her. "You really want to open these camps, don't you?"

"Oh, yes. I love having guests from all over the world, from all walks of life. It makes . . . it makes me feel part of something big."

"They brought the world to your isolated little island, didn't they?" he said, and she could tell he was looking at her. "You've been living vicariously through your guests." She felt him resettle on the mattress. "Have you ever wanted to travel to *their* world, Sarah? To participate instead of just hearing about it? Experience the world instead of just reading about it in books and seeing it on television?"

"Someday. But for now, I'm content just knowing it's out there, waiting for when I'm ready to go see it."

"And just when will that defining moment come, Sarah?"

She softly chuckled. "Probably about the time hell gets a three-foot snowstorm," she said. "Have you had a chance to look around yet? Do the cabins need many repairs?"

"I haven't left this room for more than two minutes. I didn't want you waking up alone, not knowing where you were."

"Thank you," she whispered, feeling the blankets until she found his arm. She patted his sleeve. "I appreciate that you're being open-minded about the sporting camps. And when you check out Cabin One, you'll see how I intend to decorate them."

"It would be a daunting task for a small army of people, Sarah. How can you hope to pull it off with a baby demanding your attention?"

"I'll get one of those baby backpacks, and I'll hire a couple of high school girls in the summer to help me. I ran the inn on Crag Island while tending both my mother and father. I can do this, Alex. I can make it work."

He covered her hand on his arm. "I don't doubt you can," he said. "How about we put some salve on your eyes? Then I'll take a look around upstairs, feed us lunch, and head out to check the cabins while you have another nap. Sleeping is good for both your injuries and our baby."

Sarah shivered all the way down to her toes. *Our baby*. "Okay," she said, her hand going to the gauze over her eyes.

He lifted her into a sitting position and brushed her hand aside. "Let me," he said, gently working the tape free.

"Alex, did Charlotte take Delaney and Tucker with her when she left you?"

His hands stilled, then started gently tugging again. "No," he said. "She walked away from them, too. She was worried they'd hinder her search for a new deep pocket to pick."

"How old was Delaney?"

"Five. And Tucker was just a few months shy of two."

"Would you have fought for custody?"

His hands stilled again. "It wouldn't have reached court. I could have bought Charlotte off, and probably would have had to eventually, if she hadn't died." His hands cupped the sides of her face. "I would never take your child from you, Sarah."

She lowered her head. "I wasn't worried about that."

"Yes, you were," he said, lifting her face and kissing her forehead. "Because the first thought that crossed my mind when I heard you were pregnant was that you might run back to Crag Island and take my child with you."

"I wouldn't."

"I know. I dismissed my worry because I just as quickly realized that I trust you," he finished softly, his hands going back to her bandages. "If you need to use the bathroom, I melted some snow and filled the tank of the downstairs toilet." He lightly tapped her nose, then slowly pulled off both patches of gauze. "So that means we have indoor plumbing."

"I wondered about water if I moved here in the middle of the winter," she said, thankful they were on a safer subject.

She immediately started blinking, able to see a very fuzzy face squinting back at her. She rubbed around her eyes, but Alex grabbed her hand and pulled it down to her lap.

"I have some water heating on the stove across the room," he said as he got up. "I want to wash around your eyes before I cover them again."

Sarah looked around the room, her blurred vision taking in the vaulted pine ceiling supported by thick, hand-hewn logs. Then her blinking gaze traveled down the pine walls to the floor-to-ceiling stone fireplace large enough for half a dozen people to fit inside. She looked at the fireplace for several seconds and then down at the blanket-covered mattress she was sitting on.

Alex had built her a cozy little nest in front of a crackling fire, started up the woodstove across the room, and got the toilet working, and he was tending her as if she were a princess. If he had been even half this thoughtful to his first wife, Charlotte had been an idiot for running away.

"Where did you find the firewood?" she asked, closing her eyes when she saw him walking back with a wash-cloth in his hand. "The few pieces I found in the wood-shed didn't put out much heat when I came here before. And it felt spongy."

"It's at least five years old," he said, and Sarah sensed him kneeling in front of her. "So it's dry-rotted, which turns it into a sponge that soaks up moisture. I brought wood from home."

"Oh. Oh!" she said again when the warm cloth touched her face. "Sorry, I wasn't expecting that."

He cupped the back of her head to keep her still, and Sarah felt a lot like Tucker must have felt when she'd had to get the giant bubble of gum he'd blown—and burst—out of his hair. Alex carefully washed around her eyes, then her cheeks, her nose, her chin, finally ending up softly brushing the damp cloth over her lips.

"I—I washed up this morning," she said with a nervous laugh, pulling away. "How often did Dr. Betters say I needed to put on the salve?"

"Twice a day. I'll do it again before we go to bed tonight."

There was something about the way he said "we go to bed" that made Sarah shiver again. It had sounded so . . . married. "How long do I have to keep my eyes covered?" she asked, trying to ignore the thumping ache in her chest.

"At least today and tomorrow. The day after tomorrow, you can try leaving them uncovered, but you have to keep them moist with the salve." He splayed his hands across the sides of her face, and Sarah opened her blurry eyes enough to see a tube in his right hand. "I've had welder's flash twice," he continued as he carefully oozed the thick gel into her right eye. "Don't blink," he instructed, using his thumb to hold her eye open. "I know it's uncomfortable, but it doesn't sting, does it?"

"No. Did you really duct-tape socks on Delaney's and Tucker's hands?"

She could just barely make out his grin. "It was the only way to keep them from making their rashes worse." He shook his head. "I hadn't realized we had a large patch of poison ivy so close to the house. They both waded through it when they went searching for the baseball Paul had hit to them. They were miserable for nearly two weeks, and Paul felt guilty as hell." He grinned again. "Actually, I had to double up the socks, so they could rub without digging."

Sarah grinned back, picturing Tucker and Delaney walking around scratching themselves with socked hands. "That was devious of you."

She could just make out Alex's bobbing eyebrows. "I'm a very devious guy," he said, letting her eyelid drop and lifting the other one.

Sarah took a deep breath in an attempt to relax, but she only managed to make her breasts rise and fall against Alex's arm. His hands stilled. "We're going to have to play doctor more often," he whispered.

If her cheeks got any hotter, she would have to run outside and jump into the snow to cool off. Sarah cleared her throat. "Is it still snowing outside?"

"I hope so. I'd hate for it to be snowing inside. Don't laugh," he said when she did, causing him to squirt salve on her nose. "Now see what you made me do."

"Sorry," she said contritely, sitting up straighter and inadvertently shoving her breasts into his arm again.

Alex leaned away, dropping his hands. "Tucker's a better patient than you are."

Sarah blinked, spreading the salve through her eyes as she reached up to rub it off her nose with her gauze-covered hand. But she only ended up smacking Alex in the chin just as he leaned forward with the cloth. "Sorry," she said again, trying not to laugh.

Alex sighed, took her injured hand in his, kissed her broken fingers, then pushed it back down to her lap. "You move again, and the next time you wake up from a drugged sleep, you will be naked. Got that?"

She actually felt a bit drugged right now. Sarah brought her good hand up to her forehead and saluted. "Aye-aye, captain."

He was just reaching up with a gauze patch this time, when he sighed yet again and pushed her hand down to her lap. "We're playing *doctor*, not captain of the high seas. Keep with the program, will you? And I'm charging you double for being an unruly patient."

"Double?" she asked, leaning away just as he came at her with the patch again. She narrowed her blurry eyes. "How much is double?"

"Two kisses instead of one."

Either she was getting brave, or she was starting to get used to his kisses, because Sarah found herself not only willing to pay his fee but boldly upping the ante. "I'll give you three kisses if you leave the bandage off one eye," she said, trying to bat her eyelashes at him, but they kept getting stuck to her bottom lashes.

He had once again started forward with the bandage, but he stopped and sat up straight. "Three?" His own eyes narrowed. "How long does the bandage have to stay off?"

"Just long enough for me to see what I'm eating for lunch."

"Deal," he said, starting to cover her right eye but stopping yet again. "I want a down payment. One kiss now, then the other two when I'm done."

Sarah licked her suddenly dry lips, and that throbbing in her chest suddenly kicked up three notches.

Sarah saw Alex drop his gaze to her lips. Her tongue got stuck to the roof of her mouth, but she nevertheless reached up, cupped his face with her good hand, and leaned toward him. He obligingly met her halfway, and Sarah closed both eyes, tilted her head, and kissed him.

It wasn't a tentative kiss she gave him, either. No, it was a bold, Rachel Foster kind of kiss, involving full contact, a little bit of tongue, and just a hint of passion boldly thrown in for good measure.

Only Alex didn't kiss her back. He stayed leaning into her, his own eyes closed, his lips slightly parted to allow her access. She pulled away just far enough to say, "Kiss me back."

"Uh-uh," he murmured just as she made contact again. He pulled back this time. "It's your debt, you do the kissing."

"But kissing requires two people, to work properly."

He said nothing, leaning forward until their lips touched again, and her mind's eye immediately shot back to five weeks ago. Sarah might be a bit blind, but she could quite plainly see the image of Alex braced above her, his heated body pressing her into her bed, the memory so vivid of him moving so deeply inside her.

She darted her tongue into his mouth as she held his face, tilting her head and snuggling her body against his. She could actually taste his male heat, feel it surrounding her as her head swam with sensations so exciting that being drunk on whiskey didn't even come close to the intoxicating power of anticipation. Her own confidence grew when he wrapped his arms around her, and she moved her tongue against his, boldly wrapping her arms around his neck.

She felt his chest rumble against her breasts, just before his groan erupted into her mouth. He lifted his head, and Sarah opened her eyes to find him staring at her, looking . . . looking . . . he looked a bit angry, actually. Sarah snapped her eyes shut.

"Have you decided yet?" he asked, his voice thick.

"Decided what?"

"How you feel about being pregnant."

She looked up. "Why do I have to decide that now?"

"Because happily pregnant women make happy babies," he said a bit more evenly as he looked around the mattress. He found the new gauze patches and held them up. "You need to keep both eyes covered until your lunch break."

Sarah wanted badly to take a deep breath but didn't dare for fear her still tingling breasts would touch him again. "All right," she whispered, closing her eyes.

He set the gauze over her face, gently pressed the tape around her eyes with trembling fingers, then was gone.

"I need to go out and do some plowing," he said, and

she felt a draft of cold air enter the room. "I'll feed you lunch in twenty minutes. Just lie down and keep your eyes closed. And don't move from that mattress."

"Aye-aye, doctor!" She gave him another salute.

Sarah dropped back onto the pillow as the door closed, and she smiled. Imagine that. She had the power to make Alex Knight run from *her* kisses. Well, spit, this heroine business really was powerful stuff.

Chapter Twenty

✦

"*Who the hell is seducing whom?*" Alex muttered as he stomped through the snow to his truck. Sarah had actually *kissed* him. And it hadn't been one of those shy, tentative kisses, either, but a full-blown kiss that women gave men when they wanted to make love. He'd very nearly obliged her, too, but that would have ruined his carefully orchestrated plans.

Or else he was dumber than dirt for not accepting her unwitting invitation.

Alex jerked open the truck door, slid into the seat, and stared at the solid wall of snow covering the windshield. *Unwitting* was the key word here. Sarah couldn't possibly have realized the signals she'd been sending him; she was too damn naive. She might know what her smile did to a guy, but she sure as hell didn't realize the power of her kisses.

And it hadn't been all that experienced a kiss, either.

But when a woman spent most of her time fighting off men's kisses, she probably didn't have much of a chance to practice giving them. He suddenly grinned. She'd be a quick learner, he bet, if she had a really dedicated teacher.

Alex reached out and turned the key in the ignition to heat the glow plugs, then turned it further. He heard the starter crank over with a loud, protesting whine, but the engine didn't start. He released the key, then turned it again, and again all he got was a screeching whine. What the hell?

He tripped the hood release and got out, lifting the hood to stare at the engine. Why hadn't it turned over? He wiggled several cables, then suddenly realized he could smell something he shouldn't be smelling anywhere near a truck. It was sweet, like their kitchen used to smell whenever his mother had scorched a pot of fudge. He climbed back into the truck, turned the key to open the electric system, and grabbed the radio mike.

"NorthWoods Two calling NorthWoods One," he said. "Dad, Ethan, Paul, any of you out there?"

He released the mike and waited. "I'm here," Grady said after a few moments. "And so are Ethan and Paul."

"Are you at the cutting?"

"Oh, yeah," Grady said through the static. "And we're stuck here because we couldn't get one single engine started after we stopped for our morning break. Our pickups won't start, the delimber and harvester won't start, and not one of our skidders will crank over."

Alex stared at the snow on his windshield. "Dammit, our fuel was sugared! Did everything get fueled up last night? And all the pickup trucks?"

"Yup," Grady said. "Paul's Mustang is the only thing that's not diesel. He's thinking of walking home to get it."

Alex snorted. "It'll take him three hours to get home, and you know his car won't go in this snow. Call Tate."

"I tried. Tate's at an accident fifty miles from here. And Daniel's in court in Dover all day," Grady explained. "I called in one of our rigs, and Jason's on his way out to get us."

"So what's the plan?" Alex asked.

"As soon as we get home, I'll do some calling around to find us temporary transportation." There was a hesitation on the other end before Grady said, "Then I'll have to start calling around for new engines."

"Send someone out here to get us," Alex said.

"What for?" Grady asked. "There's no need for you and Sarah to rush home, since there's nothing any of us can do except get madder and madder by the minute."

"Where was our fuel tanker parked?" Alex asked.

"Right beside our machine shed. They must have seen our guards watching the equipment at the cutting, so they hit our diesel fuel in our own damn yard." There was a short silence. "This means it wasn't teenagers messing with us after all. Sugaring our fuel tanker is too calculated. They must have done it sometime yesterday, while you were at the hospital with Sarah and before we got home."

Alex stared out the open truck door at the quickly accumulating snow. Dammit, they *were* dealing with an organized group of men. But smugglers? That still sounded surreal to him. The most exciting thing that ever happened around here was when someone's wife suddenly ran off with someone else's husband. Alex sighed and keyed the mike again. "Sarah and I will stay here for the night, then. But see what John can find out."

"Will do," Grady assured him. "And we'll be out to get you first thing tomorrow morning. Meanwhile, try not to let this ruin your plans, okay? Sarah means more to all of us than a few engines."

Well, hell. "Okay," Alex said into the mike. "But I'll check in with you again this evening, to see if there's anything new. Try to keep your blood pressure in check, will you?" he ordered. "One ornery patient is more than I can handle."

Grady chuckled. "Sarah have a bit of a roar, does she?"

"And claws," Alex shot back. "I'm out," he said, releasing the mike and snapping it into its cradle as he heard Grady's own "Out" reply.

Alex slid back out of the truck and slapped the hood down with a solid thud, pulled up the collar on his coat, and stared at the lodge through the falling snow before lifting his gaze to the smoke billowing out of the two chimneys.

This rapidly escalating mystery was getting serious, and just when he needed to stay focused on Sarah. Alex tramped back to the lodge, stamping snow off his feet before he opened the door just in time to catch Sarah scrambling back onto her mattress. She stretched out, folding her hands over her belly.

"Am I going to have to hobble you?" he asked, shedding his jacket. "If you want that knee to heal, you have to stay off it."

"Actually, it feels quite a bit better," she said. "A good deal of the swelling's gone down. You weren't gone long enough to plow, and I didn't hear the truck start."

"That's because it won't," he told her, walking over and dropping into a chair at her feet. "Do you know how to use a gun, Sarah? Have you ever shot a rifle or a shotgun?"

She lifted herself onto her elbow. "No. Why?"

Alex shrugged. "I just wondered. I should probably teach you to shoot if you're going to live out here. You never know when a gun might come in handy."

"Handy for what?" she asked in alarm. "I'd never shoot anyone."

Alex grinned. "You wouldn't have to. Any guy who sees a gun in a woman's hand usually runs the other way at mach speed. The loud crack of a rifle will scare off a bear nosing around, too." He leaned forward, setting his elbows on his knees. "You need to get comfortable handling a gun, Sarah, for your peace of mind as well as my own."

"Okay," she said, lying back down. "I'll learn. How come the truck won't start?" She suddenly sat up again. "Does that mean we're stuck here? Can we at least use the radio?"

"I just talked to Grady. They've got a bit of a problem out at the cutting, so they can't come get us right now. None of the trucks or equipment will start."

"Why? Engines don't break all at the same time."

"They do if they've got sugar in their fuel and are seized."

"But we drove here this morning. Our truck obviously ran okay."

"That's because the sugar hadn't reached the engine yet. When I started the truck this morning, the contaminated fuel spread to the engine and coated the cylinders with sugar. The moment you shut off the truck and the engine cools, the sugar hardens the cylinders tight."

"Can you rebuild the cylinders?"

He shook his head. "No. The sugar has gone all through the engine and fuel system and created a bond as strong as a metal weld. It's cheaper just to put in a new engine."

"In all three trucks?"

"And in all our harvesting equipment. We fueled all our equipment last night, so everything is seized." He stood up and rubbed his hands together. "How about lunch?" he said, changing the subject because he didn't want to worry her.

Sarah didn't respond for several seconds, her frown saying she didn't care for his changing the subject, but then she sighed. "I was about to start gnawing on my arm," she said. "What's for lunch?"

"Leftover stew from last night," he told her, laughing when she groaned dramatically. "And toast from this morning to sop up the broth."

Alex walked over to the reception counter and started rummaging through the bin of food. He smiled when he found something that would surely redirect her interest. "Oh, I forgot. You got some mail yesterday, and I just threw it in with the food so I'd remember to give it to you."

"I got mail? From who?"

Alex picked up the two letters and read the return addresses. "One's from a law firm in Machias, and the other one is from some gallery in New York City."

"Oh! That's from Martha's lawyers. They must have found Brian Banks." Alex looked over to see her sitting up again. "Open it and read it to me. See if they found Brian and he wants to buy me out."

Alex opened the envelope and shook out the letter, only to have a check go floating to the floor. He reached down, read the amount of the check with a silent whistle, then unfolded the letter and read it.

"Well?" Sarah asked.

"They found Brian," he told her. "And he sent you a bank check for fifty thousand dollars as down payment to buy your half of the inn."

"Fifty thousand?" she squeaked.

Alex looked over at her. "Exactly how much is your inn worth, Sarah?"

He saw her shrug. "One and a quarter million dollars, maybe even a million and a half by now. Last time it was appraised was five years ago, just after Roland died."

"That much?" Alex said in surprise, carefully tearing open the other envelope.

"Like you, I'm land-rich but cash-poor," he heard her say as he scanned the next letter with a frown. "The inn itself isn't that valuable, but the nine acres of prime waterfront land it's sitting on is. Island property doesn't exactly grow on trees, and the more remote the better for rich out-of-state buyers," she explained. Alex looked up when he saw her motion with her hand. "You can give me the other letter," she said, wiggling her fingers. "It's not important. I'll read it later, when I can see."

"Too late, Sunshine," Alex said, walking over and sitting down in the chair by her feet. "I already opened it. I thought you wanted me to read them both to you."

Alex frowned when Sarah immediately lowered her head and started picking at her bandaged hand.

"The gallery envelope contains a check for four thousand dollars and a note from a Clara Barton that says she's expecting your other hanging to sell for nearly double that. She has an interested client who's already been back twice."

No squeak of joy this time; Sarah merely continued to pick at her hand.

"What's a hanging?"

"It's a small quilt that you hang on a wall instead of putting it on a bed." Her hair hid her face from him.

"What kind of quilt is worth eight thousand dollars?"

"One that looks like a painting, only it's made of hundreds of tiny pieces of hand-sewn fabric."

Alex remembered the quilt he'd found in Sarah's box in the attic. "That quilt of the bouquet of roses I bought you is a hanging? And it's worth thousands of dollars?"

She nodded, still picking at her bandage.

Alex smiled. "You're quite a talented artist, then, if your work commands that kind of money. Why aren't you so excited you can't contain yourself? As Martha Stewart would say, isn't this a good thing?"

She mutely nodded again.

"Sarah?"

Her shoulders squared, and her chin rose. "I *am* talented," she said. "And if I wanted to devote more time to my hangings, I could make a good living."

"Then why don't you?" he asked curiously.

Just as suddenly as her hackles had been raised, she deflated. "The first time I got a check in the mail and I showed Roland that I could supplement our income, he came unglued. It was the only time I was ever actually afraid of him."

"But why?"

"Because men who want the world to think they're macho certainly don't want their wives earning more money than they do. I also think he was afraid that if I became financially independent, I would leave. He carried all my fabric out to the lawn and burned it."

"I see," Alex said softly, fighting to hold his outrage in check. "So the phone call you got last week when I was laid up, the one where you ran into your bedroom to talk, that was Clara Barton? And you didn't want me to know you made good money selling your quilts because . . . because why? You weren't worried about making money running these camps."

She shrugged. "I don't know. The camps are different. Roland never had a problem with my running the inn."

Alex decided he'd like to have five minutes alone with Roland Banks. "So what's this check for, if you stopped quilting after Roland came unglued?"

"I met Clara when she stayed at my inn one summer, shortly after I'd gotten married. She saw one of my quilts and asked if she could take it back to New York to sell in her gallery. That was the one that ignited Roland's temper when she sent me the check for it. I kept quilting, only I hid them in the attic at home. After Roland drowned and I had two bad seasons in a row because of rain, I sent several of my quilts to Clara." She nodded at his hand. "That's the fifth one she's sold for me, although the other checks were only for two thousand and three thousand dollars. They make up most of the eight thousand dollars I have tucked away for my camps budget."

Alex still couldn't get past the fact Sarah had been afraid of his reaction to her earning honest money. "Well, now you have twelve thousand in your budget. No, wait. Sixty-two thousand," he said, waving the check from Brian Banks.

He stood up, walked over to Sarah, and put the checks and the letters in her good hand. "Congratulations, Sarah. I'm really proud of you."

"Th-thank you," she whispered.

Alex walked back to the food bin, grabbed a box of crackers, a can of cheese, and a bag of pepperoni. He started assembling little sandwiches, placing the pepperoni on a cracker, squirting it with cheese, then capping it off with another cracker and pressing it flat. He made at least a dozen, arranged them on a paper plate, and grabbed her bottles of medicine before heading back to the mattress.

He uncovered one of Sarah's eyes as he had promised. "You're supposed to take your pregnancy vitamin with food," he told her, handing her a bright pink pill big enough to choke a horse. "And I know for a fact that the pain pill settles better with food in your stomach," he added, breaking one in half and handing half to her. "And your antibiotic," he finished, handing her one of those. "I'll get you a soda to wash them down," he said, jumping up and going back to the counter.

"Is it still snowing?" she asked, her voice subdued.

"Yes. And the wind's picking up. We might be trapped more by snow than by engine trouble," he said, sitting back down and handing her the can of soda.

She grabbed his wrist. "I-I'm sorry, Alex. I reacted

without thinking earlier," she said. "I know you're not like Roland." She gave him a tentative smile. "I'm pretty sure you're secure enough in your manhood to accept women being financially independent."

"Still," he said with a sigh, "even manly men can get their egos dented." He tapped his cheek. "Best way I know to soothe a dented ego is with a kiss." He turned his cheek toward her. "It eases the pain."

She touched his face with her fingers, then leaned forward and softly kissed where she'd touched. "Is that better?" she whispered.

"A little," he said. "But if it starts hurting again, I'll be back for another one," he teased. "Now eat, before that half a pill knocks you out."

Alex added another log to the fire as she ate, stoked the stove across the room, then picked up the book he'd been reading earlier and started reading out loud.

"I think I'd like to sleep now," Sarah said before he'd even finished one paragraph.

"But this is getting interesting," he said. "Willow Foster just locked herself in a pub bathroom and is climbing out the window."

"You're supposed to be checking out my camps."

"But it's storming."

"You have boots, a hat, and gloves. Be a mountain man like Paul Bunyan, and brave the storm."

"Paul Bunyan was a lumberjack. You need to work on your character profiles." He walked over and knelt down to pull up the blanket around her, then replaced the second eye bandage. "Will your broken fingers stop you from creating your quilts after they heal?"

"No. Dr. Betters said that if I had to break them at all,

I did a good job of it. They're just hairline fractures from where I smacked the dash. He said twisted breaks might have needed surgery."

"That's good." He kissed her cheek. "Sweet dreams, Sunshine."

Chapter Twenty-one

✦

Sarah decided she wasn't taking any more pain pills, not even a quarter of one. She was sorely tired of waking up to a solid wall of blackness, her mind stuffed with cotton and her muscles feeling like lead. And then there was the fact that someone was sleeping beside her again. Actually, he was surrounding her, more than lying beside her.

"Good morning," Alex whispered next to her ear, his arm tightening around her waist.

"It is *not* morning. We just had lunch."

"Oh, that's right." The hand attached to that imprisoning arm slid up her belly. "But then, you can't see, so you really can't tell what time it is, can you?"

Sarah halted his hand by covering it with her own, though his fingers continued to caress her ribs. "Your real name is Frankenstein, isn't it? I shudder at the thought of Delaney and Tucker enduring your doctoring for two weeks."

He used his lightly stubbled cheek to move her hair so his lips could touch her ear when he spoke. "Careful, Sunshine, or you'll have to soothe my dented ego again."

His warm breath sent a wave of heat all the way down to her toes. "Is it still snowing?" she asked.

He snuggled closer. "Last I looked," he said, again into her ear, again making her toes curl. "Aren't you glad you're snowbound with Paul Bunyan? I chopped wood all afternoon just so you'd be warm."

But it wasn't the fire in the hearth making her hot. "I need to use the bathroom," she told him. "And I need to get up and move around. My muscles are screaming to stretch." *Almost as loudly as my hormones are screaming.*

Alex kissed her cheek, then unwrapped himself from around her and sat up. "It's almost four o'clock, if you're wondering," he said. "The storm's gotten worse, and it's dark out."

Sarah rolled onto her back. "Is someone home with Delaney and Tucker?"

"Everyone's home," he said, the mattress moving as he stood up. "Have you decided yet?"

It took Sarah a minute to realize what he was asking. "No, not yet," she said, not quite ready to admit her feelings to him. She sat up and held out her good hand. "Help me up?"

Her hand was pushed aside, the mattress dipped, and he picked her up. And she was right back to feeling his warm breath and smelling his woodsy male essence.

"Are you hungry?" he asked as he carried her across the room. "Our menu tonight is fire-toasted popcorn, melted chocolate and marshmallows served on cinnamon graham crackers, and spit-roasted hot dogs slow-cooked over glowing coals. To complement tonight's three-course dinner, your chef has chosen a sparkling grape juice imported from . . . Massachusetts, I think." He sat her on a hard chair in a much cooler room.

"The powder-room attendant seems to be on break at the moment," he added, his voice sounding as if he were looking around for said attendant. "Will madam be okay on her own?"

"I'll be fine," she said, dismissing him with an imperial wave. "I shall call when I need your services."

She heard his footsteps move to the door. "Don't try peeking past your bandages. There's no light in here. I found some old lamps in the kitchen, but the kerosene had evaporated. I brought a gas lantern, though. Do you want me to get it?"

"No," she said. "I'll be fine."

"Then I shall have a fresh towel waiting for madam when she's done. Just give me a shout."

Sarah heard the door click shut. Holy smokes, how was she going to survive a night alone with Alex? He was nearly irresistible when he was so playful.

Sarah slapped her good hand to her chest. Now she was on to him—they were on a date! He'd brought her here to get her alone, not to check out her camps. And she'd bet there was absolutely nothing wrong with the truck. It probably wasn't even snowing anymore, either.

Trapped, hah! The man was staging a seduction.

So . . . was she going to let him? Could she go back out there and play his game, eat his three-course meal and drink his sparkling grape juice, and act innocently but pleasantly surprised when he made his move?

Then she remembered Alex's reaction when *she* had

kissed *him* this morning. She had caught him completely off-guard with that kiss, and he'd run into his imaginary snowstorm like an overheated teenager.

Why not turn the tables on him again and let him see what it was like to be on the other end of a well-orchestrated scheme? After all, how hard could it be to seduce a man who'd already admitted he wanted her and had worked so hard to set the stage for her?

Images of their first night together suddenly ran through Sarah's mind, making her shiver as she remembered the heat of Alex's body covering hers, the exciting sensations that had sent her soaring to wondrous heights, the feel of him deep inside her. She'd been so close . . . so close . . .

Why not just put them both out of their misery and simply go for it? She could no longer deny that she wanted Alex just as much as he wanted her. Sarah thought she might explode with repressed desire.

And, by God, she would experience *it* this time, and finally become a fully realized, completely satisfied woman. Sarah lifted her bandaged hand and gave the fictional Rachel Foster a high-five just as she heard footsteps stop outside the door.

"You okay in there?" Alex asked.

"I'm just great! In fact, I'm feeling positively energized from all that napping."

There was a moment's hesitation. "O-kay. Call me when you're done," he said just before she heard him walk away.

Sarah stood up on her good leg and eased her weight onto both feet, discovering that her knee barely hurt anymore. She groped around and found the toilet, did her business, then threw back her shoulders as she smoothed down her clothes with a Cheshire Cat smile, wondering how Alex liked seducing a woman who was wearing ratty old jogging pants and an even older sweatshirt.

She snorted. The guy was only interested in what was *under* the clothes. "Okay," she muttered. "Let's see if I can pull this off stone-cold sober." Sarah groped for the doorknob and opened the door with an innocent smile plastered on her face. "I'm done, Alex."

She heard him walking over and was quite prepared when he swept her off her feet and settled her against his chest. She was not prepared, however, when he sat down with her still in his arms and carefully positioned her on his lap.

"I don't get my own chair?" she asked, figuring this meant their game must be on.

"I've decided I should feed you," he said. "I realized the menu was messy when I did a taste test."

"And my fresh towel?" she asked, holding out her hand.

He leaned away momentarily, then set a warm, moist cloth in her upturned palm. "How's your knee?" he asked, gently caressing it. "It seems like the swelling's gone down."

"It has. I guess all that rest worked," she said, awkwardly washing her good hand. She started washing her face next, but Alex took over.

She hadn't read all those romance novels without learning one or two things about men. She leaned into his hand, parting her lips when the cloth reached her mouth. "Mmnn, that feels wonderful," she whispered, letting her tongue dart out just as his fingers went brushing by.

The cloth suddenly disappeared, and she heard it plop into a bowl of water. Alex cleared his throat. "Our first course tonight is hot dogs," he said, his voice a tad edgy.

A warm hot dog was pressed against her mouth, and Sarah parted her lips again, touched the hot dog with the tip of her tongue, then slowly pulled it partway into her mouth with a moan—which was completely drowned out by the stifled rumble coming from the chest she was leaning against.

She bit off the end of the hot dog with a snap of her teeth and felt Alex shudder beneath her, the tiny quake empowering her to lick her lips and say in a drawn-out whisper, "Mmmnnnn, that tastes sooo good."

She heard the remains of the hot dog hit the floor. "Maybe I should start with the s'mores," he said, the edge in his voice now decidedly pained.

The gooey marshmallow and dripping chocolate cracker was pushed a bit more abruptly between her lips, and Sarah quickly took a bite, chewed, then turned her face toward him. "Do I have chocolate on my face?" she asked, running her tongue over her lips.

It wasn't a stifled groan she heard this time but an ominous growl, warning Sarah of his impending strike. His mouth completely covered hers, adding the taste of sparkling grape juice to the marshmallow and chocolate she had just swallowed.

Holy smokes, she'd overplayed her hand! Sarah's head swam in dizzying circles, and it wasn't until she could breathe again and she felt her back press into the mattress that she realized what was happening.

Alex landed heavily beside her, his mouth again covering hers just as one of his broad hands slid up under her shirt and closed over her breast, his other hand twined through her hair so he could deepen his kiss.

But everything stopped, including time itself, it seemed, when he suddenly reared up, cursed softly, and pulled his hand from under her shirt. "I need to see your eyes," he growled.

Trembling with her own blossoming need, Sarah reached up and touched his clenched jaw. "No, you don't. I'm wide awake, I promise. Make love to me, Alex," she whispered. "For real this time."

That was all the encouragement he needed. He grabbed the hem of her shirt and worked it up over her breasts, lifting her with it as he carefully pulled it over her head. Sarah immediately began helping him pull his own shirt out of his pants and heard several buttons pop and clink to the floor when he yanked it off. Her breath caught in her throat when she reached up and felt his down-covered chest, which he used to press her back into the mattress as his mouth returned to hers, her thin lace bra little defense against his naked heat.

Her own body was generating plenty of heat, too. Sarah's pulse quickened as her fingers explored his powerful body, her sock-covered toes curling with the urge to run up the length of his legs and wrap around him. Her nerves crackled with high-tension energy as blood roared through her veins to pool in the pit of her stomach.

So this was passion—this urgent need to feel, to taste, to *become* part of someone else. It was little wonder she felt as if she were being consumed. Sarah wanted to taste every inch of Alex. So she suckled his tongue and slid her feet up his pant-covered legs, all while her body continued to coil in anticipation. She flexed every one of her unbandaged fingers into his naked shoulders, arching her back to push her breasts into his heat.

His mouth left hers so unexpectedly that Sarah cried out, her protest turning to a moan when his lips moved down her throat to find several sensitive places, sending shivers crashing through her like waves.

Alex muttered something just as she felt the flimsy lace of her bra rip away to expose her breasts, and she gasped in surprise when his mouth closed over her nipple. He started to suckle, rocking her with pleasure, making her arch upward again.

Except for an occasional curse when his wandering mouth got stopped by the drawstring on her pants, and intermittent growls when she would grab his hair and try to steer his salacious journey, Alex was proving to be a man of few words.

There was a short wrestling match with her jogging pants, and when Sarah tried to help, she realized she was actually working against him, and she uncurled her toes when he pulled off her pants and socks in one fluid motion.

Her tachometer shot up past the redline when Alex settled between her thighs to nestle against her. He'd taken off his pants, and there was nothing—*nothing*—between them but solid, glorious heat.

"Say you want me again," he growled.

"I want you."

"Say my name."

"Alex. I want you, Alex."

He reached down and touched her ever so intimately, his fingers sending a wave of even more focused, more intense pleasure rippling through her. "Hold my shoulders," he ordered, moving firmly against her as his fingers continued to do magical things. "That's it, Sunshine, relax and let me inside you."

Dammit, he was moving too slowly! Sarah shot him a beatific smile, gave it time to sink in, and said in a sultry voice, "I want you, Alex." She lifted her hips. "Now," she growled, pulling him closer to lick one of his nipples. "I want . . . oh, just do it!" she ordered.

He went still. "I'm pretty sure I've been trying to *do it* for the last ten minutes."

Well, spit. Alex was all but inside her, for crying out loud, and she was blowing her great seduction by practically yelling at him to hurry up! She reached up and cupped his face, rubbing her thumb over his lips. "It's just you, me, and our baby, Alex," she whispered, placing his hand on her belly. "I've finally decided. You're the only man I ever want to have a baby with."

Sarah felt his hand on her tummy tremble as he softly kneaded her sensitive skin. She arched up with a moan of pleasure and feathered a finger along his clenched jaw. "I want you, Alex. I ache to feel you inside me."

That, too, was what he needed to hear, apparently, because he lowered himself, setting his elbows on either side of her head as he covered her mouth with his. Sparks of pleasure returned with the swiftness of a summer squall, battering Sarah with a blazing heat that shot straight to her pelvis. He moved then—deliberately and maddeningly slowly—easing into her while gently kissing every inch of her face. Her own muscles tightened as Sarah stretched to take him inside. His weight lifted slightly, and his magical fingers started their erotic dance again, just as he began moving in a wonderfully gentle rhythm.

Sarah buried her face in his neck to stifle her moan.

"Don't hold back, Sunshine. If I can't see your eyes, then let me hear what you're feeling," he whispered raggedly.

And Sarah finally let go. With his heated body reflecting her own raging desire, every nerve, every muscle, every cell in her body suddenly convulsed with violent pleasure, and Sarah's long, keening scream rose to the rafters. Alex's answering shout cannonaded like thunder as he drove into her, each commanding thrust carrying her beyond anything she could have ever imagined.

It went on forever, this amazing melding of passion; she could feel, even taste, Alex's pleasure, which only served to heighten her own. A succession of spiraling convulsions rocked her world, shattering her control and soundly shattering her safe little cocoon wide open.

There was no sealing it back up, Sarah realized as her mind slowly tilted back into balance, but she didn't care, lingering spasms of pleasure making her melt into the mattress with a deeply contented sigh. Trembling fingers brushed the hair off her face, and warm lips gently kissed her forehead between ragged breaths.

Long after the last tremor of pleasure faded, Alex continued surrounding her with his heat, staying deep inside her. His weight felt wonderful; he was being so careful not to crush her.

But she mustn't let him get too pleased with himself. Not when she couldn't stop blushing so hard. "Don't think this means I'm moving to your bedroom," she warned in a panting whisper. "Because we can't ever do this when the kids are home. I *screamed*."

"I noticed," he drawled, and kissed her forehead with a satisfied sigh. "It's something we'll have to work on, I guess." He grinned briefly, then turned serious. "Will you marry me, Sarah?"

"I already did."

"For *real*."

She hesitated. "I'll have to give it some thought."

"You decided you're glad you're having my baby."

She tried shrugging, but his elbows were in the way. "One doesn't necessarily have anything to do with the other."

He must have realized he wasn't going to get the answer he wanted, so he simply asked another question, seemingly unaware that he was still inside her. "Was it better for you this time, sunshine? All that you'd hoped lovemaking could be?"

Sarah heaved a huge sigh, forcing Alex to lift his chest enough to accommodate her before he lowered his weight again, pinning her in place. Oh, yeah, he was feeling much too smug—obviously overlooking the fact that *she* had seduced *him* and that she should be the one asking that question. Besides, wasn't he supposed to roll onto his back now, take her with him, and they'd fall asleep cuddled in each other's arms?

She sighed. "It was wonderful," she whispered, lazily patting his shoulder. "Even more than I'd imagined."

He suddenly but gently moved his hips forward and upward at that admission, then slightly withdrew before thrusting forward again. Sarah's entire body shot awake, especially the sensitive spot he started kissing at the base of her ear. Holy smokes, he was ready to do it again?

Apparently! His mouth moved along the base of her throat, rekindling her passion, and his hips started rocking her world all over again. Mmm, she could easily get used to this. . . .

Chapter Twenty-two

❈

"*How much will new* engines cost?" Sarah asked, sitting in front of the crackling fire, eating God knew what for breakfast. She couldn't tell by taste or smell whether Alex was trying to cure her or kill her.

"We're insured against vandalism, which this certainly is," he said from someplace near the reception counter. "But it'll probably cost more for the new engines than all our equipment is worth. Two of the skidders and the delimber are old, the harvester's considered ancient, and insurance only covers their actual value." She heard him walking across the room. "At least our newest skidder escaped the tainted fuel. It's been in the shop waiting for a part to repair it."

"So how much will you have to pay out of pocket?"

"All total? Probably sixty, seventy thousand dollars for the trucks, delimber, and skidders," he said, this time from the woodstove. "And another two hundred and fifty thousand for a new harvester, since we might as well replace it instead of repairing it."

Sarah looked toward him even though she couldn't see anything. "Do you have that kind of cash?"

She heard his sigh all the way across the room. "Not if Grady cleaned out our account to make that down payment on Loon Cove Lumber. Our credit will also be tied up in that mill."

Holy smokes—they could be put out of business. Without stopping to think what she was doing, Sarah took a bite of her breakfast and immediately gagged. She spit her mouthful into her hand and scraped her tongue on her teeth. Alex might make love as if there was no tomorrow, but he couldn't cook his way out of a wet paper bag.

"Here's some grape juice," he offered, holding a bottle up to her lips.

Sarah took a large swig, forgetting it was *sparkling* grape juice, and started choking so badly some of the juice bubbled out her nose. Her chin was suddenly lifted and . . . good God, he was using his sleeve to wipe her nose!

"I need to go to the truck to call home," he said, his thumb rubbing something off the corner of her mouth. "Do you think you can eat your breakfast without killing yourself if I leave for a few minutes?"

"Probably not," she muttered, tossing the remains of her sandwich down. Her hand was sticky, and she groped around until she found Alex's chest and wiped her fingers on his shirt. "I'm not very hungry, anyway. Is it done snowing?"

"The sun's shining. We got two feet of new snow."

"So how are we going to get out of here if all the plow trucks won't start?"

"Maybe we'll have to stay another night," he suggested, his voice close. "That wouldn't be so bad, would it? We can work on your lessons," he said just before his mouth covered hers.

They had worked on her lessons enough last night that she should pass all her tests with flying colors. Sarah sighed into his mouth and was just starting to kiss him back when she suddenly found herself kissing empty air.

"Don't do that," he said from someplace above her. "Or I'll keep you here until the spring thaw."

"You started it."

His face came close to hers again. "And I intend to finish it," he whispered. "Just as soon as you give me your answer."

"My answer to what?" she asked, totally confused.

"I believe I asked you to marry me last night."

"Oh." She leaned away and nodded. "I'll let you know just as soon as I decide."

The air in front of her was empty again, and Sarah heard footsteps heading for the door. "Stay put," he ordered just as a waft of cold air blew across the room and the door shut with a bang.

Sarah touched the wedding band on her left ring finger. She had discovered it there when she'd awakened this morning and decided Alex was making sure no one poached his proxy wife while she was deciding whether she wanted to become a permanent fixture in his life—and, of course, in his bed.

If she had any conscience at all, she'd put him out of his misery and tell him what he wanted to hear. But then she'd be doomed to spend the next fifty years married to a man who thought he could get his way simply by seducing her with mind-blowing sex. That was *not* the foundation she wanted for their marriage, and it definitely wasn't a good precedent to set. Alex couldn't just cart her off and make the rafters shake with her screams whenever he wanted something. Though he would certainly try, she thought with a crooked smile, because the apple hadn't fallen very far from its daddy's scheming tree.

Sarah slowly got to her feet. Her knee protested slightly, but not enough to keep her an invalid any longer. Well, except that she couldn't see. How dumb was she, to give herself welder's flash? She had read the warning label on the box that housed the bulb, but the new bulb hadn't been hot or even all that bright when she'd bent close to see if it smelled like ozone. Sunburned eyeballs; who would have guessed?

Sarah shuffled to the reception counter, blindly rummaged through the large bin, and found what she thought was a box of crackers. She also found what felt like several chocolate bars, and she hungrily tore into the candy instead.

"Ethan's coming to get us on the snowmobile," Alex told Sarah when he returned to the lodge ten minutes later. "Or I can call him back and say we'll wait until tomorrow if you want. They're putting the engine from my wrecked truck in one of the other pickups today, and your SUV can be fixed at least enough to drive by—" He came to a halt in front of her. "What in hell are you eating?"

"Breakfast," she said as she reached up and wiped

chocolate off her chin, then licked her finger. "And as much as I've been enjoying this little vacation, if we stay another night, I'll starve to death." She gave him a thoughtful look—at least, it looked thoughtful to Alex, even though he couldn't see her eyes. "Unless you're Davy Crockett and can shoot us a bear to eat."

Alex plucked what was left of the candy bar out of her sticky hand. "It's Daniel Boone who shot the bear, not Davy Crockett. And bear meat is rank and tough."

"Whatever," she muttered, blindly rummaging through the bin until she found the box of crackers. "I just need something *edible*. Who did the cooking before I came along, anyway?"

"Between housekeepers, you mean? Whoever was the hungriest or the least tired," he said, snatching the box of crackers from her. He took her face in his hands and bent down to kiss a spot of chocolate on her chin. "You've gone and dented my ego again," he whispered, sliding his lips across hers. "I've been cooking my heart out for you for two days."

"Poor baby," she crooned, giving him a soothing, motherlike kiss. She patted his cheek. "Does that make it better?"

"Hell, no," he muttered, folding her into his arms and covering her mouth with his. "Dammit, Ethan will be here in twenty minutes," he said once he found the strength to tear himself away from her luscious mouth.

"Your vocabulary becomes quite limited when you . . . when you get . . ."

"Horny?" he finished for her, just before he kissed her again, not coming up for air for at least five minutes this time. And then it was only long enough to say, "You do make me horny, Sunshine," before he picked her up and carried her to the mattress.

The minute he set her down, she rolled away and scrambled to her feet, groping to put the chair between them. "I don't want Ethan walking in to find us rolling around on the floor," she said somewhat raggedly. She took a deep breath and brushed down the front of her chocolate-smeared sweatshirt. "I've never ridden on a snowmobile," she told him, her voice still shaky, and she shook her head as if to clear it. "And I never expected to be blind the first time I did."

"Did what?" Alex asked absently, watching her lovely breasts rise and fall with each breath.

"Ride a snowmobile," she snapped. "Are you staring at my chest?"

"Uh-uh," he said, his eyes nearly crossing when she took another deep breath.

She came back to the mattress and started feeling around the blankets. "Help me find my bra," she demanded. "I need to finish dressing before Ethan gets here."

Alex stopped her by dragging her against his own chest. "Shhh," he crooned, touching his smile to her hair. "You can't be self-conscious around Ethan, Sarah. He's really okay with our being married. In fact, he's very happy for both of us."

"That doesn't mean we have to rub it in his face. He has to realize what we've been doing here all night."

Alex grinned over her head. "I imagine even Delaney knows what we've been doing," he said with a chuckle. "Everyone considers our marriage real, Sarah." He dropped his forehead to hers. "Except you."

He could feel her braless breasts pushing against him, her lovely nipples provoking him unmercifully. Alex muttered a curse and set her away when he heard the distant sound of a snowmobile approaching. "Here's your bra," he said, picking it up off the floor and handing it to her. "It's . . . ah, it's a little ripped."

Sarah must have also heard the snowmobile. "Just give it to me," she hissed. She snatched the bra away and said, "Point me toward the bathroom."

He did, holding her hand so she didn't run into anything.

As she dressed, Alex pushed the dying embers to the back of the fireplace, then covered them with ashes. He was putting the poker back on its peg when he noticed the large map hanging beside the mantel. He stepped closer when he saw WHISTLER'S MOUNTAIN printed in small, black letters beside a drawing of a mountain bumping out of a pencil-sketched forest.

Alex leaned away to view the entire map and realized it wasn't a scaled map but a collage of drawings pointing out wildlife habitats, geographical places of interest, and natural landmarks surrounding the sporting camps. Tiny beavers had been drawn near some of the ponds, an old cabin was near one of the other mountains, and moose, deer, and bear were scattered throughout the five-by-four-foot map.

But what caught Alex's eye were the caves drawn on the side of Whistler's Mountain—the series of caves that had formed in the talus when part of the mountain had broken off, likely when the glacier fields had receded thousands of years ago.

Someone knocked on the porch door. Alex spun in

surprise and walked over to open it. "You knocked?" he said. "Why?"

"Because I didn't want to embarrass your wife by walking in on something I shouldn't," Ethan said, stepping inside as he brushed snow off his shoulders. He lifted an inquiring brow. "She is your wife now, isn't she?"

Alex shrugged.

Ethan gave him a crooked grin. "Did you leave your charm in South America, or have you forgotten how to seduce a pretty mouse?"

Alex pointed at the closed bathroom door. "That is not a mouse, that's a—"

The bathroom door shot open, and both men turned to see Sarah standing in the doorway with her sweatshirt held against her naked chest.

"Dammit, Alex, you ripped my bra, and I can't fix it with only one hand," she scolded, her bra dangling in her good hand. "And so help me God, if you even hint to Ethan what went on here last night, I will shoot you as soon as you teach me to use a gun."

"Too late, sister-in-law," Ethan said softly.

Sarah gasped, gathering her shirt tighter to her chest, then darted back into the bathroom, slamming the door behind her so hard that the walls rattled.

Alex sighed. "You couldn't have just kept quiet?"

"Not on your life," Ethan said with a chuckle. "She walked straight into that one."

"Now I'll never get her out of there." Alex eyed his brother. "Unless I can tell her you walked home. There's a set of snowshoes hanging on the porch."

"Uh-uh. I'm driving, Sarah can sit behind me, and you can ride on the tow sled."

Alex grabbed Ethan by the arm and shoved him out the door. "You know, I've been thinking about it, and I've decided you should get a job at Loon Cove Lumber for a couple of months before we take it over. Without letting anyone know who you are, of course, so you can get a feel for the crew."

"Half this county knows who I am."

"But they don't know you're about to become the new owner," Alex countered. "You can tell them we're thinking of opening our own sawmill."

"I am not going to Loon Cove Lumber one day sooner than I have to, and sure as hell not as a worker. Those guys would have a field day giving me all the grunt work."

"Best way to learn a new business is from the ground up," Alex reminded him, and slammed the door on Ethan's black look.

Alex walked over to the bathroom and opened the door to find Sarah sitting on the straight chair. She was holding her eye bandages in her lap, her sweatshirt was back on, and her bra was on the floor.

"He was only teasing you, Sunshine," Alex told her, brushing her hair over her shoulder. "Ethan's sense of humor is a bit rusty."

"Where is he?" she asked, leaning forward to look into the main room.

"Outside, waiting for us."

"I'm not wearing my eye patches. I don't need them anymore."

"They have to stay on for the ride home; the cold wind will dry out your eyes. Once we get home, then we'll see." He lowered to his haunches, once again smoothing back her hair. "Making love to your husband is nothing to be embarrassed about, Sarah. It's what married people do."

"Our marriage license is forged."

"It's only forged if you say it is, otherwise it's as legal as if I signed it myself. It's not just Ethan that's bothering you. What else?"

"Everyone knows why you brought me here yesterday, don't they? Paul and Grady were in on your plan."

"Only because they love you."

She finally looked at him, but Alex couldn't have read what she was thinking if he'd had a crystal ball. "You planning on making Ethan stand out in the cold all day?" He took the bandages out of her hand. "How about if I dump him off the tow sled a few times on the way home? Will that satisfy your sense of revenge for embarrassing you?"

He finally got a faint smile from her. "I'd feel even better if he had to run to catch up with the sled each time he fell," she suggested. "Or if he didn't catch up with us at all about a mile from home."

Alex nodded. "I think I can make that happen." He gently kissed her, then carefully set the bandages back over her eyes and smoothed down the tape to secure them. He picked up her bra and stood, bringing Sarah with him. "Let's finish getting you dressed," he said, turning her around and lifting the hem of her shirt. "With any luck, Paul's got a stew cooking."

"Paul can cook?" she mumbled from somewhere in her shirt as she held it up for him.

Alex wiped the sweat suddenly beading on his brow. He knew how to take *off* a bra, but he'd never paid much attention to putting one on. But then he made the mistake of peeking at the beautifully full breasts that were just waiting for him to touch and decided it was a shame to bind up such perfection. Alex pulled the hem of her shirt back down to her waist with a curse of defeat. "You'll have enough layers on that nobody will notice if you're missing some clothing," he said, tossing the bra and sweeping Sarah into his arms.

He carried her over to the door, stuffed her into her jacket, pulled a cap down over her head, and shoved a mitten over her good hand. "You'll have to put your bandaged hand in my pocket for the ride home," he said, hustling her out the door.

He picked her up again to carry her off the porch and through the deep snow, stopping when he reached the idling snowmobile. It took only a threatening glare to make Ethan scramble off the seat and plod to the dogsled attached to the rear bumper. Alex set Sarah down on the seat, climbed aboard, and tucked both her hands in his jacket pockets so she could hold on.

"I'll go slow," he promised in a whisper, "until I see a good place to dump Ethan."

That got him a full smile. Alex patted her hand in his pocket, revved the engine in warning, and drove down the steep bank of the shoreline and onto the lake.

It took every bit of courage Sarah possessed not to blush like a new bride when she walked into the house on Alex's arm. Grady greeted her with a hug, and Paul greeted Sarah by pulling her away from Alex and leading her over to the stove. He held a spoon to her lips and asked why his venison stew didn't taste like hers did, since he had followed her recipe exactly. Sarah thought she'd died and gone to heaven to be tasting something edible and said she'd have to eat an entire bowl in order to figure out where he'd gone wrong.

"You added the potatoes at the start," she told Paul once she'd finished her second bowl. "You're only supposed to add them an hour before you intend to serve the stew, or they'll make the broth too thick and starchy."

"But I watched a show about cooking in crock pots this morning," Paul said. "They just throw everything in at once, so you can come home at the end of the day to a fully cooked meal."

"Crock pots are designed to cook slowly," Sarah explained, trying to see him through the excessive salve Alex had gobbed on her eyes when he'd taken off her bandages. "You made your stew on the stove and set the heat too high. That makes the potatoes mushy."

"If we're done with the cooking lessons," Grady said, shoving his empty bowl away to rest his elbows on the table, "we need to get down to business before the kids get home from school. I don't want them realizing the pickle we're in. It'll only make them worry."

"What pickle?" Ethan asked, dropping his spoon into his bowl and also pushing it away.

Sarah stood up and started stacking the dirty bowls inside each other with her good hand, but Alex reached out and pulled her back down into her chair. "We'll get those after our meeting. Sit down and listen. It's your pickle as much as ours, Mrs. Knight."

Sarah kicked him under the table, just hard enough to make him grunt—and her smile.

"I found an engine for one of the skidders," Grady said. "Jason and Harley believe they can put the diesel engine from our generator into the delimber with a bit of retrofitting. And I've found us a nearly new tree harvester for a very sweet price." He blew out a tired breath and rubbed the back of his neck. "But even with the insurance check that's coming, we'll still have to come up with forty-six thousand dollars to be back in business."

"Then find an *old* used harvester," Alex suggested.

Grady shook his head. "I think we should buy this one. The price is too good to pass up."

"How much?" Ethan asked.

Grady folded his arms over his chest and rocked back on the rear legs of his chair. "It'll only cost us permission to rebuild eight miles of our roads."

"No," Alex snapped. "Porter isn't touching one inch of our roads."

"This feud has gone on long enough," Grady said, dropping his chair onto all four legs. "The man did you a favor by stealing your wife, Alex. And you know damn well that if it hadn't been Clay, it would have been someone else. Hell, Charlotte left *him* within a month."

Sarah sucked in her breath. No wonder the Knights didn't like Porter.

"The bastard's blackmailing us," Ethan protested.

"No, he's buying permission to rebuild our own roads," Grady returned with a growl, his patience obviously waning. "And the price is two hundred thousand dollars for only the permission. He'll have to pay for the cost of the improvements. We win both ways: we get a harvester and ten miles of new roads."

"No," Alex repeated softly. "We'll sell off some land."

Grady shook his head. "I didn't scrape and scheme to buy land just to sell it off the first time we find ourselves in difficulty. That's moving backward, and that's against company policy."

"It doesn't matter," Paul interjected. "Even if we get Porter's harvester and get the delimber up and running, we're still forty-six thousand short."

Sarah fingered the wedding band on her left hand. Did she dare find out just how her second marriage was going to work?

"I know where you can get forty-six thousand dollars, interest-free," she said, looking over at Grady but seeing Alex stiffen.

"Where?" Grady asked.

"From me. I received a couple of checks in the mail two days ago, one for fifty thousand dollars as down payment on my half of the inn and one for four thousand for . . . for some artwork I sold."

Grady immediately shook his head. "That's your personal money, Sarah. We're not touching—"

"We'll take it," Alex countered before Grady had finished, his intensely focused gaze locking on Sarah's. "Interest-free."

"No," Paul said, echoing his father. "We're not touching Sarah's money. That's most of her entire savings."

"She's a Knight now, isn't she?" Alex asked, still looking at her.

"We can work around our money problems," Ethan said. "We just have to go back to using chain saws instead of a harvester, we'll get the delimber up and running, and we still have one working skidder in the shop. We can operate with what we have."

"Then I guess you don't really consider me part of this family," Sarah said softly, looking at the others.

"That's not it," Ethan snapped. "We do not marry women for their money."

"I kind of like the idea of marrying a woman for her money," Alex drawled, warming Sarah's heart with his smile.

She lifted her chin. "But I have one condition."

He lifted one brow.

"You take Clay Porter's tree harvester and let him rebuild ten miles of your road."

"Done," Alex said quickly. He suddenly stood up, slid his arms under her knees and around her back, and lifted her out of her seat. "Sarah needs a nap," he told the others. "Pregnancy is very tiring."

The last thing Sarah saw before Alex carried her through the swinging door were the stunned expressions on the three Knight men. She smacked Alex in the chest as he carried her through the great room. "We agreed to keep the baby a secret," she hissed, smacking him again when he smiled.

He started climbing the stairs. "All's fair in love and war, Sunshine. You start throwing money and ultimatums at me, and I'm going to counter with whatever ammunition I have." He stopped at the top of the stairs, his grin a bit sinister. "You're not the only one who can get a few ideas from romance novels. That Keenan Oakes guy didn't worry about playing fair."

"He's not even *real*," Sarah ground out. "He's a figment of some demented woman's imagination."

Alex headed down the hall. "She certainly seems to know something about men."

"Hey!" Sarah yelped, just now realizing where he'd carried her. "I am not moving into your room."

He stopped beside the bed. "Why not?"

"Why—because it will confuse Delaney and Tucker, that's why," she said, wiggling to make him set her down.

He held her firmly against him. "You're the only one who's confused, Sarah. We're married, we're having a baby together, and you like being in my bed. So what's the problem?"

"You're the problem! You're assuming I'm going to move in with you just because we slept together."

"I don't remember getting much sleep last night," he said with a wicked grin. "In fact, I think I need to go to bed myself," he added, kissing her in a way that said he was anything but tired.

Chapter Twenty-three

❈

$\mathcal{S}$*arah spent the next eight days* worrying about which was going to give out first, her sanity or the clothes washer. The Knights were running a marathon of engine replacement and retrofitting, and she'd been trying to feed them and keep them clean with the use of only one hand. The men came into supper each night covered in grease from head to toe, their fingers wrapped in Band-Aids, and their eyelids drooping with fatigue. Even Tucker helped, heading out to the machine shed immediately after school to hand them tools. Delaney, bless her heart, was a great help to Sarah, especially when it came to moving Sarah's stuff up to Alex's bedroom. The girl had been positively beaming as she'd lugged clothes and toiletries upstairs.

The only point Sarah had won in the last eight days was a promise from all the men that they wouldn't tell the kids about the new baby. She wasn't even seven weeks pregnant, and things could still go wrong in the first trimester.

"You and Daddy should have a real wedding," Delaney said as she opened the oven door to peek at the brownies she was baking. "Was your wedding to Mr. Banks fancy?"

"No. It was just Roland and his mom and a justice of the peace," Sarah told her. "But Alex and I don't need a wedding, sweetie. Our proxy marriage is legal as long as no one says anything."

Delaney turned with her hands on her hips and frowned. "But you need a real wedding," she argued. "It's the last one you're going to have, and I want to be in it and wear a long dress and flowers in my hair. I can be your maid of honor."

Delaney walked over to the table and picked up one of the carrots Sarah had peeled. She took a bite, chewed, and swallowed. "You're driving Dad nuts, you know. Don't you want to stay married to him? You're sleeping with him."

This was exactly why she hadn't wanted to move into Alex's bedroom, Sarah thought with a sigh. "Has that boy at school tried to kiss you again?" she asked.

Delaney's face turned bright red. "Daddy told you."

Sarah nodded. "So if you woke up tomorrow morning and found out you were married to this boy, how would you feel?"

"Grossed out," Delaney immediately answered. "But Daddy's *nice*. He doesn't smell like a wet dog, and he's handsome and strong and smart."

"Okay, then suppose you woke up tomorrow and found yourself married to a handsome, strong, smart, nice-smelling boy who also happened to be a complete stranger. Would that make it okay?"

"Well . . . no," Delaney said with a frown. She shook her head. "But Daddy's not a stranger to you anymore. And if you're sleeping with him, that means you must like him."

Sarah reached out and tucked a loose strand of hair behind Delaney's ear. "I do like your daddy," she admitted. "But I've only known him seven weeks." She cupped her palm over Delaney's cheek. "Sometimes when men want to get a girl's interest, they mask their true personalities to make a good impression. I'm not saying your daddy's one of those men; I'm just saying that I was hurt pretty bad once, and it's going to take longer than seven weeks for me to get over it."

"Are you talking about your first husband?"

Sarah nodded.

"But if he took off his mask after you were married, why didn't you just leave him?"

"It's complicated," Sarah said, positioning another carrot in the three usable fingers on her right hand so she could peel it with her left. "I didn't have anyplace to go, and no money even if there *had* been relatives I could run to." She stopped peeling and smiled. "That's part of why I fell in love with you and Tucker. I've always wanted to be part of a big family."

Delaney smiled back. "And now you are. You've got us and Daddy, and Ethan and Paul and Gramps, and you've got a new baby on the way."

Sarah stopped peeling again.

Delaney smiled. "I know what morning sickness is."

"Please don't say anything to Tucker," Sarah pleaded.

"There's enough craziness going on around here without adding my pregnancy to the mix."

Delaney held up her hand with three fingers pointed at the ceiling. "Scout's promise," she said. "I'm old enough to babysit, and I'm willing to share my room with the baby." She suddenly frowned. "But what about your camps? How will you run them with a new baby?"

"I'll hire help." Sarah gave her a crooked smile. "You ever think about working at a sporting camp?"

"I can do that," Delaney said, straightening her shoulders. "If the pay's good."

"I pay top dollar for good workers. The girl helping me on Crag Island was only thirteen years old. You remember meeting Karen last August, don't you?"

"She was kind of shy. I tried to get her to explore the tidal pools with me, but she said she had to get home right after she got done with work."

"Karen comes from a large, very poor family. She's the youngest of six kids, and she's always been intimidated by the children who stayed at my inn, because she thought they were rich and . . . and more worldly than she was. I know how she felt, because I felt the same way when I was growing up," Sarah softly confessed as she started peeling again.

"And that's why you came here to live with us—because you figured our woods would be just as safe as your island."

Sarah gaped at Delaney. From the mouths of babes, as they say. *Was* that why she had come here? Was she really afraid of venturing into the big world, as Alex had suggested?

The buzzer on the stove told them the brownies were

done, heavy footsteps came tramping through the door like stampeding cattle, and Sarah blinked wildly to fight back tears as she vigorously started peeling again. Dammit, she hadn't been fooling anyone but herself. There obviously wasn't one feisty, confident bone in her body.

"We're not here for supper," Alex said, giving her a cold and likely greasy kiss on the cheek. "We're done with the delimber and the older skidder, so now we're heading over to get the tree harvester from Porter. We'll be back in two hours, three tops."

"I'm going with them," Tucker said, snatching a carrot off the table and biting into it. "I'm the radio man on the wide-load truck. It's my job to watch out for mailboxes, so they don't get flattened by the rear wheels of the trailer."

"Make sure you do a good job then," Sarah said, rubbing a smudge of grease off his face. "Because I'm betting your daddy will dock your pay for every mailbox that gets flattened."

Tucker swung to face his father. "Will you?"

Alex nodded, his expression serious. "One dollar a box. You and Delaney okay here alone?" he asked. "We should be home just after dark. We have to be off the main roads by sunset."

"Then get going," Sarah told him, giving him a shove when he stole one of her carrots. "We'll be fine."

"We're taking your SUV, but the plow truck is here if you need it."

"We'll be fine," she repeated, shoving him again. She looked at Ethan and Paul standing by the door, holding steaming brownies in their hands. Grady was by the sink, popping pieces of raw turnip into his mouth. "If you don't all get out of here, there won't be anything left for supper."

Every male in the room scrambled out the door except Alex. He bent close to her ear and whispered, "You better not fall asleep on me tonight. We're just getting to the good part of our novel, where Duncan is sneaking Willow out of the house to take her on the schooner so he can get her alone." He darted a glance to see that Delaney was busy in the pantry, kissed Sarah on the lips, and whispered, "I'm learning a trick or two from Duncan."

Sarah shoved him away again, and Alex finally left, his laughter trailing behind him as she stared at the swaying curtains on the back door. That was another battle she'd lost, and for the last seven nights she'd had to lie in bed beside Alex and listen to him read Willow Foster and Duncan Ross's story out loud. Sarah figured her cheeks were permanently stained from blushing so much.

Tuesday morning arrived with a cold, wind-driven snow, and Sarah was glad the sun wasn't shining, since her eyes were still sensitive to bright light. She could see quite well now, since she was putting on the salve herself instead of letting Alex administer it in globs. As for morning sickness, well, some mornings she woke up fine, and sometimes she barely made it to the bathroom in time.

She felt pretty good this morning as she lounged in bed and watched Alex dress. The guy wasn't at all shy about parading around their bedroom naked. In fact, Sarah suspected he did it on purpose.

She had tried parading around naked herself a few

mornings ago just to tease him but had found herself right back in bed when Alex had jumped up and started making love to her before they'd even hit the sheets. Everyone had been sitting at the kitchen table, eating cold cereal and looking sorry for themselves, when she and Alex had finally made it downstairs half an hour later.

"You're not dressing for work," Sarah said when she saw Alex slip into the silk undershirt he usually wore for ice fishing.

He turned to face her as he pulled on silk long-john bottoms. "Ethan's leaving for Loon Cove Lumber today, and Grady and Paul don't need me to help the crew clean up at our old cutting. So I thought I'd take a little hike up that trail on Whistler's Mountain before we move our equipment over there tomorrow."

Sarah sat up, holding the blankets to her naked chest. "Why? I thought that trail didn't lead anywhere."

"I saw a map at your sporting lodge that showed caves up there." He turned to rummage through his sock drawer. "I just want to check them out and see if there's been any traffic on that trail."

"Alone?"

He turned with his socks in his hand. "It only takes one person to look around."

"Daniel Reed should be that person. Or someone from the border patrol."

Alex walked over and sat down on the edge of the bed so he could brush her hair off her face. "I'll stay out of trouble, Sunshine. If I find anything up there that doesn't look right, I promise I'll come straight home and call John and Daniel. But things have been pretty quiet around here lately, and there's a good chance the bad guys have moved on since they haven't been successful shutting us down."

"I still don't like it. And why not take one of the snowmobiles?"

"Too noisy," he said. "Snowshoes are quiet and just as quick when the terrain is rugged."

"Ethan can go to Loon Cove tomorrow. Take him with you."

Alex bent over and pulled on his socks. "I'm not giving Ethan any excuses to avoid going to Loon Cove." He straightened, leaned back on one elbow, and tugged on her hair. "You're sounding very wifely this morning. Careful, Sunshine, or I might think you've finally decided to accept my marriage proposal but just forgot to tell me."

Sarah rolled out of bed, grabbed her nightgown off the floor where it had landed last night, and kept her back to him as she slipped it over her head. She heard him sigh and walk around the bed just before he took hold of her shoulders and turned her to face him.

"Just tell me what you're afraid of, so I can fix it."

"I'm not a piece of equipment you can fix. I have to fix myself."

"But fix what? What's keeping you from taking that final step?"

"Twelve years of conditioning can't be erased in seven weeks."

"Ah," he murmured, gently folding her into his arms. "Then if it takes another twelve years, I'll wait. As long as you stay here and give me a chance to compete with your demons."

Sarah slid her arms around his waist and buried her face in his silk shirt. "My hero," she said with a sigh.

Alex kissed her breathless, lifting her off her feet and carrying her over to the bed. Sarah rolled away the minute her back touched the sheets and scrambled off the opposite side. "Oh, no you don't," she said, pointing at him. "We will not be late for breakfast again. I couldn't stop blushing all morning the last time."

He puffed out his chest. "We heroes like making our women blush."

Sarah grabbed the romance novel on the nightstand and threw it at him. He caught it in midair and turned it faceup, thumbing through it until he came to a dog-eared page. *"He captured her hands, gently pinning them over her head as he leaned back and looked down at her so fiercely, Willow stopped breathing. His dark emerald gaze—"*

"You marked the sex scenes!" Sarah yelped, rushing over and swiping the book out of his hands. "You pervert," she snapped, opening their bedroom door and heading down the hall, the sound of Alex's laughter following her into the bathroom.

Chapter Twenty-four

❈

Two hours later, the snow had stopped, but the wind continued to howl down from the threatening sky. The house felt unusually empty, and Sarah felt unusually edgy, to the point that she hadn't answered the phone both times it had rung. Worried about Alex, she was in no mood to talk to anyone, much less deal with brokers trying to find the last skidder engine and truck motor.

There wasn't anything worth watching on all one hundred and fifty satellite channels, and every country-western video that came on was too damn maudlin. Sarah finally sat down on the couch with her sewing scissors and started snipping off the bandage on her right hand. Surely she could remove most of the gauze around the two metal splints in a way that would let her use her fingers for more than propping up stuff.

The phone rang again, but Sarah ignored it and kept snipping, again letting the answering machine pick up.

She heard Grady's message, silence, a click, and then the dial tone, just like the first two times. "Get a phone book and look up the right number," she told whoever had hung up as she continued to snip.

It took her twenty minutes, but Sarah was finally satisfied. She held up her right hand and opened and closed her thumb and first two fingers, thankful that it was her ring and pinky fingers she'd broken. Now she could do some real sewing.

When she heard some snowmobiles pulling into the dooryard, she frowned. They must be lost. She walked into the kitchen but stopped when she saw three men pulling off their helmets as they climbed off three snowmobiles.

Two of them were the men who had chased her through the woods! Sarah looked at the doorknob and noticed the door wasn't locked. She ducked down, scurried over, and twisted the dead bolt. Staying bent over, she headed back through the great-room door, turning to stop it from swinging just as the men stomped onto the back porch.

"I called three times," she heard someone say, the voice muted through the two doors. "No one's home, I tell you."

"I'm still checking the place out," another voice said

Sarah heard the doorknob rattling, first softly, then violently, and decided that pretending no one was home might be wise. She grabbed the portable phone and ran up the stairs. She rushed into her and Alex's bedroom but froze when she heard wood splintering and the back door crashing open.

Sarah dropped to the floor and slid under the bed. She

tugged the quilt down to hide her and hoped they would quickly find what they wanted and leave.

Something crashed downstairs. "Jesus, we're not here to loot the place," a menacing voice said almost directly beneath her, which told Sarah they were in the kitchen. Then she heard the swinging door snap back on its hinges and bang into a chair, followed by heavy footsteps in the great room. Something else fell to the floor with a dull thud, and then Sarah heard someone walking up the stairs.

Don't panic. Don't panic, she told herself, trying to dial 911, only to realize there wasn't a dial tone. That must have been the phone's base she'd heard crashing to the floor when they'd ripped it out of the jack. Sarah sucked in her breath when she saw a pair of boots walk past her bedroom door. She heard the boots go into Tucker's room and then Delaney's, and she felt like throwing up.

"Come on!" someone shouted from the foot of the stairs. "The place is empty. We need to get out of here."

But the man continued to work his way methodically back down the hall, going into every bedroom and even the bathroom, opening and closing doors, before finally walking into Sarah's bedroom. Not even daring to breathe, she waited for what seemed like forever while he looked in her closet before finally walking back into the hall. Sarah closed her eyes and balled her hands to control her trembling. She'd almost hidden in that closet!

"We can at least take a couple of these guns," she heard someone call out from Grady's office. "Some look expensive."

Glass shattered in the office, and the man searching Ethan's bedroom ran down the stairs. Sarah's stomach lurched when the floor beneath her shook with his heavy footsteps.

"Grab what you can carry on the sleds, and let's get out of here," one of the men shouted, sounding as if he was running from the kitchen into the great room. "It's gonna move fast through this old relic. We'll go out the front and leave the door open to feed it."

Feed it? *What* was going to move fast?

"There," somebody said in a loud growl just as Sarah heard a crackling sound coming from the kitchen. "That ought to keep the bastards out of our hair for the rest of the winter. Come on, Spencer's waiting up at the caves."

A stark silence descended over the lodge, broken only by an ominous snapping sound that turned Sarah's trembling to violent shudders. As the three snowmobiles started up with high-pitched whines and sped away, the crackling grew louder, and Sarah got a whiff of smoke as it swirled up the stairs.

Oh, God—they set the house on fire! They'd meant the *fire* would move fast!

Sarah bumped her head on the box spring when she scrambled out from under the bed and quickly ran down the stairs, over to the front door, and slammed it shut. She rushed through the thickening smoke to the kitchen, pushed open the swinging door, and was met by a solid wall of flames. She cried out in surprise and spun back toward the front door, only to see flames licking at the windows and the door on the front porch. They had set fires on both sides of the house.

"Oh, my God, the caves!" Sarah cried, rushing into Grady's office. Alex was headed to the caves. He was headed straight to their hiding spot!

She tripped on something lying on the floor, fell to her knees with a startled yelp, and discovered she'd tripped on a shotgun. She grabbed it and scrambled to her feet just as a loud explosion came from the kitchen, shaking the floor beneath her. She made sure the shotgun wasn't the one without the firing pin, ran to the gun cabinet, grabbed a fistful of shotgun shells, and stuffed them into her pocket. Blinking against the smoke filling the office and starting to cough uncontrollably, she used the butt of the shotgun to break out one of the windows, threw the gun outside, and slid out behind it. She pawed through the deep snow to find the shotgun, then headed toward the machine shed, shielding her face from the wind-whipped flames shooting out of the downstairs bedroom window.

Once inside the machine shed, Sarah ran to the phone on the back wall, praying the fire hadn't reached the phone lines yet. She dialed 911. "This is Sarah Knight from Oak Grove," she said the moment an operator came on the line. "Our house is burning."

"Knight, you said?" the man asked as Sarah heard a keyboard clicking. "In Oak Grove?"

"Yes. We're eight miles out on the private Knight road by the general store. But tell the firemen they have to turn left seven miles out. Hurry! The house is fully engulfed."

"Anyone inside?"

"No, everyone's out. Can you get hold of Sheriff Tate and tell him that Alex Knight is up on Whistler's Mountain and that the smugglers are heading up there right now? Tell him he needs to hurry. Wait, call Daniel Reed, too! And the border patrol, and tell them the same thing."

"Just a minute, lady," the man said calmly. "You have both a structure fire and . . . did you say smugglers?"

"Yes! The smugglers set the fire. And they're going by snowmobile up to the caves on Whistler's Mountain. You have to tell John Tate and Daniel Reed that Alex Knight is also up there. You got that?"

The keyboard pounded furiously. "I got it, lady. Where are you calling from?"

"I'm in the garage next to the house."

"Get out of there," the dispatcher calmly ordered. "Walk down the road several hundred yards, and wait for the fire trucks to arrive."

"How long before John and Daniel can get up to Whistler's Mountain?"

"Quickest they can be out there is half an hour, maybe even an hour, depending on where they are. Leave the phone off the hook, and get out of the garage right now," he said.

"Okay." Sarah dropped the receiver and looked around the machine shed. Even half an hour was too long! Which meant it was up to her to warn Alex.

Unless she could stop the men before they reached the caves. Sarah eyed the skidder in the garage. It wasn't Alex's Mean Green Machine; this was their newer skidder, the one waiting for some stupid part.

Sarah grabbed the shotgun she'd set next to the phone and prayed the skidder wasn't missing anything critical as she climbed up the ladder and opened the cab door. She tucked the shotgun inside and sat down, then frowned at the dash. Damn. Some of the dials and gauges were different.

But she could do this; she *had* to do this. Alex's life depended on her.

Sarah turned the key and held down the starter button until the yellow monster came awake with a grinding sputter that slowly smoothed to a deep-throated idle. But when she looked up, she saw that she'd forgotten to open the overhead doors. "Double damn," she hissed as she eyed the pedals, trying to remember Alex's lesson. Sarah pushed down on what she hoped was the clutch, then shoved the hand throttle all the way up, filling the machine shed with dark, smelly exhaust as the deafening roar of the powerful engine bounced off the walls and ceiling. She ground the gears trying to engage them, took a deep breath, then popped the clutch and smashed right through the doors. She quickly turned the wheel once she opened her eyes and steered the shuddering, screaming monster past the burning Knight homestead.

It took every bit of concentration she possessed to stay between the snowbanks, as well as a few prayers and some luck, but Sarah quickly reached the main hauling artery and turned right.

Dammit, where was the tachometer? The engine sounded as if it was going to explode. "Don't blow up, don't blow up," she begged the large diesel engine, which screamed in protest as she swerved down the road toward the new cutting site.

She almost missed the turnoff because of the wind blowing snow off the trees, causing nearly white-out conditions. Sarah cut the wheel to make the turn without even touching the brake. The skidder protested the sudden change of direction, its blunt chains digging into the icy road. The two left wheels lifted off the ground when the skidder slammed into the snowbank, before dropping back onto all four wheels with a jarring thud.

The skidder shook and shimmied and slowly inched its way out of the snowbank. "Come on!" Sarah shouted, slapping the steering wheel impatiently. She yelped in triumph when it finally broke free and concentrated on steering as she roared up the winding narrow road toward the stream where she and Alex had shot grades.

Oh, God, the stream! Well, if she could get across it, this huge skidder sure as hell could. She approached the sharp corner much too fast, bounced off first one and then another snowbank when she overcorrected, and straightened out just as she sped over a knoll—and saw three snowmobiles sitting in the middle of the road.

She recognized them as the arsonists, two of whom were standing beside their snowmobiles, staring at her in shock, as the other guy bent over Alex's sled on top of a snowbank, doing something to its engine.

Sarah aimed the skidder straight at the three smugglers' snowmobiles, not closing her eyes until she heard the explosive crunch of metal connecting with metal. The skidder reared up as its massive tires rolled onto the sleds, bucking violently when it crushed them with a sickening screech. When Sarah finally opened her eyes, she realized that not only was she heading toward the frozen brook, but the collision hadn't even slowed down the skidder.

She heard shouts behind her and guessed the men had jumped clear. Sarah screamed when something suddenly shattered the rear window above her head, and she instinctively ducked. Another sharp crack exploded through the air, and something ricocheted off the metal beam to her left, showering the cab with glass from the door window.

Holy smokes, they were shooting at her!

Sarah had a good mind to turn around and take another run at them. But she cut the wheel to the right instead and plowed into the woods—just as another bullet hit the skidder's solid metal frame. Sarah pulled the hand throttle all the way back to slow down once she was in the woods, yet the engine continued to race.

The skidder wouldn't slow down. She ran over small trees, managed to dodge most of the larger ones, and bounced off those she couldn't dodge, until the forest suddenly opened onto a trail rising up the side of the mountain.

The trail wasn't much wider than her yellow monster, but she was getting damn good at steering. Her heart lurched when she spotted Alex's snowshoe tracks.

"Okay, Hero Man," she sang out as she steered up the center of the narrow trail like a seasoned logger. "Let's see if I can't save you from the bad gu—" The roof of the cab suddenly slammed into a thick branch overhanging the trail.

But the skidder kept on growling forward, seemingly undamaged other than the spidery cracks in the windshield. "Oh, yeah!" Sarah shouted. "Who said heroines can't rescue their heroes?"

Alex stopped in the middle of the single snowmobile track he'd been following and looked back with a frown, absently unzipping his jacket to release some of the heat his climb had built up. He kept catching a whiff of smoke now and then, and it was puzzling him. He was too far from home to be smelling wood smoke from their hearth, even if the wind was blowing from that direction. And a forest fire was virtually unheard of in the middle of the winter, unless . . . unless it had been intentionally set.

Alex retraced his tracks a short distance down the mountain to a high knoll, then stopped to look at the forest below. He could barely make out Frost Lake, since his elevation was just touching the low-hanging clouds, and what forest he could see looked fine. But then he caught another whiff of smoke at about the same time as he heard the distant, muted sound of a large engine coming from the direction of their main hauling artery.

Had Grady decided to move their equipment today instead of tomorrow? But they had to clean up their old logging yard first, and that should have taken the entire day. The deep, heavy whine sounded as if it was moving closer, and Alex recognized it as a skidder engine. It was on the road of their new site now, but something wasn't right. The pitch was off—instead of the give and take of a working skidder, this one sounded as if it was traveling at full throttle without a load behind it. In fact, it reminded Alex of his hair-raising ride with Sarah the day he'd discovered she didn't know the first thing about driving.

The skin tightened on the back of his neck.

No. It couldn't be. Sarah was home safe and sound, probably elbow deep in a bowl of dough as she watched one of her cooking shows. She was not climbing Whistler's Mountain in a skidder. The one in the machine shed had an electrical problem, and he wasn't even sure it would start.

A loud crash rolled up the mountain toward him like muted thunder, and Alex flinched when it was followed by three sharp gunshots. Shit! Paul must be trying to find him because the smugglers had set the forest on fire!

Alex repositioned the rifle strap across his chest and started tramping back down the mountain, going as fast as his broad snowshoes would allow. But he stopped less than five minutes later when he realized the skidder was heading up the trail toward him, snapping off trees in its path, the engine revving so violently he expected it to throw a rod at any moment.

The ground began rumbling beneath him as the air filled with an increasingly loud roar, and Alex decided he'd better get the hell out of the way. He tramped well off the trail and into the protection of trees just as the large yellow skidder crested the rocky knoll not twenty yards away. He jumped behind a large tree and covered his face with his arms to protect himself from the rocks, tree limbs, and chunks of ice the tires churned up as the skidder went roaring past.

Alex could only gape in disbelief—his crazy, suicidal wife was behind the wheel! And the really scary part was, he didn't know if she was actually controlling the skidder or just hanging on for dear life.

He stepped back onto the trail and quickly tramped after her, torn between putting the woman over his knee when he caught up with her or kissing her until he stopped shaking—about a hundred years from now.

Alex heard a sickening crash up ahead, followed by the sounds of snapping branches and smashing boulders. He broke into a run and saw the skidder jammed up against a giant pine tree, its four massive tires still chewing up the frozen ground and spewing debris into the air.

He swiftly unlaced his snowshoes and kicked them off, then ran over and jumped onto the skidder's ladder. Sarah was frantically yanking on the throttle with her bandaged hand and pushing every damn button on the dash with her other one.

"The electrical system shorted out!" he shouted over the roar, grabbing the cab door as the skidder dangerously chittered sideways toward the cliff. "Just sit still!" he hollered, working his way forward to reach the cowling covering the engine. He didn't dare risk pulling Sarah out while the tires were churning, afraid her clothes might get caught in the chains and she'd be pulled beneath them.

Ignoring the heat billowing from the overworked engine, Alex threw open the hood and started ripping out wires, nearly falling into the grinding front wheel when the machine suddenly lurched sideways.

Sarah grabbed his coat sleeve with a scream of warning and tried to tug him back over the ladder. But Alex kept ripping out every wire he could reach, until the large diesel motor gave one last shudder and sputtered to a coughing death. He then reached through the broken window into the cab, plucked Sarah out of her seat, and jumped to the ground—just before the lifeless skidder began to roll backward, its right rear tire sliding off the edge of the cliff.

As Alex backed up the trail with Sarah safely tucked against him, the other three tires slowly lifted into the air with a groan of twisting metal. As if watching a film in slow motion, Alex saw the skidder tilt, turn belly-up, and then disappear over the edge. Trees snapped and boulders shattered as the ten-ton machine rolled down the steep embankment, the loud crashing thuds suddenly stopping with a sickening silence.

Alex tightened his hold on Sarah, unable to get the image out of his head of her rolling down the mountain with it. If he'd been two seconds longer getting her out, she'd be dead now.

Chapter Twenty-five

❄

Sarah twisted and squirmed until she could face Alex and grab the front of his jacket. "It's the smugglers!" she told him. "They burned our house and are headed up to the caves where somebody named Spencer is waiting for them. We have to get out of here!" she cried, tugging harder when Alex didn't even acknowledge he'd heard her. "Come on!"

But he still wouldn't budge or say anything; he just mutely lowered his gaze to hers, his face ashen gray and his dark navy eyes haunted.

Sarah smacked his chest. "There's *three* of them, Alex. We have to get out of here!"

He finally moved, only to grab her shoulders and violently shake her before crushing her against him, his arms locking around her like a vise.

"Alex," she yelped into his jacket, squirming to get free. "Will you listen to me? I smashed their snowmobiles down at the stream, but they're going to come after us. And they have guns!"

His arms only tightened more, and Sarah was forced to quit struggling because she couldn't breathe. She could still hear, though, and Alex's heart was pounding so violently it hurt her ears.

Then he suddenly started pulling her over to the large pine tree she had driven the skidder into in order to stop it. Sarah dug in her heels to explain they had to get off the trail, but she snapped her mouth shut when Alex turned and gave her a lethal look. He let her go to pull his rifle off, appearing ready to pounce if she so much as blinked. He took off his jacket next, mutely stuffed her into it, then zipped it up to her chin. Still silent, he took her hand again and led her around the tree, then forced her down against the back side of the trunk.

Sarah's breath caught when he hunched down and she found herself looking into his dangerous eyes. "I need you to stay here," he said ever so softly. "You got that, Sarah?"

Sarah said nothing, merely pressing into the tree when he brought his face even closer.

"No matter what happens, no matter what you hear, you stay curled up here like a rabbit hiding from a pack of wolves until I get back."

"But—"

"*You need to stay here until I come back for you, Sarah.*"

She nodded.

"Good," he said, standing up to look past the tree at the trail. He turned back to her, his face chiseled from granite and his eyes even harder. "If they get this far, all they'll see is the mess the skidder made. They might come close enough to look over the edge of the cliff, but they won't be able to see you back here."

He reached down and picked up his rifle, then slung it over his back. "They won't bother looking for you once they see that skidder down in the ravine. You stay perfectly quiet and still, and they'll think you went over the cliff with it." He hunched down in front of her again, this time his hand spanning her face more gently. "You understand what I need you to do, Sarah? No matter what you hear in the next couple of hours, and no matter what those men say if they do make it this far, you can't let them know you're alive."

"Wh-what are you going to do?"

He merely stood to look up and down the trail again. Sarah rose to her feet, but Alex spun around in warning, and she immediately halted. Good God, he was angry.

Sarah reached out and touched his chest. "I know I just gave you a terrible scare," she quietly told him. "And that you don't like how I put myself in danger coming up here to warn you. But, Alex, no one else could get here in time. There wasn't anything else I could do. And at least they're on foot now, thanks to me."

His eyes narrowed, and his face darkened, but then he suddenly covered her hand on his chest and blew out a ragged breath. "You're not going to stay here and hide like I want, are you?"

"I would try very hard to stay here," she said, "because I understand your need to know that I'm safe so you can concentrate on the bad guys." She shook her head. "But no, I can't just sit up here while you go after them alone."

"You need to trust me, Sarah."

"I *do* trust you."

"Then let me take things from here, Sunshine. Do as I ask, and I'll be back within the hour, I promise."

Sarah suddenly remembered the man named Spencer up at the caves. She nodded and started to turn back to the large pine, but Alex stopped her by squeezing her hand. "Promise me," he whispered.

"I promise," she said, rising on her toes to give him a kiss on the chin, then giving him a nudge. "So get going, already."

He stood watching while she tucked herself between two of the pine's massive roots, then settled a few broken branches around her to conceal her further from the trail before hunching down to cup her cheek. "I promise I'll be back, Sarah," he said softly. "We haven't finished our novel yet. I still don't know if Willow is going to marry Duncan."

"Of course she is," Sarah whispered, leaning into his hand. "It's a romance novel. Everyone always lives happily ever after."

His intense gaze locked on hers, Alex slowly shook his head. "I'm not so certain about that. There's a chance Willow is too afraid to risk her heart."

"She will. Sh-she loves him."

"You sure about that?"

Sarah cupped her hand over his. "I'm sure,"

Alex rubbed his thumb across her lips, kissed her forehead, then stood up and walked around the tree. Sarah bent forward to see him scuffing over their footprints with a branch he'd picked up, backing away until he reached his snowshoes. Then he looked at her. "I'm counting on you to stay safe, Sarah."

"Only if you do the same," she said, waving him away.

Alex picked up his snowshoes and started jogging down the trail toward the smugglers. Sarah watched until he was out of sight, then leaned back against the tree and closed her eyes, hugging her knees to her chest to stop her shaking. Yeah, she would stay here—but only because she needed to guard Alex's back. The man up at the caves wasn't getting past her, no way!

A fistful of snow blew off an overhead branch and landed inside her collar, the wind carrying the acrid smell of the Knight lodge burning flat to the ground. Sarah buried her face in her hands. She'd achieved her goal of warning Alex, and if she had insisted on going with him, she probably *would* have gotten in his way. So she stayed curled in a ball and prayed for her husband's safe return while she guarded the trail leading up to the caves.

Her head snapped up at the sound of a gunshot not ten minutes later, the sharp noise echoing up the mountainside. It was followed by another shot less than five minutes later, then two more in rapid succession just minutes after that, the piercing echoes fading to an ominous silence. As the chill wind howled in the trees, Sarah shuddered in fear. Had Alex been shot? Had he been forced to shoot those men?

A few minutes later, she realized she was no longer hearing just the wind but the distant whine of a snowmobile engine. Only it wasn't coming from below, it was coming from above her. Sarah tucked herself into the pine's large roots as the snowmobile drew closer and watched as the speeding sled came to a stop not thirty feet from where she was hiding.

With the sound of the idling engine covering any

noise she might make, Sarah turned and watched the lone man get off and walk over to the edge of the cliff.

Okay, it was now or never. She could do this. She *could*. Sarah moved around the pine and silently crept up behind the man just as he stepped forward to look over the edge—and shoved him with all her might.

The guy spun around off-balance with a shout of surprise, waved his arms like windmills, and fell back into empty air. Feeling as horrified as he had looked, Sarah watched him tumble down the steep hill, bouncing off bushes and snow-covered outcroppings, until he came to an abrupt halt against the mangled skidder. With a sense of surreal detachment and no small amount of guilt, she saw him slowly sit up and try to stand, then fall back and grab his twisted leg.

Relieved that she hadn't killed him, Sarah eyed the snowmobile sitting in the middle of the trail, quietly idling. Then she looked down the trail, trying to gauge how much time had passed, flinching when another single shot suddenly cracked up the mountain.

Should she go after Alex or stay up here out of his way? She'd only promised to stay here in order to cover his back—and she had accomplished that quite nicely, hadn't she? Sarah walked over to the snowmobile, slid her leg over the seat, and grasped the handlebars.

Damn, nothing looked familiar. She didn't know which lever was the throttle or which one was the brake. She finally settled her right thumb over the right lever and her left fingers over the long lever on that side and squeezed both hands closed. The snowmobile shot forward, and she grabbed at the handlebars to keep from falling backward, just as the engine died and the sled came to a skidding stop, sending her forward into the handlebars with a grunt of surprise.

"Now I've stalled the damn thing," she muttered, searching the dash for the key, which she finally found and turned. Nothing happened. The sled remained silent beneath her. Well, that decided whether or not she'd stay put.

Then Sarah caught the distant wail of sirens coming from the main hauling road from town, and her heart lifted with hope.

She had told the dispatcher to tell John and Daniel the smugglers were on Whistler's Mountain. And when she heard one lone siren break away from the others and turn up the road to the new site, she smiled broadly. Help was on the way—she only hoped that John Tate had arrived in time.

Alex wiped the blood running into his eye and stepped out of the woods, just as the sheriff's cruiser came to a skidding halt in front of the tangle of snowmobiles littering the road. John climbed out of his car, and Alex walked across the frozen brook to meet him, avoiding the area where Sarah's skidder had broken the ice.

"What in hell went on here?" John asked, assessing the snowmobiles before turning his gaze on Alex. "I hope that blood belongs to someone else."

"Some of it's mine," Alex said raggedly. He jerked his thumb toward the woods. "But most of it is from one of the two men I shot about half a mile up the trail."

"They dead?"

Alex shrugged. "I got the bleeding stopped on one of them, but without medical help, he'll likely die from exposure within an hour."

"And the other one?" John asked.

Alex shrugged again. "There's also a third guy, but last I saw, the bastard wasn't having much luck outrunning the rock slide I started." Alex strode over to his undamaged snowmobile sitting on the snowbank. "Sarah's still up there, John," he said, straddling the seat and taking the key out of his pocket. "And she mentioned a fourth guy waiting up at the caves."

But just as Alex started to put the key in the ignition, he noticed the wires hanging out of the side of the hood. "Shit," he hissed, lifting the hood to find that they'd cut the plug wires.

He felt a hand on his shoulder. "Reed's on his way," John said. "He'll have his snowmobile in the back of his pickup. Where is she? Is she hurt?"

"I hid her behind a pine tree about two miles up the trail," Alex told him, climbing off the sled and walking toward the brook. "We can't wait for Daniel. The guy up at the caves must have heard the gunshots."

John stopped him. "Listen. That's a truck coming," he said, looking past his car. "It could be Daniel," he added, drawing his gun as a precaution.

Daniel Reed came tearing up the road in his pickup, slamming on the brakes behind the cruiser and jumping out of his truck. "What's going on?" he asked.

"We need to go after Sarah," Alex said as he ran to the back of Daniel's truck and started undoing the tethers holding the snowmobile in place. "I stashed her two miles up the trail, and there's supposed to be a fourth guy up at the caves. Back up to the snowbank," he ordered, jumping into the truck bed.

Daniel climbed into the cab and backed the truck up

to the snowbank, shut off the engine, and tossed the sled's keys to Alex. "We're going with you," he said, pulling his rifle from the gun rack in the rear window. "We'll drop you off at Sarah, then John and I will head up to the caves."

Alex started the snowmobile and backed it off the truck, then slid back on the seat to make room for John so that Daniel could squeeze in front of them to drive. Alex was more than willing to let the lawmen take care of the fourth guy. He was focused only on getting back to Sarah—hoping like hell she was still tucked behind that pine when they got there. If he lived to be a hundred, he'd never get the image out of his head of Sarah cresting that knoll at full throttle or of the skidder rolling over the side of the cliff just seconds after he'd gotten her out.

Alex snorted to himself just as the sled shot across the brook. Who was he kidding? The chances of finding Sarah still hiding behind that tree were about as good as hell freezing over. Which was why Alex wasn't at all surprised when they crested a knoll about a quarter-mile from the pine and saw his wife running down the trail toward them.

"Alex!" she shouted, rushing toward them. "Oh, my God, you're okay." She came to a skidding stop when he climbed off the sled and faced her. "You're covered in blood!" she cried. "You've been shot!"

"Only the blood on my face is mine," he growled, walking over and taking hold of her shoulders. "Dammit, Sarah, you're supposed to be hiding," he snapped, using every bit of willpower he possessed not to shake her.

"I heard the sirens," she snapped back. "And I

thought—" She stopped with a choked cry and threw herself at his chest.

Daniel and John walked up to them, and Alex spoke over Sarah's head as he hugged her against him. "We'll be fine here," he told them. "Keep going."

Sarah's head popped up. "It's not over?" she asked, looking at Daniel and John.

"Alex mentioned a fourth man up at the caves," John said. "We'll go deal with him."

"He's not there," Sarah informed them, effectively stopping the two lawmen.

Alex closed his eyes on a deep sigh. Why wasn't he surprised? "Do you happen to know *where* he is?" he asked.

"He's at the bottom of the cliff," she said softly. "I think he broke his leg when he, ah . . . when he tripped and fell over the edge."

Alex counted to ten, but when that didn't work, he simply pulled Sarah against him as Daniel grabbed a coil of rope off his sled and trotted up the trail toward the cliff with John. "You're going to be the death of me, Sunshine," he growled into her hair.

Honest to God, he wanted to . . . he wanted to . . . aww, hell! "Dammit, Sarah, quit crying," he ordered, rubbing his thumbs across her tear-stained cheeks. "And tell me where you're hurt."

"In here," she cried, thumping her chest. "In my heart."

"Your heart?" he repeated in alarm. "You're having a heart attack?"

"Yes," she said, glaring up at him. "And *you* gave it to me. You scared me spitless, you jerk!" she shouted. "And if you don't quit growling at me and tell me you love me right now, I *will* die."

Relief washed through him. "I seem to remember saying that hell would be covered in three feet of snow before I'd say those words to you."

Sarah suddenly gave him a smile that made him go weak in the knees. "I've been sitting in hell for the last hour—and the snow looks about three feet deep to me."

He started to tell her the words she wanted to hear, then snorted. "Oh, no you don't. That smile isn't going to work this time, Sarah. You're not distracting me from the fact that you probably helped that guy over the edge of the cliff. Not to mention that you had no business coming up here in a skidder in the first place."

"Even if I came up here to tell you what I've decided?"

Alex groaned. Following his skidder over the cliff might be safer than hitching himself to this maddening woman for the next fifty years. He ran his fingers up the back of her neck into her hair. "So what have you decided?"

"That I want a honeymoon."

"What?"

"In England. Then I want to take one of those hovercraft ferries to Europe and make the grand tour."

Alex opened his mouth, but nothing came out.

"We'll have to go in the summer when the kids aren't in school," she continued, "because they're going with us. They need to realize there's a big, wonderful world outside these woods." She frowned. "But it'll have to be next year, because I'll be too pregnant this summer."

Alex looked toward the cliff, then looked back at Sarah, who was smiling up at him again. "Say it," he demanded as he pulled her toward him.

"I love you, Alex Knight."

"I love you, Sarah Knight," he said at the same time, just before covering her mouth with his.

And damn if she didn't kiss him back with all the passion of one hell of a feisty woman. Alex folded her against him and deepened the kiss, letting her know just how glad he was about her decision—that is, until she muttered something into his mouth.

He leaned back. "Now what?"

"You taste like blood," she said, still succeeding in keeping him off-guard with that damn smile as she reached up and touched the crusted cut on his forehead. "I think it's time we headed home, don't you?" She suddenly sobered. "But we don't have a home to go to anymore. They burned it down."

He gave her an encouraging smile. "Your sporting lodge is about to have its first guests, Mrs. Knight. We'll move everyone over there."

"But Delaney and Tucker will be devastated. They've lost everything but the clothes they wore to school today."

"We'll make them see this as an adventure."

"And all your mother's beautiful things—Grady's going to think he's lost Rose all over again."

"Grady's tougher than all of us put together," Alex assured her, looping his arm around her shoulders to guide her up the trial. "His grandfather came here from Norway seventy years ago with nothing more than a double-bladed axe and a hundred dollars in gold." He looked over at her and bobbed his eyebrows. "You didn't know you fell in love with a Viking, did you?"

She gave him a sultry smile. "I've read a few Viking romance novels."

"Really? I wouldn't mind reading a story with a Viking hero. Out loud, of course," he added with a wink, only to stop short when he spotted the fourth man's snowmobile sitting half off the trail, its nose buried up to the windshield in the bushes. He looked down at Sarah and stifled a sigh. "I suppose you're going to tell me that just before he *tripped* over the edge, the guy crashed his sled into the trees?"

She gave him a maddeningly guileless smile. "Lucky for us he's a bit of a klutz, huh?"

"Why don't you take Sarah down on the guy's sled?" John suggested, walking over to them as he brushed snow off his pants from his climb out of the ravine. "Then you can take my cruiser to the hospital and get both of you checked over. We'll haul this guy up and bring him down on Daniel's sled. I radioed for backup, and when they get here, we'll find the other three men."

Alex led Sarah over to the snowmobile, yanked it out of the bushes so that it was pointed down the trail, and turned the key.

"I broke—I mean, *it* broke when it crashed," she said when it didn't start.

Alex reached down on the handlebars, lifted the emergency kill switch, turned the key again, and the engine immediately started.

Sarah glared at the button on the handlebars. "What did you do?"

"The *guy* must have accidentally hit the kill switch when he crashed," Alex explained, setting Sarah on the seat. He sat behind her. "This is the throttle," he said, placing her thumb over the lever on the right handlegrip. "And this is the brake," he added, placing her left fingers over the lever on the left handlegrip. "And that," he said, pointing to a dial on the dash, "is the tachometer. Try to keep it below 2500, will you?"

She turned to look at him over her shoulder. "You're going to let me drive us down?"

He lifted his feet onto the running boards, securing her legs inside his. "You managed a runaway skidder well enough. I think you can handle this little sled."

She shot him a beautific smile that outshone the sun, turned forward and nestled into his chest, and squeezed the throttle with all her might.

Alex winced at the pain in his right thumb wedged under the throttle, and kept his left hand within inches of the kill switch as his heroine wife finished rescuing him.

Chapter Twenty-six

❦

S*arah couldn't seem to* get comfortable in the lumpy old chair; she couldn't stop fidgeting, needing to get up and *do* something. But after the sixth time Alex had threatened to tie her down, with Grady and Paul backing him up, she had decided to let the men deal with the results of living in a town full of generous people. The growing piles of donations included not only enough food to feed a small nation but also mattresses, bedding, personal items, and clothing. At the rate stuff was accumulating, the Knight household was going to have more possessions than it had before.

Most of it was stacked in the huge main room of the sporting lodge, spilling over into the kitchen while they waited for the electricity to be turned on and the whole lodge to be made livable.

The rooms upstairs needed to be cleaned; many of the old mattresses were filled with more mouse nests than stuffing, the windows were so dirty even light couldn't get through, and there were enough cobwebs hanging from the rafters to weave an entire wardrobe from spider silk. And the four bathrooms couldn't be used until the well was primed and the pipes flushed, which couldn't happen until the electricity got turned on. Sarah didn't even want to think about the condition of the kitchen. And the old furnace in the cellar hadn't run for five years and more than likely had racoons living in it. They were probably cousins to the racoons Alex had relocated from the kitchen to Cabin Eight this morning.

Along with the donations had come several offers for them to stay at different houses until the sporting lodge was habitable, but everyone had decided they didn't want to be separated. So the family being warm and safe and *together* was all that mattered.

"Earth to Sarah," Alex said, waving his hand in front of her face. "John and Daniel are here with some men from the border patrol," he told her once he had her attention.

"Huh? Oh!" she said, jumping up when she saw the four officers standing by the door. "Please, come in and sit down," she said, moving some of their new possessions off the couch so the men could sit.

Daniel had to nudge the guy in a border patrol uniform to get him moving, since he seemed unable to when Sarah gave him an apologetic smile.

"I'm sorry everything is such a mess, but it's going to take us a while to settle in," she told her guests as she cleaned off the other chair. "I can at least offer you cake and coffee," she finished, turning toward the kitchen.

Alex swept her off her feet and sat down in the chair,

then locked his arms around her so she couldn't leave his lap. "They aren't staying," he said as he gave some sort of silent signal to John Tate.

Sarah pinched his arm out of sight of the men, and Alex merely slid his thumb up her ribs, way too close to her breast. She got the message and immediately quit squirming. She smiled at their guests sitting on the couch and the opposite chair, the border patrol guy and the man in the suit quietly grinning at her.

"We just stopped by to let you know what we learned about the smuggling ring you two closed down yesterday," John said. "This is Peter Nadeau from the border patrol and Raymond Smith from Homeland Security."

"Homeland Security?" Sarah looked at the man in the three-piece suit, who appeared so out of place next to the three local law officers.

Raymond Smith nodded. "Yes, ma'am," he said, his expression turning serious. "I'm here because of the explosives the men were smuggling into the country."

"Explosives?" Alex said, his arms tightening around Sarah. "They were bringing in explosives?"

Smith nodded. "We've been hearing chatter for over a year that something was in the works, but we couldn't get anything specific—until John Tate called our office last night and told us we might want to see what he'd found in the caves on Whistler's Mountain."

Sarah frowned. "But why stash them up there? Why not just bring them to where the snowmobile trail crossed a road and load them into a car to take them to wherever they were going?"

"Because the explosives weren't going to be used until next summer, we've learned, and the people bringing them in wanted a remote site to stash them on their route. Next summer, they were going to bring in some men by the same route, pick up the explosives, and head to their targets." Smith looked at Alex. "What they hadn't counted on was for you to start cutting on Whistler's Mountain this winter."

"Then why not just move the explosives?" Alex asked.

Smith shrugged. "They'd been planning this for a couple of years, near as we can tell, and they probably thought they were dealing with a bunch of backwood nobodies they could scare off, rather than change their plans. You two are heroes. We'll never know how many lives you saved by stopping this pipeline of explosives and terrorists coming into the country. A lot of people likely owe you their lives, and your government owes you its gratitude."

"There was nothing altruistic about what we did. We were only protecting ourselves," Alex said.

"And to set the record straight," John Tate interjected, looking at Alex, "the guy who died actually shot himself. Near as we can tell, his finger jerked on the trigger when your bullet caught him in the leg, and he shot himself with his own gun." John leaned forward, his elbows on his knees. "The man at the bottom of the rockslide likely won't ever walk again, but he'll live. And we life-flighted out the other guy you shot in the leg."

Alex stood up. "I appreciate your driving out here to fill us in," he said to the four gentlemen, who rose and put on their coats.

After the men drove off, Alex pounced like a hungry lion, sweeping Sarah into his arms and striding down the porch steps to the short path leading toward the cabins.

"Where are we going?" she asked.

"As soon as I got rid of Paul and Grady and the kids this morning, I came over and built a fire in the stove," he said, leaping onto the porch of Cabin One.

"Why?"

He opened the door and stepped inside. "Because I need to get you naked and in bed in the next ten minutes," he said, covering her mouth with his own to kiss her quite thoroughly. "As much fun as it was sleeping in front of the hearth with everyone else last night, it was a little crowded. Tell me again that you love me."

"I love you."

"And that I'm your real, live hero."

"You're my *only* hero."

"Now we're getting somewhere," he said, laying her on the bed and pinning her down with his weight as he started to tell her exactly what he intended to do with her for the next two hours.

Sarah's eyes widened with each salacious and provocative description, wondering if some of them were even possible, as he ignited a bonfire deep inside her. She started to squirm beneath him, running her feet up his legs and twisting to free her hands to touch him.

"Feeling a bit hot and bothered, are we?" he whispered, sending an even stronger wave of desire crashing through Sarah when she felt his own desire pushing against her. "Well, Sunshine, let's see if we can't compose our own memorable love scene."

Alex stared down at his thoroughly exhausted and utterly satisfied wife with the smile of a very contented man. He softly kissed her forehead, then gazed up at the ceiling of the quaintly decorated cabin.

Sarah was determined to open the sporting camps come spring, and he intended to back her one hundred percent, even if it meant moving his kids three miles deeper into the woods. Grady and Ethan and Paul could rebuild on their old site, but Alex was keeping his expanding family right here so they could help Sarah realize her dream.

Besides, if he didn't get his brothers weaned off her cooking, they would never find wives of their own. Maybe they could even find Grady a woman.

Holy hell, he had to stop reading romance novels, or he'd be trying to marry off John and Daniel next!

A truck came skidding to a halt in the lodge yard, and Alex climbed out of bed with a sigh and started dressing. "Wake up, Sunshine," he told Sarah. "It's time to return to the real world."

"Who's home?" she asked, sitting up with a yawn and brushing the hair off her face just as a truck door slammed.

Alex put on his boots and looked out the window. "Dammit, Ethan's back," he said, checking his watch. "And it's only one o'clock. He didn't even last half a day at the sawmill!"

Alex opened the door and strode onto the porch of the cabin, buttoning his shirt as he gave a sharp whistle at Ethan. "What are you doing home?"

Ethan glared across the yard with his hands on his hips. "I was fired."

"Your first day?" Alex asked in disbelief as he tucked in his shirt. "How in hell can you screw up bucketing sawdust?"

"I never got to the sawdust," Ethan said, striding across

the yard and up onto the cabin porch. "In fact, I never even set foot inside the mill. I'd just come out of the office and was walking across the yard when I got fired."

"Bishop wouldn't fire you; he set it up for you to work there. And what happened to your face?" Alex asked, looking at Ethan's swollen left eye.

His brother gently touched the darkening bruise. "Bishop didn't fire me, his foreman did."

"Why?"

"Because I hit her."

"You *what?* Wait a minute. You hit a *woman?*"

Sarah stormed out of the cabin. "You did *what?*" she asked, her face flushed with anger.

Ethan shook his head. "I didn't know she was a woman. She was wearing a hard hat and coming at me with a tire iron; I just defended myself. It wasn't until she fell down and her hat fell off that I realized she was a woman." He looked at Sarah beseechingly. "I thought she was a short man."

"Why was she coming at you with a tire iron?" Alex asked.

"I—uh—stepped in front of the loader she was driving. It was carrying a load of logs at the time, and she had to ditch the machine to avoid hitting me. It rolled over, dumping the logs and landing on its side." Ethan closed his eyes. "She came climbing out of that rig cursing and waving a tire iron. I just reacted."

"Bishop has a woman foreman?" Alex asked.

Ethan nodded. "And from what I can tell, the crew respects her." He touched his battered face again. "I thought they were going to kill me."

"Ethan would cut off his right arm before he'd knowingly hit a woman," Alex told Sarah, heading back into the cabin. "So let's just keep this to ourselves."

Ethan snorted. "The whole county probably knows by now." He looked around the cabin in surprise. "Wow, you've fixed this place up real nice, Sarah."

Sarah merely scowled at him. "You apologized, I hope."

"I was sort of busy fighting for my life." He suddenly grinned. "But I'll apologize in two months, when I return to Loon Cove as her boss," he said, anticipation lighting his one good eye. "So, what needs to be done to whip the lodge into shape?" he asked, rubbing his hands together as he looked at Alex. "I seem to be free for the next two months."

"You're going back," Alex said.

Ethan shook his head. "In two months," he repeated, turning and walking out the door.

Alex grinned at Sarah. "Do you think there's any chance that Dad didn't know Bishop had a woman foreman or that he simply forgot to mention that interesting little fact to Ethan?"

Sarah leaned back in surprise. "You think Grady set him up?"

Alex nodded.

She made a sound of disgust. "We really have to do something about that scheming man. He's been running unchecked for too long."

"Spoken like a true Knight, considering I had that same thought." He kicked the door shut with his foot, reached out and turned the lock, then lowered his mouth to within inches of hers. "You up for another driving lesson, Sunshine?"

Sarah twined her arms around his neck and touched

her lips to his. "You'd better fasten your seat belt, because I have every intention of redlining your tachometer. And this time, there won't be a block of wood taped under my gas pedal."

Alex leaned away. "Who told?"

"Delaney," Sarah said sweetly. "She knows we women have to stick together."

"Oh, Lord," Alex groaned, sweeping Sarah into his arms and carrying her to the bed. "I just aged a hundred years, thinking about Delaney at sixteen."

"Don't worry, hero man." Sarah pulled him down onto the bed, then straddled his hips. "You'll have me backing you up." She gave him a thousand-watt smile and started unbuttoning his shirt.

Letter from Lake Watch

Dear Readers,

Not long after I met my husband—more years ago than I care to acknowledge—I found myself wondering what mysterious force could make a man sit on an ice-covered lake in below-freezing temperatures, and spend hours patiently waiting for a flag to signal that a fish had just taken the bait. Summer fishing I could understand; who wouldn't enjoy spending a sunny day in a boat on a beautiful lake, having nothing to do but read, snooze, snack, and jump in the water to cool off? But when my future husband grabbed his ice-fishing traps and bait pail, and offered to take me with him one surprisingly bright winter morning, sheer curiosity had me trudging beside him onto the frozen lake. And that was the day I not only became hooked on winter fishing, but saw the entire world through new eyes.

The magic began with the sound of a gasoline-powered ice auger as it bore through the frozen shroud of ice to suddenly well up a gusher of slush-laden water. I distinctly remember peering down into that dark, seemingly bottomless hole, trying to imagine the watery world a mere ten inches beneath my feet. How could any ecosystem survive five months of numbingly cold, sunless living? Or was the ice really a cleverly designed shield, protecting the lake's inhabitants from the harsh winter weather? But even more bothersome to me at the time, had my husband-to-be just opened a painful wound by drilling ten holes in the lake's protective mantle? (On our lake, each fisherman is allowed five traps—which is why, I inadvertently learned, lots of men encourage their wives or girlfriends to go fishing with them; the more traps set, the better the chances of catching supper. And here I thought my guy just wanted to spend some quality time with me!)

The regulation book that came with my fishing license that long-ago Christmas stated that I must tend my own traps; so I was taught how to bait my hooks with tiny minnows, feed the thick lines down those dark holes, then set the flags. (A big fish comes along and eats the little fish, the flag shoots up, and—hopefully—I pull up the line with the big fish still attached.) But instead of five traps, I was told only to set four. Then I was handed a very short rod as well as a plastic bucket to sit on, and shown how to *jig* over the fifth hole. (Jigging is actually bobbing the line up and down to attract a hungry big fish with the movement of the little fish. I jigged slowly, afraid of making my poor little minnow seasick.)

But here's the *really* magical part. I was sitting in patient bliss on that bucket in the middle of that frozen lake for maybe an hour, munching down a perfectly cooked hotdog (I still can't figure out why food tastes better if it's cooked and eaten outdoors), when something suddenly tugged on my line! I don't mean a sharp jerk, but a barely perceptible tug that hardly moved the tip of my tiny rod. I didn't jump to my feet in excitement, but sat staring down that dark hole in awe. Some unseen creature (hopefully a large trout or salmon and not a cousin to the Loc Ness Monster) tugged again, and with a smile of delight I gently returned the gesture. A subtle tug-of-war ensued, and I can't begin to describe how sparring with something unseen, a mere ten inches below me but an entire world away, made me feel. Words conveying my heart-thumping joy, anticipation, and up until then, dormant desire to do battle—and win!—seem inadequate.

I was coached on how to pull up the line without jerking the bait out of the big fish's mouth, only to find myself suddenly scrambling back with a yelp of surprise when a huge landlocked salmon shot free of the hole and angrily began flopping on the ice. My delighted fishing partner palmed the beautiful salmon, gauged its size, and proudly (as if *he* had battled the beast himself) declared it a keeper.

I immediately began pleading for him to throw it back.

I don't know who gaped more, my future hubby or that displaced fish, but with a sigh of resignation the wonderful man bent down and let the salmon slide free, its tail giving a happy splash as it disappeared back into the dark watery depths with its belly filled with my bait. (I've been ice fishing for nigh on thirty years now, and though I've had many fine meals of freshwater fish, I still more often than not plead that my catch be released. Which is why my husband always packs hotdogs in our cooler, or simply refuses to take me with him when he has a hankering for baked salmon.)

But I still remember my first experience on the ice as a day of many lessons: about ice fishing, about how my then future husband's mind worked, and about my own mind-set. How does that old adage go? *Before you judge a man, you should probably walk a mile in his shoes?* Well, I spent that day seeing winter fishing through another's eyes. And I learned that in their own way, men are just as spiritual, inspired, and compassionate as we women. But instead of a suit and tie and wing tips, some men might prefer to dress in long johns, a bomber hat and warm boots, and connect with the universe in the ultimate cathedral.

This was quite an epiphany for me. I learned not to assume that people are weird simply because they have a passion for living each day as it's given, rain or shine, thunderstorm or blizzard, forty degrees above or twenty degrees below freezing, with nothing more than a gently rocking boat or a plastic bucket to fish from. (I've never admitted this to him, but when Robbie released that beautiful fish just to appease my soft soul, I knew I had found the man I wanted to spend the rest of my life with. But please keep this our little secret, because he still thinks it was his manly charm that captured my heart.)

So how does one magical day of ice fishing become a romance novel almost thirty years later, appropriately titled *The Seduction of His Wife?* Each of my stories begins with some tiny insight on my part, that somehow lends itself to a whole host of questions. (And Lord knows, I have more questions about life and love and the human spirit than is healthy!) So . . . if spending one simple day with my guy can give me a glimpse into *his* mind while teaching me something about myself, how might a man attempt to get into a woman's head, and therefore learn more about himself?

And being not only a writer but an avid reader, this train of thought eventually led me to wonder what men think about romance novels. Do larger-than-life, tough, sexy heroes threaten men? Intrigue them? Or are guys just plain curious about why we women stay up until the wee hours of the night reading romances? Then again, do men think that if *they* were to read a romance novel, they might come to understand us women better?

Another consideration I had when penning this book (see how the questions keep multiplying?): Do romance novels ever influence a *woman's* everyday life? Do they make us see things differently as we experience the world through our fictional female characters? If not, then what happens to all those romantic tales after we've read them? Do they simply evaporate into the ether, never to be thought of again, or do they ruminate someplace deep inside us, giving us a sense of . . . oh, I don't know, hope maybe? Anticipation?

Every romance author's dream is that our work will strike a chord and tug a few heartstrings. I like to call it the "aahhh" factor, where a reader closes one of my books and softly sighs, knowing all is well in that fictional world, so surely there's hope for the real world.

The heroine of *The Seduction of His Wife*, Sarah Knight, certainly feels this way. In fact, she lives in constant hope that one day she will become a feisty, confident woman just like the heroines in the books she reads. Sarah's only problem though is that she's so caught up in her fictional worlds she probably wouldn't recognize happily ever after if it walked up to her and kissed her on the nose.

Thinking back to my first day on the ice, I wondered what sort of hero it would take to pull Sarah out of her books and into the real world. That was when I remembered this really nice guy by the name of Alex Knight (who happened to be ruggedly handsome and conveniently single) living in the deep woods of Maine. I thought he just might be brave enough (he'd certainly be motivated when he saw her) to challenge Sarah's deeply entrenched fears about life and love and happily ever after. So I decided to marry Sarah and Alex to each other before they even met, then have a bit of fun watching *them* figure things out on their own.

Until later, from LakeWatch . . . happy reading!

Janet

Pocket Star Books
Proudly Presents

THE TEMPTATION OF HER LOVE

Janet Chapman

Available in Paperback
February 2007
from Pocket Star Books

Turn the page for a preview of
The Temptation of Her Love. . . .

Chapter One

The man stepped out of nowhere, directly into the path of the loader Anna was driving. She jerked the wheel to the right and hit the lever that lowered the forks to drop her center of gravity, but she couldn't stop the heavy load of logs from shifting. Tires screeched for purchase on the frozen ground as the loader skidded into the ditch, causing her cargo to scatter like giant toothpicks.

Anna barely had time to cover her head as she was tossed against the side of the cab, then down to the floor as the massive machine rolled onto its side with a jarring thud. A log crashed through the windshield, raining glass down over her like hail as several more logs slammed into the cab with deafening bangs, drowning out Anna's scream.

Then everything went suddenly still but for the

rapping knock of the huge diesel engine. Anna cautiously lowered her arms. She was alive apparently, and except for the throbbing pain in her right shoulder, she didn't seem to be hurt. She reached over and turned the key in the ignition to put the beast out of its misery, hearing it cough once before it fell silent. Anna closed her eyes, seeing again the man's horror when he realized he was about to be crushed by several tons of logs and machinery.

Lord, that had been close.

Trembling with delayed shock and anger, Anna climbed around the heavy log wedged in her seat and pushed at the cab door. It wouldn't budge. Feeling the cold February air on her face, and realizing the side window had blown out as well, she popped her head out and looked toward the loading ramp. The man she'd barely avoided was just picking himself off the ground, brushing dirt, snow, and bits of bark off his pants.

Anna grabbed the tire iron wedged behind the seat. A lumber mill was no place for idiots, and that stupid fool had nearly killed them both with his inattention. Using the tire iron to knock away what was left of the glass, Anna scrambled out the window and climbed to the ground. She waved away several men running toward her, hefted the tire iron like a weapon, and stalked toward the idiot gaping at her. He took a step back as she advanced, held up his hands in supplication, and sheepishly grinned.

A log suddenly fell behind her. Anna turned just in time to see it roll off the loader, taking the headlights with it and forcing two men to jump out of the way to avoid being crushed. What a mess. The expensive loader was laying on its side in the ditch, its cargo strewn around like scattered bowling pins. And to her experienced eye, Anna knew there were several thousand dollars of damage to the big rig.

She turned back to the man, repositioned her grip on the tire iron with a growl of anger, and stepped straight into his oncoming fist. Anna's brain rattled inside her hard hat again as her head exploded in pain, lights flashing in the back of her eyes as she crumpled to the ground amid angry shouts.

"Aw, shit! I didn't know she was a woman!" she heard above her, the voice backing away. "She was coming after me with that tire iron. Dammit, I didn't know!"

Anna wanted to stay right where she was, curled up in a ball, knowing that the less she moved the less it would hurt. But as much as she'd like to see the idiot taught a lesson, that lesson might turn into murder if she didn't get up. So she rolled to her side and pushed herself up on her hands and knees, then stood, finally opening her eyes to see four men from her crew backing her attacker against the saw shed. Two other men rushed to her side to hold her up, but she shrugged them off.

"Leave him alone," she said through the pain in her jaw. She stepped up to the four men just as one of them drove his fist into the idiot's belly. "Back off, dammit!" she snapped as she shoved them away.

Anna pointed at the hunched, gasping man. "This

is a sawmill, not Disneyland. You can't walk around here with your head in the clouds. Do you know what happens to a body when twelve tons of timber and steel run over it?"

"Yes, ma'am," he acknowledged with a gasped cough. "Look," he said, stepping toward her and holding out his hand, "I wouldn't have hit you if I'd known you were a woman."

Anna took a step back before he could touch her, and pointed at the mangled loader. "That piece of equipment costs more than you can earn in two years, but I had to ditch it so your heirs couldn't sue us right out of business. Now who the hell are you, and what are you doing walking around my mill yard?"

"I'm Ethan. I work here."

"Not anymore you don't. You're fired."

"What!"

Anna reached down and picked up her tire iron before she turned and looked back at him. "We don't pay people to be stupid. You're a walking accident, and next time someone could be killed."

"I hired Ethan this morning," Tom Bishop said as he rushed over. Her aging boss wrapped one arm around her, moved her hand so he could examine her jaw, then turned and frowned at Ethan.

Tom Bishop owned Loon Cove Lumber, and he had the right to hire and fire anyone he wanted. But she was his foreman, and Anna was angry that Tom hadn't told her he was adding to her crew.

"I'm sorry, Tom. I didn't know she was a woman,"

Ethan repeated. "And she was coming at me with that tire iron." He pointed at her right hand.

Tom took the heavy tool from her and gave it to one of the men. "Haven't I told you that piece of hardware would get you in trouble?" he said, sounding more like a father than her boss.

Anna gaped at him. "The man just wrecked your loader and struck one of your crew, and you're scolding *me?*" She stepped out of his grip. "I'm firing him, Tom," she said with all the grit she could muster, then turned to Ethan. "I want you off this property in sixty seconds."

It was the idiot's turn to gape. He looked at Tom. "She can't fire me."

"Now, Anna," Tom said, looking as shocked as Ethan. "Don't be rash. Maybe you can give him another chance. It was an accident."

"You know my rules: There're no second chances when it comes to safety. I run a tight yard."

"But Anna," Tom entreated, darting a worried glance at the man in question.

Anna cupped her swelling jaw. She had to get some snow on it soon, or she wouldn't be able to open her mouth tomorrow. "It's either him or me, Tom. Your call."

"But Ethan's worked in the woods all his life. The Knights own a logging operation on the other side of the lake. He knows his way around machinery."

Anna shot her gaze to Ethan on an indrawn breath. Good God, this hard-punching, devil-handsome idiot was Ethan Knight? *Her* Ethan Knight? It took all of

Anna's willpower to merely raise a brow at the man who stood as tall as a mountain and looked to be made of steel.

He also looked like he couldn't believe his fate rested in the hands of Tom Bishop's female foreman. She looked back at Tom. "He's probably here because he stepped in front of a skidder at home. It's him or me," she repeated.

Tom looked around at the gathered men waiting to hear which worker he chose, but Anna spoke first. "Davis, escort Mr. Knight to the gate, and make sure he doesn't destroy anything else on his way out." She turned toward the wreckage. "Come on, people. We have a mess to clean up."

There was a heartbeat of silence before a dozen or more men scrambled to follow her orders.

"Jeeze Louise," Keith said as he fell into step beside her. "You've got balls, lady."

Anna kept walking, not looking at him. "Tom needs me more than he needs to worry about some accident-prone idiot. I know it, and he knows it."

She suddenly stopped and bent at the waist, propping her hands on her knees and taking deep breaths. The throbbing in her head was only slightly worse than the throbbing in her shoulder, and she felt like she was going to pass out.

"We can take care of the loader, boss lady. There's only an hour of workday left. Go home," Keith told her, putting an arm around her waist, obviously afraid she was going to fall flat on her face—which was fast becoming a possibility.

Anna closed her eyes and took shallow breaths. "Is Knight headed for the gate?" she asked, not daring to move her head even an inch.

"Yeah. He's leaving. And if looks could kill, you'd be one dead foreman right now."

"Good. I'm just going to sit here a minute," she whispered, sidling over to a low stack of lumber and letting Keith help her sit down. "And I think I *will* go home. See what you can do about righting that loader."

"You going to be okay to drive, boss lady?"

Anna attempted to smile. "I'll be fine, thanks. I just need a minute."

Keith examined her with a critical eye. "That was a mean punch he threw. Your jaw's already turning purple."

Anna touched her jaw as she looked over to see Ethan Knight spinning out of the parking lot. She also saw Tom Bishop, his face a mask of concern, headed her way. Damn. She didn't want his coddling. Ethan may have caused the accident, but she'd equally been an idiot to go after him with a tire iron.

"Just look at you, girl," Tom said, the worry evident in his voice. "Come on. I'm taking you to see a doctor."

"No, I'm going home." She motioned for Keith to get to work on the loader, then looked back up at the owner of Loon Cove Lumber. "I'm fine, Tom. Really. I just need an ice pack and some of Samuel's tea."

Tom frowned. "Your grandfather's tea could skin the hide off a beaver. Don't tell me there's still some of that old rot-gut hanging around."

She nodded. "I seem to have inherited a whole case of it right along with Fox Run Mill."

Tom rolled his eyes. "Samuel must have figured you'd need it, if you intended to keep that ghost camp."

Anna lifted her swollen chin. "I'm keeping it."

"But it's no place for a woman alone, Anna."

"It's my heritage."

"It's falling down around your feet."

"The main house is sound."

"Which is why the animals have taken it over," he shot back. He took hold of her shoulders to help her stand, and held her facing him. "Sell the place, Anna. Save out a couple of acres on the lake, if you're determined to stay here, but sell the rest."

Anna stepped back and tucked her balled fists in her jacket pockets. "We've had this conversation before, Tom. My grandfather left Fox Run to me, and I'm keeping it."

Tom put his own hands in his pockets with a tired sigh. "It was Samuel's dream you'd come back here someday and restore Fox Run Mill," he admitted. "But you were eleven when he made out his will, and no one was planning to build a resort next door back then. Just a few months before he died, Samuel said he was reconsidering putting you in the middle of this mess. They're going to keep up the pressure, you know. You can't fight big business."

"Sure I can. I just won't sign on the dotted line."

"You think that will stop them from putting up their condos? Anna, they'll just build around you."

"Then let them. I have enough land that I won't even see the resort."

"But they need your mile of lake frontage, too. How about the historical society? Couldn't you work out a deal with them, to protect yourself from the developers?"

She shook her head, then immediately regretted it. "I'm keeping Fox Run," she repeated.

"Then at least get a dog to scare away your ghost."

Anna walked over and picked up her hard hat. "I have a dog," she reminded Tom.

He snorted. "The most Bear could scare off is himself if he looked in a mirror."

She started walking toward the gate. "Keith can handle things here tomorrow, Tom. I'm going home, taking some aspirin and going to bed, and I'll be back to work on Monday."

"You need a keeper, Anna Segee."

"I can take care of myself," she said automatically, not taking offense. Tom was, after all, a man. She got into her truck and put the key in the ignition, but looked back at Tom without starting the engine. "Why did you hire Ethan Knight without talking to me first? Didn't his house burn down yesterday? It was the talk of the mill yard this morning. Someone said the Knights were moving into those old sporting camps farther up the lake."

Tom nodded.

"Then why isn't Ethan helping his family get settled?"

"I asked him that same question," Tom said. "He told me his dad and brothers insisted he show up his first day of work here, since there wasn't anything for him to do that they couldn't do themselves."

"You still haven't explained why you hired Ethan without telling me."

"I was doing his father a favor." Tom looked down at the ground, then back at her with serious eyes. "Ethan didn't recognize you. Is that the real reason you got mad and fired him?"

Anna would have scowled if it wouldn't have hurt her face. "I'm relieved he didn't recognize me."

"Somebody's bound to put two and two together one of these days," Tom warned. "Then what are you going to do?"

"I'm not eleven anymore."

"Samuel sent you to live with your father in Quebec because he knew it was impossible for you to live here." Tom shook his head. "And nothing's changed in eighteen years, Anna. Hell, half the men in this town have a history with your mother."

Anna glared at Tom. "You've spent the last three months convincing me Samuel sent me away because he loved me. So maybe you should consider that he brought me back for the same reason."

"He never stopped loving you, Anna," Tom said in a whisper, his eyes misting. "You were all he talked about."

"Yeah, well," she growled, looking out the windshield, "he didn't love me enough to stay in contact." She looked back at Tom. "He sent a confused, heartbroken little girl to live with complete strangers, and he never once came to see me. He didn't even write or call."

"That was your father's doing," Tom countered.

"Jean Segee insisted that if he took you, the break had to be clean." He lifted a brow. "I don't recall you trying to contact Samuel, once you came of age."

Anna twisted the key in the ignition and started her truck. "I wasn't about to chase after someone who didn't want me."

Tom touched her sleeve. "Samuel loved you more than life itself, Anna, and spent eighteen lonely years living with his decision to send you away. He didn't dare call or go see you once you grew up because he preferred to live with the hope that you could forgive him, instead of risking the reality that you never would."

Anna closed her eyes. "I forgave him," she whispered. She looked back at Tom, her eyes filled with tears. "I was simply too stubborn to make the first move."

"Not stubborn," Tom said, squeezing her arm. "Scared. You were just as scared as Samuel." He rocked back on his heels. "Ethan Knight was . . . twelve, thirteen when you left?" he asked. He shook his head. "That boy spent the entire summer with his arm in a cast because of you. He'll recognize you eventually; then what are you going to say to him? 'I just thanked you for rescuing me eighteen years ago by firing you?'"

"Then why did you put me in such a terrible position?" Anna snapped. "Of all the people you could have hired to work here, why Ethan Knight?"

"Because Grady Knight asked me to."

"You can't run a business hiring men as favors, Tom."

"I hired you as a favor to your dead granddaddy," he said, puffing up his chest.

"No, you hired me because I'm the best damn foreman you could ever hope to have."

Tom let his chest sink back into his belly with a sigh of defeat. "Dammit, Anna. What am I going to tell Grady Knight?"

"You tell him to keep his son away from large machinery."

"But you don't know Ethan. He's more competent than most men. All the Knights are. Hell, half our saw logs come from NorthWoods Timber."

"Then what's he doing at your mill? Why isn't he seeing to his own business, if he's such a hot-shot logger?"

"Grady said Ethan wanted a change of scenery," Tom muttered, his voice so low Anna had to strain to hear him.

"I haven't got time to babysit idiots." She gave Tom a hard look. "What would you be telling Grady right now if I'd run over his precious son?"

All the color drained from Tom's face. "Hell, Anna. You saved Ethan's life."

"For all the thanks I got," she muttered, touching her jaw.

Tom's eyes grew misty again. "Thank you for being the best damn foreman I could ever hope to have," he said thickly.

Good Lord, she had to get out of here before she started bawling. She ached from head to toe, and this conversation stirred uncomfortable memories for her. "Go back to your office," she gently told him. "Call

Grady Knight if it will make you feel better, and tell him to be thankful his son is alive. And tell him that I fired Ethan, not you; that it was out of your hands."

She closed the truck door, then rolled down the window. "Oh. And while you're at it, tell him he might want to keep his son away from their wood chipper. Ethan's liable to get eaten up." She put the truck in gear and headed for home.

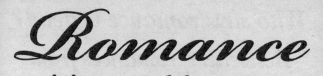

Who says romance is dead?

Bestselling romances from Pocket Books

Otherwise Engaged
Eileen Goudge
Would you trade places
with your best friend if
you could?

Only With a Highlander
Janet Chapman
Can fiery Winter
MacKeage resist the
passionate pursuit of a
timeless warrior?

Kill Me Twice
Roxanne St. Claire
She has a body to kill
for...and a bodyguard
to die for.

Holly
Jude Deveraux
On a starry winter night,
will her heart choose
privilege—or passion?

**Big Guns Out
of Uniform**
*Sherrilyn Kenyon, Liz
Carlyle, and Nicole Camden*
Out of uniform and
under the covers...three
tales of sizzling romance
from three of today's
hottest writers.

**Hot Whispers of
an Irishman**
Dorien Kelly
Can a hunt for magical
treasure uncover a love to
last a lifetime?

Carolina Isle
Jude Deveraux
When two cousins switch
identities, anything can
happen. Even love...

POCKET BOOKS
A Division of Simon & Schuster
A VIACOM COMPANY

**POCKET
STAR BOOKS**
A Division of Simon & Schuster
A VIACOM COMPANY

Available wherever books are sold or at www.simonsayslove.com   13446